I, LUCIFER

By Peter O'Donnell

The Adventures of Modesty Blaise:

MODESTY BLAISE

I, LUCIFER

Peter O'Donnell

SOUVENIR PRESS

FOR

JIM HOLDAWAY

'I EXPECT my people to be prompt in making their reports,' Seff said musingly. 'It is hard to believe that any of them could be unaware of my feelings in the matter.'

Bowker, a big man, rather fleshy and with a fuzz of thin fair hair, put a cube of ice in his vodka and coke, then moved away to the long couch on the far side of the room. The cotton shirt and lightweight slacks he wore were sticking to him, even though the windows which almost filled one side of the big room were fully open to the slight breeze from the sea.

Seff looked at the watch on his bony wrist. 'It is now almost thirty minutes since Mr. Wish returned to the house, and he has not yet presented himself to me. I am most displeased.'

There was no anger in the precise voice with that tinny quality which always reminded Bowker of a voice from an old gramophone, but the word 'displeased' was among the strongest in Seff's vocabulary. Hearing it, Bowker felt the sweat-damp shirt grow clammy against his back.

'It's hot,' he said, and lit a cigarette though he did not want one. 'Jack Wish has been pretty damn busy for three days, and travelling for the last six hours. Not surprising if he wants to shower and change as soon as he gets in.'

Before Bowker finished speaking he had begun to despise himself. At the same time the professional part of his mind stood ready to observe his own behavioural response to stimuli in what would now follow.

He had blustered. Now Seff would slowly turn and look at him, just look, with the head tilted a little to one side, query-ingly. Bowker would see the thin, long-limbed figure in the black suit with the wing collar and pearl tie-pin; the narrow face with sunken cheeks; the black hair spread so carefully that it might have been painted on in streaks.

The Adam's apple in Seff's scrawny neck would jump up and down two or three times, then Seff would speak, and Bowker's suprarenal glands would pump adrenalin into his bloodstream as his body reacted to fear. The moment of bluster would end, and he would crumple as he had crumpled a hundred times before.

'*Physician, heal thyself,*' Bowker thought bitterly.

Seff turned slowly and stared at Bowker, his head on one side, queryingly. The protuberant Adam's apple jumped up and down two or three times.

'I would not like to think that your remarks mean that you approve of Mr. Wish being dilatory, Dr. Bowker,' Seff said with grave courtesy.

'No, I don't approve.' Bowker ground out the cigarette with a shaking hand, looking away. 'I was only saying ... well, it's hot.' He gestured meaninglessly.

After several seconds Seff turned and stood with his long-fingered hands loosely clasped behind his back, facing out of the open windows. From them a broad flight of steps led down to a sandy path with low dunes on either side. The path ran for fifty yards and ended in a large square terrace of pastel-coloured tiles jutting out into the sea some ten feet above the quiet waters of the bay. To one side of the terrace lay a long finger of water, an inlet forming a natural pool.

'Will you come here please, Dr. Bowker?' Seff said. Bowker moved across the room to stand beside the thin black figure. His eyes searched the empty terrace then moved to the pool. He saw a flash of movement as a glistening brown body in red swim-trunks surfaced and swam lazily down the length of the pool before submerging again.

'I am concerned about our young friend there,' said Seff. 'Over the past six months his results have fallen from eighty per cent accuracy to seventy-five per cent.'

'It's not a lot.' With an effort Bowker stopped his voice sounding petulant.

'It is too much.' The gramophonic voice was without inflexion. 'It means more killings, Dr. Bowker. That is undesirable—not in itself, of course, but to the extent that it increases Mr. Wish's task, and hence our vulnerability. This matter of our young friend's efficiency is very much to your address, I feel.'

Bowker wiped his face and said, 'I'm doing all I can, Seff. I've maintained his delusion, even strengthened it.'

'Does one have to maintain a delusion in such cases? You have given me to understand otherwise.' Seff was musing again. He did not wait for a reply. 'It is his work and his accuracy that concern me.'

'The psychiatrical side is only part of it,' Bowker said quickly. 'As for the other part, I've been meaning to talk to you about that. It's not really my field——' He broke off and turned as the door opened. Seff turned with him.

A short man with very broad shoulders and a barrel chest came into the room. His hair was rather long and sleeked back from a low brow above a face that seemed flattened almost to the point of being concave. He wore only boxer shorts and open sandals.

'I have been waiting for you, Mr. Wish,' Seff said coldly.

'Sorry. Been busy.' Jack Wish had a low, growling voice. He was American, highly skilled in his own particular trade but slow-witted in almost anything else.

Bowker felt a flash of envy as he watched Jack Wish roll across to the bar and pour himself a drink. The man could be frightened by Seff, but only when the fact penetrated that Seff was displeased with him, and it would not penetrate unless Seff put himself to the task of making sure that it did. Bowker would have liked to run an I.Q. test on Jack Wish. It baffled him, professionally, that a man could apparently possess a selective intelligence which made him brilliant in one field only.

Drink in hand, Wish came towards the other two men now, a grin creasing his face. 'The Büchner boys knocked off Werner in Hamburg, Tuesday,' he said. 'Nice job. I paid 'em off.'

'We read of it,' said Seff, and Bowker realised with a pang of

A*   9

disappointment that Seff was not going to put the screws on Jack Wish this time.

Wish nodded. 'I figured you'd read that bit. But I got the Paris killing laid on too. Sometime this week it'll be. Only three thousand dollars.' He paused and drank, then looked expectantly at Seff and Bowker.

'You have something to tell me, something else?' Seff said.

'You bet I got something else.' The flattened face gleamed with pride. 'Remember we had a Danish kid with us on the ship when we were working around the Med?'

'Larsen?'

'That's him. Well, he must've peeked a little when he shouldn't. And he saw enough to make a few crazy guesses about us. Or maybe not so crazy.'

Bowker felt cold, but Seff's voice held no emotion as he said, 'How do you know this, Mr. Wish?'

'Ran into him in Hamburg. He'd been doing a lot of adding up, and he reckoned he might earn himself a pension. But when he sees *me*, he just can't help doing a little digging before he starts putting in the squeeze.'

'I hope to God you played it innocent,' Bowker said hoarsely. 'Dammit, he's only guessing. He's got nothing to tell anybody.'

'Lot of folks are interested in his kind of guessing right now, Doc.' Jack Wish grinned smugly. 'Sure I played it innocent. Made like I was just a bum around the place and didn't even know as much as he did. So in the end we figure we better operate together on this, do a little shamus work, me on the inside, him on the outside. It's like a movie, see? He laps it up. Once we know the full score, then zowie! We're rich.'

There was silence in the room.

'And where is Larsen now, Mr. Wish?' Seff asked at last.

'Here.' Wish jerked a thumb over his shoulder. 'We came back together. I was to drop him in Westerland, but I chilled him and brought him on here. Reckoned maybe you'd like the boy wonder to see him off.' Wish nodded towards the open windows with his last words.

Bowker let out a long exhalation of relief. For a moment he felt a rush of something akin to affection for Jack Wish. Seff was walking slowly up and down the room, cracking his knuckles, a sure sign that he was pleased.

'You have done very well indeed, Mr. Wish,' he said approvingly. 'And I agree with your suggestion. I take it that since you returned you have been preparing Larsen for his departure?'

'Uh?' Wish stared blankly. 'Surely to God he ain't going any place, Seff? Hell, I only just brought him in——' He broke off, light dawning slowly on his face. 'Ah, you mean I been getting him fixed up for the boy wonder? Sure! He's all ready.'

'That was indeed my meaning.' Seff continued his slow pacing. As he moved, the joints of his body creaked and clicked faintly. This was something that always set Bowker's teeth on edge, and he spoke loudly now to shut out the sound.

'You wanted to run a work-session this afternoon, Seff.'

'Yes.' Seff stopped pacing. 'Would you advise dealing with that before or after attending to Larsen?'

Bowker thought for a moment. 'Before. The killing is bound to create tensions, and he's more accurate when he's relaxed.'

'Should we attend to Larsen ourselves, perhaps?'

'No.' Bowker was on his own ground now, and he spoke positively. 'It's quite a while since the last demonstration, and Larsen provides a good opportunity.'

'Very well.' Seff looked out of the window. A tanned figure in red swim-trunks lay relaxed on the terrace, basking in the hot sun. 'Perhaps you will respectfully ask our young friend if it will please him to attend upon us now, Dr. Bowker.'

In a big upper room of the house Jack Wish flopped into an armchair and stretched out his thick bare legs.

'This stuff slays me,' he said.

'Do not let that fact be manifest, Mr. Wish, or your words may prove prophetic,' Seff answered. He was opening a metal filing cabinet. The shutters were closed and the blinds lowered. A fluorescent strip lit the room.

Jack Wish stared, puzzled, and said, 'Come again, Seff?'

'I mean do not let our young friend see your amusement.' Seff lifted his head and his lips drew back in a smile which revealed a set of very white but slightly ill-fitting false teeth. 'Or you may not live very long.'

Jack Wish stirred uneasily. He had given up wondering why Seff could sometimes make him afraid. 'Hell, you don't have to worry,' he growled sulkily. 'I know the score.'

Seff did not trouble to reply. He was busy setting out a row of long card-index drawers on the table, each containing four or five hundred sealed and numbered envelopes.

The door opened and Bowker stood aside for a man to precede him into the room. The man was bronzed by sun, tall, superbly built and with an unblemished skin. He wore red swim-trunks and monk sandals. The body was that of an athlete in perfect condition. The face was young, unlined, and slightly rounded, with very bright blue eyes. The hair was short and black, a cap of tight curls. There was about him a strange air of innocence—strange, because behind it one could sense the steel of absolute authority.

Seff bowed slightly, his body creaking.

'Lucifer,' he said. 'I hope we have not distracted you from important matters?'

'No.' The voice was strong yet mellow. 'I have been talking to Pluto and Belial.'

'Faithful servants,' Seff acknowledged deferentially. 'I regret placing any burden of work upon you, Lucifer, but in the special grades of humanity it is for you alone to decide who shall die.'

'Die?' There was disapproval in Lucifer's repetition of the word. Bowker felt quick delight that Seff had slipped for once, and moved smoothly in to repair the error.

'We mean transference to the lower levels of your kingdom,' he said, smiling. 'But since the world calls it dying, we sometimes use the term ourselves, Lucifer. You have always insisted that our operations for you must be on a mundane level, and so we school ourselves to think in mundane terms.'

'Of course.' Lucifer turned upon Bowker a sweet sad smile, then looked again at Seff. 'You have no need to be troubled at laying the burden upon me. There was a time long ago, before I called you from the lower levels and gathered you about me, when the whole task was mine alone ... to take millions of decisions each day.'

'Your subjects increase by millions each day now, Lucifer,' Seff said politely. 'It is our honour that you can now delegate all but the most important decisions to us.'

Lucifer inclined his head graciously, then moved to the table where the long card-index drawers were laid out. His eyes went blank and he rested one powerful hand gently on the stacked envelopes in the first drawer. Moving the hand very slowly, he began to riffle through the stack, letting his fingertips rest for a few seconds on each envelope in turn. After a little while he paused, drew out an envelope and dropped it on the table.

Jack Wish sat watching as a child might watch a conjuring trick. It was a long time before another envelope was selected and withdrawn. Seff paced slowly, creaking. He did not glance at Lucifer until the first full drawer had been dealt with and three envelopes selected. Then he nodded to Jack Wish, who got up and restored the drawer to its cabinet.

Lucifer began to work on the envelopes in the second drawer. Bowker watched, hiding his anxiety. There were moments of relief when Lucifer selected without hesitation, and moments of sharp tension when his hand rested long and uncertainly before drawing out an envelope. From two of the drawers Lucifer made no selection at all.

An hour passed before the last drawer of envelopes had been dealt with, and no word was spoken during that time. From just over three thousand envelopes, seventeen had been selected.

13

Lucifer stepped away from the table, and his eyes slowly focused on his surroundings as Jack Wish put away the last of the drawers. Again the sad gentle smile touched Lucifer's youthful face as he looked at the small stack of envelopes left on the table.

'There. You have my decisions, Seff.'

'Thank you.' Seff interlaced his fingers and cracked the joints. 'There is one further matter for your attention, if you would be so good ... ?'

'Yes?'

'The time is due for one of your lesser servants to return to the lower levels. He would be greatly honoured if you would dispatch him personally.'

A slight frown touched Lucifer's brow, and Seff's tinny voice went on quickly. 'As our friend Dr. Bowker—to use his worldly name—has pointed out, you prefer always to perform your operations within the natural flow of events. But for a good servant we hoped you might perhaps make an exception ... as you have done before.'

Lucifer smiled reminiscently. 'I dislike being more obtrusive than my celestial colleague. There was a time when we both used our powers more openly, but he has long ceased such activities as dividing the waters and causing the sun to stop in its path. I have chosen to follow suit.'

'There is strong evidence,' Bowker said thoughtfully, 'that he still, on occasion, operates beyond the laws of nature in a minor way, for the benefit of an individual.'

'True.' Lucifer folded brown arms across his chest and considered. 'Very well,' he said at last. 'The favour is granted.'

Jack Wish went out of the room. Lucifer stood like a statue, eyes distant, and Bowker wondered for the hundredth time in what strange reaches the mind behind those eyes was floating.

Seff had stopped pacing and stood with one hand in the pocket of his black jacket. Bowker felt his stomach tighten a little at what was to come.

Three minutes passed before the door opened and Jack Wish entered, lightly holding the arm of a fair young man in

14

slacks and a dark green shirt. This was Larsen. Bowker remembered him now. He moved slowly, obediently, without resistance. His arms hung limply by his sides and he seemed unaware of his surroundings. The pupils of his eyes were abnormally contracted by the injection of chloral hydrate which had numbed his brain.

Lucifer lifted his smooth, handsome face with the cap of black hair. 'Your greater colleagues have petitioned me on your behalf, Larsen,' he said quietly.

The man looked back at him, dull-eyed.

'He is over-awed in your presence, Lucifer,' Bowker murmured. 'This one is a very small creature in your kingdom, no more than an incubus, fleshed by you for a few brief centuries. But he has served you well.'

Lucifer nodded gravely and lifted a hand, the index finger pointing directly at Larsen's chest across the width of the room.

'I release you to the lower levels, small one,' he said in a deep voice. 'Join your brethren in darkness. Be free of the flesh now.'

With the last word a small circle of fierce white heat appeared in the centre of Larsen's chest, as if a burning-glass of unimaginable power had suddenly been focused there by Lucifer's pointing finger. Larsen jerked and started to cry out. The flash of fire vanished, leaving a charred circle in the material of the shirt. Larsen choked as if his throat had suddenly closed. He twitched violently, then toppled to the floor and lay still.

Lucifer lowered his hand.

Seff said, 'May I thank you for him? It was a great honour.'

'The Prince of Darkness has a duty to the least of his servants,' Lucifer said with quiet dignity. 'One day, Seff, in eons yet to come, I may do the same for you, the greatest of my servants. And then, once again, you will be free to roam the lower levels as your true self. As Asmodeus.'

He moved to the door, the perfect muscles rippling smoothly beneath the golden skin. Pausing, he smiled at

Bowker, inclined his head fractionally towards Jack Wish, and went out.

Jack Wish looked down at the body and scratched his jaw, puzzled. 'Who's this As-something he said about, Seff?'

'Asmodeus. A very powerful demon in Lucifer's hierarchy,' Seff answered. 'Mentioned in the Apocrypha. In the third chapter of the Book of Tobit, I believe.'

'And that's you?'

'So our young friend has recently decided.' Seff nodded towards Larsen's body. 'You had better get that wrapped up and weighted ready for disposal tonight, Mr. Wish.'

'Sure.' Jack Wish knelt by the body and stripped off the shirt. Strapped round Larsen's chest was a broad leather belt, and in the centre of this a small round disc protruded slightly, a dome of half-melted plastic now. Wish unstrapped the belt and removed it very carefully. At the back of the burnt-out disc jutted a hollow needle, half an inch long, mounted on a short spring.

Seff took a black metal case, flat and oblong, from his jacket pocket and placed it on the table. 'Very satisfactory,' he said. 'The occasional demonstration must be a potent factor in strengthening our young friend's paranoia.'

Bowker wiped his brow. 'It wouldn't be so good if that transmitter of yours failed one time when you pressed the switch. Or if the belt gadget didn't work. No magnesium fire, no cyanide injected into the body.'

'The instruments I make are extremely efficient, Dr. Bowker,' Seff said, beginning to open the little pile of envelopes. 'But if such a thing did occur, it would of course be your task to rationalise it for Lucifer. Would you be so good as to help me with these envelopes?'

Jack Wish put the belt down gingerly at one end of the long table. 'I'll leave this to you, Seff. Boy, that Lucifer ... how does a guy get to be a solid, machine-tooled, chromium plated nut like *that*?'

'You must ask Dr. Bowker to explain it to you on another

16

occasion,' said Seff, and looked up with a smile that showed his ill-fitting teeth and held no hint of humour. 'Now kindly get that stiff out of here, if you please.'

Jack Wish did not answer. He opened the door, hefted the body in powerful arms, and went out.

Bowker closed the door after him and returned to helping Seff with the envelopes. Each one carried a reference number on the inside flap. The contents varied a little. One envelope contained only a lock of hair; another held a scrap of paper with a few words of handwriting on it; another a photograph. Some contained more than one item.

Seff checked the reference numbers against a list in a register and wrote down seventeen names together with details of nationality, occupation and status.

'Are you going to have Regina send out warnings for all seventeen?' Bowker asked.

Seff did not reply at once. He was checking through another register. At last he said, 'No. Sixteen only. One is an Argentinian gentleman who is on our squeeze-list and who, on your assessment, Dr. Bowker, would be likely to pay what we might demand of him. You give a seventy per cent probability.' Seff passed a hand over his streaky veneer of hair. 'It would harm our image if a client paid up and then died after all.'

'Sixteen, then,' said Bowker. 'So if Lucifer is a little better than eighty per cent accurate we'll need only three killings.'

'A manageable number for Mr. Wish, no doubt.' Seff closed both registers. 'But if Lucifer is only seventy-five per cent accurate it will mean four killings. That is *not* so acceptable. Give thought to it, Dr. Bowker.' He got up. 'I will tell Regina to prepare the usual lists for circulation to governments and selected individuals as soon as we have chosen clients from the squeeze-list.'

Bowker hesitated, then said, 'We've been here eight months. When do we move to a new base?'

'At the end of this month.'

Bowker stared. 'You've already found a good location?'

'An excellent one. And on land again. I disliked it when we

17

used a mother ship. Yes, I surveyed it from all aspects after my last trip to Macao. You had better begin psychological preparation of Lucifer to the end that he decides we should move to some other part of his domain shortly.'

'All right.' Bowker was relieved that the conversation had turned from Lucifer's accuracy to more concrete matters.

The door opened and Jack Wish came in. 'I got Larsen all ready for a long dive tonight,' he said. 'Look, Lucifer called me a minute back. Says to tell you he wants some entertainment.'

Seff tugged at his fingers, cracking the knuckles with pleasure, and a rare hint of excitement showed briefly on his sallow face. 'Our routine work here can be completed later,' he said. 'Will you inform Lucifer that we shall attend upon him with all speed if you please, Mr. Wish? I will call Regina.'

In a well furnished bedroom, on one of the twin beds, lay a woman of fifty with greying hair piled in an old-fashioned bun. Her face was thin and fragile, the skin very pale. She wore a long-sleeved flowered dress and thick lisle stockings. Beside her was a big, shabby handbag.

The woman was dozing. She opened her eyes at once when Seff touched her shoulder. 'Lucifer has asked for entertainment, my dear,' he said softly.

The pale eyes and pale lips smiled up at him with shy pleasure. Her voice held a quavering note of gentility. 'How very nice. I'll come at once, Seffy. Just let me put my shoes on.'

The blinds had been lowered, bringing the room to twilight. Lucifer had put on dark slacks and a red shirt now, and was leaning back in an armchair. A little behind and to one side of him, Bowker and Jack Wish sat at each end of a long low couch.

They faced a marionette theatre at the far end of the room. Seff and his wife were out of sight behind the black curtain surrounding the framework of the proscenium arch. The tiny red curtains of the arch were closed.

There came the sound of soft, reverent music. The curtains rose and the miniature stage was bathed in light. The painted back cloth showed, at a distance, an ancient building set in a forest. The line of painted nuns moving out from an arched doorway, and the sound of a bell superimposed on the music, identified the building as a convent.

Two puppet nuns moved in from the wings, heads bowed in meditation. The music faded a little and the nuns began to chant. Bowker never ceased to marvel at the voices that the Seffs could produce when manipulating their puppets. Seff's thin metallic tones could become high yet mellow, the sweet voice of a woman, or could descend to the deeper registers of a male bass voice such as he never used in normal conversation. Regina's voice, too, could cover a remarkable range. Often Bowker could not tell which of them was speaking.

Now the man appeared, a young negro in ragged shirt and trousers. He did not speak, but began to dance and cavort lasciviously about the two shocked nuns. Bowker watched intently before he could decide which of the two nuns had been hooked in position on the invisible rail above, to leave either Seff or Regina free to operate the two wooden controllers from which hung the ten strings activating the negro.

Most puppeteers used only seven strings, but the Seffs were masters. Soon one forgot the strings, and it was as if the puppets lived. This owed much to the dolls themselves. It was Seff who carved and articulated them, Regina who dressed them. Some were beautiful, some ugly. Some were innocent, some malevolent. Each had a personality which made immediate impact on the viewer. But the greatest wonder of all was that by a change of angle and a subtlety of manipulation the personality could be altered.

Perhaps it was the different poise of an innocent head which suddenly gave the impression of leering salacity. More likely it was in the carving of different profiles for the same head. Bowker did not know how it was done. Seff never allowed anyone to examine the dolls.

Now one of the nuns had slowly changed her shocked pose

and was watching the dancing negro with rigid fascination, like one hypnotised. The other nun approached and plucked pleadingly at her arm but she did not move.

The negro began to sing in a deep, ribald voice as he danced. The melody was that of a spiritual, but the words were obscene and inviting. He jerked at the habit, wimple and veil of the first nun. They fell to the floor. She was young and beautiful in her white shift. Her companion turned away and dropped to her knees, head bowed, hands clasped.

Now the first nun began to move. Slowly at first, then with more abandon, she danced in unison with the negro. They moved off into the wings. The kneeling figure swayed agonisingly in her distress, then was still.

The tempo of the music changed. The negro and the nun reappeared, dancing with heightened frenzy. Her shift was gone now. So were the man's clothes. Both puppets were covered in some stretch material, of suitable colour, which hid the joints in the limbs. They appeared to be naked. Male and female physical characteristics were detailed.

The dancing girl froze, waiting. Slowly the negro gyrated around her, drawing closer. His chanting grew yet more vile. The praying nun lifted her head and wailed.

Bowker leaned forward to look across at Lucifer. He saw that the blue eyes were intent but melancholy. Satisfied, Bowker leaned back. The boy had not tired of his favourite piece. He always liked this one best. 'Liked' was perhaps the wrong word; it was more accurate to say that this piece gave Lucifer the most satisfactory suffering to endure. Satisfactory, because suffering was a part of the eternal burden imposed on him by his delusion. The content of the piece was the portrayal, with simple blasphemy, of evil corrupting good and of evil overpowering good by force.

Now the black body and the pink-and-white body merged, writhing on the tiny floor of the stage. They rose, broke apart, and the girl fled—but not to escape. Her face seemed alight with sensuality as she moved in a circle, the negro pursuing. There came the sound of her tittering laughter and of the negro's deep chuckle. She stumbled, fell, and the man was upon her.

The bodies heaved in prolonged union. The deep panting and the shrill ecstatic cries ceased at last. The negro rose and began to dance slowly, languorously about the prone girl. Music swelled as he did so.

Bowker's professional mind turned to the unseen Seff, the puppet-master. Seff pulled the strings and the puppets obeyed. But when the dreadful dolls had been laid in their boxes and the little theatre had been dismantled, the situation remained. Seff plucked the strings of fear and greed, of flattery and of menace, of life and of death. And live puppets danced to his command. Of the live puppets, only Lucifer knew nothing of the strings that activated him.

Again the music faded. The negro bent to touch the nude girl. She lifted her head. He pointed to the kneeling nun and made a crude gesture, then looked invitingly at the girl again. Her head wagged from side to side in merriment and she rose to her feet.

Together the two of them began to stalk like animals towards the robed figure. They pounced, dragging her over backwards, bearing her down. Tiny wooden hands fitted with minute hooks, invisible to the eye, tore at her habit.

The nun shrieked.

Behind the black curtain, Seff and Regina stood on the low bridge, arms resting on the waist-high rail, hands smoothly manipulating the controllers. Their faces were rapt with the concentration and pleasure of their work. From their lips came sounds and words to match the scene below.

With the toe of his shoe Seff touched a button, and jungle music rose in a rhythmic crescendo of eroticism for the climax.

'Congratulations, Regina,' Bowker said politely. 'It was quite splendid. Lucifer was very satisfied.'

She touched her hair into place coyly, walking along the passage beside Bowker. 'Oh, you're always very kind, Dr.

Bowker.' Her waxen skin flushed momentarily with pleasure. 'I do hope that *you* enjoy our little entertainments, too.'

'Always,' Bowker lied with a charming smile.

Regina paused by the door of her room. 'I must finish my rest,' she said. 'And I expect Seffy's waiting for you in the office. You'd better hurry along.'

'Of course.'

Bowker smiled again and moved on down the passage. He found the puppet shows nauseating. The eroticism did not stir him and the obscene blasphemy did not distress him. If the play had been acted in a blue movie with live characters he would have been merely bored.

It was the Seffs who roused loathing in him. He feared but respected Seff; found Regina nothing more than tedious. But when they came together to operate their disgusting dolls he felt sick. No doubt his revulsion sprang from that old familiar trick of the mind, substitution. He despised himself because he, too, was a puppet; but the mind could not long tolerate self-hatred, and so it transferred the emotion to the Seffs and their dolls——.

Bowker broke off the train of thought and swore softly. Self-analysis served no good purpose here. He knew from experience that it only reduced his skill in handling Lucifer. He moved on more quickly and went into the office. Seff, working at the table with a pen poised in his bony fingers, glanced up. 'I have been waiting for you, Dr. Bowker.'

'Sorry. I was talking to Lucifer. Wanted to find out how confident he felt about his selections.'

'And?'

'I got nowhere. I didn't expect to. A paranoiac is bound to have total belief in his delusions.'

'A waste of time, then?'

'You sometimes have to waste it when you're dealing with an inexact science.' Bowker showed a flash of irritation. 'Anyway, Lucifer's made his selections. We'll just have to hope a good percentage of the people die and leave us as few killings as possible.'

'We have also to choose our real clients for the demand-notes,' Seff said, and looked at a list in front of him. 'I propose to choose five for the moment. And I want five who, in your professional opinion, are at least seventy per cent probables for making payment. Otherwise there will be further killings for Mr. Wish to arrange in another few months.'

'I'll need to study the dossiers.'

'Of course. I have made a short list of eighteen for you to select from.' Seff put down his pen and stared into space. 'But before you begin, there is another question. You said earlier today that Lucifer's—ah—psychic abilities are not really within your field of competence.'

'I've never pretended they were,' Bowker said defensively. 'I'm a psychiatrist. I can handle Lucifer. But you need an expert in psychic research to get the best out of his talents.'

'Some gullible fool eager to believe in any manifestation? I hardly think——'

'You've got it wrong.' For once Bowker interrupted Seff. 'The real psychic research people are the toughest of all to convince and the smartest at exposing fakes. That's why they're good at handling the real thing when they find it.'

'Like Lucifer?'

'I doubt if they've ever found anyone as good as Lucifer—even with his accuracy down to seventy-five per cent.'

'We have strong reasons for maintaining and improving that, Dr. Bowker. Could an expert such as you speak of help in this?'

'I'd think so.'

'And do you know of any particular person?'

'There's a man called Collier who used to be at Cambridge,' Bowker said slowly. 'I knew him slightly. He came to psychic research from the statistical and mathematical side. Laws of chance and all that sort of thing. Then he got interested in the phenomena themselves. I've read several of his papers in specialist journals.'

'Could you get hold of him?' Seff asked.

'I might.' Bowker rubbed his chin thoughtfully. 'He's very

much a free agent now, I think. But Collier wouldn't come in with us, Seff. I mean, not on the squeeze-game and the killings.'

'I did not expect him to. He need know nothing of that.'

'It would need careful handling. Even then he might stumble on something. What happens if he does find out?'

Seff picked up his pen. 'We would take all possible precautions, of course,' he said absently. 'And you would have to absorb his expertise as rapidly as possible. But if Mr. Collier found out too much it would be necessary to transfer him to the *lower* levels of our young friend's domain.'

2

STEPHEN COLLIER said, 'Modesty.'

After a moment or two he said very slowly, dwelling on each syllable, 'Modesty Blaise.'

He was quite alone, wearing pyjamas and dressing gown, sprawled in a folding chaise longue on the tiny balcony of the little flat just off Place du Tertre, on the heights of Montmartre. Across the rooftops he could see the white dome of Sacré Coeur shining in the floodlights.

Collier was a thin wiry man of thirty. He had a lean, intelligent face, mousebrown hair, and mournfully humorous eyes. Inwardly shy, he concealed this by his manner and speech, which were dry and held an element of self-mockery. He was slightly short-sighted and wore spectacles for reading. With or without spectacles, clothed or naked, Collier had never considered himself particularly attractive. He lounged in sleepy contentment, wondering what Modesty Blaise could possibly see in him.

This was her flat, a small pied-à-terre in Paris. The kitchen was very modern, the rest of the flat furnished simply with pleasant old French pieces and half a dozen paintings, all of small value, bought from the many artists who plied their trade daily in Place du Tertre.

Apart from the kitchen and living room there was only a bathroom and two bedrooms. The second bedroom was spare and presumably unused, unless perhaps Modesty sometimes had a girl-friend staying with her for a while.

Collier thought of Modesty's bedroom. It was still hard to believe that for the last week he had slept in that big brass bed with her and known all the joy and comfort her splendid body gave.

'You lucky bastard,' he said to himself softly.

Above and beyond the wonder of making love with her there was the excitement of simply being with her day by day. She had shown him Paris, which he knew moderately well and she knew intimately; and because she had shown it to him, it had become a city touched with gold.

She could talk easily on a sometimes surprising range of subjects, and she could maintain a companionable silence for hours. During a long afternoon in the Louvre they had not exchanged a word, each absorbed in the marvels it held, sharing them, yet content to let those marvels speak for themselves. Not only could she talk or be silent, she had also the priceless gift of listening well. Sometimes Collier had become so absorbed in watching her listen that he had lost the thread of his discourse.

He had known few women closely, and beyond all question Modesty Blaise was the most fascinating. Of herself she spoke very little, and perhaps this heightened the fascination she held for him, yet he did not at any time have the impression that she was deliberately being enigmatic.

He knew that she was of British nationality and of foreign extraction; that she was rich and independent, without ties. He knew that she was widely travelled and had a curious range of friends and acquaintances. He had accompanied her to a party of remarkable opulence given by a wealthy French industrialist of much charm and culture; she had also taken him to a dive which Collier would have hesitated to enter on his own. It lay in a mainly Algerian quarter of the city and its clientèle seemed to be drawn from the underworld, the real underworld of quiet, dangerous men and hard-eyed women.

Yet Modesty Blaise, in the same dress and jewellery she had worn only an hour before when they dined at Maxim's, was clearly at home in this very different company. She had been greeted respectfully and as an old friend, and because Collier was her escort he had received nods of welcome.

How such things could be intrigued Collier, but he would have felt it the grossest discourtesy to ask questions about her background. It would also, he believed, have been fruitless to do so. Whatever she wanted to tell him she would volunteer. To probe for answers to the questions in his mind might spoil things, and Collier did not want that. He was content, and more than content, with all that she gave him of herself.

He knew, instinctively, that in time it would end. He thought she would end it gently and without needless hurt when that time came. Until then he was happy to live in this dreamlike world, in a state that ranged from contentment to ecstasy.

'Modesty Blaise...' Collier said again, softly. He smiled at his own smugness, and thought about putting on the lights in the flat and fixing himself a drink.

The buzzer on the door sounded. Collier frowned. It couldn't be Modesty. She had told him she would be back around midnight or later, and in any case she had her key. His French was above schoolboy standards, but he did not fancy coping with a chance visitor. Since the lights were out there was no indication that the flat was occupied at the moment. Whoever was at the door would soon go away.

There came the faint sound of a key turning in the lock, and Collier stiffened. He heard the door open and close, the click of switches as light flooded the living-room. Hidden in the darkness on the little balcony, Collier strained his ears to follow the sounds. Something was dumped on the floor and footsteps moved across the room towards the spare bedroom. The click of another switch.

Collier rose to his feet. He was not particularly nervous, only curious and perhaps a little annoyed. There was in him that tough streak of temperament which sometimes marks the shy Englishman.

The intruder cleared his throat. It was a man, and he was coming out of the bedroom now, whistling softly Bert Kaempfert's *Swingin' Safari*. The penny-whistle melody was an extraordinarily difficult one to produce, and some part of Collier's mind registered that it was being whistled beautifully.

The footsteps moved to the kitchen and the light there was switched on. Quietly Collier walked in from the balcony. A large, well-worn pigskin suitcase stood on the floor. The man was clattering with the pots and pans hung on the kitchen wall. There came the soft pop of the gas stove being lit.

Collier walked to the open kitchen door. A pan with a lump of fat in it stood on the stove; two chops and two eggs had been taken from the fridge and placed ready on the kitchen unit. A big man was cutting slices from a French loaf.

As Collier reached the door a board creaked under his foot. For a moment the man's figure seemed to blur. Then he was facing Collier; and, strangely, the breadknife was held by the blade now instead of by the handle.

Collier's nerves jumped with the sharp awareness of danger. Then the moment passed. The man relaxed, flipped the knife so that the handle slapped into his palm again, and smiled with genial apology.

'*Je m'excuse,*' he said. '*Je ne savais pas qu'il-y-avait quelqu'un ici.*'

Collier understood, but he did not intend to put himself at the disadvantage of using an unfamiliar language if it could be avoided. 'You speak English?' he asked tersely.

The man's eyes twinkled. They were very blue. He was even bigger than Collier had first thought, fair-haired and with a weather-beaten face. His clothes were casual and expensive.

'Some people don't reckon it's English,' he said with a strong Cockney accent, 'but I can usually make meself understood.'

'You *are* English.' Collier's cool manner did not relax. 'Then just what the hell are you doing here?' He was at once irritably aware that the first word of the question made no sense. If the big man noticed, he gave no sign.

'Name's Garvin,' he said amiably. 'Willie Garvin.' He returned to slicing the bread. 'I was going to cook a bit of nosh then go to bed.'

'Bed?'

'M'mm. But there was no answer when I rang, so I didn't know you were 'ere. I'll just 'ave a quick bite then push off.'

'How did you get in?' Collier asked.

28

'I got a key.' Willie Garvin moved to the stove and inspected the pan of hot fat dubiously.

'I have a key, too,' Collier said. 'I didn't know there were two of us.'

'There aren't. That's my room.' Willie Garvin nodded vaguely in the direction of the spare bedroom. 'Look, are you any good at cooking? I got a diabolical blindspot for it. Everything burns. I was 'oping the Princess was in, so she could fix me a meal.'

'Princess?'

'Just a courtesy title.' The big man glanced up with a friendly smile. 'I mean Modesty.'

'You're a relative?' Collier was feeling out of his depth. He could not imagine this man being related to Modesty Blaise, but it was the only idea that covered the situation.

'No,' said Willie Garvin, and put the two chops in the frying-pan. 'I used to work for 'er, then she sort of took me into partnership. And then we retired. We're old friends.'

Collier was no less baffled than before. He drew back from the danger of prying into Modesty's affairs and changed his ground. 'So she wouldn't mind you walking in here, helping yourself to a meal, and going to bed?'

'That's right. She wouldn't mind.'

Willie Garvin watched the sizzling chops with an anxious frown. There was a long silence.

'If you know her that well,' Collier said at last, 'why haven't you asked who I am and what I'm doing here?'

Willie Garvin glanced at him briefly in mild surprise. 'If you were a villain you wouldn't be wandering around in pyjamas and a dressing gown, matey,' he said reasonably. 'Outside that, it's none of my business. Be a liberty, me asking questions.' He returned to the chops and flipped them over with a knife.

Collier relaxed. He did not understand how this man fitted in as an old friend of Modesty's, but, remembering the strangeness of some of her friends, he believed it.

'My name's Collier,' he said. 'Stephen Collier.'

29

'Glad to know you. Any idea what time Modesty'll be back?'

'Sometime around midnight.' Collier moved into the kitchen, took a bottle of red wine from a cupboard and began to open it. 'She's dining with somebody who rang up earlier today. Chap called René Vaubois.'

Willie nodded. 'He's been wanting to meet 'er.'

'You know him?'

'Met 'im a couple of times way back, on business for the Princess. Nice bloke. Civil servant, about fifty-five.'

'Thanks.' Collier smiled. He was beginning to like Willie Garvin. 'She told me that herself, but in fact I don't presume to be jealous.'

Willie Garvin nodded approval, his eyes still on the pan. Then his expression changed to one of high indignation. Smoke was rising in a thick coil. He whipped the pan away from the flame.

'See?' he said bitterly. 'Look at those little bastards. I never took my eyes off 'em, did I? And suddenly they frizzle up on me.'

'I'm sorry,' Collier said regretfully. 'I'd help if I could, but you're a good two grades above me. I'd have had the whole bloody pan on fire by this time.'

'Go on?' Willie Garvin looked pleased. 'I'll give you a tip on that. If it won't blow out, don't try an' douse it in the sink. Whip a big saucepan lid down on top of the 'ole pan, that's the best way.'

'That sounds like cordon bleu standard to me,' Collier said respectfully. He poured two glasses of wine and brought them over to the stove. Willie Garvin speared the chops on to a plate, rested it on the rack over the grill, cracked the eggs into the pan, then took one of the glasses.

'Thanks, Mr. Collier.'

'Steve. Cheers.' They stood watching the eggs turn brown and then black round the edges, while the yolks remained liquid.

'I don't think you have enough fat there,' Collier suggested

30

after a while. 'Back-seat driving is gross impertinence of course, but an observer does sometimes have a more objective view of the game.'

'No offence taken,' Willie said moodily. 'But it's too late now. Put more fat in and they'll just go greasy. I've tried it all ways.' He scowled. 'Besides, I'm not going to be dictated to by two unborn chickens. They'll cook my way and like it. I'll trim the edges off afterwards.'

'That, I like,' Collier said happily. 'You have principles, Willie, and you're ready to suffer for them. Allow me to refill your glass. An inexpensive but full-bodied red burgundy is better than a bullet to bite on.'

Five minutes later Willie Garvin sat down to a meal of charred chops and crumbled egg he had scraped from the pan.

'Will it trouble your taste buds unduly if I smoke?' Collier asked gravely, sitting down across the table from him.

'It's a bit 'ard on a subtle palate like mine, but I don't want to be fussy about it. Have one of these.' Willie slid a cigarette case and lighter across to Collier.

They were both of solid gold. Collier had already noticed that the shirt and slacks Willie wore, and the light jacket he had taken off now, were handmade. So were his shoes. On his wrist was a Rolex Oyster perpetual chronometer in stainless steel.

Collier took a cigarette, lit it, passed the case and lighter back.

'You needn't worry about me getting under your feet,' said Willie. 'I'll be going as soon as I've finished this lot. You might tell Modesty I looked in——' He paused, sniffed the air and shook his head resignedly. 'No, don't bother. She'll know, soon as she smells the kitchen. Just say I'm in town and I'll be staying with Claudine tonight. I expect.'

'Another old friend of yours?' Collier asked politely.

Willie shook his head. 'Bedfellow,' he said simply. 'Nice and friendly with it, though. *Une petite amie*, as the French say. They've got a way of putting things.'

'Very charming. I must remember it.' Collier inhaled. 'How do you find retirement, Willie? I'd have thought you were rather young for it.'

'I keep meself amused. Got a pub in England, "The Tread-mill". Nice old place on the river near Maidenhead. Drop in any time.'

'I'd like to. You run it by remote control?'

'My manager runs it. I'm only there a few months of the year. What's your own line, Steve?'

Collier barely hesitated before answering. 'I'm a metal-lurgist. Very dull profession, I'm afraid.'

'I dunno. Technical, I suppose, but not dull if you're in it.' Willie put down his knife and fork. 'Doing any work with beryllium?'

'Er ... not at the moment.'

'Going to be a big thing, I'd say. Half the weight of steel, more rigid, and easier to rivet.'

'Yes.' Collier smiled apologetically. 'But I'm not going to talk shop if you don't mind. I'm on holiday.'

'Sure.' Willie carried his empty plate out, scraped it clean and put it in the dish-washer. There was a half puzzled, half amused look in his eyes. When he went back into the living-room Collier was putting a record on the radiogram in the corner, a Jacques Loussier interpretation of Bach.

'I'll just smoke a fag, then leave you to it,' Willie said, sinking into an armchair.

'Don't go on my account. Hang on for Modesty if you'd rather.'

Willie nodded absently. He sat smoking as the soft, mathe-matical perfection of *Fantaisie et Fugue in G Minor* filled the room. Collier shared the last of the wine and lounged back on the couch. It seemed that Willie Garvin had the same capacity as Modesty Blaise for being silent when there was nothing to say. But after a few minutes Willie got up and prowled to the little balcony. Grinding out his cigarette, he stood looking into the darkness for a while, then moved back into the room, hands thrust in trouser pockets, pacing very quietly but with a restless air. Twice, uneasily, he rubbed an ear with the palm of his hand.

'You said Modesty was 'aving dinner with Vaubois?' Willie's voice cut through the music, different, no longer relaxed.

'That's right.' Collier lifted an eyebrow in mild surprise.

'You know where they were going?'

'On one of the bateaux-mouches. You know. Cruise along the Seine, dine in style on deck under a transparent canopy——'

'I know.' Willie scratched his chin, eyes thoughtful. 'They'll be coming off at Pont de l'Alma around eleven-thirty. I think I'll get down there.'

Collier stood up, puzzled. 'Is something wrong?'

'There could be.' Willie was rubbing his ear again, and answered automatically. His earlier amiability had been replaced by brusqueness, and Collier found his own coolness returning.

'I don't want to be inquisitive,' he said, 'but you've been here for the last hour and now you suddenly say something might be wrong. Like what?'

'Like trouble.' Willie picked up his jacket and put it on.

'But how do you know?' There was sudden interest in Collier's face. His question did not contradict Willie Garvin, it was simply a question.

The blue eyes came back from a distance and focused on him. 'I don't know for sure.' Willie hesitated, then went on curtly, 'And how I know doesn't make sense. But my ears are prickling.' He turned away. His manner showed that he expected laughter or incredulity, and didn't care anyway.

'Wait,' Collier said quickly. 'I'll only be three minutes.'

Willie stopped. 'You want to come?'

'Yes.' Collier was taking off his dressing gown as he moved into the bedroom. Willie followed him. As he pulled on trousers and a shirt Collier said, 'Has this happened before, this ear-prickling?'

'Often enough.'

'And it means something to you? Some kind of warning?'

'Yes.' The voice was impatient. 'I don't mind if you laugh so long as you get a bloody move on.'

'I'm not laughing. I'm interested. What's the percentage accuracy?'

'Eh?'

'If you get this warning, do you *always* find there's trouble later, or do you sometimes get a false alarm?'

Willie said slowly, 'You're a funny kind of metallurgist, aren't you?'

'Never mind that.' Collier's lean face was intent, with the air of a hunter pursuing a quarry. 'Does the warning ever prove to be false?'

'Not so far as I can remember.'

'Right.' Collier pulled on socks. 'Now the other way round —have you ever run into trouble *without* being forewarned in this way?'

'M'mm? Yes, often.' Willie was barely paying attention to the questions now. His mind was elsewhere. Collier pulled on his shoes and stood up. There was absorbed interest in the dark eyes as he studied Willie Garvin.

'You know a bit about trouble, don't you, Willie?'

'A bit.'

'Do you tend to get this kind of warning when you're relaxed and not expecting anything, or is it more likely to come when you're keyed up and anticipating that something might happen? What I'm trying to get at is—when are you most receptive?'

Slowly Willie's full attention focused on Collier in a baffled, almost angry stare. 'For Christ's sake, what does it matter?' he said impatiently. 'I'm going down to the Pont de l'Alma to wait for Modesty, and I'm going now. Are you coming or not?'

The heat of the day still lingered, and it was pleasantly warm under the great plexiglas canopy which covered the long, brightly lit restaurant-deck of the bateau-mouche.

René Vaubois, head of the Deuxième Bureau, watched the waiter pour two glasses of cognac, then quickly switched his gaze back to the woman who sat across the table from him. Her head was in profile as she looked out towards the Ile de la Cité.

Vaubois was happily married, and with a daughter only two or three years younger than his companion, but that did not prevent him quietly revelling in the pleasure of being the envied escort of a young woman whose strong dark beauty drew the eyes of men and women alike.

Her black, shining hair was drawn up in a chignon on the crown of her head. The eyes were midnight blue, the face smoothly tanned, the neck long and graceful. She wore a white silk blouse with short sleeves and a skirt of deep blue velvet. A loose jacket, matching the skirt, hung over the back of her chair. Her shoulders, broad for a woman, tapered to a slender waist. Her legs were long and very beautiful; especially so, Vaubois thought, when she walked, for then one saw the long easy stride, the leg swinging fully from the thigh.

Sir Gerald Tarrant, Vaubois' friend and opposite number in England, had said: 'You'll find her restful to be with, René. I know that sounds unlikely but it's true. There are no tensions. She gives you an extraordinary sense of peace.' He had added drily, 'I wouldn't say she has the same effect on an enemy, mind you.'

It intrigued Vaubois that throughout the evening he had been quite unable to discern the dangerous potential in Modesty Blaise; but he knew more than enough about her to be in no doubt that Tarrant's final words were valid in their implication. Now, content in the warm tranquillity that encompassed him, he knew that Tarrant's earlier words were also true.

She turned her head, smiled, and picked up her cognac, lifting the glass to him. Vaubois responded.

'I am a poor host,' he said. 'I should have cigarettes to offer you. In fact, I would enjoy one myself. On very rare occasions, when I am in a state of utter contentment, I smoke a cigarette.'

Her eyes sparkled with amusement. 'Sir Gerald tries to say things like that, but he hasn't the Frenchman's gift for it and he usually ends up by turning pink.' She reached for the handbag beside her chair. 'I've some Gauloises if that would suit you?'

'Admirably,' said Vaubois. 'And thank you for the sidelight on our good Sir Gerald. I am delighted that the old fox has some small deficiencies.'

Vaubois had practised a slight deception in the matter of the cigarettes. There were several in his case. But he simply wished to give himself the pleasure of watching Modesty Blaise move, and his eyes dwelt now on the play of her arms and hands as she opened her bag, took out a small gold case and a lighter, offered him a Gauloise, and passed him the lighter.

'Thank you.' He lit her cigarette, then his own. They sat smoking in silence for a while. At last Vaubois said, 'Would you think it impertinent if I used your first name, mam'selle?'

'I'd prefer it, René.'

'Thank you. Tell me, are you expecting Willie Garvin here in Paris? I should like to renew acquaintance with him. A very remarkable character, that one.'

'More remarkable than he ever suspects.' Modesty's smile looked back into memory and Vaubois wondered what fleeting images of past battles were touching her mind as she spoke. 'But I've no idea whether he'll suddenly turn up here.'

'He is at his pub in England?'

'I don't think so. I had a card from him just before I left Tangier. He was in Tokyo then. He said he'd gone there for a hot bath.'

'A hot bath?' Vaubois stared.

'He likes the Japanese style. The masseuses are very good.'

'Ah.' Vaubois nodded his understanding. The bateau-mouche glided on, turning now beyond the eastern point of the Ile de la Cité.

'There is something I would like to ask you,' said Vaubois, 'but I'm afraid of offending you.'

'You won't. What is it?'

'During the days when you ran *The Network*,' Vaubois said carefully, 'you operated in a number of fields which were not exactly legal——'

'I was in crime,' she broke in, and her eyes were laughing at him. 'I was selective in the rackets I operated, but they were certainly criminal. Go on.'

'Did you ever find yourself involved in ...' Vaubois paused, then went on apologetically, 'in protection?'

'Not as a racket,' she answered simply. 'It's the next worse thing to drugs and vice. But sometimes we were asked for protection and were offered a price for it. Laroche found that some big boys were trying to wreck his chain of casinos and he came to me about it.' She shrugged. 'We didn't have to do very much.'

'How much?'

'Willie Garvin snatched the biggest of the big boys. We put him on one of the m.f.v.'s we used for smuggling.'

'I'm sorry, m.f.v.'s?'

'Motor fishing vessels. So the big boy worked as a greaser under a very tough captain for three months. That was the end of it.' She sipped her cognac. '*The Network* gave genuine protection here and there, but we didn't force it on anybody.'

'I see.' René Vaubois ran a finger thoughtfully round his glass.

'Is that all?' She looked at him curiously.

'No.' He was silent, arranging his thoughts, and she waited without impatience. 'The protection racket,' he said at last, 'normally consists of collecting small sums of money from a large number of people. Shopkeepers offer the simplest example. Do you think this system could be operated in a different way, Modesty—by collecting large sums of money from a few selected people?'

'Under threat of what?'

'Death.'

37

She shrugged. 'That's something you might get away with once. Like a kidnapping. You couldn't make a racket of it.'

Vaubois eased the ash from his cigarette and nodded. 'Let us suppose,' he said, 'that your government in London receives a threat that the—ah—the Minister of Housing, shall we say, will die within six months unless a sum of one hundred thousand pounds is paid for his life. What would be the result?'

She laughed and shook her head. 'You're joking.'

'Of course. But assume that I am not.'

She looked at him sharply, and the amusement faded from her face. 'The threat would be taken as coming from a crank,' she said at last. 'It would be passed to the police, and filed.'

'And if the Minister died within six months?'

'Died how?'

'Let us say by violence in this instance. And then a new warning is received, threatening somebody else. A minor civil servant, perhaps. What then?'

'It would be taken seriously.' Her voice was quiet. 'Are you saying this has happened?'

'I am putting a hypothesis,' Vaubois smiled. 'Blackmail of rich individuals, blackmail of a government in respect of its servants. Can you see any way that this could be made to work?'

'Not unless you can kill without detection and threaten without the source of the threat being traced back—and arrange some foolproof way of picking up the money from anybody frightened enough to pay up. But it doesn't make sense any way you look at it. Why make trouble for yourself by tackling governments? Why not just stick to rich individuals?'

'If you could kill without detection, and make your threats good, you would want your prospective victims to *know* that fact, so that they would more readily pay up. Therefore you would want the limited publicity that would come from involving government authorities.'

'Limited?'

'To avoid panic. And of course there are certain governments who might pay, once they were sufficiently impressed by earlier results. None in Europe, perhaps, except for one or two dictatorships. But surely you could get a good yield from some of the African countries, the new ones. If Mr. Umbopo, the Prime Minister, thought he might be killed, he could very easily raid the treasury. But private individuals would provide the best crop, I think. An oil sheikh here, an Indian millionaire there, a South American playboy ...'

Vaubois smiled and made a little gesture. 'You would have to convince them that your threats were valid, of course, and the simplest way would be to circulate all likely clients when your first threats were made, so that they could see for themselves what happened to those who failed to pay up.'

Modesty was watching him uncertainly. 'You'd have a whole lot of countries chasing you, including the Interpol countries. Threatened people would be given protection, and you wouldn't get away with many more killings then. And how do you collect, if and when anybody pays up? Collecting means there has to be a point of contact. It's always the problem for kidnappers collecting ransom money. The point of contact is where they come unstuck.'

'Very true.' Still smiling, Vaubois stubbed out his cigarette. 'The whole thing is quite absurd.'

'Perhaps you didn't give me all the details,' she said slowly. 'Details can make an extravagant idea possible.'

He laughed and gave her a look of apology. 'I have supplied the extravagant hypothesis, Modesty. I hoped you might devise the all-important details.'

She sat back in her chair, looking at him, a little frown on her brow. 'René, I'm sorry if I'm being slow. I don't know if you're trying to ask me something, or tell me something, or if this is just some kind of fashionable fantasy-game that I haven't learnt the rules of yet. But you've lost me.'

Vaubois looked out over the dark waters of the Seine. 'It is a fantasy game,' he said after a while, 'and I was both foolish and discourteous to begin it. Please forgive me and let us talk of other things. Ah, look now...'

She followed his gaze. They were passing close to the western end of the Ile de la Cité. Here the bank was low. A slack wire, invisible in the darkness, had been fastened between two trees. On the wire, seeming to float in the air, a white, phantom figure danced to and fro. It went down on one knee, the wire swaying, then rose and turned, gliding smoothly. The sheeted arms flapped and the head with its crude horror-mask wagged from side to side.

There came laughter and a cheer from the watchers on the uncovered imperial deck above.

'How pleasant,' said Vaubois, 'to be a young man, a student I would think, with such an excellent sense of values. He dresses himself up as a ghost. He sets up his wire, and as the boat passes he performs his little pantomime to amuse us, with the Ile de la Cité for his stage and the Seine for his auditorium. There is no payment. He enjoys himself by giving to us something of his exuberant spirits.' He spoke with a mock philosophical air, and Modesty laughed.

'It must be fun to do nice crazy things when you're young,' she said.

Vaubois looked shocked. '*Chère amie*, if you do not class yourself as young, then you make me a greybeard. Please show more kindness.'

'I'm twenty-seven, René. At least I think so. The early years are a little confused.'

'Twenty-seven? Nonsense. You put your hair up, wear expensive clothes and shoes with elegant heels; you sip cognac and you smoke a cigarette. But this is all deception. You are a child, making pretence.'

'I was much older when I was a child,' Modesty said idly, and he knew what she meant, for her early years had been spent in a fierce and lonely struggle for survival as a refugee in the Balkans and Middle East during the war and its aftermath. She went on with a half smile, 'But if I seem young to you now, René, it's because I do what that young man was

40

doing.' She nodded towards the lights of the Ile de la Cité, now dwindling to pinpoints in the darkness.

'That young man?' Vaubois was puzzled.

'Yes.' She looked at him. 'I sometimes walk a tight-rope. It's a necessity for me.'

'Ah.' Vaubois understood. She had not been deceived by his pretended fantasy-game. She knew that something real lay behind it, and whatever that reality might be she was offering help if he wanted it.

Vaubois thought resignedly, 'Well ... thank God I am not so bloody ruthless as Tarrant. At least, not as far as this girl is concerned. Twice he has come close to getting her killed.'

Putting out a hand, he rested it on Modesty's hand for a moment and said, 'I have just remembered something I meant to speak of. When I telephoned you yesterday a young Englishman answered. I have been worried in case he is annoyed that you came to dine with me tonight.'

Modesty knew that her offer had been understood, received with gratitude, and gently refused. She smiled to show that she was in no way put out by the refusal. It was a quick, warm smile that lit her face with a sudden air of mischief.

'I don't think the young Englishman was annoyed,' she said. 'He has no reason to be dissatisfied with me in any way.'

René Vaubois laughed and took away his hand. 'I am sure of that,' he said, and looked westward along the Seine. 'Now, there stands the abomination we call the Eiffel Tower. I have devised a magnificent scheme for blowing it up. Perhaps we could go over the technical details?'

3

'Do they still prickle?' asked Collier.

'Eh? I don't know. Stop bloody well talking about my ears, will you? It puts me off.' Willie Garvin's voice was curt, yet he seemed completely relaxed as he stood with Stephen Collier, leaning against the wall at the top of the long slope which led down from Pont de l'Alma to the embarkation stage beside the Quai de la Conférence.

To their left, at the foot of the slope, some fifty cars were parked in a line. The two men had travelled down from Montmartre in Willie's hired car, a big Simca, now parked just off Place de l'Alma. For twenty minutes they had been waiting here by the wall, watching for the return of the bateau-mouche.

'Why don't we go down to the landing-stage?' Collier ventured. 'That's where they'll be coming off.'

'You go and wait where you like.' Willie's eyes moved constantly as he spoke, watching every car and pedestrian that came near the head of the slope.

Collier shrugged and remained where he was.

'How did the Princess get down 'ere?' Willie asked after a brief silence. 'She didn't take 'er own car. It was still in the garage.'

'No. She took a cab to an office somewhere. That's where she was meeting this chap Vaubois. I don't know how they came on here.'

Willie grunted.

There was another silence, broken by Collier. 'I'm not going on about the ear-prickling,' he said, 'but tell me something else. You sensed trouble brewing. Well, all right—I wouldn't stagger back in amazement if an irate French husband or father came looking for you with a shotgun. But you seem to be worried about Modesty. I really don't see why she should be running into any kind of trouble.'

Willie surveyed him briefly, and Collier saw a glimmer of amusement behind the clear blue eyes before they turned away again to keep up the seemingly aimless surveillance.

'How did you meet her?' Willie asked.

'By chance, when I came off a night flight a couple of weeks ago at Orly.' Collier felt embarrassment creeping into his voice and was annoyed by it. 'As a matter of fact I had my pocket picked somewhere just after leaving the reception lounge. Wallet, with all my money and traveller's cheques. Felt the chap jostle me, but didn't catch on till a minute later. By then he was gone. But Modesty had just come off some other flight, and she spotted it apparently. Went after the chap.'

'Went after 'im, eh?'

'Yes. I didn't know it at the time, of course. I've told her since that it was a crazy thing to do. She might have got hurt. Anyway, she didn't. I was just getting frantic about the wallet when she came up and handed it to me. It seems the chap had dropped it as he scooted across the car park.'

'Dropped it,' Willie echoed solemnly. 'That was a bit of luck, eh?'

'I don't see what there is to be bloody sarcastic about,' Collier said stiffly. 'And I don't see what all this has got to do with the question.'

'What question?'

'The one I asked. Why on earth should Modesty be in danger of any kind?'

'She might see someone else getting their pocket picked,' Willie suggested blandly. 'Then maybe if she chased after the dip, she might catch 'im up before 'e dropped it this time.'

Collier swallowed his anger. 'I don't know what you're getting at, and I don't much care. Can I have another question?'

'Go ahead.'

'You sensed trouble. What made you think it was something to do with Modesty, and not with you?'

43

'Don't know.' Willie's voice was disinterested. 'Look, why don't you talk about riveting beryllium? Then I can just listen. I'm getting a bit tired of——' He broke off, and Collier saw that he was staring at a figure coming up the slope from the quayside. As the figure drew abreast of them a pool of lamplight revealed a small man with a wrinkled brown face. He wore a beret and a shabby grey suit.

Willie drew a deep breath and murmured, 'That's more like it...' He lifted his voice. *'Hé-là. Chuli. Ça va?'*

The man's head jerked round. He saw Willie Garvin, and in the same instant he was running like a startled mouse. Collier felt a gust of air as Willie took off from a standing start and went streaking in pursuit. A horn blared. The quarry skidded in front of a taxi, missing it by a hair's breadth.

Willie swerved, but his shoulder touched the side of the taxi and he staggered for a moment. Two more cars passed before he could take up the pursuit. Collier, who had followed, heard Willie swear savagely.

On the far side of the *place*, the small man dived into the back of a waiting car, a black Panhard. The engine roared and the car flashed away towards Avenue Marceau.

Willie turned back across the *place*, walking slowly.

'What the hell was all that about?' Collier asked.

'I'm not sure.' Willie's anger had gone. He was thoughtful, but his manner was amiable again. It was as if the appearance of the man Chuli had in some way provided a mental handhold where previously his mind had been groping in a void.

'The boat's coming in,' Collier said.

Willie looked past him down the slope. The long bateau-mouche was edging up to the landing stage. 'Right,' he said, and moved quickly to the parked Simca. Opening the boot, he took out a roll of tools. 'Let's get down there.'

Collier followed him down the slope. They halted by the long line of cars parked with their noses to the wall. Already the first passengers were coming ashore, some walking away up the slope, others moving to their cars. Willie's eyes

44

searched the shadows along the quay and the faces of the people who lingered before moving away.

'What are we looking for?' Collier said, aware of suddenly increased tension in himself.

'Anything that smells. Leave that bit to me. Just watch for Modesty and tell me as soon as you see 'er.'

Five minutes plodded slowly by. Cars drove away and the stream of disembarking passengers dwindled.

'There she is,' Collier said.

She was moving towards the broad gangway, her hand linked through the arm of a well-dressed man beside her, a man in his late fifties, with a smooth, placid face and a leisurely manner.

Collier drew quietly back for several paces, into the shadow of the wall. He wondered why he had done so, then realised with a touch of wry self-knowledge that he wanted to watch the meeting of Willie Garvin and Modesty Blaise unseen by her.

Modesty and her escort were moving across the gangway. She saw Willie at once. Her face showed no surprise, only quick pleasure.

'Willie Garvin's back from Tokyo,' she said to Vaubois. With a sudden gamine grin she put a finger to each side of her face and drew her eyes to oriental slits, putting her head on one side in query.

Willie Garvin lifted a hand and made a circle of the finger and thumb, in acknowledgment.

Collier, watching, did not understand the brief pantomime. He saw Modesty and her escort move forward, heard her voice.

'Willie, love.' She put out both hands. He took them and lifted one until the backs of her fingers just touched his cheek, then released her. They had not embraced, he had not even kissed her hand, yet there was a special, almost ritual intimacy about the greeting that sharpened the tiny pang of jealousy in Collier as he watched.

"Allo, Princess.'

'You know René Vaubois,' she said.

Willie nodded. 'M'sieu.' The two men shook hands.

'It must be almost four years now, Mr. Garvin,' Vaubois said pleasantly. 'How nice to meet you without having to talk business.'

'I'm not so sure of that.' Willie looked at Modesty. 'I think there's trouble around, Princess.'

Her face quiet, she put out her hand to run the palm over his chest, as if feeling for something beneath the jacket and shirt. One eyebrow lifted a little. 'You're not tooled up?'

'I know.' Willie's grimace was one of disgust with himself. 'I started feeling edgy, so we came down in a hurry. Should've unpacked me gear first, but I 'ad to answer a nonstop quiz——' He broke off, looking round. 'Where's he gone?'

Collier moved forward. 'His ears prickled, Modesty. Is it a joke?'

'No. It's not a joke, Steve.' She gave him a quick, automatic smile of greeting and looked at Willie again.

'We waited up top,' said Willie. 'Saw Chuli coming up from down 'ere.'

'Chuli.' Some kind of understanding passed between them as she repeated the name. Vaubois was watching them with deep interest.

'I tried to nail 'im,' Willie said, 'but the little bastard ran like a rabbit. And there was a car waiting for 'im.'

'Never mind.' She looked at Vaubois. 'You know Chuli?'

'No. He is probably better known to the police than to my people. Does he specialise?'

'Yes. Let me have your car keys please, René.'

Vaubois took some keys from his pocket and handed them to her. She passed them to Willie and said, 'It's over there. The 1963 Citroen DS 19.'

They moved east along the quayside towards the car. It stood alone now. The last stragglers from the bateau-mouche had disappeared. Willie walked all round the car, surveying it thoughtfully. He unlocked the off-side front door, put his roll of tools down on the seat, and pulled the bonnet release catch.

46

'Nonplayers off the green I reckon, Princess,' he said.

She turned to Collier. 'Darling, go with René and wait at the top of the slope, will you?' She touched his arm.

'No,' Collier said stubbornly. 'I don't know what the hell's going on, but I'm going to stand here and find out.'

René Vaubois cleared his throat. 'I do have some idea of what is happening, Modesty, but I support our young friend in the matter of remaining here,' he said apologetically. 'Would you like me to call in an expert?'

'We have one thanks, René.' She turned away and joined Willie by the front bumper. He was kneeling, releasing the catch in the off-side recess. The bonnet rose slightly. He said, 'Right, Princess,' and stood up, resting both hands on top of the bonnet.

Modesty knelt and put her hand under the front edge to release the safety catch beneath. She nodded to Willie, and he allowed the bonnet to rise fractionally. Very carefully she groped underneath it with one hand.

'Wire,' she said quietly.

'Chuli always did lay 'is bets each way.'

With nothing more said, Modesty took over Willie's place, holding the bonnet so that it could not rise. Willie slipped his jacket off, took a pencil torch from the inside pocket and selected a pair of pliers from the tool kit.

Collier, standing six paces away and with an unbelievable suspicion dawning in his mind, became aware that the man at his shoulder was speaking. 'My name is Vaubois. René Vaubois. I am afraid Modesty has been too preoccupied to introduce us yet.'

'Oh. Collier. Stephen Collier.' He tore his eyes away from the car to look briefly at Vaubois' bland, speculative face. 'Are they doing what I think they're doing?'

'Yes, Mr. Collier. It is possible, but not probable I think, that we may be blown up at any moment. Please do not imagine that I remain here as a heroic gesture. The fact is that my fears are far exceeded by the fascination of seeing these two at work.'

Collier looked back at the car. Willie was shining the torch through the gap of the slightly raised bonnet and easing his other hand through, holding the pliers. To Collier the whole scene seemed suddenly unreal. It was as if he were dreaming, but knew that this was a dream, and therefore felt no sense of danger.

'At work?' he repeated vaguely. 'I don't understand.'

'It is not necessary to understand,' Vaubois said politely. 'We are observing a mystique, two persons performing a complex task without verbal communication. This is a very minor example of it, of course. It would be fascinating to see them more actively engaged, but...'

The words became meaningless to Collier. A dozen half-formed questions crowded his head but he said nothing. For the moment he felt a sense of almost total exclusion, and it tasted bitter in his mouth.

Willie's arm tensed, and there came a faint snip from under the bonnet as the pliers bit through wire. Modesty lifted the bonnet a few inches. Willie scanned the interior with his torch, then straightened up. Modesty lifted the bonnet so that it was fully open, turned away and came back with the roll of tools.

Willie was standing by the wing now. She held the roll open for him. He selected a spanner and began to unfasten the nut on one of the battery terminals. After a few turns he passed the spanner back to her and jerked the heavy lead free of the terminal. Reaching down inside the chassis he was busy with both hands for a long two minutes. Twice Modesty passed him the pliers and twice received them back again.

He straightened up at last, holding a flat box about the size of a large cigar box. There was a small hole at each end, and from the holes protruded the ends of metallic cylinders. Very carefully Willie eased out the cylinders and passed them one at a time to Modesty. He cut the thick wire securing the box, opened the lid, then relaxed.

'P.E.,' he said, and tossed the box on to the front seat of the car. 'No sweat.'

Taking the detonators from Modesty, he walked along the quayside and tossed them far out into the river. Modesty joined Collier and Vaubois, wiping her hands on a rag from the tool kit.

'What was it, *chère amie*?' Vaubois asked quietly.

'P.E. Plastic explosive. Two different types of detonator. One worked electrically off the battery, the other worked mechanically by a wire attached to the bonnet. Chuli's always cautious.'

'Was this for your benefit or mine, do you think?'

'Yours, René. You're still in business.'

'What kind of business?' Collier said. His voice was louder than he had intended.

Vaubois made a deprecating gesture. 'I have some connection with the authorities,' he said vaguely. Then, to Modesty, 'Believe me, I am truly appalled that you might have been killed with me.'

'You'd never have lived it down.' Her quick grin lasted only a moment. She added soberly, 'It's a good thing Willie Garvin turned up.'

'He knew,' said Collier, and there was a blend of awe and excitement in his voice now. 'He really *knew* that something was going to happen.'

Modesty looked at him with a touch of mock surprise. 'You seem quite thrilled about that bit, darling. Does it interest you more than the idea of me being spread all over the Quai de la Conférence?'

'God, no. I'm sorry.' Collier ran a hand down his lean face. The skin was suddenly damp and he was inwardly shaking. 'I'm still in a daze. I just don't know what it's all about, Modesty.' He looked at her, baffled, as if she had become strange to him.

'Later, Steve.' She was looking past him. Willie came back from along the quay. Seeing him, Collier was shocked. Willie Garvin's manner was relaxed, but the brown face was hard with fury and the blue eyes so cold that their gaze seemed to blister. In silence he picked up his jacket.

49

Vaubois said, 'A description of Chuli would be useful.'

'Small man, Algerian,' said Modesty. 'About five feet three, round head, wrinkled face, early forties.'

Vaubois looked at Willie. 'What was he wearing, Mr. Garvin?'

'Same clothes they'll bury 'im in,' Willie said bleakly, and settled his jacket in place. 'I'll be in touch, Princess.' He turned away. Modesty shot a quick glance of query at Vaubois, who gave a slight shake of his head.

'Willie,' she called. He halted and looked back. 'Leave it, Willie love.'

'Leave it? Jesus, I can't let 'im get away with doing a plastic on you, Princess!'

'It was meant for René.'

'The plastic don't pick and choose.'

'Leave it, Willie.' Her voice was sharp. Collier felt his bafflement increase. During the de-fusing of the bomb it had seemed to him that Willie Garvin was in command. But now, clearly, dominance between the strange pair lay with Modesty.

Willie Garvin stood still, not resentful, not sulking, only distressed. Modesty moved towards him and took him gently by the lapels of his jacket. She spoke quietly, neither in English nor in French. Collier had the feeling that the language was Arabic. The tone of her voice was reassuring, a little coaxing. Willie's troubled face relaxed slightly. She smiled, and said something that made him laugh in spite of himself. He shook his head and shrugged acquiescence.

Modesty put an arm through his, and together they moved back to where Collier and Vaubois stood watching. 'We'll all go back to the flat for a drink,' she said. 'Willie has to pick up his bag there, anyway.'

Collier said, 'If you're taking that box of explosive, I'll walk.'

She laughed. 'That stuff's not sensitive. We'll make a call on the way. René can hand it in to the police and start them looking for Chuli.'

'Better leave the Citroen 'ere for them to check,' said Willie. 'Chuli might have left some prints.'

'I would prefer to leave it,' Vaubois agreed. 'You have a car?'

'Got a Simca up top.'

Modesty said, 'Steve, you go on with Willie. We'll be with you in a moment.'

Collier hesitated, then began to walk with Willie along the quay.

Modesty looked at Vaubois. 'Chuli's only a tool,' she said. 'Who's after you, René?'

'*Ma chère*, I truly do not know.'

'Is this the first attempt?'

'Of recent years, yes.'

'But it didn't surprise you.'

A smile. 'I have lived too long to be surprised.'

Her eyes were troubled. 'I'm worried about you.'

Vaubois looked away. The simple statement moved him deeply, but he did not want to show it. 'You are very kind,' he said. 'Please be still more kind and forget about this matter, Modesty.'

'It could almost fit in with that fantasy game you were playing earlier this evening.'

'Ah, that.' He spread his hands. 'A mere *bêtise*. Please forget that also.'

She studied him in silence for a while. When she spoke at last it was with a wry smile. 'All right, René. It might be a little awkward for you to be connected with me officially. I won't embarrass you.'

Vaubois wanted to protest, but it was simpler to let her mistake his motives. Better for her to mistake them. He moved to the car, picked up the box of plastic explosive, and locked the door. 'Your friend Mr. Collier seems a very pleasant young man.'

'A rather bewildered one at the moment. He doesn't know much about me.'

'And now you will have to tell him?'

51

'Why?' A smile, very feminine and rather wicked, lit her face. 'Shouldn't he be satisfied with what he does know about me?'

Vaubois laughed and took her arm to begin the walk along the quay and up the slope. 'More than satisfied, I think. He should count himself very fortunate. Would you ask that question of Sir Gerald Tarrant?'

'Heavens, no. It would embarrass him. He's very British.'

'And I am very French?'

'Well—I know I don't shock you.'

'Far from it. Do you know that your Mr. Collier is a little jealous?'

'Of you?'

'Ah, no.' Vaubois was amused at the idea. 'Of Willie Garvin.'

Modesty sighed. 'That's usual. I can never think why.'

'Is it so surprising?'

'I think so. If a man could choose between defusing a bomb with a girl and going to bed with a girl, I'd think he'd be glad to settle for the bed. Don't you?'

'Not necessarily.' Vaubois' voice held laughter. 'The bomb has a special intimacy. It is, after all, so much more unusual.'

She shook his arm and looked up the slope. 'Now you're back to your fantasy game. I thought you wanted me to forget it.'

4

VAUBOIS had spent much longer than intended at the police station. It was nearing one-thirty a.m. when Willie set the Simca to climb the dark streets which led up to the heights of Montmartre. Vaubois sat beside him, Modesty and Collier in the back.

'You are sure it is not too late for us to join you for a nightcap?' Vaubois asked, turning his head.

'As long as it's not too late for you. Willie, you'll run René home afterwards?'

'Sure, Princess.'

Collier had not spoken for a long time. His mind was trying to guess the answers to too many questions at once. He wondered who René Vaubois was. He wondered what Modesty Blaise was. And he sought hopelessly to grasp the nature of her relationship with Willie Garvin.

He thought about the extraordinary business in the flat with Willie. That was one thing he could follow up now, anyway. He leaned forward a little.

'Willie, when you get this danger signal, the ear-prickling—how far ahead does it work?'

'Blimey, he's off again,' Willie said with weary good nature. 'Crazy about my ears, he is, Princess.'

'I'm crazy about them myself, Willie love. They don't quite match, but they've got character.'

'I'm serious,' Collier said with a touch of exasperation.

'All right, darling. Willie's got an instinct. It's very useful. That's all.'

'Sorry, I won't buy it.' Collier shook his head. 'Instinct arises from knowledge provided by one or more of the five senses, but below the threshold of awareness. We know something without consciously realising how we know it. That didn't apply to Willie this evening. He was three or four miles away in space and an hour or more ahead in time.'

Modesty looked at the lean, intent face beside her with surprise. 'You're being very technical.'

'I'm only saying it's not instinct. It's foreknowledge. Precognition. I haven't seen anything quite like it before.'

'Been too busy with metallurgy I expect,' Willie said blandly.

Collier shot him a quick look, then sat back and gazed idly out of the window. 'I just felt it was interesting,' he said, his voice casual as if dismissing the subject.

There was silence for half a minute. Collier was aware of Modesty's curious gaze. The car turned a corner, and Vaubois coughed. 'It is probably unimportant at this time of night,' he said, 'but you are going down a one-way street in the wrong direction, Willie.'

'I know.' Willie spoke thoughtfully. 'So's the car that's following us. I just wanted to make sure. It's a Panhard, too.' He glanced at the mirror again. 'Could be the same one. Twice in a few hours is a bit saucy. They must be dead keen to see you off, René.'

Modesty was looking back through the rear window. 'Keep the speed steady, Willie. Better if they don't know we're on to them yet.'

'Right. Which way do we play it, Princess? You carrying anything?'

'It wasn't supposed to be that sort of evening. Just the kongo.'

Staring, Collier saw her hand grip the dumb-bell shaped clasp of her handbag and jerk hard. The polished wooden clasp came off, gripped in her clenched first, the knobs protruding at each end.

'Pity I didn't bring me blades,' said Willie, and turned another corner. With one hand he fumbled in the roll of tools he had tossed into the car between himself and Vaubois. 'Got a couple of nice spanners 'ere, though.'

Again Collier felt a dreamlike sense of unreality descending upon him. Vaubois was looking back, his face a little drawn and tired.

'I suggest you try to head down into the centre of the city,' he said quietly. 'This is an unpleasantly suitable area for an attack.'

'No.' Modesty's voice was cool. 'If we lose them now they can try again tomorrow. Or next week. I'm sorry, René, but we're going to put a stop to this.'

'Modesty, I am beyond the age when I might be an asset in such a matter. And I think Mr. Collier is not perhaps experienced. There will be at least four in that car, perhaps six.'

'Yes. What about their tools, Willie?'

'Knives or coshes mostly, I reckon. They don't want a lot of noise, even around 'ere.'

'Silencers?'

'Not for the 'ole carload. They've 'ad to start this caper in a hurry.'

'All right. Make for Claudine's. The alley and the court-yard.'

In the mirror Collier saw a grin spread over Willie Garvin's face. 'The courtyard. Just the job, Princess. I was reckoning to stay at Claudine's, anyway.'

The Simca surged forward, swung round a corner and plunged down hill. Willie whipped down through the gears, swung right, right again, and set the car snarling up a gradient.

'May I have a spanner, too?' Collier asked politely. He was suddenly afraid, but more afraid of showing it.

'You won't need one. And don't get under our feet, darling.' Modesty leaned forward to speak to Willie. 'I'll draw them through, you keep them penned. Have you got a key to Claudine's?'

'No. But it's just a rimlock. There are two bolts, but she never shoots 'em. Just turns the key.'

'Right.' Modesty looked back at the lights of the following car. 'I'll need thirty seconds.'

Willie nodded, and settled down to drive. The pursuit car

was no longer tailing them, it was trying to catch them. Collier had lost all sense of direction, but when they passed the same junction twice, with broad steps occupying the road leading up to the left, he realised that Willie was manoeuvring in a comparatively small area, and gradually gaining.

'Steady ... don't lose them,' Modesty said. She was half kneeling, looking back. 'All right, they've seen us. Cut off from Rue Feutrier and head for Claudine's place, Willie.'

Vaubois turned round in his seat. The drawn look had vanished. 'Tarrant will be gratifyingly envious about this,' he said with pleasure. 'May we have instructions please, *chère amie?*'

Modesty spoke without looking round. 'Yes. Steve, you listen carefully. When we stop we'll be in a narrow street of old terraced houses, with only a strip of pavement. Willie will stop with the nearside of the car only an inch from the wall. René will be able to open his door, because there's an arched passage which runs through for about ten yards into a courtyard. Clear?'

Collier nodded. 'So far.'

'We go out fast. René first, then me, then you—all out of the front nearside door. Halfway along the passage, on the right, there's a door. A front door. I'll open it. There's just a tiny hallway with a flight of stairs leading straight up from it. Steve, you follow me. Fast. René, you shoot the two bolts on the inside of the door, then follow us.'

'*Entendu.* And Willie?'

'Don't worry about him. I'll see that Claudine doesn't get scared and start screaming. It takes plenty to scare her anyway. You get on the phone to your people, René. Not the police, please. I don't want to get involved on that side.'

'It will take my people some twenty minutes to get here,' Vaubois said.

'That doesn't matter. It'll be over long before then. Play this quietly please, René.'

'I would prefer to.'

'Good. That's all then.'

Collier said a little dourly, 'What do I do when we get up to this girl's flat?'

'Nothing, Steve. This isn't your kind of business.'

'Is it yours?'

'Yes,' she said briefly. 'Now get set.'

The car swung left and swooped down a steep, narrow road of dark houses with a few shops dotted here and there. It lifted on to the pavement and came to a swift but smooth halt, with no squeal of brakes or tyres. The door where Vaubois sat was precisely level with a narrow arched opening. The rear door was within an inch of the wall to one side of the opening.

Vaubois flung open his door and disappeared. Modesty went over the back of the seat in one smooth movement, and was gone.

'Sharp!' said Willie, and Collier scrambled after her, his heart suddenly pounding. At the far end of the covered passage he glimpsed a wrought iron gate. It stood almost as high as the arch and was open. Beyond lay some kind of courtyard with a derelict fountain on the far side, set in a shallow concrete bowl and rimmed by a low parapet. There was a certain amount of light in the courtyard but Collier could not see its source.

Halfway along the passage, on the right, stood a front door. Modesty pressed the bellpush beside it, twitched her skirt above her thighs, and lifted one leg. Now Collier saw that she must have kicked off her evening shoes in the car. The flat of her stockinged foot slammed against the door, just above the escutcheon of the lock. Something snapped, and the door wavered open. She pushed it wide and vanished within.

'With her bare foot ...' Collier thought dazedly. Vaubois' hand gripped his shoulder with surprising strength and thrust him into the hallway. 'It is a knack, Mr. Collier,' his voice whispered, 'but please let us concentrate on our instructions.'

A single low-wattage lamp burned on the landing above. Collier started up the stairs after Modesty. He heard the front door close behind him, the bolts shoot home. A wedge of light

shone suddenly down as a door above opened. He heard
Modesty's voice: *'N'aie pas peur, Claudine. C'est moi,
Modesty. Je t'expliquerai plus tard. Faut qu'on se dépêche.'*

Collier entered a small living-room, Vaubois at his heels.
The décor surprised him. It was fresh, tasteful and very
modern. A door leading to a bedroom stood open. Another,
closed, presumably led off to a bathroom and kitchen at the
front of the house.

A girl in her middle twenties, with red hair and a small
round face, stood drawing a dressing gown about her. Beneath
it Collier glimpsed a short, expensive nightdress in pale green.
She had clearly been roused from sleep, but though she looked
a little startled she showed no alarm. Taking in Collier and
Vaubois with one glance, she looked towards Modesty, who
was opening a casement window at the rear of the house
where the courtyard lay.

'Une bagarre?' the girl said. *'Tu es seule, Modesty?'*

Collier's French was adequate for that. A fight? You're
alone? Evidently the girl did not feel that he and Vaubois were to be considered.

Modesty said in French, 'No. Willie Garvin's below. Put out
the lights, Claudine.'

The girl moved quickly to the switch and obeyed. Modesty
had the window open now. Collier glanced towards Vaubois.
He was crouched over the telephone, dialling, peering for the
numbers in the pale moonlight that shone through the open
window. Collier looked back towards Modesty. She had vanished.

Shaken, he ran to the window. The drop was twenty feet;
thirteen, even if she had hung from the sill by her hands. He
saw her moving fast across the courtyard towards one of two
chestnut trees which stood on the far side beyond the crumb-
ling surround of the fountain. Now he realised that apart from
the arched passage the courtyard was completely enclosed. On
two sides it was hemmed by high walls, the rear of a school, a
baker's yard—he did not know. On the other two sides stood
the backs of the terraced houses, in darkness now. The light in

58

the courtyard came from a single lamp fixed high on one of the walls.

Collier jumped as there came the faint screech of a car coming to a crash stop in the road at the front of the house. The evening had held a succession of bewildering shocks, yet some part of his mind could still register, incredulously, that only thirty seconds had passed since the moment when Willie Garvin halted the car outside the arched passage leading under the row of houses.

'Yes,' Vaubois was saying quietly into the phone. 'The van as well.' He looked at the red-haired girl. *'L'adresse s'il vous plaît, mam'selle?'*

Willie Garvin crouched in the back of the Simca. He had watched the big Panhard halt and five men pour out of it. The driver was manoeuvring the car up on the pavement, to leave the narrow road clear.

The off-side front door of the Simca was jerked open. The car swayed as a man clambered through and out of the far door into the passage beyond. Four more followed. There was the sound of their quick breathing, an impatient curse. Fifteen seconds passed before the driver left his car and started to scramble across the front seat of the Simca. Willie knelt up and hit him hard across the back of the head with a spanner, the business end wrapped in a handkerchief.

The man slumped. Willie climbed over him and went along the passage. In one hand he held two spanners, in the other a slim tommy-bar some eighteen inches long; it was, to Willie's annoyance, the only weapon the driver had been carrying.

From the open window Collier was looking down on the courtyard with a growing sense of horror. The feeling of unreality had passed now, and he knew that violence and brutality and perhaps death inhabited the courtyard below.

Five men, well spread out and moving warily, came into view, dark figures in the half-light. Collier caught his breath.

Five. His stomach churned.

'That one is holding a gun, I think,' Vaubois murmured at

his shoulder. 'It is hard to tell, but——' He broke off as the figure of Modesty rose from behind the low parapet of the fountain and darted to cover behind one of the two chestnuts.

The man in the middle waved his hand in a signal. He moved on towards the fountain. The remaining four split up in pairs, circling to each side.

Collier was shaking, whether with rage or fear he was not sure. He had glimpsed the gun when the man signalled, and he had seen the glint of bright steel in the hands of the other men.

'They'll kill her,' he whispered huskily. 'I'm going down, Vaubois!'

'Keep quiet please, Mr. Collier,' Vaubois said softly. 'It is a long drop for untrained muscles. You would break an ankle, I think. Also Modesty gave clear instructions—ah!'

The head of the man with the gun had jerked violently. He toppled forward, his body folding over the parapet of the fountain. There came a clink of metal as something bounced to the moss-grown cobbles surrounding the bowl.

'For God's sake, who did that?' Collier whispered.

'Willie. A spanner. He is a specialist, but with the throwing knives normally.'

'Normally! What does Modesty specialise in normally?'

'I understand she is very expert with a revolver or automatic. But she prefers the kongo—that little wooden thing which formed part of her handbag.'

The remaining four men had paused uncertainly, looking from the chestnut tree to the gate behind them. Willie Garvin stepped into view, and at the same moment Modesty moved out from behind the chestnut.

Collier was startled to see that she had taken off her skirt. It hung from her left hand. As she moved, light gleamed on the fine stocking-tights clothing her long legs.

'So there was only one gun,' said Vaubois. 'Now the affair begins.'

Staring, Collier saw that the figures in the courtyard had divided into two trios—Modesty and two men, Willie and two men. Vaguely he was aware of Claudine saying quietly to him in halting English, 'You know if Willie brings baggage with him, m'sieu?'

It was Vaubois who answered. 'I think not, mam'selle. This was unexpected.'

'No matter. I find pyjamas. And I will make a bath ready for him. He will be hot afterwards.'

'That is very possible, mam'selle. But please do not put on any lights.'

Vaubois had not taken his eyes from the courtyard while he spoke. Collier heard a door open, heard water running. Below him the sinister yet strangely elegant dance went on—the shifting and manoeuvring, the glitter of blades, the smooth evasive twist of bodies.

Modesty had twirled her skirt in a bundle about her left hand and forearm, as a guard. Her right hand was clenched, presumably gripping the kongo, as Vaubois had called it. Willie held a spanner in his right hand and had shed his jacket.

'One must be cautious against the knife,' Vaubois breathed. 'It is a waiting game, you understand. To commit oneself rashly to an attack or a counter is to invite immediate defeat——'

'Oh, Christ,' Collier said shakily. 'I've got to go down.'

'You have some experience after all, perhaps?'

'No!' A savage whisper. 'I boxed at school, I was no good, and I hated it.' Collier tore his eyes from the scene below and moved towards the door.

'She will be angry,' said Vaubois.

'Or dead. *I've got to go down.*'

Collier opened the door and stumbled down the dimly lit stairs. He clawed at the bolts, cursing, flung open the front door and ran along the passage towards the courtyard. The wrought iron gate was closed now and barred his way. He jerked at it, then saw that a slim steel bar had been passed through a metal stanchion grouted to the wall and then bent round the thick frame of the gate itself.

61

'... I'll draw them through, you keep them penned,' Modesty had said to Willie.

Gripping the ends of the bar he strained with fury to force them apart. Vision blurred, and he gave up at last with a gasping sob, hating himself because his anger was shot through with relief at having failed.

He stared through the bars. Incredibly, the scene seemed hardly to have changed. The six figures still performed their silent arabesques in the blend of moonlight and lamplight. A waiting game, Vaubois had said.

On the far side of the courtyard Modesty had her back to him. She was just beyond the fountain and the two men were edging closer to her at an obtuse angle. Willie was on the near side of the fountain and his attackers were interposed between him and the low parapet.

Abruptly Modesty turned, jumped with one long stride into the dry bowl, came up on the parapet on the near side, and launched herself feet-first at the closer of Willie's attackers. She caught him from the flank, her feet slamming violently against the side of his head. The man was hurled sideways, cannoning into his companion as he went down.

Collier remembered Modesty kicking the door open and wondered briefly if she had broken the man's neck. But there was little time to speculate. She had landed catlike, crouched on the balls of her feet, hands just touching the ground. Willie was already moving in. There came the sharp ring of steel on steel, then Willie's free arm swung, the hand open like an axe, and the second man went down in a heap.

Willie picked up a fallen knife. It was a good twelve inches long. Collier wondered why Modesty did not take the other knife. Surely it would be more use than the skirt and the kongo?

The two remaining men had split to either side of the fountain and were running hard. One raced for the gate, but Willie was moving fast to cut him off. It was the other man who held Collier's attention, for as Modesty had dropped her victim with that flying kick this man had cried out in a voice soft yet shrill with anger, and now he was launching himself directly at her, stabbing and slashing fiercely.

She backed away, weaving and swaying, sometimes blocking a vicious thrust with a sideways sweep of her skirt-swathed left hand. They were nearer to Collier now, and he could see the man clearly. Broad shoulders and a narrow waist. A lace-frilled shirt under a light jacket. The hair was long, dyed blonde, and crimped in the curls of a recent perm. The face was smooth, but twisted now in a mask of feminine fury. He wore lipstick and eye-shadow.

There was nothing feminine or fragile in the way he fought. He was strong and terrifyingly quick.

Collier's hands hurt from the intensity of his grip on the bars. He had heard of people being petrified with horror and now he experienced it. The pansy radiated a killing hatred. Collier had never before seen such naked ferocity. Yet it seemed to make no impact on Modesty. Her movements were fast, smooth, and controlled. Her face held only a strange severity of concentration.

Suddenly the coiled skirt swirled free and flicked sharply at the painted face. The man's head jerked back, and in that instant Modesty pivoted on one foot, perfectly poised, leaning away from him, one long leg flashing out in a sidekick to his groin. He gave a muted squeal and doubled up.

She stepped in and struck with the kongo, once to his knife arm, once to his head. The blows seemed light, yet the knife flew from his hand on the first, and his body folded limply on the second.

Collier let out his breath. He had held it so long he felt dizzy. His eyes turned to Willie. For a moment he thought the last of the attackers had escaped in some way, but then he saw the still figure lying on the ground, face to the sky. The hilt of a big knife grew hideously from the man's chest.

'The bastard got set for a throw, Princess,' Willie said indignantly. 'I 'ad to beat 'im to it.'

'Can't be helped. You can get killed, pussyfooting around

too much.' She pushed a fallen lock of hair away from her brow. 'Do you know any of them, Willie?'

Both were speaking softly. They were unaware of Collier's presence.

'No.' Willie sounded puzzled. 'They're a new lot.' He walked over to the man Modesty had felled, put out a foot and rolled the limp figure on to its back. The painted, vixenish face showed clearly in the lamplight.

'Blimey! A daisy,' said Willie. 'When they're nasty they're really nasty.'

'Yes. I think that must have been his boyfriend I took with the dropkick. Go and see if he's alive, Willie. And check that one who had the gun.'

'Sure.' Willie glanced down again at Modesty's victim as he moved off, and grinned suddenly. 'This one shouldn't sweat too much about where you gave 'im the boot, anyway.'

She laughed, a bare whisper of sound. Then her face grew suddenly hard and she was looking directly at Collier.

'Steve! What the *hell* are you doing there?'

'I came down.' He was ashamed to find his voice shaking. 'I couldn't just watch. For God's sake, I might have been a little help, even if I only got in their way.'

'Or ours. You could have got us killed if we'd had to worry about making sure you didn't get hurt, damn you!'

'All right. I'm duly humiliated.'

Her eyes sparkled with anger and she was about to speak again when René Vaubois called softly from the window above, out of Collier's sight. He spoke in French, very quickly and much too fast for Collier to follow. Slowly Modesty relaxed. The anger faded and at last she shrugged. '*Bien, René. Je n'y avais pas pensé. Vous voulez descendre maintenant?*'

'*Je viens.*'

She moved towards Collier, looking at him through the bars of the gate. 'Steve, don't be silly. I wouldn't feel humiliated if you told me to give you elbow room while you were mixing a new alloy or whatever it is metallurgists do.'

'That's a little different.'

'No.' She made a gesture taking in the tiny battlefield of the courtyard. 'There's nothing clever about it. This is just something Willie and I happen to know about.'

'Yes. I've seen that. It's still different.'

Willie came back. He was carrying the pistol he had picked out of the fountain. It was a 9 mm. Luger.

'I never like the sights on these,' he said confidingly. 'Bad combination, the narrow V backsight and the barleycorn inverted V frontsight. What you want to do is cut a Partridge square notch 'ere,' he tapped the backsight with his finger, 'then fit a little Redfield Sourdough front from a Mauser rifle. Makes a lovely job.'

'It sounds fine, Willie. If you use sights.'

'There's always that.'

He passed the gun to Modesty, gripped the ends of the twisted tommy-bar and heaved with slow, steady pressure. The bar straightened and he withdrew it from the gate.

'What about the three by the fountain?' Modesty said.

'One was coming round, but I've seen 'im off for another ten minutes.' Willie swung the gate open. 'Oh, and the daisy's going to need a new boyfriend. The old one's neck got separated.'

Collier was astonished to feel fierce satisfaction. Modesty and Willie had each killed a man. He should have felt revulsion. But he remembered the five figures stalking Modesty in the shadows of the courtyard, stalking her with long knives and with a gun. He thought of edged steel and soft lead driving into her body. . . .

So two were dead. They had bloody well asked for it.

René Vaubois came through Claudine's front door as they moved along the passage. 'A van and a car should be here in a few minutes now,' he said.

'We'd rather be gone by then, René.' Modesty gave him the Luger. 'Can you see that we don't get involved in any inquiries?'

'From my own side, yes.' Vaubois looked towards the courtyard. 'But these men must be questioned, and they may well talk of you. Do they know you?'

'It's hard to say. We don't know them.'

'Well ... if I have to report to my Minister I will imply that I was attacked when accompanied by two of my own people, a man and a woman, and that between us we managed to—ah—disarm and secure the assailants.'

'You managed to rub out two of 'em,' said Willie cheerfully. 'You want to be a bit more careful in future, René.'

'Not at all. My Minister has an old-fashioned prejudice against assassins. He does not believe it is the fault of society that they kill people.'

Willie grinned, moved along the passage to the Simca and returned carrying the driver, still unconscious. He dropped the man at Vaubois' feet and said, 'This one won't remember anything. He never got started.'

Modesty had put her skirt on. There were a dozen rents in it. Claudine appeared, her dressing gown wrapped about her.

'*C'est fini?*' she asked in an inquiring whisper.

Modesty answered in English. 'Yes, it's finished. And thank you, Claudine. Willie will repair the lock of the door for you tomorrow.'

'And nobody is hurt?'

'Only the others.' Willie slipped an arm about the girl's shoulders and looked at Modesty. 'Think we can count on a quiet night from now on, Princess?'

'I think so.' A quick smile. 'Not as quiet for Claudine as it might have been, maybe. Off you go, Willie. I'll ring you tomorrow.'

'Mam'selle Claudine has a hot bath ready for you,' said Vaubois. 'I am surprised that you trouble to go to Tokyo, Willie.'

'Ah, well...' Willie ran a hand gently up to the back of Claudine's neck. 'The girls there give you time to get out of the bath. Still, I'm not sure it's any better, come to think of it.'

Together they went inside and the door closed. Vaubois

looked at Modesty and gave a small helpless shrug. 'I did not even thank him.'

'It doesn't need saying. I'm just glad we were with you tonight.'

'So am I,' Vaubois said soberly. 'This was not a small affair.' He indicated the courtyard. 'Six men.'

'I'm sorry if you were anxious, René.'

'He wasn't anxious,' said Collier. 'He bloody well enjoyed it.'

Vaubois' lips tightened. For a moment he seemed about to speak angrily. Then he relaxed and looked suddenly rueful. 'I will not admit to enjoyment, Modesty, but our young friend is not perhaps entirely wrong. I was deeply interested. The manoeuvre for the two groupings, then the switched attack, this was really excellent. And your final coup with the foot, the sidekick. Most beautifully executed.'

'It has to be, against a knife. Or you're cooked.' She spoke a little absently but her voice was serious. 'The secret lies in the standing foot, though. I remember Willie had me working on that for months to get it just right——' She broke off, glancing quickly at Collier, then went on. 'We must go, René. Your people will be along any moment. Thank you for the bateau-mouche and the dinner.'

'Goodnight, Modesty.' He bent to kiss her hand.

'Goodnight, *mon cher*. Ring me if you learn anything worth knowing.'

Vaubois smiled and inclined his head in agreement. She took Collier's arm and moved to the car with him. Her leg showed to the hip through a long knife-cut in the skirt as she slid across the front seat to the steering wheel. Collier got in and closed the door. She let the car roll down the hill a little way so that the start would be silent.

Collier said, 'Are you sure he'll be all right?'

She let in the clutch and the engine woke to life. 'Yes. He's got a gun. He's got four unconscious men and two dead men to watch for a few minutes. And he's René Vaubois.'

'What does that last bit mean?'

'It means you needn't worry about him. There they go.' A car followed by a tradesman's van came past, going up the hill.

'I haven't been too much worried about him,' Collier said. 'I've been worried about you.'

'Don't, darling. It's a waste of time.'

'Is it? You could have been blown up, shot, or knifed. All in the last couple of hours.'

'I wasn't. Forget it, Steve.'

'No. I want to know about you. And about Willie Garvin. And men who put bombs in cars, and chase mysterious friends of yours with knives and guns.' Collier's lean body was very tense. 'I don't know where the hell to begin asking questions, but I'll start somewhere. Tonight. I want to know.'

But half an hour later, when he sat waiting impatiently on the bed, wearing only pyjama trousers because the night was still warm, she came from the bathroom fresh and clean and glowing, with her hair hanging loose over her shoulders and only a towel wrapped around her waist; she took the cigarette he was smoking and stubbed it out; as he started to speak she bent over him, letting the towel fall, and stopped his mouth with her parted lips.

Then all the tension of the past hours suddenly exploded within him and he dragged her down angrily. She resisted, struggling against him.

Collier had seen a little of what she could do. He knew that she could defeat him if she wished. But she was using only her strength against him, not her skill or speed, and her eyes looked at him with challenging laughter.

His anger soared, and he fought with all his wiry strength, forcing her to resist to the limits of her power. She was very strong for a woman, but Collier was heavier by a good twenty-five pounds and there was hidden stamina in his sinewy body.

At the end of the long struggle, when she lay soft and panting beneath him, he knew that victory had been given to him and he thrust the knowledge away. She was helpless, exhausted, vanquished ... he believed the lie, knowing that it was a lie and that she had created it for him.

She lay on her side, and he held her arms locked behind her in a harsh grip as he bent to kiss her lips, her long neck, her body. She stirred feebly, but could not—would not?—prevent him.

When he had shown his fierce mastery for long enough, he took her in a mounting wave of angry passion, a wild, furious, joyous frenzy that seemed to go on almost beyond endurance.

Then there was peace at last, and he was barely conscious of her drawing the covers over their bodies and taking him gently into the warmth of her arms as he fell swiftly, helplessly into the dark chasm of sleep.

5

It was nine o'clock when Collier woke. Bright sunlight slid between the half-closed slats of the blinds. Modesty Blaise stood over him, wearing a white chiffon négligé. Her hair was tied loosely back and she held a glass in her hand.

'Your fruit juice, sir.'

He sat up and took the glass, a hundred memories of the night before flooding through his mind.

'There's a letter for you,' she said, 'forwarded from London and again from the hotel where you were staying. Shall I bring it for you now, darling?'

'I'll read it later.'

She nodded and sat down on the edge of the bed. He drank some of the fruit juice and said without rancour, 'Thanks for the ego-building performance last night. I needed it. Very clever of you.'

'Clever? Don't spoil it, Steve.'

'Impossible. Let's say generous, then.'

'No. It wasn't that either.'

'Don't tell me your need was as great as mine. You didn't have a damaged ego to be restored.'

'Maybe I need to have my ego damaged occasionally.'

'Meaning what?'

She patted the bed. 'This is the only way I can let myself get beaten. It's good to lose sometimes.'

Collier thought about that. He was wide awake now, his mind very clear. He said, 'You certainly couldn't afford to come out second best in that courtyard last night.'

'That's what I mean.'

Collier drained his glass and put it down. She gave him a cigarette and lit one herself. He rested a hand gently on her thigh and said, 'I won't spoil anything. But I've got to know about you, Modesty.'

'Is it important?'

'Yes. Mysteries worry me. Who are you?'

She ruffled his hair and made a little grimace. 'I don't know, Steve. I was a refugee from somewhere in the Balkans when I was very small. I lived alone and on the run from the war for several years. Then I got to the Middle East—refugee camps, bedouin camps. I wandered all over the place. The details don't matter.'

'They're exactly what matters.' He was looking at her blankly, as if half convinced that she was joking.

'No. There are too many of them. When I was eighteen I was in Tangier running a gang. A small one. I built it up worldwide and it was called *The Network*. I got rich, and I retired.'

Collier waited, but apparently she had finished.

'It leaves a lot out,' he said.

'Nothing important. I'm not going to give a blow-by-blow account, Steve.'

'That seems a very suitable adjective. All right, who's Willie Garvin?'

'I found him when I was twenty. He came out of the gutter but he's very, very clever. He became my right arm in *The Network*. We retired together.'

Collier drew on his cigarette. He found to his surprise that he was in no way shocked, only deeply fascinated.

'What's Willie Garvin to you now?' he asked, watching her.

'You haven't any right to ask that, darling, but I don't mind answering. He's an old friend.'

'That's what he said himself. A close one, judging from the way he marched in here last night.'

'He'd have pressed the buzzer first, to make sure I wasn't here with company.'

'Well, yes. He buzzed. I didn't answer. Then he just walked in and started cooking himself a meal as if he owned the place.'

71

'He does.'

'What?' Collier sat up, his jaw hanging a little.

'We've got pied-à-terre here and there. Italy, Austria, Spain —oh, quite a few places. We both use them as we need. Willie just happens to have bought this one.'

'Oh, my God. I was bloody starchy with him at first.'

She smiled. 'He won't mind.'

After a moment Collier said, 'When he was dealing with the booby trap in the car last night, he was in charge. When that Panhard full of thugs was chasing us, he asked *you* how to play it. Who's the boss?'

'Neither one of us now. But he worked for me for several years. He still looks to me when it's a question of how a caper's to be played. That's if we're together. If he's solo he can figure a play just as well as I can.'

'Yes. I didn't miss the note of confidence he strikes,' Collier said with a dry smile, then added quietly. 'Do you love him?'

'What a question. Define love for me, will you?'

'Dammit...' He gestured impatiently. 'You know what I mean.'

'I don't. If you mean do we sleep together, the answer's no. We've got stronger bonds than that. We've worked together, fought together, saved each other's lives. Sorry if that sounds corny but it's simply true. We've had a fair taste of hell together, we've been hurt, we've nursed each other, and we've won together. Everything but this.' She laid her hand on the bed.

'Why the solitary omission?'

'Maybe we know it would change all the rest. It's never arisen anyway, Steve. Willie would consider it ... I don't know.'

'A liberty?'

She laughed. 'That's about it.'

'Does he love you?'

'There you go again. He needs me. I'm his talisman.'

'Princess. That's what he calls you. I'd say he worships you.'

She shook her head. 'He knows everything there is to know

72

about me, including the faults. That puts worship out of court for anyone.'

'I still think I'm right.'

She shrugged. 'Whatever he feels, it makes him happy. Should I want to change that? I know I wouldn't want Willie changed.'

Collier ground out his cigarette and held the ashtray for her to do the same. He was getting a tantalisingly incomplete picture, yet she was giving direct answers to his questions. He began to realise that the canvas was too big to be quickly or easily comprehended. Besides, the picture was lacking a thousand small but vital details.

'Who's Claudine?' he asked at last. 'She knew there was a fight on last night, and she simply went and drew a hot bath for Willie.'

'Yes, she's a thoughtful girl. She worked for me, carrying packets of diamonds. Smuggling. When Claudine was twenty-two she could pass for a schoolgirl of fifteen. And she's got steady nerves.'

'Willie stayed with her last night.'

'He's always welcome there. No strings when he comes, no questions when he goes.'

'You don't mind?'

'For heaven's sake, no. I've no right to. Anyway, do I seem the possessive type?'

'Hardly,' Collier acknowledged, 'About Claudine. Has she retired too?'

'From crime? Yes. I set her up with a little boutique. The dresses are her own design and she's good at it.'

'That leaves only René Vaubois. Who's he?'

'I can't tell you that, Steve.'

'Two attempts were made on his life last night, and he obviously has authority with the police and with "his own people" as you call them. I don't have to be a genius to guess he's someone important, and on the right side of the law. How does he come to be friends with...?' Collier hesitated.

'With ex-criminals?' Modesty supplied. 'Don't boggle at

words, Steve. In *The Network* days we had a section operating in a field that concerned René Vaubois. We had dealings with him occasionally. And he helped us in a job we got involved in a few months back.'

'A job? I thought you'd retired.'

'This was different. A virtuous caper.' She smiled and gave a little shrug. 'Willie and I found that a quiet life wasn't very satisfactory. We need an occasional break.'

'Like last night?'

'It's not always as crude as that.'

'You actually enjoyed last night?' he said wonderingly.

'Enjoyed? I don't know. We didn't go looking for it. Do people enjoy climbing mountains? The actual climbing, I mean—frostbite, muscles cracking, lungs aching, and long periods of danger?'

'I hadn't thought about it. I suppose they get satisfaction afterwards, from the achievement. Some kind of release. They've faced something and beaten it. But that's climbing mountains. It's a bit different.'

'Not very. But I didn't grow up climbing mountains. I can only do what I know how to do.'

'Yes.' Collier hesitated, then said awkwardly, 'You killed a man last night. So did Willie.'

'You think it should trouble me?' She was not angry or defensive, as he had feared she might be. Her tone was quiet and serious. 'Those men were trying to kill René. Then they tried to kill me. And Willie. Have you any idea of the risk you take by pulling your punches against odds of three to one? It's cold logic to put a man down for good in that kind of rumble. Yet we left four of them alive. Don't ever call me hard, Steve.'

Collier thought of her facing the queer with the long blade in his hand, remembered her leg flashing out. The edge of the blade had wavered within an inch of her thigh, where the great artery runs. If her timing had been anything but perfect...

He shivered inwardly.

She said, 'I've never killed anyone who wasn't trying to kill me—or one of my friends.'

Collier looked at her helplessly. 'It seems a reasonable system,' he said at last. 'Were you serious about pulling your punches last night?'

'Of course. Too many dead would have been embarrassing for René, anyway. There's also the point that he wanted some left to question.'

'My God,' Collier said weakly. He sat still, propped against the pillows, staring at her for a long time. Then he said, 'Let me look at your foot.'

She was puzzled. 'Which one?'

'Either one.'

She lifted her left foot on to her right knee, the chiffon falling away from her leg. He took the foot in his hands gently. It was a broad foot with a strong arch, attractive in shape, but the sole was like leather.

'That explains one or two things,' he said, looking up, still holding the foot. 'Like kicking a door open and jumping out of a window on to cobbles. How did they get like that?'

'I wasn't shod till I was almost seventeen. And I'd walked a long way in that time.' She was smiling again now.

Collier frowned. Something deep in his mind had suddenly surfaced. He said, 'Last night, when I was at that bloody gate. You were angry when you saw me there. Then Vaubois called something to you in French, too fast for me to follow. What did he say?'

'He asked me not to be angry with you for trying to help.'

'Just that?'

'He said you'd *had* to do it, because...' She hesitated. 'Because you were scared.'

Collier looked at her for several seconds. 'I was,' he said softly, remembering. 'Scared stupid. It was disgusting. I could *feel* one of those knives rasping on my ribs as it went in.' He made a grimace of distaste. 'I'm sorry, Modesty.'

'Sorry?' She took her foot away and knelt on the bed, taking

75

his face between her hands. 'But you did come down, Steve. That's what René meant.'

' "Despite his knocking knees and quaking bowels, our hero hurled himself into the fray." That sort of thing?' Collier spoke with self-mockery but without bitterness. The warmth in her eyes made his heart suddenly light.

'Something like that,' she answered. 'It was the wrong move, but you couldn't be expected to take my word for that. It wasn't your kind of business.' She studied him for a moment. There was a touch of curiosity in her gaze, and it seemed to Collier that she was about to ask a question. Then she changed her mind, and instead a sudden urchin grin lit her face.

'Come on, you metallurgist, you,' she said. 'Make love to me.'

His blood sang. 'Do I have to fight?'

'Not this time.'

He unfastened the négligé and drew it away from her as she knelt on the bed before him. 'You're a splendidly earthy creature, aren't you?' he said.

'Define earthy for me.'

'You and your definitions. I mean you like making love.'

'That's bad? Or wrong?'

'Not as long as you're selective.'

'I am. Very, Mr. Collier.'

'Delighted to hear it, Miss Blaise.' The phone rang as he reached for her, and Collier cursed. She grinned, stretched across to the bedside table and picked up the phone.

'René. How are you? No, you're not interrupting breakfast.' She flickered an eyelid wickedly at Collier. 'Did you learn anything from our friends?' Vaubois spoke at some length and she listened, frowning. 'I see. A pity. Look, take care of yourself, René. He may try again.' A pause while Vaubois spoke, then, 'No, I'm afraid not. I'm leaving for London this evening.'

Collier did not take in the rest of the conversation. He was staring at her as she put down the phone. Thoughtfully, look-

76

ing into space, she said, 'They were hired for the job. Fifteen thousand francs in advance and the same on completion. First contact by phone, first instalment handed over at night by a man in a car wearing a stocking over his head. No description. No name. René can't get any lead back to him.'

Collier wasn't listening. He said, 'You're leaving *tonight*?'

'Yes. There's something I have to see about. I was going to tell you at breakfast.'

'Can I come with you?'

She shook her head. 'No, darling. I don't know how long this will take.'

He looked round the bedroom, then at Modesty again. 'You mean this is finished, then?'

'Not quite, if you remember.' She took the phone off the hook and laid it down. 'There, that's better.'

'I didn't mean just that!'

'It wasn't meant to last, Steve,' she said patiently. 'You know that. I have things to do.' She reached out and ran a finger down the line of his jaw affectionately. 'And your metallurgy won't wait for ever, will it?'

He sighed and looked away. 'Modesty ... I'm not a metallurgist.'

'I know. Willie told me. The big problem with beryllium, it seems, is that you *can't* rivet the stuff. It's too brittle.'

Collier rubbed a hand over his brow and stared. 'My God. He caught me out, then? But what made him wonder?'

'Willie's got an instinct.'

'Yes.' An eager light came into Collier's eyes. 'I want to talk to him about that.'

'He's coming to London with me.'

'Oh.' Collier frowned, then gave a little shrug. 'A pity. Still, he's asked me to drop in at his pub any time.' He lifted an eyebrow in query. 'Well?'

'Well what?'

'Aren't you going to ask me what I am?'

'I know all I need to know about you, Steve. My own instinct isn't too bad. What you do is your own business.'

77

'And boring compared with yours.'

'Then let's think of something not boring. A trip to the moon?'

He was baffled, and patted the sheet between them. 'Our hero would rather stay here.'

'That's what I meant.'

'I'm sorry. What's this trip to the moon?'

She knelt upright on the bed, looking at him with affection and a gentle, unwounding mockery. 'I can see you've always moved in genteel circles, darling.' She reached out her arms. 'Come here and I'll show you.'

6

SEFF carefully completed the line of the puppet's eyebrow, then laid down the slender paintbrush and looked up at the plump, olive-skinned man in grubby denim trousers and crumpled blue shirt.

'I wish to congratulate you, Mr. Garcia,' he said. 'The pick-up last night was a perfect operation. I am very pleased.'

Garcia had a match dangling from a corner of his mouth, as always. He shifted it across to the other corner and said, 'Theng you, señor.'

'You and your friends will shortly be moving on by air to our new location.' Seff paced slowly between the two long benches of the workroom as he spoke. 'We shall follow some ten days later. Everything is arranged for you.'

'Yes, señor.' Garcia showed little interest. His dark eyes always held a faraway look, as if his thoughts were elsewhere, but Seff knew that he had taken in what had been said to him.

'That will be all, Mr. Garcia. You will wish to rejoin your friends now.'

'Theng you, señor,' Garcia said vaguely and went out of the room, his loose sandals flopping with every step.

Regina looked up from her task of re-stringing a puppet, a girl-child with a lascivious nymphet face. 'I think Garcia is such a nice man, Seffy. Why don't we invite him to our little entertainments?'

'I'm afraid he would find no interest in them, my dear.' Seff picked up the paintbrush again. 'Mr. Garcia is completely dedicated to his own work, you know.'

Regina nodded regretfully and fixed a string to the foot of the doll. It was not normal for a puppet to have both knee and foot strings, but the movements of the nymphet called for more than usual mobility of the legs.

As Seff hung up the newly painted doll, Bowker entered the big workroom. 'Well, it worked,' he said with relief.

'Certainly it worked, Dr. Bowker.' Seff cracked his fingers happily. 'I consider last night's pick-up to be my greatest success.'

'Not our greatest return, though.'

'Fifty thousand gold sovereigns is not a small return, surely? It gives a value of well over one hundred and fifty thousand sterling.'

'But the weight,' said Bowker, and wiped the back of his neck with a handkerchief. 'Over half a ton, including the container.'

'I supplied power to offset the weight.' Seff moved creakily to a workbench on which was laid out an array of components which had nothing to do with puppetry. 'I repeat, this was a considerable achievement.'

Regina said, 'Yes, you were very clever, Seffy. I can't think why Dr. Bowker is complaining.'

'I'm not complaining, Regina,' Bowker said, controlling his nervous anger. 'But the more sophisticated the operation, the more there is to go wrong. We could have got the same yield from a packet of precious stones or drugs——'

'We must be artistic as well as commercial, Dr. Bowker,' Seff interrupted, his lips parting and stretching in the grimace which served him as a smile. 'There is also the advantage that the weight you deplore will serve to confuse the authorities as to the method we use. That is very important, I think you will agree?'

Bowker rubbed his chin, then nodded grudgingly. 'It's a point. But it wouldn't be clever to repeat that kind of pick-up.'

'I have no intention of doing so.' Seff took the controllers of the doll Regina had restrung, lowered it until the feet touched the floor, and began to manipulate the tiny figure experimentally in a series of obscene movements. 'Confusion of the authorities will serve to give us a longer run in this particular form of operation,' he went on. 'I am an artist, I hope. I could make these dolls from lathe-turned heads and a few pieces of doweling, but it would affront me to do so. I am also a realist. We can expect to continue for another fifteen months at most before the various authorities co-operate with sufficient trust and intelligence to become dangerous. Before that point, we shall stop.'

'Good. We'll have made plenty by then.'

'There you go again, Dr. Bowker. We shall certainly stop this particular form of enterprise, but I shall devise something equally artistic and profitable—and completely different.'

'It's the *work* that counts with Seffy,' Regina said, fondly proud.

'Something different, using Lucifer?' Bowker asked, jerking his eyes from the twitching doll to look at Seff.

'I doubt it. Lucifer's talents would inevitably bring a sameness into any new operation. I feel he will have to go.' Seff paused in his manipulations and looked up. 'But have no worry for yourself, Dr. Bowker. I shall find use for your special skills, and for those of Mr. Wish, of course.'

'Suppose I've had enough?' Bowker regretted the abrupt words as soon as they were spoken.

Seff shook his head slowly and the creaking of his neck set Bowker's teeth on edge.

'I really could not think of accepting your resignation,' Seff said with grave courtesy.

When night fell Seff was sitting on the couch in the big lounge, Regina beside him, going through the advertisement columns of a pile of foreign newspapers.

Bowker prowled uneasily. He wished to God he had not got caught up in this now, but it was too late to back out. Far too late.

Another fifteen months, Seff had said. Maybe. But only if Lucifer could be kept up to scratch. Bowker thought about the letter he had sent several days ago. He needed help with

Lucifer, and he hoped desperately that the carefully constructed letter would produce it.

Regina said, 'Ah, here's an acceptance, Seffy. In the London *Times*. One of our clients wants to receive instructions.'

'What is the reference number, my dear?'

Regina peered at the small print. 'It's 5071.'

Seff picked up his register and thumbed through it. 'Mr. Jafar of Calcutta,' he said. 'A banker of considerable substance. We have assessed him at two hundred thousand dollars. Shall we say heroin in this case? In that area it should be readily obtainable.'

'Whatever you think best, Seffy.'

'Very well. Arrange with Mr. Wish for the preliminary instructions to be forwarded, if you please, Regina. I see we have a Mark III container ready for collection from the warehouse in Calcutta.' He looked towards Bowker. 'This is excellent. You evidently were correct in your assessment of Mr. Jafar as a probable payer.'

'Yes. He's a hypochondriac according to the dossier.'

'Ah. A useful psychological weakness.' Seff consulted his pocket diary. 'We can decide provisionally on making the pick-up about five weeks from today. With precious stones it could be much earlier, but we must allow Mr. Jafar ample time to secure the heroin. The pick-up will be from our new location, of course.'

Regina jotted placidly in her notebook. The door opened and Jack Wish came in. He was frowning, and sweating slightly. It was a three hour run from Niebüll, on the mainland. He had made the journey to put through three phone calls. Seff would not allow any business calls from Sylt.

'The Paris job flopped,' Wish said. 'That's why there was nothing about it in the papers.'

'The Paris job?' Seff put away his diary and stood up.

'René Vaubois.' Wish poured himself a drink and swallowed it greedily. 'He was time-expired. One of Lucifer's selections who should've died a month back. But he didn't, goddamit.' Wish shook his head gloomily. 'Vaubois was a real good one to come up with, too. We make the demand, the French government won't pay—we don't expect 'em to. If Vaubois had kicked off natural it would've been a real arm-twister for a lot of people.'

'I share your regret, Mr. Wish,' Seff said in his high, monotonous voice. 'But it is your responsibility to make up for Lucifer's occasional failures. Are you saying that the people who should have killed Vaubois failed?'

'They got taken,' Wish said grimly. 'I don't know the details, but somehow they got word out to my contact man there.'

'And?'

'They tried twice in one night. Both times a man and a woman took a hand. The second time it came to a fight. We'd got six men laid on. Two were killed, the rest only half killed.'

'By a man and a woman? Either you are jesting, Mr. Wish, or you are failing to select the right people for the work that has to be done.'

Bowker expected Wish to crumple a little and defend himself, but instead he answered dourly, 'I'm the best picker you'll ever find, Seff. This mob was real hard. But the man and the woman ... my contact says it was Modesty Blaise and Willie Garvin.'

Seff frowned slightly. 'You seem to attach some significance to these names.'

'That's right.' Wish poured another drink. 'Look, no offence, but you're new to this game, Seff. You're smart as hell, by God, but you don't know the ratings. Just let me tell you a little about Modesty Blaise.'

He spoke for five minutes, and Seff listened without interruption, pacing slowly.

'Thank you, Mr. Wish,' Seff said at last. 'Since you are not given to exaggeration, I must accept that what you tell me puts a different complexion upon this unfortunate failure.'

'Yeah. And I haven't told you the half of it about Blaise and Garvin.'

Seff smiled his toothy smile. 'As you say, Mr. Wish, I have

only recently discovered my very great talent for crime. I am comparatively new to it. And that, perhaps, is one of the secrets of my success. I tread no well-worn paths.'

'Seffy's an original,' Regina quavered proudly. 'A true original. Remember our first enterprise, Seffy? Our very first, when music-hall died out and we simply couldn't get any engagements——?'

'I do not think this is a time for reminiscence, my dear,' Seff broke in with a gentle wag of his head. 'As you say, I am an original. But I take Mr. Wish's point, that I have no wide knowledge of the established underworld as such. That is why I must now ask his opinion as to what immediate steps we should take concerning this man Vaubois.' He looked inquiringly at Wish.

'Let it go,' Jack Wish said bluntly. 'If he's got Blaise and Garvin watching out for him, let it go. They're bad medicine.'

'But that means we shall have issued a threat and failed to implement it.' Seff's voice was so grave that it actually reached a lower pitch.

'Jesus, we can afford *one*,' said Wish. "Specially a straight killing. We still got 'em foxed on the naturals, Seff. Look, we've had more'n a hundred and twenty naturals since we started, right? I've fixed maybe sixteen killings where the boy wonder guessed wrong, plus three clients on the other list who we figured would pay up but didn't. Right?'

'We're trying tougher clients now,' Bowker put in. 'That means more work for you, Jack.'

It was Seff who answered. 'Not at all. The earlier examples will have softened up the tougher clients, Dr. Bowker. But please do not digress. Mr. Wish feels we can afford this one failure without materially weakening our position. Do you agree?'

Bowker shrugged. 'It's bound to have a marginal effect. But very marginal, I'd think. And that's better than asking for trouble from Blaise and Garvin—if they're likely to be really dangerous.'

'They'll be that okay,' Wish said flatly.

Seff paced the length of the room and paused, looking out over the North Sea. 'Very well,' he said at last.

Jack Wish relaxed and drained his glass. 'We need more naturals from the boy wonder,' he said, looking at Bowker. 'If he was a hundred per cent accurate I'd only have to worry about clients who didn't pay up. It'd be a breeze.'

'You'll never get a hundred per cent,' Bowker answered sharply. 'For God's sake, don't you realise what a miracle it is to get what we do?'

'Nevertheless we must persevere, Dr. Bowker.' Seff walked to a large picture on the wall and slid it to one side, revealing a television screen. 'We must get the very best from our young friend's talents.'

He switched on the set. After a few moments the screen flickered and a picture took shape, a downward angled shot of Lucifer's bedroom on the floor above.

The room was large and expensively furnished, but in stark black and white. In the ceiling a huge black mirror was set directly over the bed. The headboard and legs of the bed were white, the covers black. The thick carpet held a disturbing pattern of small black and white squares that were not quite square. Two large blasphemous pictures were hung in frames, again not quite square at the corners. The whole room held an unnatural atmosphere of deliberate perversity.

The hidden camera was set behind a grotesque and crudely fretted wall panel.

Lucifer turned from the window and lay down on the bed, looking up into the black mirror above. He wore only red shorts. He could see himself full-length in the mirror on the ceiling.

His lips twisted in a resigned smile. For a moment he thought about the little creatures downstairs who served him. They were his, but they could never be his companions. The Son of Morning was eternally alone.

And now he must go down to the lower levels. This, too, was part of his burden. By the law of his own being he must survey the whole of his kingdom. The pride which had been his undoing before Time began was still strong in him, and he did not flinch.

His eyes closed, yet still he saw himself in the mirror above. Now, slowly, the image changed. His skin became black and shiny even as his body grew larger to fill the whole mirror. His face lengthened, long teeth grew from beneath his upper lip and reached down towards the pointed chin. His eyes were elongated yellow pools, without pupils. The hands were furred, the fingers long talons. Short dark horns jutted from the jet-black dome of his brow.

Suddenly Lucifer was gone, soaring smoothly above the turning ball of dust and water that was a part of his kingdom. It shimmered and became transparent, an ethereal thing without substance. Then the world was no more.

Fire roared all about him and he was in the lower levels, where chained skeletons shrieked and the hideous little beings of his own creation scuttled to and fro about their horrible work. In the endless fiery chasms, the greater ones made obeisance to him as he passed. Asmodeus would be glad to return permanently to his true mode of existence, thought Lucifer, to be once again among his companions, the great demons. But he could not be spared yet.

The cries of a million souls beat about Lucifer's long pointed ears as he flew arrow-swift above a burning sea and on past fiery mountains and bubbling plains, endless as space itself. He thrust aside compassion for those who writhed below, and for himself. Lucifer had chosen to reign over his own kingdom rather than to serve in another. It was better so. Pride surged within him as he flew on, untouched by the choking fumes and searing heat of the realm that he was forever doomed to rule.

Jack Wish moved a little closer to the screen and studied the rigid, uncannily still figure lying on the bed.

'What's he doing?' Wish said in a low voice. 'He don't look *asleep*, somehow.'

'He's down in the lower levels of Hell,' Bowker said, and lit a cigarette. 'In the flames of Gehenna where the worm dieth not, and the fire is not quenched.'

'What worm?' Jack Wish stared suspiciously.

Seff said, 'I do not think eschatology is your subject, Mr. Wish. Our young friend is at present under the delusion that he has descended into what he calls the—ah—lower levels on a tour of inspection. This world constitutes the upper levels of his kingdom, of course.'

'That right, Doc?' Wish looked at Bowker.

'Yes. He's told me about his trips. Sometimes we go down with him. Just for a visit.'

'We do?'

'So he thinks.'

'Oh, brother . . .' Jack Wish shook his head, stared at the screen again and rubbed a hand round his heavy chin. 'It's kinda creepy, huh? What d'you figure he sees?'

'Something like the Disney portrayal of Hell in that sequence from *Fantasia*.'

'Hey! I saw that movie,' Wish said, pleased. 'Real spooky. There was this big Satan kept dropping lots of yellin' people down a kinda volcano.'

Seff switched off the closed circuit television and said to Bowker, 'You are sure that the strength of his delusion is in proportion to the efficiency of his psychic talent, his ability to predict death?'

'Yes. That's established.'

'But the delusion is weakening?'

'No. Strengthening if anything.'

'Then how do you account for the slight decrease in the accuracy of his predictions?'

'There could be a dozen other factors involved,' Bowker said. He spoke impatiently to hide his anxiety and diminishing confidence. 'I've told you, I'm not an expert in psychometry or any psychic phenomena. I don't really know whether he does better when he's relaxed or keyed up, drugged or fully conscious, physically tired or full of energy. I just don't know, Seff. Even psychiatry's not an exact science, a lot of it's a matter of groping in the dark. And the psychic stuff is a damn sight more so.'

'Maybe the guy needs a broad?' Jack Wish suggested helpfully. 'He's a hell of a hunk of man.'

'I think you should confine yourself to those matters in which you are expert, Mr. Wish,' Seff said politely.

Regina folded her fragile hands on her lap and put her head diffidently on one side. 'He *could* be right, Seffy. If that nice boy Lucifer works better when he's completely relaxed, which we don't know, of course, but if he does, well ...' She made a coy gesture and her pale cheeks became slightly pink.

Seff looked a query at Bowker, who said doubtfully, 'It might be a dangerous experiment, in view of his case history. Dangerous for the girl, I mean.'

'But on the other hand there could be something in the idea?'

'There could be.' Bowker was thinking deeply now, weighing factors, his anxiety forgotten for the moment. 'It would have to be made possible within the bounds of his delusion,' he said, speaking more to himself than to the others. 'That might be managed, with the right girl ... and as long as he co-operated. He'd have to want it himself, subconsciously anyway.'

'Bear the thought in mind, Dr. Bowker,' said Seff. 'And in the meantime you will seek expert advice on the psychic aspect, of course. That must be the first step.'

Bowker nodded. 'I've written to Stephen Collier. And I think I told him enough to whet his curiosity. With luck I'll be hearing from him any day now.'

7

'You indulge in this lunacy yourself, of course?' said Tarrant. He was sitting on a car rug beside Modesty Blaise in a big field in Kent, narrowing his eyes against the sun to watch the Rapide droning high in the sky to the west.

His eyes missed the first of the tiny black dots falling from the aircraft. He counted only three, but as the second and third overtook the first he saw that there were four, manoeuvring closer together as they fell until at last they linked hands, bodies extended almost horizontally to form a falling star.

'It's not lunacy,' Modesty said. 'Safer than crossing the Bayswater road in the rush hour, or playing Rugby League. And it's a lot more exhilarating.'

The figures swooped apart, spread-eagled, slanting down and away from each other. At 2,500 feet the white and orange gores of the parachutes began to flower.

'You've done a lot of it?' Tarrant asked.

'Quite a lot. Mostly in France. It was a big thing there before it got going over here. We thought it might be useful for a job sometime.'

'A job?'

'A Network job. Being able to drop on a small target at night was worth practising. But we didn't ever find a chance to use it.'

Tarrant smiled at the regret in her voice. Behind them, in the carpark area, stood the big open Rolls they had driven down in. Her Indo-Chinese houseboy and chauffeur, Weng, was getting the picnic basket out of the refrigerator.

Modesty Blaise lay on her back, a hand shielding her eyes. She wore a pale blue silk summer dress, sleeveless, and flat shoes. A blue suede handbag stood beside her. Tarrant let his eyes dwell on her long legs. He saw that she had caught his gaze and was smiling. Once he would have flushed with embarrassment, but not now. He laughed and ran a hand over his thick grey hair. 'Age has its compensations. It does me good to look at you, and I'm old enough to be permitted a few innocent indulgences.'

She nodded approvingly. 'You're getting better. Or worse. Have we taken you away from important work today?'

'Yes, thank God. Too much of it. But my conscience is clear. You restore my spirit, and I shall go back refreshed.'

The loud-speaker from the control marquee squawked. He looked up to watch two skydivers overtaking one another in turn, passing and repassing a smoking baton as they swooped down in free fall. The parachutes opened and he followed the angled touchdown near the big white circle painted in the middle of the field.

'Protection,' said Modesty Blaise. 'Selected people in government circles being threatened. Selected tycoons likewise. Your money or your life. It's impossible and quite bizarre—but what do you know about it, Sir Gerald?'

He frowned, plucking a blade of grass and shredding it carefully. 'Not very much. Boulter's department have got that one on their plate.'

'You can get full details, surely?'

'Perhaps.' Reluctantly.

'You don't sound very keen.'

'That's because I'm afraid,' he said slowly. 'I have a hunch it's exactly the sort of thing that would make me try to tempt you and Willie into the picture. So I'd rather not know.' He hesitated. 'I remember what happened to you last time I made use of you, Modesty.'

'I'm still here. A few months older but otherwise the same.' A hint of affectionate mockery tinged her voice. 'You'd make use of me again if it suited you, you know.'

Tarrant sighed. 'I do know. That's why I'd prefer to remain in ignorance of this business. I'm surprised you picked it up. There have been one or two garbled pieces in the newspapers, but no follow-up to them. Even a quite sensational piece in an American paper died a natural death. Not enough hard facts to keep readers interested. And governments are playing it very close to the chest.'

'I haven't seen anything in the press,' Modesty said. 'René Vaubois made me curious. He put a hypothetical case to me and asked what I thought about it. There weren't enough details to think anything except that it was crazy. I told him so. Then he sheered off the subject and pretended he'd just been playing with ideas.'

'But you weren't deceived?'

'No. And you've just confirmed that there *is* something.'

Tarrant grunted, annoyed with himself. 'I can't understand René talking about it to you.'

'He thought I might be able to give him a line to work on. He closed up when he found I couldn't. Will you find out all you can about it for me, Sir Gerald? Please?'

'Dammit, Modesty, no. I've told you why.'

She was silent for a while, lighting a cigarette. Then she said, 'René Vaubois is on their list. They tried to kill him twice, the evening I was with him.'

Tarrant turned his head slowly to look at her and said in a very quiet voice, 'René?'

'Yes.' Briefly she sketched the events of the evening for Tarrant. He listened, absorbed. Though her mood was serious she felt a touch of amusement at catching his momentary expression of envy when she spoke of the courtyard battle. He had not seen her in action against an enemy himself, and now Vaubois had. It offended Tarrant's slightly proprietary feeling towards her.

When she had finished her story he said, 'And René still didn't tell you any more? Didn't try to bring you in on it?'

'No.' She drew on the cigarette and frowned. 'I don't know why.'

'I do. He's not such a bastard as I am,' Tarrant said absently. 'That's all there is to it. René thinks he's a realist, but in fact he's a romantic. After one look at you, my dear, he'd rather have his throat cut than put you at risk.'

Modesty sat up, staring at him. Then she stubbed out her cigarette and said with quiet self-disgust, 'My God, that didn't even cross my mind. You're right, of course.'

Tarrant nodded. 'He's a much nicer man than I am,' he said with such genuine regret that she laughed.

But at once she was serious again. 'You'll get all you can from Boulter for me, Sir Gerald? I think it's going to be some time before they can lay on a new attempt against René, but I'd like to move fast on this.'

'Very well.' Tarrant shrugged ruefully. 'At least I won't have myself to blame this time. Boulter may prove a little difficult but I'll do what I can.'

'Thank you.' She lay back again and relaxed.

The loud-speaker had been squawking throughout their conversation, and other sky-divers had made their drops. A Cessna 180 was circling in from the west.

'Target drops,' Modesty said. 'There's some very hot opposition but I'll back Willie. Five to one in pounds he lands no more than three feet off-centre of that circle.'

'I never bet with rich women,' Tarrant said blandly. 'Not on Civil Service pay.'

Modesty took a small transceiver from her bag, switched it on and held it close to her lips. 'Willie?'

A moment's pause, then came the sound of Willie's voice against a background of faint crackle. ''Allo, Princess. I'm jumping third. Tell Weng to get the bottle open, will you?'

'I'll tell him. Listen, I don't know if the smoke marker down here shows it, but the wind's freshened, so allow for it.'

'Right.'

Tarrant was showing surprise. 'I didn't know that ground to air communication was normal for sky-diving.'

'It's not. But Willie used it when he was called in for some of the live tests on the new PX parachute. There was trouble with it and they did a lot of cine-photo recording of the drops, to study how the 'chute developed.'

92

'And the testers gave a commentary as they dropped?'

'Yes. Wearing throat-mikes and an earplug. Willie rather liked it, so he rigged up a link for us on club meetings like this one.'

Twice the plane circled, dropping a sky-diver each time. One landed on the edge of the circle, the other just inside. Tarrant was fascinated by the manoeuvres possible in free fall. As each man dropped, a pattern of coloured lights was flashed from below. According to the pattern, the sky-diver had to perform a particular sequence of aerobatics. By manipulating body and limbs he could roll, turn, bunt in a front somersault, loop in a back somersault, or glide at such an angle as to make a foot of ground transversely for every foot of lost height.

Over the radio they could hear Willie humming softly as the plane circled again. Modesty turned the volume right down.

'Aren't we going to listen to him during the drop?' asked Tarrant.

'He won't talk for this one. There's a lot to do.'

'Ah.' Tarrant grinned a little. 'So you just used it to tip him off about the wind. The fact is, you're cheating on this.'

'Old habits die hard. Here he comes.'

Tarrant looked up quickly and muttered a word of thanks as Modesty put field glasses into his hand. He saw the spread-eagled form of Willie sliding down from the west as if on an invisible slope. The cruciform shape swung in a flat circle to the right, to the left, then revolved smoothly in an open back somersault. A pause to gain stability, a lateral roll, then the arms and legs seemed to disappear as Willie drew them in close to the body, in the plummet position, dropping straight and fast above the western end of the field.

'He's allowing plenty of leeway for the wind,' Modesty said.

Willie half extended arms and legs, to stabilise. The parachute blossomed open. Tarrant peered hard. One edge of the canopy had not developed properly. The loudspeaker was booming and all round the field people were standing up, staring.

'He's got a thrown line.' Modesty half rose, a hand shielding her eyes, then relaxed. 'It's not bad, though.' She grinned suddenly. 'But he'll hit the ground about twice as fast as he should. I wonder if he's switched on?' She reached out and turned up the volume control of the little transceiver.

'... You pox-doctor's stringbag,' Willie's voice was saying with quiet venom. 'You nylon cow. You steaming, pot-bellied, baggy-uddered, split-arsed moo.' He developed his theme with an imagery that made Tarrant blink.

Modesty lifted the radio, pressed a button and said, 'You're on the air, Willie love. And Sir Gerald's afraid you'll singe my ears.'

'Eh? Oh, sorry, Princess.' The voice and the faint background noise cut off abruptly.

'I thought he was very moderate, considering,' Modesty said. 'He'll be lucky to hit the field, never mind the circle.'

Tarrant was watching the figure dangling from the semi-developed parachute, now only two hundred feet from the ground. 'Neither of you seem worried,' he said anxiously. 'Won't he hurt himself?'

'Not Willie. He'll be way off target, though. You should have taken that bet.'

It was only during the last fifty feet that the speed of the drop could be appreciated from below. Tarrant felt his stomach contract, and held his breath. The dangling figure hit the ground and crumpled instantly, like a rag doll. It was as if Willie had been unconscious at the moment of impact.

The parachute billowed, dragging strongly. Willie rolled over, caught the rigging lines and came up on one knee. One side of the canopy flew free as he hit the release, and at once the billowing nylon subsided.

The loud-speaker boomed its relief. Modesty turned and called towards the Rolls. 'Weng. Bring the picnic and open the wine now, please. Mr. Garvin will be thirsty.'

'Coming, Miss Blaise.' Weng moved forward with the hamper, opened it, and began to lay out plates and a cold lobster salad.

Tarrant lowered the glasses and relaxed, watching Willie tramp from the far end of the field, the parachute bundled under his arm. 'It still strikes me as lunacy,' he said.

'Thousands to one against that happening.' Modesty put the radio away. 'What odds would you give on the Bayswater Road?'

There came the pop of a cork, and a few moments later a glass of chilled white wine was put in Tarrant's hand. He turned to see Modesty lift her own glass to him.

'Santé,' she said. 'Don't forget to dig that stuff out of Boulter for me.'

'You're quite sure?'

A smile lit her face, a full and sparkling smile that came from deep within her. It was a very rare expression of hers, but one that Tarrant loved to see. If he watched for it, he always watched in vain. When it came, it always came unexpectedly.

'Quite sure,' she said. 'Don't let's waste time. You like René Vaubois and you're worried about him. If I told you to forget it you'd spend the rest of the day trying to figure some devious way of bringing me in on it. True?'

Tarrant sighed. 'True,' he acknowledged. 'I really am a most detestable man.'

Willie Garvin came up and began to strip off his jumpsuit. 'I got lumps,' he said resentfully, massaging a hip. 'That perishing 'chute...'

'Never mind, Willie love. I'll rub hell out of you with that special embrocation of yours as soon as we're home.'

'Thanks, Princess.' Willie sat down and took a glass from Weng. 'I've 'ad worse lumps. Did I ever tell you about a girl I used to know in a village near Heraklion? Aliki, her name was. She was crazy jealous.'

'He makes them up,' Modesty said to Tarrant.

'I don't, Princess. Honest. We used to sleep out on the balcony, first floor. Just a single bed with little castors on. Well, she got the idea I was after some other Cretan girl, and you know what she did?'

'No, we don't know what she did,' Modesty said with the brisk interest of a music hall comic's feed. 'Tell us, Mr. Garvin, what did she do?'

'Well, this balcony rail was just wood and pretty flimsy. So she waited till we'd gone to sleep one night, then she got up...' He paused and drank. 'She was a really big girl, see? Hefty.'

'Go *on*,' Tarrant said, fascinated. 'What did she do?'

'She gets round the side of the bed and she heaves. I wake up just as the bed an' me go smashing through this balcony railing, like I was on a dirty great roller-skate. Over the edge and down on the grass. Twenty foot. Wham! Two legs broken.'

'You broke both legs?' Tarrant stared.

'No. Two of the bed-legs. I fell clear. But I got some lumps, though.' Willie drank reminiscently. 'I've always 'ated sleeping in a bed with castors on ever since. It's a phobia. I can't get to sleep in one.'

Modesty was looking at him blankly. She said, 'Is *that* why you took the castors off the bed in the spare room at the pent house?'

'M'mm.' Willie nodded virtuously. 'I told you I wasn't making it up, Princess. It's the Aliki-complex.'

She began to laugh, and Tarrant's deeper chuckle joined her. Willie held out his glass for Weng to refill. When they were quiet again he said, 'You asked Sir G. about that business, Princess?'

'Yes. He's going to get details from Boulter's section for us.'

'Good.' Willie drank again. 'This wine's a bit of all right. Real supernacular I'd call it.' He got up and walked away to the car to put his jumpsuit and parachute in the boot.

Tarrant shot a glance at Modesty and murmured, 'What on earth's supernacular?'

'I don't know.' Her voice was low. 'And I'm not going to ask. It's one of those words he digs up now and again from God knows where. I always pretend to understand and look it up later—but he's tried this one on me twice already and I can't find it in the Oxford or *anywhere*. It's maddening.'

'Supernacular...' Tarrant rubbed his chin. 'I'll get my secretary on to it, and let you know.'

Two days had gone by. Tarrant stood in the snooker room of Rand's Club in Pall Mall, chalking his cue, feeling irritable. He and Willie Garvin had finished dining in the club restaurant half an hour ago. It was one of Tarrant's small pleasures to have Willie as a guest here in the hallowed territory of Rand's.

There were one or two members who, hearing Willie's accent, were politely offensive. But since Willie was a master of bland one-upmanship they invariably regretted it.

However, it seemed that Tarrant's ploy this evening had failed. He had contrived to bring about a game of snooker with Willie partnering him against the two men Tarrant disliked most. Their names were Fuller and Cartwright. Both were under forty, both had inherited money and position without inheriting what Tarrant, in his old-fashioned way, would have termed the instincts of a gentleman.

They were a little arrogant, a little patronising, a little overbearing. Mildly disliked by most of the members, they were hated by the club's excellent stewards—a sure condemnation in Tarrant's view. They were extremely good at snooker, and knew it. Three of Tarrant's friends in the club had approached him with an attractive suggestion for taking Fuller and Cartwright down a peg or two—with the aid of Willie Garvin.

But the idea was going sour.

Willie, neatly dressed in a dark grey suit, stood leaning on his cue, watching resignedly as Fuller smartly pocketed the last red and then the blue. Willie's eyes were not quite focused, as if he were a little drunk.

Tarrant moved close to him as Cartwright picked the blue from the rack beneath the pocket and placed it in position. 'For God's sake, Willie,' he muttered, 'what's wrong with you? We're going to lose fifty apiece on this game. I'm damn glad I didn't manage to squeeze them up to a higher stake now.'

Willie said with a vague smile, 'Always deal a mark a good 'and to start with.'

Tarrant frowned and looked at the table. Fuller had to take the yellow ball. It lay hard against the end cushion, and he would simply play to leave it safe. He could afford to. He and Cartwright were twenty-four points ahead, with only the colours left on the table now.

The cue ball moved smoothly up the table, kissed the yellow, moving it only an inch, and came back a little off the cushion. Fuller straightened up and surveyed the table. Cartwright slid the marker along the scoreboard and said in his rather penetrating nasal voice, 'Enjoy yourself, Garvin. You're going to need all the colours.'

Willie grinned foolishly. 'All of 'em?'

'We're twenty-four up,' Fuller said, 'and there's twenty-seven on the table. That means all of them, you see?' His heavy patience barely veiled the sarcasm.

'Ah.' Willie pondered. 'I'm really at me best with 'igh stakes,' he said to Tarrant with an air of self excuse. 'If we'd made it a ton instead of fifty, Sir G. . . .'

Cartwright laughed in a way that set Tarrant's teeth on edge. 'You can make it a hundred if you want to, Garvin, old man.'

'Eh? Oh, *I* wouldn't mind,' Willie said hastily, moving to the table. 'But I don't suppose your mate Mr. Fuller would fancy stumping up.'

Tarrant took quick delight in the reference to 'your mate', but it was overtaken by the surge of excitement as he realised Willie was playing his own devious game.

'Hold it,' Fuller snapped belligerently as Willie set the cue rather unsteadily on the bridge of his left hand. 'What the hell d'you mean? If you want to double the stakes now, that's splendid. But I don't imagine Tarrant will be fool enough to go along with you.'

'I'm fool enough,' Tarrant said pleasantly. 'A hundred apiece, then.'

'You're on,' said Fuller, and Cartwright nodded promptly.

'Right, then.' Willie moved briskly away, chalked his cue and picked up the long rest. His movements were precise and methodical now. He laid the rest along the baize, set his cue in the fork, sighted carefully, and played the cue ball hard, with a lot of bottom on the stroke.

The yellow hit the side cushion and doubled down the table to smack smartly into the corner pocket. Tarrant took the rest from Willie, his expression solemn. The remaining colours were all well-placed, except the black. Well-placed for a player of Willie's calibre. Tarrant felt extremely happy.

Willie trickled the green gently into a side-pocket, bringing the cue ball into position for a straight shot at the brown. Though his manner was relaxed, Tarrant could sense the fine-drawn concentration in him.

The brown went down; then the blue, and with the shot Willie put side on the cue ball so that it screwed away to strike the black and bring it clear of the cushion. A long shot to the corner for the pink. A double across the table to slam the black home. The game was over.

Willie laid down his cue. 'Talk about luck,' he said. 'Can I buy you gents a round of drinks? I know I'm not a member, but——'

'I'll see to it, Willie,' Tarrant said genially. 'You've just put a hundred in my pocket.'

'Never mind the drinks, thank you.' Fuller's face was thunderous as he spoke. Cartwright was taut with anger. Both men took out their cheque books.

'Thank you very much for the game.' Willie spoke in a pleasant, well modulated voice now, with no Cockney accent. 'Sir Gerald and I must give you gentlemen your revenge some-time.'

In silence Fuller and Cartwright passed over their cheques and went out.

'Lovely,' said Willie, and put his cue in the rack. ' "*They* 'ave digged a pit before me, into the midst whereof they are fallen themselves," like a couple of right pills. Psalm 57, Verse 6. Not the last bit.'

'Very apt. You must have left a well-thumbed psalter in that Calcutta gaol when young, Willie,' Tarrant said happily. He put the cheque in his wallet. 'I'm much obliged. This will get my old Rover rewired.'

'Blimey, I'll do that for you.' Willie began to stack the red balls in the triangle. After a few moments he said, 'Modesty's fretting a bit. She told me to ask if you'd got that stuff from Boulter's lot yet.'

'Boulter's having one of his jealous spells. He won't play.'

Willie looked up quickly, a little startled. 'Can't you make 'im?'

'Not without a major departmental clash. I can't have that.'

Willie stood frowning at the green baize. 'That's not so good.'

'It may not be so bad, either,' said Tarrant. 'I've put Jack Fraser on the job.'

'How d'you mean?' Willie knew Jack Fraser. He was Tarrant's assistant, a man with a cringing and obtuse manner which concealed a very astute mind.

'I've been asked, or rather instructed, to make a high-level security check,' said Tarrant. 'On security. It's a wide brief. I've put Fraser on the job of testing security within Boulter's department. The brief will cover him if he fails, but I don't think he will.'

'Nor do I.' Willie grinned, relieved. 'Fraser's good. He does that pathetic-little-sod act a real treat.'

It was fifteen minutes later, and they were in the bar, when a steward approached and murmured to Tarrant.

'He's here,' Tarrant said quietly to Willie. The two men got up and walked through to the lobby. Tarrant collected his hat and umbrella on the way. Fraser, in black jacket and pin-striped trousers, sat on the edge of a chair, a bowler hat on his knees, hugging a thin briefcase. He peered uneasily through his spectacles as Tarrant and Willie approached.

'I do hope I'm not disturbing you, Sir Gerald,' he said anxiously, getting to his feet. 'But you asked to see this month's trade graphs as soon as they were available.'

'Quite all right, Fraser,' Tarrant said benevolently, and watched Fraser twitch his features into an expression of humble relief. 'We'll go to the office and study them right away. I want to be fully briefed for the Minister tomorrow.'

Fraser's old Bentley stood at the kerb outside. Willie and Tarrant got in the back. Fraser hunched over the wheel and drove off. A horn blared indignantly behind him.

'Don't be alarmed,' Tarrant said to Willie. 'Fraser uses the selective system of driving.'

'Selective?'

'Yes. You confine your awareness to traffic lights and policemen, but you ignore all other traffic and pedestrians. It's a little frightening, but it works—providing you have complete faith and allow no shred of doubt to enter your mind.'

Fraser giggled. 'Sir Gerald is making fun of me, Mr. Garvin.' He carved his way out into Piccadilly. The Bentley did not move fast, but with a steady and inexorable majesty.

'They do get out of the way, though,' Willie said, impressed.

'They'd better,' said Tarrant. 'We'll go to Miss Blaise's apartment, Fraser. How did it work out tonight?'

'I think you'll find we have all you wanted, Sir Gerald,' Fraser answered diffidently.

'You were damn quick, Jack.'

With the use of the Christian name Fraser changed. He dropped his servile manner and scowled, his thin face hard.

'Bloody right,' he said. 'You'll really have to shake up Boulter's section now.'

'As bad as that?'

Fraser nodded grimly. 'You know they run that photo agency on the third floor as a front. All the works are on the fourth. No night duty officer. It's not that kind of shop. I went to the agency, chose some pics, walked out and straight up the stairs. There's another short flight leading up to the roof, but the access there is permanently sealed. So I just sat there. After a couple of hours they all went home.'

'Except the night guards?'

'Guard, singular. Except him. When he found me I was going to show my card and tell him to ring the office. I'd fixed with Boyd there to confirm my identity and to stall for ten minutes or so. I was pretty sure that one way or another I could get into the filing room for long enough to find what I wanted. I know Boulter's system pretty well.'

'So?'

'So the night guard made his rounds. *He didn't even come up that last flight of stairs to the roof.* I wanted to go and throttle the bastard. Anyway, he locked up and went down to the third floor.' Fraser shrugged. 'There's plenty of girlie pics there, and maybe he likes looking at tits. Anyway, I had a free run. Bridged the alarm, spent five minutes on the lock, got in, found what I wanted, clicked away with the camera, gum-shoed downstairs, switched off the outside alarm, and walked out. I drove back to the office and I've been blowing up prints ever since. Christ, my sister's twelve year old kid could have done it, and he's a bloody imbecile if ever I saw one.'

Willie Garvin was shaking with suppressed laughter.

'It's not funny,' Tarrant said gloomily. 'We've got enough to worry about without lax security in a security section.'

'Sorry. I was only thinking it's the same everywhere, Sir G. We always banked on that in the old days.'

'Banked on what?'

'Security departments are always too busy watching other people to watch themselves. 'Ow long is it since you made a check on your own night guards or changed all the locks on your doors and filing cabinets?'

There was a long silence. Fraser gave way to a taxi, a sure sign that he was shaken.

'Yes,' said Tarrant at last. 'Look into that, Jack.'

Fraser nodded, and turned the Bentley into the forecourt of a tall pent house block overlooking the park.

8

It was an hour past midnight. Modesty Blaise passed the last of the photostats to Willie, who took it and put down the page he had just finished reading.

The windows leading out on to the broad terrace were open, yet even so the air was humid. This had been one of those rare summer weeks which the English seem always to expect but which always takes them by surprise. Modesty got up, closed the windows and switched on the air conditioning. She was wearing silver grey slacks and a fine check shirt open at the neck.

Glasses and empty coffee-cups stood on small tables. Tarrant had finished reading and was leaning back at one end of the long chesterfield, drawing slowly on his cigar. Fraser had taken off his jacket, after asking permission, and was pacing the room, his narrow face frowning.

Willie put down the final sheet and leaned back in his armchair. Modesty came to sit on the broad leather arm and looked round. 'Would anybody care to summarise?'

The men looked from one to another.

'I'll start,' Tarrant said at last. 'It won't make sense because the whole damn thing doesn't make sense, but let's see how we go. About eighteen months back, a letter was sent to the Prime Minister. It didn't get past his second or third secretary because it was obviously a crank letter. It announced that three people, a fairly high-ranking civil servant in the Ministry of Social Security, a wealthy merchant banker and a certain M.P. would die within six months unless a sum of sixty thousand pounds was paid in each case, in a manner to be specified. The banker alone received a personal warning as well, probably because he could pay for himself. Intention to pay was to be signified by a cryptic advertisement in the personal column of *The Times*. Whereupon further instructions would be issued.'

Tarrant eased the ash off his cigar. 'We now know the method of making payment, and it taxes belief, but I'd rather we dealt with that separately if you agree.' He looked round and received brief nods of assent.

'Very well. With the letter was a list of some twenty people in other countries who were also threatened with death in six months unless payment was made.'

'Some of 'em weren't in government,' Willie put in. 'They were just rich.'

'True. And it's a point worth noting that government people threatened in the major countries were mostly small fry. In the smaller and less stable countries there were, on the other hand, some VIP's included. However, what concerns us at the moment is that nobody paid up or even asked for instructions, and within six months every person on that list was dead.'

A Tompion clock in the corner struck the quarter as if to mark his words, and Tarrant looked towards it with sardonic acknowledgment.

Fraser said, 'In the meantime a second threat-list had been sent and similar lists have followed at intervals of a few months.'

'Let's stay with the first list for the moment.' Tarrant picked up one of the photostat sheets. 'Although everybody on this list died, only three were certainly murdered, none of them our own candidates. The civil servant, Rutledge, had a thrombosis. Barnes was hurrying to a division in the House, slipped on the steps between the Central Lobby and St. Stephen's Hall, and cracked his skull; he wasn't pushed, there were a dozen witnesses. And Martindale was struck by lightning; his wife was sheltering under the same tree when it happened, but it didn't harm her. The same kind of thing was happening to victims in other countries, according to the reports which have been slowly gathered in since. And now somebody else can talk for a bit. Fantasy's not my meat.'

'After the results on the first two lists a few people started to pay up,' Modesty said. 'They paid. And they're still alive. Nobody gave them a thrombosis or struck them by lightning.'

'Major governments didn't pay though, Princess.' Willie was frowning. 'I don't know why this mob's bothered to try that angle. I mean, you'd never get a big power to fork out even if you threatened the P.M. or equivalent.'

'I hate to admit it,' Fraser said gloomily, polishing his spectacles, 'but I agree with Boulter's theory on that. He thinks the threats to government people in major countries are made and implemented simply as a lesson to others—to people who are more likely to pay. We know the Heads of State of two African countries have paid. We think it's the same with two other African VIP's, even though they won't admit it. But they were on the lists and they're still alive.'

'Three South American politicians or generals,' said Willie. 'One oil tycoon in Venezuela. One ditto in the Middle East. A jute millionaire in Pakistan. A Texan beef man whose kid was threatened. One Egyptian merchant——' He broke off and shrugged. 'Seventeen have paid so far.'

'That's only those we know about since Interpol came into the picture,' said Fraser. 'There may have been more. And the squeeze is getting tougher. The amounts are less than you'd expect, maybe, but later lists threaten people who don't scare easily, and some of them are paying up.'

'You wouldn't wonder,' Willie said shortly. 'Everyone who's been threatened and failed to pay has died. Except René Vaubois.'

There was a long silence.

'The nature of the payment has varied curiously,' said Tarrant. 'Heroin, gems, diamond dust, and in one very recent case a fortune in gold sovereigns. But leaving aside the nature and method of payment, the most baffling thing of all is to account for the extraordinarily high proportion of seemingly *natural* deaths.'

'There's no seeming about it, surely,' said Fraser, scowling into space. 'Mellini died in a restaurant from getting a chicken bone stuck in his throat. Nobody can organise that sort of thing.'

Tarrant glanced at Modesty. She still sat on the arm of Willie's chair, her hands between her knees, staring almost sleepily down at the pattern of an Isfahan rug on the tiled floor. 'What do you think, my dear?' he asked quietly.

'About fifteen per cent were definitely murdered.' She did not look up but spoke absently, her mind following its own train of thought. 'Let's call the rest natural deaths for the time being. You know, you can analyse these lists in several ways. Government people as against rich individuals; natural deaths as against killings; likely prospects for payment as against hopeless prospects. Boulter has run several analyses on different lines.'

She was silent. Tarrant was about to speak but a quick glance of warning from Willie stopped him. After several seconds Modesty lifted her gaze from the rug and her eyes focused. 'But he hasn't taken the time factor into account,' she said. 'That's more significant than anything else. Look at those lists again. All the natural deaths have occurred in the first *three* months of the six-month time limit. The rest, the killings, have occurred in the last three months of the period.'

Nobody spoke for a while. Modesty lit a cigarette. Tarrant said at last, 'Yes. It must be highly significant. But I'm damned if I see what it signifies, Modesty.'

'Neither do I, yet. Not clearly.' She stood up and began to pace the room slowly, holding her elbows, the cigarette clipped in the fingers of one hand. 'Look. We have to make assumptions. Either we can assume that a number of people in different parts of the world can be—I don't know—hypnotised if you like, into swallowing a chicken bone, walking under a truck, falling out of a window, or dying in any other of the ways Boulter's listed...' She paused.

'Or what?' Tarrant prompted, puzzled.

'Or we can assume that the people behind this business have some way of predicting natural death.'

Tarrant looked blank and said, 'Good God.'

'It's a nice trick,' said Fraser. 'Do you think they read it in the tea leaves?'

Willie drew an angry breath but Modesty silenced him with a touch of her hand on his shoulder and gave Fraser a brief smile, unoffended. 'I don't know *how* they predict death, Mr. Fraser. I'm not saying they do so. I've just put forward two alternatives. Some kind of long range hypnosis to induce suicide; or some kind of foreknowledge. Can you suggest a third?'

Fraser screwed up his eyes in thought for a full minute. 'No,' he said at last. 'Not on the facts we have. My apologies.'

'No need for them. This is a time for disputing theories. Both alternatives are highly improbable. It's also improbable that the United States would make serious tests for the possibility of using telepathy for communication with submarines, but that's a cold fact.' Tarrant nodded confirmation, and she went on. 'So we're not talking nonsense. Of my two alternatives, which will you buy as the least unlikely?'

Fraser paced to the windows and back, then halted. 'You'd have a job hypnotising anyone into getting a thrombosis. Still more into getting themselves struck by lightning, for God's sake.'

'Wait a minute!' Tarrant sat up straight. 'That time factor you spoke of just now, Modesty. Natural deaths in the first three months, killings in the second three. *It could mean that the killings are to make good any failure in the predictions.*'

Her face lit with sudden excitement, and Tarrant saw the same quick reaction in Willie Garvin.

'It makes a pattern,' she said softly. 'Good for you, Sir Gerald.'

'I'm not so sure.' Fraser spoke uneasily. 'If it was a matter of predicting deaths, then the people who paid up would die too. And they don't.'

'No problem there.' She shook her head decisively. 'You have your list of predictions, drawn from a main list of carefully selected people. You take off that list of predictions anyone likely to pay up—because they're going to die anyway.

107

But you add to it three or four people you think are highly likely to pay. If they pay, they live. If they don't pay, you have them killed. That's another good reason for the killings falling in the last three months of the six month period.'

'Ye-e-es...' Fraser grimaced. 'I like it. But aren't we getting a little unreal? I mean, we're assuming that somebody has found a pretty good way of predicting death.'

'Yes. But I prefer it to the long-range hypnosis alternative. At least there are examples of the first. Jeane Dixon in America predicted President Kennedy's death three months before he was killed. She tried to get friends to prevent him going to Dallas.'

Fraser looked unconvinced. 'That sort of thing usually comes to light only after the event.'

'Not in this case. It's on record from the people she contacted to try to stop him. That was three months earlier.' Modesty looked sombrely at Fraser. 'But if you don't trust word of mouth, there's more. Seven *years* earlier she said in an interview that a blue-eyed Democratic President elected in 1960 would be assassinated. That went into print in 1956. Anyone can still check it in the files.'

'Precognition,' Willie said suddenly. 'Remember, Princess? That's what Steve Collier called it that night in Paris. He got all excited about me knowing there was trouble around.'

Fraser stared. 'Not you too?'

'Sometimes Willie's ears prickle,' said Modesty. 'It's a sure danger signal. But predicting individual deaths is a bit different.'

'Only in degree,' Tarrant said thoughtfully. 'And as you say, we have to make an assumption of some kind. Suppose we buy your theory, Modesty. Where do we go from there?'

'I don't know. And I haven't bought it myself, yet. But it'll do to stop us groping around in the dark when we ought to be concentrating on other things.'

'I'm sorry. I don't follow you.'

'Point of contact,' said Willie. 'Never mind 'ow the caper's worked. The loot's got to be 'anded over.'

'Yes.' Modesty nodded briskly and looked at Tarrant. 'When René Vaubois put this to me, very sketchily as a hypothetical case, I said the big weakness would be in handing over the ransom. Contact would have to be made for that. So now we come to the practical side. Will you summarise that for us?'

'I'll try.' Tarrant sorted out three of the photostat sheets and ran his eye down the typescript. 'When a victim decides to pay up he inserts a cryptic advertisement in one of the big newspapers. He then receives instructions to pick up from a warehouse a crate which is awaiting collection.'

Tarrant paused and looked up. 'I need hardly mention that all correspondence, which is typewritten, and all stationery, letters, crates and contents have been thoroughly checked. Interpol have found no lead-backs. The crates seem to have been placed in storage in warehouses at various ports throughout the world many months before.'

'If routine work had produced anything we'd all be in bed now,' Modesty said. 'Go on, Sir Gerald.'

He looked at the typescript again. 'The crate holds a large buoy-shaped plastic container of a size suitable to take the radio equipment it already contains and whatever ransom has been demanded. Instructions are then sent to the effect that the container must be put over the side of a ship, into the sea, at a particular reference point.'

'Not always the same,' said Fraser.

'No. The first five pick-ups were made from a point in the Caribbean, another lot from the Mediterranean, the most recent from the North Sea, near Denmark. Several countries have acquired these containers by inserting the necessary advertisement. They did not acquire them for use, but for examination.'

'Boulter's got one,' said Willie.

'Yes. They vary slightly but the basic design is always the same. When lowered into the sea and released, the container sinks to a depth of thirty fathoms, where it is buoyed to remain floating upright. It bears a large snap-hook at the top, presumably for pick-up purposes, and also a sonar transmitting device. Specifications are given here, but I confess they're too technical for me to follow. Did you understand them, Willie?'

'M'mm. A sound job. Not all that sophisticated. But I'd like to 'ave a look at one meself.'

'Well ... we'll have to see.' Tarrant looked down at the papers again. 'The drop is always made at night, and the ship must move off immediately after having made it. Boulter assumes that the submerged container is picked up by a submarine of some kind.'

'You can't just go out and buy a submarine,' Willie protested. 'Not even a midget one. I don't get this bit.'

'Neither does anyone else,' said Tarrant. 'The Americans lowered a container with a small low-frequency tracer hidden in it. They had two or three big launches in the area and they hoped to follow the—whatever it is, after the pick-up. But that container just wasn't picked up. It was left strictly alone. They don't know how the tracer was discovered, since one would have to know the frequency to detect it. But our mysterious friends must have detected it. They made no pick-up and the victim died by violence six weeks later.'

'I liked the French idea best,' said Fraser. 'They suspended a depth charge from the container, triggered to go off when the snap-hook was operated.' He looked gloomy. 'But it only got the same result as the American idea.'

'What gets me is the homing transmitter,' Willie said. He got up and prowled the room restlessly. 'It starts operating by water pressure. It transmits on reducing intensity for two hours, then stops. So the pick-up must be made in that time. All right. But why the reducing intensity?'

'Why anything?' Fraser shrugged. 'The Italians had a sonar detector operating in a launch circling the area for two hours before and six hours after the drop. And again our little friends didn't come for their loot, which means they must have detected the launch. How could they do that when the launch couldn't detect *them*?'

'Could it be done by people, Willie?' Modesty asked doubtfully. 'I mean scuba divers working from a mother ship.'

'They couldn't work that far away, Princess. And they'd 'ave to carry better detection gear than the launch was carrying.' Willie shook his head. 'No. It's got to be a sub of some sort. But some'ow I just can't buy that.'

'I've got the same feeling,' Modesty said slowly. 'The whole of this caper is completely off-beat. The pick-up should be as off-beat as the rest.' She looked at Tarrant. 'Boulter's got one of the containers. I think Willie must have a close look at it.'

'Boulter may jib very hard, my dear.'

Willie said, 'After the way Fraser blew that security system tonight you've got Boulter over a barrel, Sir G. He'll 'ave to play.'

Tarrant fingered his chin. 'You're proposing blackmail, you know.'

'That's right,' Modesty said. 'And Boulter may know one or two things that haven't been put in the file Fraser photographed. Blackmail anything like that out of him, too. Especially on one point.'

Fraser grinned approvingly. Tarrant sighed and said, 'What's that?'

'The killings. If they follow the pattern that was tried for René Vaubois, they're made by hired killers. Somebody must lay them on. That's another point of contact. Whoever does the hiring must really know his way around in a lot of places. It's not hard to arrange a killing, and not all that expensive, but it's hard to do it anonymously. Maybe he works through stringers in different countries. René couldn't get a lead from the men we caught. But maybe somewhere, sometime, there's been a little slip. Boulter may have heard of a thread of a lead that nobody's been able to follow up.'

'But you could?'

She gave him a half smile. 'Willie and I were on the other side for a long time. It gives us an advantage.'

'Yes. Your contacts are much wider, of course.' Tarrant got up. He felt tired, and with the tiredness came a sense of unreality. All that had been said in the past hour seemed little more than a futile exercise in fantasy.

Yet there was no hint of doubt in the faces of Modesty Blaise and Willie Garvin. They were absorbed and speculative. Tarrant knew he could not have called them off the scent now anyway. The caper was real, no matter how baffling its operation, and they were fascinated by it. But beyond that, René Vaubois was still on the list to die, and they liked Vaubois.

So did Tarrant. He reminded himself that week by week people who had been promised death were dying or being killed; that tonight, perhaps, a fortune was being lowered into the dark sea under the orders of a rich and frightened man.

'Where shall I reach you, Modesty?' he asked.

'Here, please. I'd like Willie to see the container tomorrow, if you can fix Boulter.'

Fraser chuckled a little grimly and picked up the sheaf of photostats. 'We can fix Boulter,' he said.

It was chilly in the laboratory. The old-fashioned central heating plant was closed down for the summer, and overnight the temperature had fallen sharply. The container secured by Boulter's department had been carefully cut for examination. On a bench lay the two longitudinal halves of an object like a giant pear about six feet in length and of black plastic.

The bald man in the white coat was talking with quiet enthusiasm to an audience of two, a dark and very striking girl in a wine-coloured cashmere dress with three-quarter length sleeves, and a big fair man with a Cockney accent. The scientist wondered if the emerald bracelet the girl wore could possibly be real. He did not know their names, only that he had been instructed to answer all their questions.

'Beautifully simple design,' he was saying. 'Strong but light, the walls honeycombed inside for strength and buoyancy. She'll float upright at thirty fathoms, plus or minus two. The transmitter was in this section at the top, but I took it out with the other gear.'

He moved along the bench and pointed with a pencil to a metal cylinder just over a foot long and seven inches in diameter. Beside it stood a sealed metal box with heavy cables projecting through waterproof grommets.

Willie Garvin began to ask questions. The talk of amplitude and intensity became too technical for Modesty to follow. She watched Willie's face. It held a frowning, slightly exasperated look, as of a man trying to catch at some fleeting thought that continually eluded him. When all the questions had been answered Willie stood for a long time staring at the transmitter.

'Won't the bell ring?' Modesty asked quietly.

He shook his head. 'No. It ties up with something I've heard or read, but I can't put 'em together. I don't even know what it is I'm trying to remember.'

'Leave it for a while.'

He nodded and moved back to the split container. 'What's this other cavity at the bottom for?'

'Ah, now that's quite interesting.' The scientist pointed with his pencil to a very small hole in the base. 'There's a vent here, you see, and this little gadget seals it when the container is in an upright position. The cavity held several pounds of lead shot.' He waited expectantly, looking at Willie.

'Looks like the lead shot would start to trickle out once the container's turned on its side—once you started to tow it.'

'Exactly. So it runs out and the container becomes progressively more buoyant over a period of ... oh, ten minutes or so.'

'Why?'

The scientist looked startled. 'I've no idea. I can only tell you how it functions. I'd rather like somebody to tell *me* why.'

Willie grunted. 'Does it grow buoyant enough to surface?'

'Oh, no. The weights built into the interior walls at the bottom would remain. With the lead shot gone, she'd stay submerged at about a fathom or two.'

Willie ran a hand through his hair irritably. 'That's neither one thing nor the other,' he muttered.

113

Ten minutes later he sat glowering beside Modesty as she drove the Reliant Sabre Six she used for town work on the thirty minute run to 'The Treadmill'.

'Don't be broody, Willie love.' Modesty rested a hand on his for a moment. 'I didn't expect you to do a Sherlock Holmes just by looking at the thing.'

'I know, Princess. But I'm sure I've got the answer if I could only fit all the pieces together—if I knew what the pieces were.'

'Stop thinking about it. We'll have an hour's easy workout at "The Treadmill" to give your mind a rest. Then a quick lunch and on to Tarrant's office this afternoon. I want to know if he dug anything useful out of Boulter.'

'Right.' Willie relaxed. 'Can you drive an' carry on that game we started on the flight back from Paris?'

'If we take it easy on both counts.' She focused her attention on the road and held it there as if setting automatic controls. Then part of her mind visualised the chessboard. Eight moves had been made by each side. She was white, to move, and had played a Queen's pawn opening to which Willie had replied with an Indian defence.

'Knight takes knight, my last move,' said Willie.

'Yes. I've got it.' She had once found it difficult to get beyond four moves. Now she could usually finish a game without losing track of the position. For a minute she sat in thought, then said, 'Queen takes knight.'

It was noon as the Sabre Six drew up in the forecourt of Willie's pub by the river. They got out and went round the side of 'The Treadmill' to the grounds at the back, where a long windowless building of brick lay tucked away beside a tree-lined inlet.

A figure was strolling by the river. Tarrant.

He lifted his rolled umbrella in a salute, and came towards them.

'I thought I'd drive down,' he said, taking Modesty's hand. 'Did you have any luck?'

'We're not sure yet, Sir Gerald. Willie has a hunch that he can't pin down.'

Willie was unlocking the first of the double doors which gave entrance to the long soundproof building. Tarrant's expression became uneasy, and he said, 'You're not going to have one of those workouts, Modesty?'

'Not one of those.' She smiled. 'Just some practice and limbering up.'

Tarrant nodded, relieved. This meant practice on the handgun, knife and archery ranges that ran the length of the building; followed by gymnastics and controlled combat. But sometimes, at the end of such a session, these two fought seriously. He had been present on one occasion only, and had seen Modesty knocked cold. He knew that the reverse was just as likely to happen but he did not ever want to see it. The combat in itself was frightening to watch, and had left him limp with reaction.

He followed Willie and Modesty through the small lobby and the second of the doors. Willie locked the door and put on the fluorescent lights. The dojo lay in the middle of the long building, with the ranges on either side. Along one wall hung an array of modern handguns and a collection of trenchant weapons of all countries and ages.

The sandbagged wall behind the butts at the far end was pierced by a door leading to Willie Garvin's remarkable engineering workshop.

Modesty moved to a changing cubicle with a shower, in one corner. 'Talk to Sir Gerald while I get changed, Willie.'

'Okay, Princess. Pity I 'aven't got something to tell 'im.' Willie Garvin eyed the array of weapons and took down a long-bladed knife with a leather-bound horn haft. 'That's the kind they were going to carve up Vaubois with,' he said moodily. 'A Cajun knife. Don't often see 'em in Europe, but this was a new mob.'

His arm flickered and the knife flashed through the air to stand quivering in the centre of a man-shaped target by the butts.

'Does it have any significance?' Tarrant said hopefully.

'I dunno. That's the trouble with this caper. We don't know enough, yet there must be masses of stuff.'

'What do you mean?'

Willie exhaled irritably. 'Boulter's got a container. So have a dozen other countries, maybe. Same with information. Everybody knows a bit, but nobody knows the lot. Who's paying up? Who hired some little Panamanian freighter last week or last month to run out and drop what in the North Sea? Or somewhere else?'

'Everything is fed to Interpol, Willie. They have the whole picture.'

'Balls,' said Willie without heat. 'You've got forty-odd countries in Interpol, and they all feed it what they think fit. Interpol works fine for some things, but not for this. It's all too slow. I reckon it'll be another year or more before there's enough co-operation to give 'em a chance of action.'

'What's the alternative?'

'Get the governments together and set up a central control for this one thing.'

Tarrant laughed. 'That would take two years.'

'I know.' Willie relaxed and gave a wry grin. 'I shouldn't grumble. It suited us well enough during *The Network* days.' He scratched his cheek, a little puzzled. 'How's this been kept out of the press?'

'It hasn't entirely. But that's one thing the governments have co-operated on,' Tarrant said drily. 'At first the thing was too ridiculous to publicise. But when the deaths started it was too hot. As Boulter pointed out to me this morning, no government enjoys being shown up as powerless to protect its citizens. And how do you protect a man from electrocuting himself fixing a fountain in his fishpond?'

Modesty came out of the cubicle wearing black slacks and shirt, and plimsolls. Her hair was bound in a tight, short club at the back of her neck. She wore the modified Gun Hawk holster Tarrant had seen before. It was empty now.

116

'I'll get the Colt ·32, Princess,' Willie said, and moved towards his workshop.

'Did I hear you mention Boulter?' Modesty said to Tarrant.

'Yes. I saw him this morning, of course. I must say he accepted my blackmail with a degree of humour that was very commendable.'

'He's a realist. If you'd blown him for lack of security he'd have had the skids under him. Did he tell you anything useful?'

Willie was returning with the Colt revolver, thumbing cartridges into the chambers.

'You have a curious instinct,' Tarrant said to Modesty. 'You said that somebody was hiring people for the killings; that it was done anonymously in some way, perhaps using a local stringer or go-between; and that there might have been a slip-up at some time.'

'Yes?'

'Boulter gave me a name. The name of a man who ran a gang in Greece. The information is that he was approached to handle a killing, but turned it down. It's believed that he knows the identity of the man behind the contact man. A slip-up.'

'Has he talked?'

'No. Unfortunately he was double-crossed by a member of his own gang, the second in command, who disapproved of turning down the killing job.'

'How was he double-crossed?'

'He went to Yugoslavia, under an alias, to bring out the mistress of a failed politician who'd managed to get clear of the country about one step ahead of the secret police. The woman was in hiding, and the politician had offered a very handsome sum if she were brought out safely.'

'But Krolli was blown,' Modesty said. 'They were waiting for him.'

Tarrant stared. 'How did you know his name was Krolli?'

'He was one of my men in *The Network*. A good one. I gave him that area when I split up the organisation.' She looked at

Willie. 'It figures. Krolli wouldn't touch that kind of killing.'

'No. Did the Yugoslavs give 'im the chop, Sir G?'

'They were more practical than that. He was sentenced to ten years in a labour battalion for attempted political crimes and aiding an enemy of the State.'

'Ten years.' Willie looked at Modesty.

She said to Tarrant, 'Yugoslavia belongs to Interpol. Why haven't they questioned him?'

'They have, but he won't talk. They could make him, no doubt, but they're not particularly interested. It happens that no Yugoslav has been on any of the death-lists. The Interpol people there are very subordinate to the political machinery, of course.'

'Krolli would talk to me, ' Modesty said quietly.

'I very much doubt that you'd be allowed access to him, my dear.'

'I wasn't thinking of that.' She glanced at Willie, and Tarrant saw that he was beginning to smile. 'Get changed, Willie love. I'll ring Weng and get him busy on the arrangements.'

Willie went into the changing cubicle, whistling.

Tarrant followed Modesty along the length of the combat room and into the workshop, where a telephone stood on a shelf in one corner. 'What are you up to?' he asked uneasily.

'I want to talk to Krolli.' She began to dial. 'Willie and I can be in Yugoslavia in two days. We'll need that time to set everything up.'

'But——'

'Ten years in a labour battalion,' she broke in. Her eyes rested on Tarrant, and though nothing in her voice or expression seemed to have changed he felt the sudden force of her will as an almost physical shock. 'Krolli took a bullet meant for me, once. Took it deliberately.'

She spoke into the phone. 'Weng? Now listen . . .'

9

It was hard to tell that the Chevrolet Impala was green, for white dust from the narrow, unmade road clothed it like a sheet.

The woman in the passenger seat looked wearily round the tiny village square where the car had halted. She wore a head-scarf, beneath which a short fringe of bleached hair hung down. Dark sunglasses hid her eyes, and heavy make-up hid whatever ravages the years had wrought on her complexion.

A few men and women, and rather more children, stood a little distance from the car, studying it with sober interest. Their clothes were of homespun wool, heavily embroidered. They wore round forage caps and the moccasin style of shoe called *opanci*, with coloured knitted stockings or baggy trousers clasped at the ankles. Some of the women held shawls partly hiding their faces.

A few yards away a big man stood speaking in a deep American voice to a cluster of blank-faced villagers. He made frequent gestures and kept pointing to an open map he held.

'What do they *say*, Chuck?' the woman called in a nasal twang. The man turned and lifted his shoulders. He wore a straw trilby with a broad band, and a lightweight fawn suit over a blue shirt. A cine-camera hung from his neck.

'Can't get through, honey,' he said. 'I guess——' He broke off and his eyes lit up as two children began squabbling over possession of a peeled stick with a piece of string tied to one end. Chuckling, he crouched and lifted his camera. It began to whirr as he panned with the movement of the struggling children.

'For God's sake, will you leave it alone, Chuck?' the woman called plaintively. 'Just find out how we get back on the main highway.' She gave a huff of contempt and repeated, 'The main highway. All thirty goddam feet of it.'

The man stopped shooting, put his camera in its case and moved over to the car. 'Look, Janey,' he said reasonably, 'I'm trying. But I guess the population here adds up to about seventy-five, maximum. And nobody talks English.'

'What's the map say?' the woman asked, her voice getting a little strident. 'You spent ten minutes on it when we took that turn-off God knows how long back. You said we'd come out okay.'

There was a little stir among the scattered villagers as a greying man was escorted towards the car by an eager young man gabbling rapidly. The older man said, 'I talk some English. What you want please?'

'Ahh...' The American beckoned and spread his map on the dusty bonnet. 'Look. This road that cuts round the mountain. See? We should have hit it a few miles back, but we couldn't find it. You understand?'

'Understand. But is no road. Only to walk. Now they make road, but is long time. Finish in two, three year maybe.'

The woman glared bitterly at her husband. 'Two, three year. You wait that long, you'll run out of film.'

'Now don't be like that, Janey. Jesus, the thing's not marked as a footpath on the map!'

'Map, shmap. The sun's down and it'll be dark in half an hour. I'm not riding another three hours back down that road. See if they've got a hotel with plumbing and showers here.'

The grey-haired Yugoslav said, 'Is no shower. Is no hotel.'

'Oh, great.' The woman leaned back, took out a compact and began to dab at her cheeks with quick, angry movements.

'Maybe someone would let us have a room for the night, Janey,' her husband said doubtfully.

'A room?' She closed the compact with a snap. 'Maybe I'm fussy but I like to know what's sharing the bed with us. Will you get in and drive, Chuck?'

'But you said——'

'I *know*. But if we don't start back, we sleep here. I'd sooner spend the night in the car. Now will you *please* get in and drive?'

'Sure.' The American thrust a note into the hand of the English-speaking villager and climbed in behind the wheel. The Chev backed, circled, and started off down the road, a trail of dust rising in its wake.

Modesty Blaise took off her sunglasses and said, 'About five miles ... it should be dusk when we get there. Don't use lights.'

Willie Garvin nodded. 'You reckon Nedic will turn up?'

'I think so. It's only forty kilometres from his place, and he must have found the message we left this morning.'

'Bit of luck, him knowing the area.'

'We'd have had to manage without him otherwise, but this ought to make it easier.'

The last of the sun's reflected light was fading as Willie eased the car off the road and wound a cautious way deep into a stand of trees. He stopped, switched off, put on the brake, then moved back to the road to remove any trace the car had made in turning off.

Modesty was cleaning the thick make-up from her face with cream when he returned. She had taken off the headscarf, with the fringe of bleached hair attached, and the long-sleeved blouse which had concealed the young and telltale firmness of her arms and shoulders.

Willie unlocked the boot and took out a case. As he opened it Modesty stripped off the skirt and bra, stockings and pants she wore. All bore American brand names, as did every article of clothing that Willie wore.

She stood naked in the twilight of the woods, unselfconscious. Her body was the same soft golden tan all over. Willie handed her a pair of stocking-tights, the kind she invariably wore, and ran an appraising eye over her. There was nothing furtive in his appraisal. He knew her body well. At this moment he was concerned only with judging her physical fitness to meet what might lie ahead. It was an automatic glance that she had long grown used to, and it was followed by the usual little nod of approval.

She slipped into the stocking-tights, fastened on the black bra he passed her. Slacks and long-sleeved shirt now, not the usual black, but mottled grey-green for camouflage. She sat in the open doorway of the car to pull on the calf-length grey combat boots.

Willie had stripped. He pulled on close-fitting shorts with a light plastic box guard, then strapped on the slender leather knife-harness which held two sheathed knives in echelon across his left breast. Modesty in turn automatically checked his smoothly muscled body, not because there was need to check but because she never failed to wonder at, and to appreciate, the speed and power and hard-won skills his body contained; which were at her service when needed, and gladly given.

She remembered finding Willie Garvin, finding and in some strange way re-making him. No, he had re-made himself, because of her. She did not know why, for she had done no more than back a hunch and place her trust in him. It did not matter why. After all the long years of fighting alone, there had come a time at last when she had found someone able and eager to stand at her shoulder. Willie Garvin had stood there in all the years since, as sure and unfailing as if he had been an extension of herself.

He had put on shirt and slacks now, in the same grey-green camouflage colours as her own, and was sitting beside her to pull on his boots.

'Willie...'

'Yes, Princess?'

'Would you say that Yugoslav wine we had at lunch was supernacular?'

'Well ... 'ardly.' In the gathering darkness she saw his smile. 'But I 'aven't got much of a palate, really. What d'you reckon yourself?'

She pretended to think. Then, 'Difficult to say. I wouldn't claim to be too well up in oenology.'

His head turned quickly in momentary surprise before he said very casually, 'No, I suppose not.'

She laughed and went to the boot.

They sat in the darkness, eating with forks from a can of cold meat and drinking from a water bottle, talking quietly at times, at others holding a contented silence.

They did not speak of Tarrant, or of mysterious deaths and killings and plastic containers dropped in the sea. Neither did they talk reminiscently of the past, or of what was to come. At these times, waiting for a caper to begin, they spoke of ordinary things.

Of the Ptolemaic blue glass lion's-head finial Modesty had bought at Christie's; of installing an infra-red cooker in her pent house kitchen; of the anti listening-bug device Willie was making in his workshop; of a play seen, a book read, a disc bought.

Midnight came.

'The garage people can't find what's wrong,' Modesty was saying quietly. 'Weng's furious. That little Anglia is his pride and joy. But they've checked the carburettor jets, the fuel feed, the pump and the whole of the ignition. It hasn't made a scrap of difference.'

'She ought to fire first prod on the starter,' Willie said ruminatively.

'She does, once she's been run. But not if she's been standing for a while. Then you have to grind away for ages on the starter before she'll fire.'

'Ah.' Willie grinned.

'You've got a thought?'

'Wouldn't mind a quid on it, Princess. Drain-plug at the bottom of the float chamber isn't quite tight—only half a turn maybe. But the juice drips out slowly while the car's standing, so you've got to keep the starter going till the chamber's full before you get anything through the cylinders——'

He broke off and reached inside the open front of his shirt for a knife, head cocked a little. Now Modesty heard it too, the soft tread of somebody moving carefully through the trees to their left. She did not reach for the holstered Colt at her belt. If, by a hundred to one chance, the unseen walker was an enemy or stranger, Willie would take care of it. The knife was silent, and would be thrown to strike hilt first to the head. She had seen him stun a man at fifty feet with such a throw.

The faint sound of movement stopped and there came a soft, two-note whistle in a minor key. Willie relaxed and answered with the same whistle. It was an old recognition signal.

They stood up as a man came towards them, taking shape in the moonlight that filtered through the trees. He was carrying a bicycle, the crossbar resting on one shoulder. When he saw the car he set the bicycle down against a tree and moved on towards them.

He was a man of about forty, dressed in rough, hardwearing clothes. His right arm ended at the elbow, and the jacket sleeve was cut short and pinned up.

Modesty saw the weathered face as he drew close. It was a hard, square face which might once have been dangerous but which the passing years had made quiet.

'Nedic,' she said, and spoke in French. 'It's good to see you.'

'Mam'selle.' He dipped his head in a polite little bow. The single word brought her a momentary nostalgia. In *The Network* days she had always been addressed and referred to simply as 'Mam'selle' by the men who worked for her.

Nedic looked at Willie and gave a friendly wag of the head. '*Ça va, Willee?*'

'*Ça va, mon petit pote.*'

'How is the vineyard?' Modesty asked.

'It goes well, Mam'selle.'

Four years ago Nedic had been a casualty in one of the rare non-profit making operations of *The Network*—the crushing of a narcotics gang in Morocco. He had lost part of his arm. When he was fit enough she had sent him back to his homeland, set him up with the small vineyard he wanted, and added him to the list of seven disabled men who received pensions from a special fund built up for that purpose from the earliest days of her organisation.

'How is it with the arm now, Nedic?'

'Good. One quickly becomes skilled, Mam'selle.' The hard face smiled.

'There are very fine artificial limbs now. I could arrange——'

'It is not necessary, thank you, Mam'selle. Truly. I am well content.' He looked inquiringly at her. The note left at his house had been in Network cryptic and had simply asked him to meet her at this spot soon after midnight. 'There is something you wish of me?' Nedic asked.

'Yes. Krolli is with the labour battalion working on the new road.' She jerked her head towards the east.

'Krolli?' His eyes widened a little.

'Yes. He was betrayed. Do you know the new road and the area around it?'

'I know it well, Mam'selle. Each month I sell wine to the camp there.'

'A hutted camp, or tents?'

'Tents. They are easier to move as the road progresses.'

'Well guarded?'

'Very well. By the military.'

'How long would it take to reach the head of the road to-night, on foot, across country?'

Nedic thought for a moment, then said apologetically, 'If you are as you used to be in the old days, Mam'selle, three and a half hours.'

She smiled. 'We have not become soft, Nedic. Will you guide us?'

'Yes,' Nedic said simply. 'But if there is work to be done in taking Krolli out, I am not what I was.' He shrugged and lifted the stump of his arm slightly.

'You will go back as soon as you have guided us to the head of the road, Nedic,' she said a little sharply. 'You must be home before we take Krolli out. You understand?'

'But that means　you will take him out by daylight? From the working party?'

Nedic stared.

'I think we can find a way if the road runs according to the map we've been studying. Let's get in the car.'

All three climbed into the front seat, with Nedic in the middle. Modesty switched on the shielded map-light and spread the map on her knee. A pencilled line was marked on it, curving through mountains and alongside a tributary of the Lim.

Nedic nodded, took a dead match from the ashtray and placed the end of it at a point where the pencilled line ran beside the river. 'The road has reached this point, Mam'selle. They are cutting round the slope of the mountain now, above the river.'

'Good.'

'How will you take him out by day?'

'It depends. We'll have to see what job Krolli's doing and how the land lies.'

Nedic gave a little smile. 'Of course. It always depends.'

Willie said, 'Will the car be all right here till tomorrow night?'

'It would only be found by chance, Willee. You are two hundred metres from the road, and few motors use it, only small carts. You are well hidden, I think.'

Modesty folded the map, snapped off the light, and got out of the car. Nedic followed. Willie went to the boot and took out two light rucksacks. 'Let's 'ope we've packed everything we might need,' he said, and held one for Modesty to slip her arms through.

'Please, Mam'selle. I will carry it,' Nedic said.

'Don't worry. I won't slow you down.'

A gesture, brushing the idea aside. 'It is not that. But for old time's sake. I would be happy.'

She said, 'Put it on him, Willie,' and looked at Nedic with a half smile. 'For old time's sake, then. But you leave us when you've guided us to the road. *Entendu?*'

126

Nedic nodded, a wistful look in his eyes. '*Entendu,* Mam'selle.'

The late afternoon sun was still hot.

Krolli, at the controls of the open power shovel, sat stripped to the waist. Most of the labourers were busy with picks, shovels and wheel barrows, cleaning up the rocky surface where protrusions remained after the explosives and the power shovel had done their work. There were a dozen guards in sight, all wearing grey shirts and carrying rifles.

This was a wide part of the road that was being cut across the slope of the mountain. Behind Krolli it ran straight back for a hundred yards to a point where a deep vertical cleft in the mountain had left a broad gap in the newly cut surface. The power shovel, with its caterpillar tracks, had been brought across the gap on a makeshift bridge of felled trees, but no trucks could cross until the gap had been filled.

Krolli looked at the narrower stretch ahead which wound out of sight within fifty paces of where he sat. Vaguely he wondered how many more hundreds of tons of rock he would have to tip down into the gap.

It was a slow business, trundling up to the head of the road where explosives had broken the rock, lifting a load in the two cubic-yard dipper of the shovel, turning tightly, then lumbering slowly back to drop the load into the gap. Once this was filled, progress would be quicker, for then the rock torn from the mountain side could be tipped direct into the deep river which ran a hundred and fifty feet below at the foot of the sheer drop to Krolli's right.

The slow progress did not trouble Krolli. He had over nine years of this ahead of him, unless he chose to seek a quick death by attempting escape. Krolli did not intend that. He would serve his time, go back to Greece, find Lascaris. And kill him.

Krolli was a powerful, dark-haired man in his late thirties. Once he had been a hot-head. But then, in the years that he looked back on as the best he had known, he had been taught, bullied, and encouraged to find an inner quietness even in moments of high danger and fierce action. It had been a strange lesson for a Greek to learn; stranger still that his mentor had been a woman.

Now he had a quiet mind and a casual manner. He did not nourish his hatred or brood over his betrayal. He simply knew, without thinking about it, that when the time came he would kill Lascaris as a matter of simple justice and self-preservation.

From beyond the bend in the road ahead came the bellow of an explosion and the grinding rumble of rock. The engineer walked forward to the bend and vanished round it. After a few moments he reappeared, waved his arm in a signal, and came on.

Krolli started the engine of the mobile power shovel and began to grind forward along the road. To his left the wall rose sheer. There was some kind of goat track about forty feet above, running parallel with the road. Krolli had given thought to that track, but not for long.

It was always patrolled by a guard; and even if the guard could be avoided, escape would be short-lived. A foreigner, in the clothes the prisoners wore, with a patch on the shirt, with no food or friends, would stand no breath of a chance of getting out of the area, let alone out of the country.

The engineer waved Krolli on. He took the power shovel carefully round the twist in the road and saw the new fall of rock thirty paces ahead. Driving up to it, he halted with the tracks grinding on scattered rock fragments. The dipper arm swung forward, thrusting into the rubble.

Something glinted at the corner of Krolli's vision, and there came a faint sound of impact, barely audible above the roar of the engine. Krolli looked down.

A knife still quivered in the wooden planking close to his foot, a knife with a haft of black dimpled bone and with a thin fillet of brass backing the heel of the blade near the hilt. A scrap of folded paper, very thin, was wrapped round the lower part of the haft, held firmly by a rubber band.

Krolli would have known that knife among a thousand others.

He turned his head and glanced casually back down the road. It was empty as far as the bend. He looked up to the narrow track above. Sometimes, from this viewpoint, he could see the head and shoulders of the guard who patrolled it, but there was nobody to be seen now.

Krolli jerked the knife from the wood and slipped off the piece of paper. He picked up an oily rag, wrapped it carefully about the knife, pulled up a trouser leg and eased the wrapped knife firmly down the long woollen stocking.

One hand moved over the controls, swinging the boom of the dipper up and back. The other hand unfolded the note. It consisted of no more than fifty words in French, and every word was important. Krolli knew the handwriting.

He tore the note up, screwed it into a tiny ball and tossed it over the brink to his right, where the river ran below. Both hands on the controls now, he turned the power shovel and began to trundle back down the road. He passed the other prisoners and the strolling guards. Most of the prisoners were stripped to the waist. The guards wore coarse grey shirts and peaked caps of darker grey. The sergeant was looking at his watch. Another half-hour and work would be finished for the day. The prisoners would be lined up, counted, and marched off, scrambling over the makeshift bridge on their way to the camp which lay a mile down the road.

Krolli pulled the rope to open the trap in the bottom of the dipper and watched the mass of rock and rubble fall down into the gap. He turned again, and the caterpillar tracks crunched over the rough surface as he moved once more towards the head of the road.

As he passed the bend Krolli glanced casually back. No guard was following. No prisoner was within fifty paces. He lifted a hand and passed it back over his dust-laden hair in a slow, deliberate gesture.

Ahead of him a thin nylon rope snaked down from the edge of the goat track above. Krolli did not glance up. He was gauging his direction and speed carefully, edging to the right, towards the brink.

Satisfied, he jumped down from his seat and ran hard, getting ahead of the slow-moving power shovel. The rope hung down the sheer wall and ended in a small loop eighteen inches from the ground. Another loop had been knotted in the rope at shoulder height. He put one foot in the lower loop, gripped the upper loop in both hands and put his weight on the rope.

It gave an inch or two, then began to move up. Fending himself from the wall with his free leg, he wondered briefly how he could be hauled up so smoothly and swiftly when the track above was no more than two metres wide, with no room for anybody to walk away with the rope. He looked down over his shoulder.

The power shovel was almost at the sloping pile of rock, but because of the heading he had given the machine its right hand track was on the very brink. It lurched over, and the weight of the tall boom toppled the power shovel sideways. Krolli opened his mouth and gave a yell of terror.

With a snarling roar of its engine the power shovel vanished, and seconds later there came a tremendous splash from the river below.

Krolli was only six feet from the top, still moving up smoothly, and now he saw that a strip of hard leather lay between the rope and the rocky edge to prevent abrasion. The loop he gripped would save his fingers from being caught beneath the rope as he reached the brink.

In the instant that his head cleared the sheer wall he saw Modesty Blaise. She lay on her face, her right flank towards him. Her left arm was thrust into a crevice in the vertical rock beyond, and her body was pressed hard against the ground for traction, booted toes digging in. Her right arm was bent, elbow towards him, hand hooked about her neck. A broad strap was buckled round the elbow, and a small pulley was fastened to the strap. Her face was rigid with strain.

The nylon rope ran through the pulley and then at right

angles along the track ahead of her. There, forty feet away, Willie Garvin had the rope twisted round his waist and over his shoulder. He was facing towards Modesty, leaning away as he drove backwards with long, steady strides.

He stopped as Krolli's head and shoulders appeared. Krolli heaved himself over the edge and rolled to lie flat beside Modesty Blaise, bringing the strip of leather and the end of the rope with him.

So this was how he had been whisked up so swiftly.

He turned his head to look into Modesty's face, only inches away. She was breathing hard, easing her left arm out of the crevice. An eye closed at him in greeting. His response was a little nod, but his eyes said many things.

From below came the sound of shouting and booted feet running. It had been very necessary to get Krolli up and out of sight quickly. He listened intently to the gabble of voices, for he understood the language well enough now.

It was very smooth, Krolli thought. Tight, but smooth. Just as one would expect from Mam'selle and Willie Garvin. And the cut-out element in the plan was superb. Obvious escape meant a hunt and probable recapture. But nobody would hunt for a man who had gone over the edge into that deep rushing torrent and was no doubt crushed on the bottom by the twisted wreckage of the power shovel.

Mam'selle was lifting an eyebrow at him in query. He waited, listening to the confusion of talk below, then to the voice of the sergeant lifted in sudden command. Again Krolli gave a barely perceptible nod. The soldiers had no suspicions. The sergeant's main concern was with the infuriating loss of the power shovel, which would take days to salvage even if it were possible, and which might take even longer to replace.

One thing troubled Krolli. He looked ahead towards Willie, who was lying flat now, then turned his head cautiously to look back down the narrow track. The patrolling guard lay there, only a few yards behind him, sprawled unconscious. Krolli could see a thin trickle of blood from broken skin just behind the guard's ear.

131

Not so good. When the man came round, or when somebody went to find him, the trick would be suspected.

Krolli looked at Modesty again. She knew what was in his mind. He saw her teeth as she smiled briefly and gave a reassuring shake of her head.

Good enough. Krolli did not understand, but if Mam'selle said that it was all right then he was content.

Willie had started to draw the rope in, coiling it. Modesty was trying to unbuckle the strap from her arm. Krolli saw blood on the fingers of the left hand, the hand that had anchored her to take his weight. He rolled on his side, unfastened the strap for her and put it carefully in his pocket. She made a sign to him and began snaking up the track towards Willie, who turned and moved on his stomach ahead of her. Krolli followed.

After three minutes, with the curving slope of the mountain screening them, they were able to move on at a crouch. They were close together now, in line ahead, with Willie leading. Nobody spoke.

Krolli felt a great contentment which had nothing to do with the escape; reaction to that would come later. It was a nostalgic happiness, a recapturing of the good times. Mam'selle there. Willie there. No wasted questions, no arguments. Everything methodical and efficient and purposeful.

He wondered why they had come for him.

The Network had not been a benevolent institution made up of dedicated men, but a hard and dangerous organisation to handle, calling for all the qualities of a wild-animal tamer in the woman—the girl in those days—who controlled it. Krolli had been one of her favoured lieutenants, one of the small handful of men close to her, trusted men with a strange, strong loyalty to her that barely existed in the bulk of the smalltime criminals who necessarily filled the outer reaches of the organisation.

But it was not for old time's sake that she and Willie had come for him today. Krolli knew that, and did not resent it.

132

When she had split up *The Network* she had spoken plainly enough.

'You can take over the Athens branch, Krolli,' he remembered her saying on a warm summer day in her house on The Mountain in Tangier. 'I don't know how much you've stashed away over the past few years, but if you prefer to settle down I'll give you a bonus of twelve thousand dollars instead.'

'I think I would be unhappy to settle down now. After a few years, perhaps.'

'All right. I'm not offering advice. You're a big boy now, Krolli. But I won't be behind you any more. If you hit trouble, I don't want to know.'

'Understood, Mam'selle.' Krolli had smiled. 'I have learned much and I will be very careful.'

A nod of acceptance. 'I wasn't going to give advice, but I'll just say this. Don't be greedy. Don't leave it too long before you get out.'

'I will remember. Thank you, Mam'selle.'

She had shrugged and looked wryly out of the window, down the green slopes to the quiet blue sea of the Straits. 'I've changed you from a stupid criminal to a clever one, Krolli. If that's something to thank me for, do me a favour in return. Stay with the clean jobs. Keep clear of the dirt.'

'I will play it the way we have always played it, Mam'selle. No need to ask the favour.'

Krolli had kept his promise. That was why Lascaris, who wanted the quick rich pickings that dirt provided, had betrayed him. But Krolli knew that this was not the reason Mam'selle and Willie had come.

He followed them, wondering, walking soft-footed as the track wound upwards. Ten minutes later Willie turned into a broad gulley with high walls. The gulley narrowed and twisted to the right, then came to a dead end. Two light rucksacks lay on the ground in the shadow of an overhang.

Willie dropped the coiled rope and gave Krolli a grin. 'How does it feel to be dead?' he said in French.

'Good, Willie. My thanks.' Then, to Modesty, 'When they

find the guard, Mam'selle ...?' There was no anxiety in his gaze, only polite inquiry. She looked at Willie, who drew from under his shirt a long strip of soft leather with a thong at each end. A sling.

'Only started trying this out last year,' he said. 'I can fetch a bird down with it now. Lead ball makes the best ammunition, but I couldn't use that for the soldier. Didn't want the shot found if it bounced over the edge.'

'A stone?' Krolli said. 'He is dead?'

Willie shook his head with a touch of indignation. 'Two inch ball of sand, moulded with wax. Heavy, but it breaks up on impact. Just put him to sleep.'

'But when he comes round?'

Modesty said, 'Willie brought him down just one second after that last explosion, when the rock was flying. He might feel sore at the engineers for giving him a headache, but that's all.'

'Ah,' Krolli nodded, understanding.

Modesty sat down and gestured for him to sit. She gave him a cigarette, took one herself and threw the packet to Willie, who stood leaning against the wall of the gulley.

'We stay here for an hour, till after sundown,' she said. 'Then we have to cross the saddle of this ridge. Three hours and we'll be where the car's waiting, Krolli. I've got a well-faked passport, clothes and gear for you. We're American tourists and you're a French camper hitch-hiking to Athens. We're giving you a lift. We cross the border into Greece at Gevgelija.'

Krolli listened attentively. She had not changed, he thought. This was just the way she had always spoken at a briefing.

'Thank you, Mam'selle.' Pulling up his trouser leg, Krolli drew out the little bundle of oily rag and unwrapped the knife. 'Thank you, Willie.' He tossed the knife, and Willie caught it by the hilt and slipped it into the sheath under his shirt.

Krolli said, 'I will use a knife of my own to kill Lascaris.'

Modesty looked up at the sky. The first hint of twilight was darkening the blue. 'Think twice about killing Lascaris,' she said slowly. 'Revenge is a hollow thing, Krolli.'

'Not to a Greek, Mam'selle. But it is not for that I must do it. When he learns I am free, Lascaris will be afraid. He will surely kill me if I do not kill him first.'

Modesty looked at Willie and saw the tiny shrug of his shoulders. They both knew that what Krolli said was true.

'Do it before he knows, then,' she said. 'But we didn't pull you out for that, Krolli.'

'I know.' He looked at her inquiringly.

'I want a name. The name of the man behind the man who approached you concerning a killing he wanted done, some seven months ago.'

'Yes. The police have asked me this. I did not tell them.' A touch of curiosity came into his calm gaze. 'You are ... in business again, Mam'selle?'

'No.'

Krolli waited, but she said no more. His curiosity was not to be satisfied. He regretted that, but without rancour. Since the splitting up of *The Network* he had heard strange whispers about Modesty Blaise and Willie Garvin. Now he had seen them again, and knew that the power in them had in no way faded, the steel had in no way lost its edge. They were not in the old business, perhaps. But they were in some kind of business.

Krolli drew on his cigarette and exhaled.

'The name of the man is Jack Wish,' he said.

10

STEPHEN COLLIER put down his drink.

'I'm not at all sure that I can help,' he said. It was late afternoon, and only four hours since he had arrived at the big house on the coast of Sylt. In that short time he had sustained too many unusual impressions to be able to think as clearly as he would have wished.

The house itself held every luxury, but it was a tasteless piece of architecture, a rambling and fussy confection.

The inhabitants were an equally strange mixture. Seff, cadaverous and creaking in his black suit and wing collar; his wife, Regina, fragile and faintly absurd in her flowered dress which fell five inches below the knee; Jack Wish, the burly American who looked like a thug and seemed to have no particular function except to wander about in shorts and sandals.

Bowker he already knew slightly, and had some vague memory of reading about a scandal that had put Bowker out of practice a few years ago.

Then there was Lucifer, a young man with a godlike body, dark hair and a ruined mind ... a case of total paranoia. He had met Lucifer only briefly, after a preliminary explanation and warning from Bowker.

Lucifer had greeted him with regal cordiality, regretting that it had been necessary to call him from the lower levels for a short time. It would not, perhaps, be for more than a few decades, a century at most, Lucifer had said kindly.

Primed by Bowker, Collier had replied that he was happy to serve the Son of Morning in whatever way he could be of most use. Strangely, he had not felt foolish or embarrassed during the brief conversation. He had felt only pity.

Now he sat with Bowker on a small balcony leading from

one of the upper rooms—the bedroom he would be using during his stay here.

'I don't expect you to work miracles with Lucifer,' Bowker said, running a hand over his thin fuzzy hair, 'but I'm sure you *can* help us, Collier. There's also the point that Lucifer is a fascinating subject for you to study, in your particular line of work.'

'I'm not too easy about studying a paranoiac,' Collier said doubtfully. 'In psychic research we go in for controlled experiments. If we find a sensitive, a person who seems to have some kind of extrasensory perception—precognition, telepathy, clairvoyance, telekinesis—then we set up a series of carefully controlled experiments to eliminate all possibility of trickery, or even of unconscious hypersensitivity in the five normal senses. I can't see much chance of doing that with Lucifer.'

'Not right away,' Bowker agreed. 'We have to find means of getting him to do what we want him to do within the bounds of his belief that he's Satan. But you needn't worry about the psychological aspects, that's my job. What I need your advice on is the psychic side, the extrasensory perception. By the way, do you experts still call it e.s.p. or is *psi* the more up to date term?'

Collier smiled. 'I prefer e.s.p. myself. *Psi* seems to smack somewhat of science fiction, even though it had a respectable laboratory birth. But call it which you please.'

'E.s.p., then. What I need is help from you in increasing, or at least maintaining, Lucifer's abilities in this respect.'

'Why do you want to do that?' Collier asked. 'I'd have thought the main idea would be to cure him.'

Bowker smiled resignedly and shook his head. He picked up the jug of iced fruit-juice on the little table and refilled Collier's glass. 'Sure you wouldn't like something a little stronger?'

'Quite sure, thanks. It's too early.'

Bowker nodded and settled back in his chair. 'What do you know about paranoia?'

'Very little. Delusions of grandeur, isn't it?'

'In simple terms, yes. Some people believe they're Napoleon, or Hitler, or Queen Elizabeth the First. Correction. They don't just believe it. They *know* they're Napoleon, or whoever. Lucifer knows that he's—well, Lucifer. Satan. Prince of Darkness.'

'Why did he pick on Satan?'

Bowker closed his eyes against the sun and put his hands behind his head. 'Lucifer is Seff's nephew and ward,' he said. 'Twenty-five years old. When he was twenty he was studying to go into the Church. I didn't know him then, of course, but apparently he was a very earnest and dedicated young man.'

Bowker felt more relaxed now. He could afford to, because for the moment there was no lying to be done. Apart from the relationship of Lucifer to Seff, the rest of the story was true.

'Then something happened to this dedicated young man,' he went on. 'He was seduced by a woman. It happened quite out of the blue. The time, the place, the atmosphere ... you know? They all happened to be just right. Rather like Sadie Thompson in the Maugham story. She seduced the parson who was trying to save her, didn't she?'

'Only in the book,' said Collier solemnly. 'There were notable changes in the film, I recall. But anyway, I thought he seduced *her*?'

'It's always a bilateral business,' Bowker said with a touch of impatience. 'The simple fact is that our young friend tumbled a woman. Then remorse, of course, but in this case remorse of huge proportions. He had a breakdown. And he came out of it a paranoiac, convinced that he was the source of all sin. So obviously he had to be the devil himself. Satan.'

'I thought you chaps could bring a thing like that from the subconscious to the conscious and effect a cure.'

Bowker opened his eyes. 'Let me quote Kraepelin to you. *"Paranoia is characterised by the furtive development, resulting from inner causes, of a lasting, immovable delusional system that is accompanied by the complete retention of clearness and order in thinking, willing, and acting."* Lasting and immovable are the operative words, Collier. True paranoia is incurable.'

'I see.' Collier looked out over the blue-grey waves of the sea. 'But how does he make the normal world fit in with his delusion?'

'He's created his own delusional set-up which covers all the problems, and he can rationalise anything that happens,' said Bowker. 'You'd better know his view if you're going to get anywhere with him. This world is Hell, or part of Hell, anyway. It's not a new idea, you know. I think Bernard Shaw suggested that earth was in fact the Hell to which beings from other planets were consigned.'

'A Shavian joke.'

'Yes. But with a thought behind it. I don't know if Lucifer ever read Shaw, but that kind of thing would help the "furtive development" of his delusion. So here we are on Hell, or in Hell, but we all know that people die here and we all know the Dante's *Inferno* bit, so that has to be fitted in somewhere. Lucifer has encompassed it very nicely.'

'How?' Collier felt slightly ashamed to realise that he was becoming strangely fascinated by the macabre story.

'This is the upper level of Hell,' said Bowker. 'A sort of Limbo. Everybody has already died, someplace else. But they get born here to give them a short breather before being sent on down to the old fiery pits—the lower levels. Lucifer has the job of deciding who goes when.'

'Millions a day?'

'That was in the old times, a few thousand ages ago. Now he delegates all the minor decisions, and just deals with the important ones. So he believes. It doesn't matter anyway. Look Collier, you can take a paranoiac, put him in an aircraft and fly him over Paris at a thousand feet, pointing out the streams of cars and everything new in the last century and a half. But he'll still *know* that he's Napoleon.'

'I see. The delusion is unbreakable, so Lucifer proclaims himself as Lucifer, no matter what?'

'As it happens he doesn't proclaim himself.' Bowker was

about to grin but stopped himself in time. Collier would think amusement unprofessional. 'All his powers are exerted in mundane ways. Like his Celestial Colleague, as he calls him, Lucifer doesn't go in for miracles and supernatural methods these days. He doesn't consign people to the lower levels with thunder and lightning and brimstone. He just causes x-thousand road accidents a day, and everything else that brings what people call natural death.'

Bowker lifted a hand to emphasise his words. 'Always remember it's a cardinal point in Lucifer's delusion that people here *don't know* they're in Hell. I think that's Shaw again, by the way—only Lucifer knows that Hell is Hell. That's why our young friend doesn't have to grow black wings and fly around. Fortunately.'

'But *you* know all this. So do Seff and the others. Good God, even I'm supposed to know it, from the way he spoke to me.'

'Of course. But we're not people, Collier. We're spirits and demons of various kinds in earthly guise. Just like Lucifer himself. He brought us up from our enjoyable jobs of prodding souls with red hot pitchforks on the lower levels, to serve him up here.'

Collier sat back and gave a little apologetic laugh. 'Boggling,' he said helplessly. 'That's what my mind is doing, Bowker. I hesitate to use the word fantastic, but——'

'Why not use it? Lucifer lives in a fantasy world of his own imagining. He's a paranoiac.'

'I didn't mean that I disbelieved you. It's just that the idea takes a little getting used to.'

'I know. That's why I'd like you to take things slowly. Study Lucifer, and get the feeling of the whole thing before you start work on him.'

Collier was silent for a while. At last he said, 'You wrote in your letter that he had very marked e.s.p. abilities. What are they?'

'Well ... Lucifer has what I believe you call precognition. He can get glimpses of the future.'

'General or particular? I mean, does he foresee a war breaking out in a certain country within a certain time, or is his precognition confined to individuals?'

'Oh, to individuals.' Bowker swallowed the last of his drink. Inwardly he became more alert, for now lies would have to be carefully blended with truth. 'Lucifer seems to get these psychic impressions by handling objects connected with individuals. A photograph, maybe, even in a newspaper; a ring worn by the person; a lock of hair; a piece of paper with a few words of handwriting on, though he doesn't look at the handwriting.'

'Psychometry,' Collier nodded. 'Difficult line for making controlled statistical tests. What sort of things does he predict?'

'Fairly mundane things,' Bowker said casually. 'Marriage, divorce, success, failure, sickness, death—very much like a crystal gazer in a fairground. Except that Lucifer is very specific and very accurate. I'm sure you'll find him an interesting subject.'

'Yes.' Collier had been gazing out over the sea. Now he turned to look directly at Bowker. 'I understand that you can't cure the boy. But why do you want me to help stimulate and improve his extrasensory powers?'

Bowker pursed his lips. Here came the difficult part. 'I'll be frank with you,' he said. 'Lucifer is our bread and butter. And jam. A year or two ago the Seffs were penniless. So was I, for reasons you may have heard about.'

'Penniless people don't rent this kind of house in this kind of area,' Collier said drily.

'No. I spoke of a year or so ago. We're well fixed now and we'd like to stay that way.' Bowker adopted an air of open candour. 'Not just for Lucifer's sake, though that's pretty important, but for our own sakes. When the Seffs had no money, the boy had to be in a home most of the time. He's a lot happier now, believe me. And it was his e.s.p. that made it all possible.'

Collier stared curiously. 'Don't tell me he uses it for filling in football pools or predicting horse races?'

'No.' Bowker shrugged. 'We've tried that sort of thing but he can't do it. Or won't. I don't know why.'

'I can think of one reason.' Collier's lean, angular face was thoughtful. 'His psychic powers are probably keyed to his delusion. In that respect I'd have thought they would mainly be directed to precognition of death.'

'Ah ...' Bowker rubbed his eyes to hide any momentary uneasiness that might show. This man Collier was sharp. They would have to handle him carefully. 'That makes sense,' he said. 'But in fact Lucifer does go beyond that.'

'In what way?'

'Worldly success.' Bowker shook his head as if baffled. The lie would be more convincing, he thought, if he gave the impression that he could barely believe it himself. 'Seff is supposed to be Lucifer's chief servant, the demon Asmodeus. One day he carefully pointed out to Lucifer that living as people, in earthly guise, we should really use ordinary means to obtain the money necessary for living, rather than supernatural means.'

'Supernatural? What happened about money before this?'

'Oh, Lucifer would hand over a fistful of diamonds and a bag of gold dust when he heard the Seffs worrying about money. The diamonds were pebbles he'd picked up, and the gold dust was a bag of dirt. They didn't buy much in the way of groceries.'

'So?'

'Seff suggested natural means, and put the share-price pages of the *Financial Times* in front of Lucifer.' Bowker waited for Collier's look of disbelief, but it did not come. Instead Collier said quietly, 'The idea was worldly success for Seff, acting on behalf of Lucifer?'

'Yes.'

Collier nodded. 'I've no statistical proof, but I've known three very hard-headed businessmen who used a psychometrist to advise them. What happened in this case?'

'Lucifer marked five shares.' Relief expanded within Bowker as he spoke. The biggest hurdle had proved to be no hurdle at all. 'Seff took a chance and bought on margin. One share held steady, the other four shot up for various reasons. In ten days Seff had cleared three thousand pounds.'

'Eighty per cent accurate,' Collier muttered, frowning. 'It's difficult to fix a point of chance-expectation in a thing like this, but the result is very much above the highest one could expect from chance.' He looked at Bowker. 'Even so, no short run is significant. Toss a penny and it can come down heads twelve times running, or twenty times. That's wildly against chance-expectation, too. You have to go on for a long, long while before you can assume that luck or coincidence have worked themselves out and left you with a firm basis for drawing conclusions.'

'I can only tell you,' said Bowker, 'that we've done extremely well on the various European and American stock exchanges over the past eighteen months. To be honest, we're not concerned with proof or statistics, only with results. We see nothing unethical about this. I hope you take the same view.'

'It's not a very productive or useful way of living,' Collier said bluntly, 'but that's about all anyone could say against it. I'm more interested in the phenomena than in the ethics. It's unusual for anyone with extrasensory powers to be able to use them for his own direct benefit.'

'Really? Why's that?'

'Because the knowledge that you're trying to foretell something for your own benefit normally creates tensions which inhibit the extrasensory faculties. We find the best results are gained when the subject is indifferent to them.'

'Completely relaxed?'

'Yes. That, too.'

'I see. This may be the reason that Lucifer isn't quite as accurate as he was.'

'Not so accurate?'

'That's why I wrote to you, Collier. He's still getting good results, but not quite so good. We're worried in case they fall off still more.'

'What do you expect me to do?'

'Study Lucifer. Make tests. Try to find out what may be reducing his accuracy.'

'I can't help him with share prices. Or births, deaths and marriages. I can only make controlled tests, with Rhine cards and so on. The usual laboratory tests for this sort of thing.'

'But if you find ways to improve his general performance it would surely be extended to his—er—more rewarding predictions?'

'Probably.'

'That's all we ask.'

'There's another point. Will Lucifer co-operate? How do I get the devil himself to play little games with me?'

'It's my job to get his co-operation,' said Bowker. 'He can't be forced, of course. But tell me when you've decided exactly what you want to do, and I'll find some way of fitting it into his delusion. It's a question of getting him to believe that what he's doing is part of his work as the Prince of Darkness. I've had a lot of experience in that now.'

'Yes.' Collier sat in silence for some little while, thinking. He did not warm to Bowker, nor to the Seffs or the American, Jack Wish. He felt distaste at the use they were making of Lucifer, but at the same time acknowledged that his distaste was more a matter of feeling than of logic. It was better for the boy to live comfortably and happily, even if, as Collier suspected, the Seffs and their colleagues were more concerned with their own fortunes than with Lucifer's.

And if what Bowker said was true, which there seemed little reason to doubt, then Lucifer's psychic faculties would make a rich and fascinating field for study.

There was also the point, Collier thought wryly, that he was at a loose end. He was due to spend eight weeks at Duke University, working with the Americans on a long series of experiments, but that was not till late autumn. Apart from his work, there was nothing to hold his interest at the moment.

And he was feeling very much alone.

Modesty Blaise had taken him on a trip to the moon, and

kissed him goodbye and gone on her way, wherever that might lie. Willie Garvin had gone too. That was a pity, for Collier had hoped to study him. Willie had a measure of e.s.p. Not to the same degree as Lucifer, perhaps, but he had certainly foretold danger that night in Paris.

Collier wondered if Modesty had it too. He remembered the fight in the courtyard, every second of it, as if in slow motion. She had uncanny anticipation. It might have been no more than acute perception by the normal senses, and enormously high-speed reactions. All the same, it would have been interesting to investigate her. Interesting to make Rhine tests for a degree of telepathic communication between Modesty and Willie. There were strong indications of it ...

Collier dragged his thoughts away from speculation, inwardly mocking himself, knowing that he would not have wasted golden hours with Modesty Blaise in compiling pages of statistics.

Bowker was watching him, a little tensely.

'All right,' Collier said. 'Give me a few days to settle down as a demon in earthly guise. When I feel I know Lucifer well enough not to make any blunders, I'll tell you. Then if you can persuade him to co-operate, I'll see what I can do.'

MODESTY BLAISE and Sir Gerald Tarrant sat with aperitifs in the bar of Quaglino's.

'The Americans have very kindly sent over a copy of their file on Jack Wish,' Tarrant was saying. 'Apparently he was a fixer for the Mafia there, operating mainly overseas for them, to keep the narcotic lines of communication in good repair. Europe, Middle East, Far East ... a much travelled gentleman. When the Mafia took a big beating a few years ago Wish was in Europe and just stayed there. No information on him from any of the European countries. It seems he went to ground.'

'They haven't been looking for him?'

'No. There's nothing against him officially. He's just one of those people to keep an eye on if you can, but...' Tarrant shrugged. 'There's always something more important that needs doing.'

Modesty lit a Gauloise. The temperature had risen again and she wore a cream linen suit with camel shoes and handbag. Her only jewellery was a pair of deep blue amethyst drop earrings. Looking at her now, Tarrant found it hard to believe what he knew to be true, that less than seventy-two hours ago she had snatched a prisoner from a labour battalion in the mountains of Yugoslavia and brought him safely out of the country.

'Our old Network files on Jack Wish give us a little more than you've told me, but not much,' she said.

Tarrant looked surprised. 'I thought they had been disposed of when you retired?'

'We microfilmed them first. It seemed a pity to throw away years of careful work.'

'Even though it would never be of use to you again?'

She made a little face at him. 'Never mind that. These letters, the warnings and the death-lists, where are they posted?'

'In the capital or major cities of the appropriate government or individual who receives them. Ours are posted in Central London. Others are posted in Paris, Bonn, New York —but why do you ask?'

'We want to find Jack Wish. I think the only lead is through the postal arrangements he makes.'

'Assuming he's responsible.'

'Assuming that. I know the postal arrangements have been checked without result, but that was before we were looking for Jack Wish. He can hardly handle the posting himself, since the letters go out simultaneously every few months in a number of different countries. He must have people who handle it for him.'

'Dangerous, surely?'

'It depends. Our file on Wish is a little different from the usual official dossier. We were always more interested in basic character and habits.'

'So?'

'Jack Wish seems to be a kind of landbound sailor, with a girl in every capital rather than in every port.'

'Girls? Still more dangerous, I would think.'

'It depends,' she repeated. 'Jack Wish attracts a certain type of girl. They're invariably pretty little dolls. Not bright, but reliable.'

'Isn't that a contradiction?'

'No. Think about it.'

Tarrant thought. Not bright, but reliable. Success in most fields depended on a man having imagination and initiative. But Boulter's night guard, for example, would have done a better job if he had gone stolidly about his routine work, obeying orders, checking every inch of the building night after night, without growing weary of it. A sentry with imagination might not stop a car entering a restricted area, if it was a staff car flying a pennant. Another man would simply carry out his orders.

'Yes,' said Tarrant. 'Go on.'

'The girls Jack Wish attracts are also the type that get a certain kick from being frightened of a man. And judging by the file it seems he can be pretty frightening.'

'So he has these paramours in various places. He sends them the letters sealed in a larger envelope. They open it, wearing gloves, and post the letters inside. Is that it?'

'I think it's likely he handles quite a lot of his postal arrangements that way. He could have other ways as well.'

'Wouldn't these girls be curious?'

'Not these girls. And not with Jack Wish.'

Tarrant was silent for a while, then he smiled slowly. 'Well ... it's no less unlikely than predicting that certain people are going to die within the next few months. But this is an unlikely world, our stratum of it, anyway. What do you want me to do about this, Modesty?'

'Nothing. This is Willie's field.'

'Girls are, certainly,' Tarrant said with faint disapproval. 'But how does he find them in this instance?'

'He's found the girl Jack Wish stays with when he's in London. We had her name on the file, and the name of a girl in Rome. Willie's trying the London one first. He picked her up last night at the strip club where she works.'

'My God, you move fast,' said Tarrant, and thought ruefully of the paperwork that seemed to clutter all his own operations. 'Do you think Willie can get her to talk?'

'I doubt it. There isn't time for a long campaign to break her down. But I'm pretty certain he can get her to bed. And if he has the run of her flat for a day or two he may be able to find some kind of lead.'

Tarrant stared down at his drink. 'At least I can be glad it's girls,' he said rather sourly. 'I'd hate to think what might be happening now if it was men.'

'I wonder how many times you've organised seduction as part of your work?'

'It's standard practice. But they're other girls.'

She laughed, her eyes teasing him. 'Sometimes you're very

148

Victorian with me. I believe you think I'm promiscuous.'

'No! Really, Modesty.' Tarrant had flushed. 'I assure you——' He broke off, collecting himself, then went on, 'Believe me, I don't think that at all. On the contrary. You mustn't try to shock me by pretending that you'd relish doing what Willie's doing. I know you better than that.'

She put her head a little on one side, studying Tarrant with quiet affection. 'René Vaubois is still alive at the moment, isn't he?'

'René? Yes.' Tarrant was baffled by the question. 'Why?'

'It's relevant. Willie will probably quite enjoy what he's doing. It's different for a man. As you say, I wouldn't relish it. But I'd do it without a second thought if it meant giving René a better chance of staying alive. And I'd do it well.'

Tarrant nodded without speaking.

She glanced round to make sure they could not be overheard, and said very softly, 'I killed a man to keep René alive, remember? It would hardly make sense if I jibbed at going to bed with a man for the same reason, would it?'

Tarrant sighed. 'I'm glad you're on our side,' he said. 'I wouldn't like to have you against us. And I'm still more glad that I wasn't responsible for bringing you into this affair.'

'You can buy me lunch with a clear conscience,' Modesty said, and picked up her handbag. 'But I warn you, it's going to be an expensive one.'

'Good.' Tarrant rose with a bland smile. 'I hate to have an entirely clear conscience, so I shall do this on expenses. Let's go and consume some government money.'

Willie Garvin looked at his watch. It was two in the afternoon, another seven hours before Rita would have to leave for the strip club. He had moved into the little flat off Devonshire Street three days ago.

He sat in an armchair, in pyjamas and dressing-gown, leafing idly through a romantic picture-story comic. This was Rita's sole literary diet.

The door to the tiny kitchen was open. As usual, the

kitchen was a mess. Rita was making one of her vague attempts to tidy it up. He watched her pick up a stack of comics, pieces of string, brown paper, brochures, circulars and paper bags. She moved out of sight and he heard her thrusting the pile into a cupboard he knew to be already crammed with similar litter.

Rita rarely got around to throwing anything away. There was nothing in the cupboard that she did not think might come in useful or that she might not want to look at later.

Willie called, ''Ow about a cup of tea, Rita?'

She appeared in the doorway, a blonde girl with short hair and plump curves. Her eyes were large and brown, her face round and pretty like the face of a doll. She wore a cheap transparent négligé over a lacy bra and pants, fishnet stockings and high-heeled slippers.

'I'm just tidying up, Willie. Honest, I don't know where everything comes from. I'll make a pot of tea for you soon as I've finished.'

'Okay, love. When you're ready.'

'There's a good boy.' She screwed her eyes up at him affectionately, then turned away. Willie looked down at the comic again, satisfied. He was playing this right, now. At first he had been a little tough, a little menacing towards Rita, but that had been wrong.

Jack Wish was the man she liked to be frightened of. She had been hooked on Wish for a long time, as a street-walker is hooked on her ponce. Not that Rita was a street-walker. She simply liked to have a man in the background, even though she rarely saw him, and that man was Jack Wish. Probably Wish did not care whether or not she was unfaithful to him, but Rita liked to believe that he did. That was why she would let herself be picked up occasionally. She enjoyed the imagined danger. But she did not want another Jack Wish. She wanted somebody amiable and obliging. A good boy. Like Willie Garvin, now that he had fathomed how her mind worked.

In a placid, almost maternal way, Rita liked to call the tune.

Then everything was fine. After a brief false start, Willie had quickly played up to this. It was the only way to get anywhere, for there was an underlying toughness in her, and this had been bent to Jack Wish's advantage, if Modesty's guess was right.

Willie had probed Rita cautiously with a few oblique questions. They had not made her suspicious, but neither had they drawn any worthwhile answers. She acknowledged, with a giggle touched by awe, that she had a steady gentleman friend who travelled a lot, so she only saw him occasionally. There was no photograph of him in the bedroom and she had never let slip his name, always referring to He or Him with an implied capital letter.

Willie Garvin was disappointed. He had done well up to a point, but it wasn't enough. He was a good boy, close to Rita now, and well set to pump her—except that Rita wasn't going to be pumped.

He brooded, wondering about his next move. There didn't seem to be one, short of drastic measures like tying her to the bed and putting a shot of scopolamine into her. Bleakly he recognised that it might come to that.

He looked at the dog-eared comic in his hands. It was open at the letter page where, amid other problems, Doubtful Redhead was asking how far she should let her fabulous but insistent boyfriend go. She was afraid he would stop loving her if she didn't give in to him.

Willie read Mary Wisdom's standard admonitory answer. Idly he composed another answer, which would have shaken Mary Wisdom, assuming she understood it, but would have pleased the boyfriend of Doubtful Redhead enormously.

His eyes rested on the date at the top of the page. The comic was over five months old. It did not surprise him. Rita was a compulsive hoarder. He flicked over the page, and a torn window-envelope with a shopping list scrawled on the back fell out. It had once contained a gas bill, judging from the return address printed on one corner.

A thought crept into Willie's mind. He put the comic aside

and lit a cigarette, absently listening to the click of Rita's heels as she moved about the kitchen.

Yes. It was worth trying.

'What time you on at the club today, Rita?' he called, knowing the answer. 'S'afternoon?'

'No. S'evening. Nine-thirty.' She appeared in the doorway again, folding a large paper carrier-bag. 'I thought we'd go round the shops s'afternoon when we've had something to eat. I've got to get a summer dress and some things.'

'Trailing round shops gives me the dead needle,' Willie protested. 'You go, Rita. I'll stay 'ome and watch the racing on telly.'

She moved into the room and sat on his lap, slipping an arm round his neck.

'Ah, come on now, Willie. I like comp'ny.'

'Well ... all right, then.' Willie patted her thigh and yielded reluctantly.

'That's a good boy.' She put her face close to his and gave a suppressed giggle, enjoying her own daring. 'I'll make it up to you all right s'evening.'

'That's my girl.'

Another giggle. 'I'm not your girl, Willie, and you know it. Honest, I don't know what He'd say!'

'What the eye don't see the 'eart don't grieve over.' Willie kissed her on the lips.

Two weeks of Rita and he knew he would have been stone dead from boredom. But at least she was clean and wholesome, her body firm and nicely curved. That was something to be thankful for.

'Don't you go starting something now,' she said, fending off his hand, pleased.

'What d'you expect with a lovely little bundle like you sitting on me lap?'

'Ooh, you are a shocker.' She got up and drew the négligé about her. 'You're bristly, too. Go and shave while I put the kettle on.'

Later, when Rita was making it up to him, Willie wondered vaguely what she was like with Jack Wish at such times. Probably quite different, he thought.

Now, on the bed in the muted light from the small bedside lamp, he watched her moving body with an inward bafflement that held a touch of something close to hilarity. Making love with Rita was a prolonged affair. She liked to take the dominant role, at least with her occasional boyfriends. That was not remarkable. What made her extraordinary was that the whole time she kept up an intermittent conversation that had little or nothing to do with making love. It was rather like somebody enjoying a good wine and talking desultorily between sips, the unrelated talk in some way adding to the enjoyment of the wine.

'I'm glad I didn't buy that green dress I tried on,' she was saying absently. Her eyes were closed, and her firm breasts bobbed rhythmically.

'M'mm...' Willie rested his hands on her thighs. The conversation, he had learned, was more of a soliloquy than a dialogue. She rarely required answers.

Rita gave the suppressed giggle that usually preceded any remark about Jack Wish. 'Honest ... if He could see what I'm doing to you now, Willie, He'd *kill* me!'

'M'mm...'

Silence for a few moments. Then, 'I really bet He would. And kill *you*, too. He can be a real terror.' She was stimulating herself by stirring up her own delicious fear of Him.

After a while she said dreamily, a little plaintively, 'He says I'm ever so dumb. Still, I suppose He's right in a way. I was never much good at school and all that. D'you think I'm dumb, Willie?'

An answer was called for. Willie concentrated, put surprise and indignation in his voice and said, 'You? Blimey, you're smart as they come, Rita. Never mind about school, you got intelligence. The thinking man's bit of crumpet, you are.'

She paused in her steady movements, opened her eyes and focused on him, pleased. 'Ah, you're ever so nice, Willie.'

'*He* wouldn't think so if 'e walked in now.' Willie chuckled. 'What's 'e look like, anyway?'

'He won't walk in now. Don't worry.' That was all. No answer to the casual question, no hint of where He was now or when He might return. Resignedly Willie accepted that Rita knew how to keep her mouth shut when Jack Wish told her to do so.

She closed her eyes and her body began to move again. Willie knew that in the end her excitement would mount and her movements quicken, but that was a long way off yet and she would be petulant if he did not wait for her. He forget Jack Wish and addressed himself to the task of the moment.

'That dress wasn't bad really, though,' Rita said absently after a while. 'I might go and have another look at it . . .'

Tarrant said gloomily, 'It's all very well for you. Bare arms. A blouse that even a micrometer couldn't gauge, and a nice little skirt. But pinstriped trousers and a black jacket aren't quite so comfortable.'

They were sitting on the wide, L-shaped terrace of Modesty's penthouse, with the park spread below them. The mid-afternoon sun was hot.

Modesty said, 'Why don't you take off your jacket?'

Tarrant looked shocked. 'I really don't believe I could,' he said. 'I'm psychologically incapable.'

She laughed. 'We'd better go inside, then.'

'Good God, no. Your place is in the sun. I like to see you enjoying it.'

Weng came out carrying a big parasol under his arm and frosted glasses of fruit juice on a tray. He set the tray down on the low table, opened the parasol and slid the butt into a splay-footed stand, moving it so that Tarrant was in the shade.

'Ah, thank you.' Tarrant relaxed gratefully.

Weng said, 'Mr. Garvin is coming, Miss Blaise?'

'Any minute now, Weng.'

'What will he drink?'

She thought for a moment. 'I'm not quite sure. He sounded a little martyred on the phone. Leave it, Weng, I'll fix whatever he wants. You get along to Soapy's and pick up that C.E. Willie ordered.'

'Yes, Miss Blaise.' Weng disappeared.

'Soapy,' Tarrant said thoughtfully. 'Soapy who?'

'Never mind.'

'Compound explosive?'

She nodded. 'That's why I said never mind.'

'Of course. Is this for any specific purpose?'

'No. Willie's just seeing that our various pieces of gear are all in order.'

Tarrant thought of the workshop at 'The Treadmill', where Willie performed strange mysteries of micro-engineering among other things. Before he could ask another question there came the sound of voices. He turned in his chair, looking through the open glass door to the foyer beyond the long living room of the penthouse.

Willie Garvin, a jacket slung over one shoulder, stood by the open doors of the private lift, having a word with Weng. He wore a short-sleeved shirt and lightweight slacks.

'He'd get nowhere in the Civil Service,' Tarrant said enviously.

Weng, who had changed from his white jacket, went into the lift. The doors closed after him. Willie Garvin walked down the three steps piercing the wrought iron balustrade which edged the foyer, crossed the living room and emerged on to the terrace.

He bent and lifted Modesty's fingers to his cheek, shook hands with Tarrant, drew up a spare lounging chair, sat down, leaned back and closed his eyes, all in silence.

Modesty studied his face for a moment. 'Something long and cool, with a sparkle and just a featherweight kick,' she said. 'A long iced hock, topped up with soda?'

Eyes still closed, Willie nodded gratefully. 'Thanks, Princess. Blimey, it's good to be back.'

She got up and went inside, through to the kitchen. Tarrant, a little puzzled, decided to say nothing. A minute later she returned with a long amber-filled glass and set it down in front of Willie.

'You've suffered,' she said, sitting down.

Willie opened his eyes and picked up the glass. 'Thanks, Princess,' he said again. He drank deeply, then looked from Modesty to Tarrant. 'Know what I've been doing for the last —for *ever*? Walking round shops, sitting in a strip club, watching television, and reading picture stories in *Heart-Throb*. That's all.'

Modesty raised an eyebrow. 'All?'

'Well, things brightened up a bit now and again,' he conceded. 'But even then ... you wouldn't think it could be made *boring*, would you?'

She shook her head solemnly. Willie drank again and said, staring out over the park, 'You know what 'appened yesterday evening? We'd done the shop bit, and we'd watched a children's Western, and Batman, and God knows what. So it's eight o'clock, and Pet Clark comes on singing *Downtown*.' His voice grew awed as if with horror. 'And that's when Rita switches off and starts the bed bit! Honest, I could've chilled 'er, Princess.'

'Poor Willie. You've been very brave.'

Willie nodded, with the air of a man staggered by his own fortitude. 'I didn't even argue. I think I even made a joke.' He looked at his empty glass and stood up. 'Can I get meself another?'

'I'll get it for you.'

'No, it's okay. I'm feeling a bit stronger now.' He went through the door into the living room.

Tarrant looked at Modesty and said, 'Is he serious?'

She laughed. 'Half serious.'

'I hope his sacrifice has yielded results,' Tarrant said drily. 'Has he told you anything?'

'Not on the phone. Except that he'd given this girl the impression that he was only one jump ahead of the police. That was this afternoon. She was glad to get him out of the place then. But he must have got something good or he wouldn't have come back.'

Willie returned with his replenished glass and sat down.

'She's got a well-buttoned mouth,' he said. 'Couldn't get a thing out of her. But she's a hoarder. She shoves papers and bits of string in a cupboard. So I got an idea it might be worth searching. I was going to do it last night when she went to the strip club, but she wanted me along too, so I 'ad to wait till this morning, while she was at the hairdresser's.'

He fumbled in his back pocket and drew out an eight by six manila envelope, folded in four. It bore Rita's address and a German stamp, and it had been slit open.

'There was this,' he said. 'The recent pick-ups 'ave been in the North Sea, and the date on this postmark is a few days before the last lot of warnings were sent out.' He passed the envelope to Modesty. She studied the postmark closely.

Tarrant watched her, excitement beginning to stir in him. She held out the envelope and he took it in silence. The post-mark was quite clear.

Sylt.

'One of the Frisian Islands, isn't it?' Tarrant looked up.

Modesty nodded. 'Quite small. Long and thin. Off the coast near the border between Denmark and Germany. A holiday place and a retreat for the wealthy.'

'Would the coast offer suitable concealment for any kind of submarine?'

'No.' It was Willie who answered. 'It's flat. A stretch of low red cliffs along part of the west coast, but you couldn't tuck away a submarine there. You've mostly got flat beaches run-ning up to sand dunes.' He ruminated. 'I once took a girl to Sylt. Funny thing 'appened. They've got these nudist bathing beaches——'

'Does this get us anywhere?' Tarrant broke in quickly, touching the envelope. 'I mean, aren't we looking for a place from which these people can actually operate?'

'We don't know how they operate,' Modesty said, and took a cigarette that Willie offered her. 'We're looking for Jack

Wish. We think he uses Rita to post some of the warning letters. They must be sent to her from wherever he is, in an envelope like that, most probably. The date fits and the place fits.'

Tarrant turned the manila envelope over thoughtfully in his fingers, thinking of the strange, improbable theory Modesty had produced.

Predictions of death. Accurate predictions.

He had talked to several shrewd psychic investigators over the past few days, men who sought for the nucleus of truth by the most rigorous scepticism. He had not found one who was prepared to ridicule the idea of precognitive knowledge. The concept was strange and improbable. And possible.

'It's a pity we're not psychic ourselves,' he said at last. 'Failing that, I suppose somebody had better go to Sylt and take a look round.'

WILLIE GARVIN walked quickly along the wooden planking above the beach at Westerland. The temperature was high in the seventies, which meant that for the people idling or playing on the FKK, the Frei Körper Kultur section of the beach, nudity was compulsory.

Willie Garvin was not attracted by mass nudity. He felt it offended the eye, artistically, more often than it delighted. There were very few people whose appearance was enhanced by complete nudity. Good bodies were rare.

There was one, though. The young blonde girl, seventeen perhaps, jumping for the beachball...

He would have liked to stand still for a moment, watching her with a pleasure untinged by desire, for she was too young to stir him; but he moved on quickly till he came to the steps which led down to the other section of the beach.

Modesty lay on a towelling-covered mattress of foam rubber, a beachbag beside her. She wore a black one-piece swimsuit. Her hair was loose and clipped back at the nape of the neck.

Willie dropped down beside her. He wore tailored slacks and an expensive shirt with a cravat at the throat.

'You must be hot,' Modesty said. 'But you can stop looking elegant now. I'm sure you impressed the agents, Willie love. Why don't you have a swim?'

'I don't think there's time,' he said. She sat up, looking at him, and he went on, 'I was dead lucky, Princess.'

'You've found Jack Wish?'

'I'm pretty sure. They offered this big place for rent north of Wenningstedt. It's called Haus Lobigo. Belongs to a South American who's never there. The people renting it now have been there six months. Five men and a woman, and a daily staff. One of the men only joined 'em a few days ago. Another's American.'

'The right one?'

'I conned them into a description by saying I thought I might know 'im. It fits Wish. But the place is rented under the name of one of the others. Bloke called Seff. Oh, there was another, but he went off a week or two ago.'

'The agent offered you this place?'

'Yes. As from tomorrow—because they're leaving today. I said I'd think about it, and shot back to tell you.'

'Damn.'

'More or less what I said meself. It doesn't give us much time.'

'Do you know how they're leaving, Willie?'

'Sorry.'

She sat thinking. The party could be going out by air, or by car on the train across the Hindenburg Causeway to Niebüll, or by the sea ferry from List.

'It's just the kind of place, this Haus Lobigo,' Willie said. 'On the west coast facing the North Sea, and set in a bit of a bay with high dunes and rock behind it, so it's secluded.'

'If it's the people we want, they're shifting their base again. The sixth man's gone on ahead as advance party.'

'Looks like it. I was thinking, we could drive up the List road now and walk across the dunes.'

'Yes.' She unclipped her hair from behind her neck, divided it in two and began to plait. 'Do the other plait for me, Willie.'

'Sure.' His fingers became busy with the skein of hair. 'Jack Wish doesn't know you, does he?'

'He may have seen a photograph. But if I roll the plaits into earphones and talk with an accent I doubt that I'll register on him. There's no time for anything fancy, anyway.'

Willie said, 'You just going to 'ave a look round?'

'If I can. I might find out where they're going. That's the big thing. Or I might spot something significant in Haus Lobigo. I'll just have to play it the way it comes, Willie.'

'Where d'you want me?'

'Watching. Not too close. This is just a recce to get the feel of the set-up. We'll decide what to do when I come out.'

'How long do I give you?'

'I don't see what can go wrong, but if I'm not out in an hour you can take it I'm in trouble.'

Willie grinned faintly. 'They'll 'ave to be good.'

'They may well be. So don't rush in. Play it carefully.'

She finished rolling the second plait into a coil, and pinned it in position.

Haus Lobigo was big and rambling, with the windows of the upper floor set in a steeply pitched roof. Modesty walked along the brick path which ran between one end of the house and a sloping sand dune with thick tussocks of coarse grass.

She wore dark slacks and a cream tunic with a round collar. The tunic was loose and fell to a few inches below her hips. Beneath it, belted higher than usual, she wore the Colt ·32. A band of buckram stiffening under the lower part of the tunic prevented the shape of the gun showing. A handbag hung from her arm.

When she turned the corner of the house she saw the open French windows with the steps leading down to the sandy path which ran to the spacious terrace. The house was on her right now, and on her left lay the little bay protected by low rocks and sand dunes. A small wooden landing stage lay at the end of a track which wound from the terrace to the sea.

A stocky man in a light jacket came through the French windows carrying a suitcase. He set it down beside the steps, turned to go inside, and stopped short as he saw her. She knew that this was Jack Wish, even though the photographs she had studied had been four or five years old. Watching the fall of his jacket as he turned, she knew also that he carried a gun holstered under his left arm.

He said suspiciously, 'Who are you?'

She gave a polite smile, halting in front of him, and spoke in good but carefully accented English. 'Excuse me, please. I am from the agency.'

'The agency?' His eyes narrowed fractionally. 'We've already had someone round to do the inventory.'

She changed her plan smoothly. 'I am sorry. I do not explain myself well. I am not of the agency. I am from them. They send me to look at Haus Lobigo on the part of Herr Weise, who may wish to rent it. I am Hilde Geibel, his secretary.'

Wish ran his eyes over her. 'We're busy packing, doll. Moving out, see? You better leave it till tomorrow.'

'Herr Weise says I must telephone him tonight.' She looked anxious. 'He will be angry with me if I have to say I have not seen the house.'

Jack Wish grinned and said, 'Well...' He took her arm and turned her towards the open windows. 'Your boss'll be angry, eh?' He moved his hand to her buttocks and let it rest there for a moment as he steered her up the steps and into the room.

She did not pull away, but turned to him with a worried smile. 'Herr Weise is an important man. He likes everything to be done as he says. If you will show me the house I will not disturb you and the other persons.'

'You can disturb me any time, doll,' Wish said, and looked at his watch. An hour to go. There was only the hand baggage to be brought down. Everything else had been sent on. Seff might not like it...

To hell with Seff. No harm in showing the doll around. He didn't expect to make her, not in an hour, even if she was easy. But it looked like she didn't mind a little handling. It might be kind of interesting....

He stood watching her and said, 'You scared of your boss?'

'He is a little, how do you say? A little strict.'

'A doll like you ought to know how to smooth him down.'

'Please—a doll?'

'A girl.'

'Ah.' She smiled and gave a shrug in which there was subtle provocation.

Wish was ready to show her round in the hope that he

might get a little way with her. Clearly there could not be anything dramatic for her to discover, but they would probably run into the other members of the party, and it would be useful to have a sight of them. With Wish looking for opportunities, she might be able to get some hint of where they were going.

She regretted now that she had put on the gun. She would have to make sure that Wish didn't feel it. At the first chance she would ask to use the bathroom, and slip the gunbelt in her bag.

'It will be very kind if you will show me the house,' she said.

'Okay. This way.' He started towards a door on the far side of the room. It opened, and Steve Collier came in. He looked at Modesty with mild curiosity but without immediate recognition, and his eyes had started to turn towards Wish when they snapped back to stare at her in astonishment.

'Good God!' he said. 'Modesty! I didn't recognise you for a moment. What on earth are you doing here?'

Wish spun round to face her. She stared past him at Collier and kept moving forward, a look of polite puzzlement on her face.

'Please?' she said. The hope of a bluff died even as it was born. Collier had spoken her name, and Wish had heard. It was the wrong name, even if Wish failed to associate it with Blaise. There was nothing slow in his reactions. His hand was darting to the shoulder holster beneath his jacket. Her own gun was in no position for quick use.

She kept her eyes on Collier's startled face beyond Wish, and took another step forward, then pivoted slightly and swung one sandalled foot in a raking upward kick. The toe drove into Wish's solar plexus. He made a wordless sound and started to buckle at the knees, his empty hand falling away from the gun.

The kongo was in her fist, wrenched from the clasp of the handbag. She caught Wish under one arm to muffle the sound of his fall, and in the same moment struck with the kongo.

163

He went limp, and she eased him to the floor. Collier was gazing open-mouthed, speechless. She said in a fierce, demanding whisper, 'Do you know what goes on here, Steve? Do you?'

'Goes on?' he said blankly. 'What do you mean, for God's sake?'

She bent and flipped Wish's jacket aside to show the gun, a Colt Commander seven-shot .45 automatic tucked snugly in a Berns-Martin holster. Collier shook his head dumbly. He had no further capacity for surprise.

Her mind raced. She could not believe that Collier's bewilderment was a pretence. Whatever he was doing here he had no knowledge of the set-up. And she had other reasons to believe that Stephen Collier could not knowingly have any part in the same kind of activities as Jack Wish. She calculated the next move. Wish was out, for the next five minutes at least. She could explore the house further, and deal with trouble as it came. She might find some hint of what was going on. But Steve Collier would know more. He did not know the truth, but he must know the people here, what they purported to be doing, where they were going now. And how.

A second had passed since Collier shook his head at sight of Wish's gun. She straightened up and said, 'We have to get out fast, Steve. The way I came, round the side of the house. Keep close behind me till we're out front. And if I say "run", bear left into the dunes and keep going.'

His eyes asked a dozen questions, but she said sharply, 'I'll explain later.' Turning, she moved towards the French windows. She had taken only three paces when from behind her there came a brief soft sound, followed by a grunting gasp. She whirled.

Collier was on his hands and knees facing her, head bowed as he fell slowly sideways. Behind him stood a big man in a cool white shirt and dark slacks. His face and arms were golden, his hair short and black. He was young, astonishingly handsome, yet very masculine.

He stood just within the open doorway, one clenched fist

164

poised from the hammerblow he had just struck. There was no alarm or tension in his face, not even an element of alertness. His blue eyes were relaxed and intrigued.

She had the extraordinary feeling that this man was not dangerous. But that was absurd. He was moving past Collier, past Wish, coming towards her now. His smile had a completely unselfconscious charm.

'A rebel,' he said wonderingly. 'One of the little people raises the flag of revolt in my kingdom. Strikes down one of my servants. Suborns another. You are a brave woman.'

He was making no attempt to guard himself. She moved in smoothly, feinted, then struck with the kongo. The blow did not find its mark. His hand was there, cupped to take the impact.

Shock ran through her as she realised that he had not moved with extraordinary speed; he had moved *before* she launched the blow. His other hand reached out to catch her. She weaved under it easily and struck again—into the hand that was now cupped close to his jaw.

Collier lay on his side, his eyes open. He was conscious, but his muscles would not obey his shrieking mind. As if in a nightmare he watched the strange scene. Modesty had struck twice, very fast, and each time Lucifer had moved to guard himself an instant before the blow was irrevocably launched. He had ignored feints. It was as if his own simple defensive movements were attracting the blows; as if effect was preceding cause.

Precognition.

'*God Almighty, he's ahead of her!*' Collier thought wildly, and tried to call out, but Lucifer's untutored fist crashing against his head seemed to have deadened every nerve.

The action between Modesty and Lucifer could have lasted only brief seconds, but to Collier it seemed to endure interminably, as if his paralysed body had given heightened perception to his mind.

On the third lash of the kongo Lucifer caught her wrist. She went with the jerk of his arm, her knee driving for his groin, her free hand chopping to his throat, but a muscular thigh had moved to block her knee and the chopping blow was struck aside. Instantly her leg straightened and swung to trip him, but did not carry through. She jerked back and thrust forward again for a head-butt; stamped hard down for his instep; jabbed with stiffened fingers for his solar plexus. And each move was thwarted.

Lucifer was still smiling. He seemed a little surprised, and hardly aware of his own movements.

'A rebel...' he said again in wonderment, then held her fast with one great hand gripping her shoulder close to the neck, blocked an upward swing of the kongo with his forearm, and struck a ponderous blow with his clenched fist to the side of her imprisoned head.

She flew sideways as he released her with the blow. Collier saw her hit the wall, bounce back, and go sprawling limply across Jack Wish. The kongo fell from her hand and she lay quite still. Her tunic was rucked up, showing her bare waist and the holstered Colt belted at her hip.

With a frantic effort of will Collier drove a little strength into his numbed sinews. Shakily he got to his hands and knees.

'Lucifer...! The word croaked from his throat. 'Lucifer, listen——'

Seff came through the door with Bowker at his heels. They stopped short.

'The first rebel,' Lucifer said, looking at Modesty, and his eyes sparkled with pleasure. 'Imagine! The first of the little people to rebel against me is a woman. This one is her ally.' He indicated Collier, who was swaying on all fours, then looked at Wish. 'She even defeated one of my servants.'

Bowker's face was grey. He moved forward and snatched the gun from Modesty's holster, then straightened up.

'Who the hell is she?' he said roughly, staring at Seff.

'I am not in a position to answer that, Dr. Bowker.' Seff creaked forward and stared down at Modesty Blaise, his

166

sallow face looked more bony and hollow-cheeked than ever. 'Perhaps Mr. Collier can tell us. Or Mr. Wish, when he recovers. I will take the gun while you bring some cold water. I suggest you also ask Regina for some smelling salts, but tell her there is no need to disturb herself.'

Bowker passed over the gun and jerked his head imperceptibly towards Lucifer. Seff nodded. Inclining his head politely he said, 'I am sure you will feel content to let us deal suitably with this rebel, Lucifer. There is no need at all for you to be troubled further. Perhaps you would care to—ah—talk with Regina for a while?'

'No,' Lucifer said quietly, firmly. He sat down in an armchair and leaned back, his eyes on the still figure of Modesty Blaise. It was the first time he had ever given Seff or Bowker a flat refusal.

She was lying on a couch, her hands tied behind her. Her neck and head ached.

Memory came back. The big golden man with black hair. The shock of that brief, incredible struggle was still with her. He had not been skilled. Fast, perhaps, but not very fast. Yet he had always been ahead of her.

She opened her eyes. He sat in an armchair watching her. Steve Collier stood facing the wall with his hands lifted and pressed flat against the panelling. Jack Wish, in shirt-sleeves now, sat on the arm of another chair, the Colt Commander in his hand, very watchful.

There were two other men in the room, one with fuzzy fair hair and the other an older, strangely decrepit man in an old-fashioned black suit. The first man held her Colt .32. Her eyes moved to the electric wall-clock. It was only just over ten minutes ago that she had entered the house. Another fifty minutes before Willie Garvin would think about taking action. Carefully she felt for mental balance, achieved it, and waited.

Seff linked his hands behind his back and rocked up and down on his toes. He was annoyed, disturbed even. Not so much by this young woman as by Lucifer's sudden and un-compromising refusal to be persuaded.

'That's Blaise okay,' Wish said, looking at her. 'I can see it easy now. But soon as Collier called her Modesty——'

'Quite so, Mr. Wish,' said Seff. 'You were no doubt vigilant, if perhaps unfortunate.' He showed his teeth politely in the direction of Lucifer. 'As Lucifer himself has said, she is a rebel. I am sure we ought to find out what—ah—led her to rebellion before we decide what is to be done.'

He looked at Modesty. 'What brought you here?'

She did not answer. There was something eerie in this set-up. Instinct told her that Seff was the big man, yet he was to some extent, and in the strangest way, deferring to Lucifer.

Lucifer? Why use that name? No matter. He was different from the others. Seff was bad. Bowker was weak and danger-ous. Jack Wish was strong and dangerous. But this boy they called Lucifer ... why was she thinking of him as a boy now? It could only be the almost unearthly quality of innocence that dwelt in his face. Genuine innocence?

But what was this strange talk of rebellion?

And where did Steve Collier fit in?

'Perhaps you can answer for the young woman, Mr. Col-lier?' said Seff.

Collier half turned his head, keeping his hands against the wall. He was still a little pale but he had control of himself now. 'Does she need answering for?' he said coldly. 'Wish is the one who started pulling out a gun. It's you and your friends who should bloody well be answering questions, Seff.'

There was silence. Bowker said uneasily. 'We haven't got much time.'

'We have over forty-five minutes before the yacht arrives, Dr. Bowker. That gives ample time for decisions to be made and implemented. What are your views on Collier? If we keep him, is he likely to be of use?'

Bowker nodded. 'If he co-operates.'

'He will co-operate,' Seff said with an assurance that shook

Collier and made him crane his head round further to look at Modesty. Her face was quiet and told him nothing.

Seff said to her, 'Who sent you?'

'Nobody.'

'That is unlikely.'

Wish said, 'No. It's likely. Nobody sends Blaise any place. Garvin, he'll be around. But they'll be working solo.'

'Then you feel we can——' Seff glanced at Lucifer, 'dispatch her to the lower levels without further concern, Mr. Wish?'

'Sure. But watch out for Garvin.'

'We shall be gone very shortly, leaving no trace. I think the sooner this young woman is dispatched the better.'

'Okay.'

Lucifer stood up and said with complete authority, 'No. She is to remain here on the upper levels.'

Seff smiled toothily and gestured with skeletal hands. 'This is too small a matter for you to be concerned with, Lucifer. It is surely within the competence of your faithful servants to decide——'

'I have given my decision, Asmodeus.' Lucifer spoke with austere patience. There was finality in his voice. He looked at Modesty, and a smile came to his lips. 'A small matter? Oh, no. She is the first rebel. I have much in common with her. I am a rebel myself, remember.'

The calm gaze turned to Seff again. 'She is to remain with us. She is to accompany us on this journey, Asmodeus. I, Lucifer, have given my irrevocable decree.' He crossed to the door and went out.

There was silence in the room. Collier dipped his head against his upper arm to wipe away the sweat that beaded his brow.

Seff said in a harsh, high voice, 'She has to go. You must rationalise this for him, Dr. Bowker.'

'I can't! For God's sake, you heard the way he spoke, Seff!'

'Kindly take care not to use that expression in his presence.

It is most inappropriate. Now, you have told me that no matter what happens, Lucifer is bound to rationalise it within the framework of his own delusion. Therefore if the woman vanishes, Lucifer will persuade himself that he so ordered.'

'Yes, he'll make it—he has to! But the strain will be enormous. It might even send him into withdrawal for a time. And how do you think he's going to make out with predictions then?'

Predictions. Modesty registered the word. It seemed her guesswork had been somewhere on the right lines. Lucifer suffered from a delusion; she half guessed its nature now. And Lucifer was certainly the one with psychic powers. He had shown that, during the brief and incredible fight.

There was a host of new factors inviting speculation. She shut them out and put her mind to the sequence of action that would follow if Seff decided to kill her.

He would want no blood-letting in the house. Somebody would have to get close to her for the kill. Her feet were still free. Steve Collier was free, and with luck he might be anticipating a burst of action if the worst seemed imminent. But Wish held a gun, and he would use it if he had to. The best hope was Willie Garvin ... if the outcome could be delayed long enough.

'You feel her departure might affect Lucifer's powers adversely?' Seff was saying.

'I know it will.' Bowker's voice was rough with fear.

'I know something too,' said Wish. 'Whatever Lucifer wants, you can't hold this dame on the kinda trip we got ahead. Not even when we get there. She's smart and she's sneaky. First thing you know, she'll have the drop on you.'

Seff half closed his eyes, swaying thoughtfully back and forth. Bowker glared with hatred at Modesty and said, 'Suppose we put one of the magnesium and cyanide straps on her? She couldn't bloody well get sneaky then. And put one on Collier, too.'

Seff cracked his knuckles absently. 'An excellent idea in principle. But a strap can be quickly removed unless the

wearer is supervised every second.' He paced across the room,
creaking. 'No, not the strap. But I have something far better.'
He turned with an inquiring smile. 'I hope you recall your
basic training, Dr. Bowker. We shall need a small measure of
medical skill.'

13

WILLIE GARVIN lay on his stomach by a ridge of ochre-coloured rock sunk in the dunes to the north of Haus Lobigo, binoculars to his eyes.

He was deeply worried. Something had gone wrong. He would have known that by now, even if his ears had not been prickling almost painfully. It was just an hour since he had seen Modesty on the path at the rear of the house. She had spoken to Jack Wish, and gone inside with him.

Then ... nothing, until ten minutes ago, when a seventy-foot twin screw diesel yacht had anchored a hundred yards out from the little landing stage and put down an outboard motor boat. On the first trip from the landing stage to the yacht it had carried a number of suitcases, a frail grey-haired woman, and Jack Wish.

Now it was returning. Willie swung the glasses towards the house. Modesty came out, and he felt a moment of relief at the sight of her. Beside her was a splendidly built young man with short dark hair. Now another man...

Christ! It was Steve Collier!

Willie bit his lip and drew in his stomach. Impossible to see the expression on a face, even with the binoculars, but Collier looked very white against the tan of the other man. Now came two more, an old man in a black suit and a man of about forty, carrying Modesty's handbag under his arm. That was bad.

Willie rubbed the sweat from his eyelids and adjusted the focus carefully as the little group moved down to the landing stage. Nobody seemed to be speaking. Modesty's hands were free, and there was no indication that anyone was holding a gun on her.

Willie breathed deeply to ease his aching nerves, and waited for the unobtrusive signal Modesty would give if she wanted him to move in. They were on the landing stage now, and the motor boat was moving towards them. Modesty had her back to the area where he lay. She put both hands on her hips for a moment, dropped her right hand, turned her head slowly to the left, then bent it to flick at her ear as if a fly were bothering her. She returned the hand to her hip for a moment, then folded her arms.

Willie Garvin swore softly, incredulously.

Two minutes later all four were in the motor boat and heading towards the yacht. The anchor came up as they approached. Willie watched them climb the short gangway. The motor boat was lifted aboard. The screw churned, the yacht came round and began to move smoothly away to the north.

Willie checked the name painted on the bows once again. *Riorca*. He watched until the yacht passed out of sight beyond the rising dunes that lay between him and the sea, then lowered the glasses. Turning on his back he rested a damp forearm across his eyes.

North. To Oslo? Copenhagen? Any small port? No way of telling. He would have to guess. But Tarrant should be able to trace the yacht for him. Willie Garvin got up and began to walk steadily through the dunes to the point where he had left the car, willing his mind and nerves to absorb the brutal shock.

They had taken her. Just like that. He did not know how. Or where, or why.

Quite suddenly, and before there was any sense of a battle having begun, he was groping in the dark, alone, with Modesty lost.

It was twenty-four hours later that Tarrant put through a call from his office to Willie Garvin at a small hotel in Stockholm.

'That yacht,' Tarrant said without preamble. 'We've checked the Lloyd's Register and all foreign classification societies. They have nothing called *Riorca*. Probably a false name painted on the bows.'

'All right. Thanks.' Willie's voice was neutral, without disappointment.

'You say she headed north?' Tarrant asked.

'Means nothing. She could've come round in any direction. I've checked Stockholm, and I've rung contacts in Oslo and a few other ports, but there's no joy.'

'On previous form they're probably moving to a new base a long way off, Willie.'

'That's what I reckoned. I doubt if the yacht's for more than the first leg, then they'll switch. Can you get eyes watching for 'em at ports and airports?'

'At main ones. But they'll be using false names, surely. What will they do about a passport for Modesty?'

'Wish has likely got a dozen passports. With a camera, he could fix one for Modesty in a couple of hours.'

'They may well use minor ports and airports,' Tarrant said. 'I can't get a big coverage. People tend to ask why I want it.'

'I know, Sir G. Just do what you can. But for Christ's sake don't let anyone take action if they pick up a lead. Just observe and report back.'

'Yes. How do you think they're holding her, Willie?'

'That's what I can't figure. She didn't 'ave time to give me much of a signal. But if they'd just been using a gun she'd have found some way of making a break for it. Same thing if she'd thought they were going to give 'er the chop on the yacht.'

Tarrant pinched his eyes. He felt as old as God. 'What's your next move?'

'I'm going to think. I've got an answer to this submarine pick-up business, if only I can fit the pieces together. Listen, did you find out what I wanted to know about that last pickup—the fifty thousand gold sovereigns?'

'Yes. And you were right, the container was different. Bigger, and it carried a long cylinder running through it with a torpedo type of motor. No gyros or steering. Nothing sophisticated. Just a simple drive to a small propeller.'

'Ah.'

'What made you ask about it, Willie?'

'The other times it's been diamonds, drugs—small stuff. Valuable but lightweight. This didn't fit the pattern. Those sovereigns, with all the rest of the gear, would weigh over 'alf a ton in air. There wouldn't be any weight, floating in water, but there'd still be too much inertia'.

'Too much for what?' Tarrant said, baffled.

'I don't know. But it didn't fit the pattern, and now it does. That's why I asked about a motor.'

'I don't follow the logic, but you guessed right. Does it help?'

'Anything 'elps. This keeps the towing power in the same limits.'

Tarrant was going to say, 'The towing power of what?' But the answer to that was the answer Willie was groping for, and to put the question now would be stupid. He picked up a sheet of paper and said, 'There's been a new death-list sent round. Much the same pattern as before, but there's a point of personal interest. Our American friend, John Dall, is on it.'

There was silence from the other end. Tarrant could guess the run of Willie's thoughts, for his own thoughts had traced the same route. If Modesty's ideas were right, which category did Dall come under? Was he one of those whose death from natural causes had been psychically predicted, or was he in the blackmail category?

'Dall won't pay up,' Willie said slowly. 'But this lot don't know 'im like we do. They're bound to reckon there's a chance, 'specially now they've got plenty of examples.'

'I agree,' said Tarrant. 'On past success they can expect tougher clients to knuckle under. But if Dall isn't on the natural death quota, and if he doesn't pay, they've set themselves a big job when it comes to having him killed.'

'Not so big. John Dall won't put up with bodyguards under the bed and in the loo. Wish might know that much about 'im.'

'True enough.' Tarrant sighed and put down the sheet of paper. 'But it's not our main problem at the moment.'

'No. Call me if anything comes up, Sir G. I'll be 'ere till tomorrow.'

'And after that?'

'Depends what I come up with when I've done a bit of thinking.'

Willie Garvin put down the phone and looked out of the window across the harbour. It was early afternoon. He drew the curtains and moved across the semi-dark room to the bed. He laid out cigarettes and lighter on the bedside table, then stretched out on his back with his hands behind his head and closed his eyes.

Carefully, over a period of ten minutes, he stripped all anxiety and speculation about Modesty from his mind, creating a quiet void. In the void he assembled a number of questions.

First he thought about the sonar equipment in the container. It occupied only an eighteen inch cube of space. The twelve volt battery provided eight kilowatts in short pulses of one tenth of a second every five seconds, over a period of three hours. The intensity was mechanically reduced towards the end of that period. Power was fed into an acoustic transducer which converted electrical energy to acoustic energy. Transmission was omnidirectional on the horizontal plane and covered a thirty degree spread on the vertical plane.

Why the mechanical device to give diminishing intensity? Why were the pulse signals so powerful to begin with? It seemed the wrong way round. The general position of the sunken container was known anyway, and the final physical contact was a much greater problem than homing in from a distance to a location already known.

What kind of underwater craft could approach, sense any ship in the area, sense any addition to the container which made it suspect, and then, if all was well, tow it away undetected?

The answer had to be simple. Willie Garvin did not believe

176

in the criminal genius who could produce fantastic machines unheard of by the world's scientists.

Why was the lead shot system used to increase buoyancy as soon as the container was on tow?

When all the questions had been posed, Willie put them aside. Concentrating on the known facts he began to shape them in a variety of patterns. Every pattern was incomplete, meaningless. He smoked a cigarette and settled back again. Deep in the memory-banks of his mind he began to search for the stored knowledge which he knew must complete and make meaningful one of those patterns.

Six o'clock in Stockholm.

Noon in New York. John Dall sat at the head of the long boardroom table on the top floor of the great skyscraper which housed Dall Enterprises. He was a man not yet forty, with a strong brown face beneath black hair that was cut short and stood up slightly from his head. There were a dozen men of power in the room, but Dall's was the dominant personality. One man was speaking, referring occasionally to a file in front of him. Dall listened, his wide-set grey eyes fixed on the speaker. He had the gift of total concentration, and was unaware of the muted buzz of the telephone on the table where his secretary, Jane Dunster, sat.

When the speaker hesitated, looking past him, Dall frowned and turned to see Jane about to put a slip of paper at his elbow. He was surprised. She had firm instructions that he was not available until this long meeting ended. But Jane had been with him for ten years now, and her judgment was infallible.

He took the slip of paper. Three words were scribbled in her bold handwriting. *Willie Garvin—urgent.*

She said, a little anxiously, 'I thought——'

'Sure, Jane. That's right.' His tone was reassuring. He stood up. 'You gentlemen will excuse me for a few minutes.'

As she walked with him along the corridor to his private

office suite she said, 'I did ask if he could leave a message, but he said it was urgent.'

'Then it is.' Dall felt a twinge of unease. 'Did he say anything about Modesty?'

'No.' Jane Dunster looked sideways at the man she worked for. Because he trusted her, and because he knew that it made her a more competent private secretary, he hid nothing of his business or private life from her. She had been with him at the time, some years ago, when he had made use of Modesty Blaise and her organisation to recover a valuable industrial secret stolen from the Dall Chemical section of his empire.

Jane Dunster knew how Dall had first met Modesty Blaise in person, only last year, and how he had pulled strings with C.I.A. to help her, and Willie Garvin, in a strange and nightmarish struggle in the mountains of Afghanistan. She had met Modesty Blaise only a few months ago, in the early spring when, recovered from her wounds, Modesty had spent six weeks with Dall on his ranch near Amarillo and at the cabin on the lake in Idaho's Sun Valley.

Jane Dunster had seen Dall's happiness during that time, and she had been happy for him. But now she was afraid, for she alone in the Dall organisation knew that he was under threat of death. For the past two days she had been sick with worry for him.

She said now, 'I wonder if he could be calling about that threat?'

'Could be.' Dall held the door for her and followed her into his office. 'But I wonder why it's not Modesty calling.' He picked up the phone and said, 'Dall. Switch that call through, please.'

A moment later Willie's voice said, "Allo, John?'

'Hallo, Willie. What's new?'

'Tarrant tells me you've 'ad the bite put on you.'

'That's right. Half a million dollars' worth of industrial diamonds.'

'They've told you that in the first warning?'

178

'Yes. Not a very big bite, as these things go. Film stars never sue for less than twenty million. But this is an odd business from what my friends in high places tell me.'

'Yes. It's that. You paying up, John?'

'Like hell I'm paying up.'

'I'd be glad if you would.'

'What?'

'Then I can get a lead. We were nosing around on this and Modesty got taken. I don't know where she is now.'

Dall felt a chill in his stomach. He said harshly, 'Taken?'

'Just that.' Willie's voice was expressionless. 'I don't think they've signed 'er off. She wouldn't 've gone quietly if they were going to do that.'

'Quietly?'

'I saw it.'

Dall sat dazed for a moment. With an effort he focused his mind on essentials. 'If they've taken her they're out in the open now. You saw it, you know who they are. Or maybe you don't, but you must have enough to start the wheels turning, Willie. Big wheels, internationally.'

'It's not like that, John. I've got to 'andle it solo.'

'Solo? Why, for God's sake?'

'Because there's a bugger-factor. If a lot of big feet start tramping around she'll be cooked.'

'How do you know?'

'I was watching through glasses when she was taken. She gave me the high sign, loud and clear.'

'Meaning what?'

'Meaning don't start anything till you know the score. And she put a top priority on it.'

Dall was silent. He did not ask how or where she had been taken. If it was of any importance Willie would have told him. He did not ask how she had conveyed the message. She and Willie would have a system for it.

'You still there, John?'

'Just thinking. You want me to answer this bite?'

'Yes. I'll put up the dough. There's about two 'undred grand in dollar holdings with the Chase National, and I'll get the rest switched from Switzerland——'

Dall broke in angrily, 'You think I care about the goddam money?'

'No.' Willie's voice was oddly formal. 'But she wouldn't want me to take anything for granted.'

Dall closed his eyes, marvelling, then said gently, 'I know. All right, Willie, you haven't. But forget about the money and tell me what you want done.'

'Thanks. First thing, put whatever advert they've called for in the papers, as an acceptance. After a bit you'll be told where to pick up a container and where it's to be dropped. And when. Make the dropping arrangements, and let me know. I want to be there.'

'So do I. I don't know how their communications work, but this could take three or four weeks.'

'I know. We'll just 'ave to sweat it out. I'll be at "The Treadmill", getting some gear together, so call me there.'

Dall's voice held a rough edge of anxiety as he said, 'What do you aim to do, Willie? Tracking them back from the pickup has been tried several ways, according to C.I.A. Everything's failed.'

Willie said, 'There'll be a difference this time. I know 'ow the pick-up's worked.'

'You *what*?'

'Save the questions, John. I'll tell you when I see you.'

Dall drew a deep breath. 'Okay. You're playing it. Are you dead sure you're right to play it solo?'

'It might go wrong. But I'm dead sure it's the only chance to get Modesty out alive.'

'I'll let you know as soon as I've had instructions and fixed the drop.'

'Thanks again. So long, John.'

Dall put down the phone and stared into space for long seconds. Jane Dunster said, 'I couldn't follow everything. Is it bad?'

'Yes. It's bad. But somehow it hasn't registered yet.' He

shook his head impatiently, then unlocked a drawer of his desk and took out a typewritten sheet of cheap paper. 'I'll tell you about it later. Phone this advertisement through to the *New York Times*. It has to go in the Help Wanted Male column.'

'Yes, Mr. Dall.' She took the sheet of paper as if it were contaminated.

'Then call Torsen and tell him to get a packet of industrial diamonds ready. Value, half a million dollars.'

'Yes.' She hesitated. 'Arrangements will have to be made about a ship. For the drop, I mean.'

'We'll leave that till we know where the drop's to be made, Jane.'

She said impulsively, 'I'm glad you're paying. I know you didn't want to, but I'm glad. I've been so frightened.'

'I know. Sorry.' He looked up at her with a barren smile. 'I'm frightened now.'

14

TODAY Modesty Blaise wore the red cheong sam. She had two others, green and yellow, that Bowker had picked up for her during the two-hour stop in Macao, and nothing else. The red cheong sam was wet now and clung to her body, for she had been swimming, but the thin fabric would quickly dry in the hot sun.

Fifty paces from where she sat cross-legged on the white sand stood a dark-skinned man in a green turban, G.I. slacks, and thonged sandals made from a motor tyre. His torso was bare, and an old Winchester carbine was slung over one shoulder.

He was a Moro. There were thirty-two of them and twelve Moro women here on this neck of land which jutted into the South China Sea.

Moros were killers. In centuries past they had come to the Philippines from the southwest, pirates of awesome violence and ferocity. Just under seventy years ago they had fought a war against the might of the United States Army. It had taken seventy thousand well armed and highly trained soldiers to defeat them. In recent times, during the Second World War, they had formed the core of the communist inspired guerilla resistance to the Japanese. 'Huks', they had been called then, an abbreviation of Hukbalahap; and for some years after the war they had fought to secure domination of the country. But with defeat, political motives had withered. The Huk movement had splintered. They had reverted to their old ways, and the name of Moro was used again. Equipped with arms pilfered from U.S. stores, small bands raided coastal villages and towns from powerfully motorised converted sailing boats.

The Moros here, guarding Seff's new base, were one such

band. Seven Moro boats lay at anchor by the wooden landing stage on the long southern arm of the bay. Behind Modesty, and to her left, where the low cliff dipped down to a tangle of rock, stood a cluster of Moro huts with matting walls and roofs of palm leaves.

The Moros were here under a deal made between Seff and Mr. Wu Smith of Macao. Modesty knew Mr. Wu Smith from days gone by, and it did not surprise her that he was the man who handled Seff's takings—the gold, the drugs, the precious stones. He and Seff made a wickedly powerful combination. It was small wonder that the Moros showed no sign of following their natural instincts and slaughtering the little group of Europeans here. They feared few men, but Mr. Wu Smith was one, and his arm was long; and Seff had quickly and effortlessly established himself as another. Even Sangro, the leader of this group, was uneasy in Seff's presence. It was perhaps the unease of the hotblooded carnivore faced by the cold menace of a venomous snake.

Modesty did not know whether this point of land was part of Luzon, or Mindanao, or one of the seven thousand smaller islands composing the Philippines and strung out for over a thousand miles. She had seen nothing during the last leg of the journey, when the seaplane had set them down by night in the bay and taken off again.

Before her now the waters of the bay lay between two long, steep ridges of volcanic rock. There was no reef across the entrance. According to Bowker the reef had been blasted away by the Japanese during the war, for they had used this point for a shore battery. She had seen the concrete gun-platforms herself, overgrown now by bamboo twigs and creepers.

Because there was no reef, tall breakers swept into the bay. They came at an angle, rolling along the northern arm and sweeping round one end of the crescent of beach, reaching right up to the sheer cliff for half the length of the beach before swirling on and round to be absorbed by the calm waters of the bay's southern side, where the Moro boats were moored. The calm was deceptive, for here the current ran swift and strong; but in the middle, just beyond the curving sweep of the rollers, lay an area of placid water safe for swimming.

Immediately behind Modesty the cliff rose thirty feet to a stretch of flat ground where short coarse grass struggled for life in the paper-thin skin of soil which covered the rock. Two hundred yards from the cliff edge stood the house.

It was a piece of folly built by a Spanish noble towards the end of the three centuries when Spain ruled the Philippines. One of those remote and solitary dwellings which appeal to rich eccentrics, it had been maintained and occupied from time to time during the half century of American rule. The Japanese had used it as a billet for their small force of artillery, and after the war it had been bought and restored by a rich Malayan who had wearied of it after a year or two.

Now Seff had rented it. The house was built in the shape of a T, with a long front facing towards the sea and a stem running back into a wide cleft of the cone-shaped mountain which towered directly behind.

On either side, the slopes of the mountain plunged into thick jungle, a dark tangle of trees and vines set in dank humus and extending down to the rocky and convoluted shoreline, so that mountain and jungle between them formed a massive barrier across the neck of land, isolating the house and the bay. The only access was by sea.

The house was in two storeys, the upper storey of the long front being set back to provide a terrace. The roof was flat, with a low parapet of stone. All windows carried bars, a precaution taken by the rich Malayan against the danger of a Moro raid. A water tank was set on the short steel tower that rose from the roof at the far end of the stem of the T.

At some time an attempt had been made to establish a garden to the right of the house, so that poinsettias, hibiscus and brilliant orchids rioted in a great wave of colour against the dark jungle fringe.

It was three days since the party had arrived here, after a four day journey through the side-routes of Europe and Asia.

It had begun on the yacht *Riorca*, but that leg of the journey had lasted only a few hours, for the yacht had doubled back to the south, to Wesermunde, Modesty believed, where two cars had carried the party to a small airfield where a charter plane was waiting.

Thinking back, Modesty decided quietly that Willie Garvin could have had no hope of tracing the tortuous route, even with Tarrant's help. She wondered briefly what angle Willie would be working on, then put speculation aside as profitless.

For the moment her main concern was Steve Collier. They had been given little chance to talk together, though it was not in fact forbidden by Seff. She had tried to give Collier reassurance with a look and with a word whenever opportunity offered, but she was still afraid that he might crack.

He was not a weak character, but neither was he a fool; he had enough intelligence to assess the future objectively, and he must know that when his usefulness to Seff was ended he would die. He knew, too, that her own life hung even more tenuously on Lucifer's good will. For the moment that still remained, and in this one thing Lucifer could not be manipulated, either by Seff or Bowker.

She thought that the strain showing in Collier's face arose out of fear for her rather than for himself. But perhaps the thing that gnawed more viciously at him was not so much the knowledge that sooner or later they would die, as the more nerve-snapping knowledge that they both carried instant death with them in their bodies every second of the day and night.

Bowker had placed it there, under Seff's supervision.

She remembered lying face down on a blanket-covered table in a small room of the house on Sylt, with Jack Wish holding a gun to her head. Stripped to the waist, she had felt the prick of a needle under her left shoulder blade; and then, sixty seconds later, Bowker had taken a scalpel to the area numbed by novocaine and worked in silence while Seff explained to her and to Collier exactly what was being done.

A half-inch incision, a quick separation of the muscle fibres, and the thin plastic capsule was inserted, embedded in the muscle. Swab, an alum coagulant, a stitch; a strip of plaster over a dry dressing, and the thing was done. It had taken six minutes.

Then it was Collier's turn. She remembered his face, pale with shock as she rose from the table and began to put on her tunic, incredulous horror in his eyes. She had subdued her own shock, holding it down, sealing off her emotions and watching impassively as the thing was done to Collier, glad to watch because the knowledge might later be vital.

She had seen the second capsule, held between tweezers in Seff's bony fingers. It was white, lozenge shaped, and no thicker than a match; an inch long and perhaps a quarter of an inch across.

She had heard Seff's voice as Bowker bent to make the incision in Collier's back: 'You will not be incommoded by this. The small incision will heal in a day or so. But you will, of course, be effectively compelled to obedience. It is best that you should have no doubt of this, so I will tell you precisely how the capsule functions . . .'

Willie Garvin would have understood the detailed technicalities. Modesty's own knowledge of miniaturisation was sufficient for her to know that Seff was not speaking in the realms of fantasy.

Each capsule contained simple, standard components. A ferrite rod an inch long provided the aerial and was connected to a piece of miniaturised circuitry which would, when triggered, discharge a Mallory mercury-cell battery no bigger than a waistcoat button. The trigger for the discharge would be a hard signal of high frequency, tone modulated for safety, so that the modulation would have to be filtered out by the encapsulated circuitry before the trigger signal would cause the battery to discharge. This prevented any random transmission acting as a trigger.

When the signal came, from the pocket transmitter Seff carried, the Mallory battery would fire a primer from an ordinary flash bulb. The primer was no bigger than a match-head, but its firing would be sufficient to pierce the thin plastic casing of the capsule.

And a few grains of cyanide would then be released into the bloodstream, to bring immediate death.

There was a different frequency for each capsule, and the transmitter was so built that Seff could kill either captive at the touch of a switch. Throughout the journey Modesty Blaise and Steve Collier had never been more than fifty paces from Seff, and the effective range of the small transmitter was over half a mile. Also, they had never been allowed within attacking distance of Seff, and there had been supervision day and night.

Little supervision was needed now. Somewhere in the house was the transmitter Seff used for maintaining contact with Mr. Wu Smith in Macao. It had enough power to trigger the release of the cyanide at fifty miles. Seff still continued to carry the small transmitter with him, like a loaded gun. Bowker also had one now, and so did Regina.

The two prisoners were held as effectively as if their feet had been nailed to the ground.

Modesty moved her shoulder, flexing the muscles. She could not feel the presence of the capsule. The little cut had healed and the stitch had been taken out three days ago. Inserting the capsules had been a simple operation. Removing them would require great care and a steady hand, for they would first have to be accurately located in the muscle fibre.

It was impossible for her to remove her own capsule, very difficult to remove Collier's without killing him by cyanide poisoning, but she believed she could do it for she had watched Bowker closely. It was far less likely that Collier could do the same for her. Still, the chance might have to be taken. She had stolen a razor blade from one of the bathrooms and kept it hidden in the sole of her sandal, but she had never yet been left alone with Steve Collier.

Modesty's eyes rested unseeingly on the big bamboo raft which lifted gently on its mooring ropes fifty yards from the beach. Her mind quietly turned over the situation, exploring every facet in the hope of finding a flaw she could turn to her advantage.

Many mysteries had been unravelled for her in the past few days. She knew what Lucifer was, and what he believed himself to be. She knew how Seff used Lucifer's powers of e.s.p. to predict death, and how he used those predictions. She knew the structure of the little group Seff had gathered about him, knew the part played by Bowker, the part played by Jack Wish. All this fitted into the pattern of the strange yet logical guesses she had made that night in London.

But she also knew now the astonishing answer to the mystery of how the submerged containers were picked up from under the sea. That was where the plump, gentle Spaniard in rumpled slacks came into the picture. Garcia.

There was no doubt that Seff was one with the rare gift of finding strange talents in men and blending those talents to serve an equally strange purpose. He had found Lucifer and Garcia, and the part that each played in Seff's scheme staggered the imagination.

But all that she had learned offered no factors on which to build a plan for escape. An attempt to steal one of the Moro launches was pointless, for by Seff's orders the engines were kept immobilised. There was no landward route; behind the house lay mountain and jungle and unknown territory, the *bundok* area of east central Luzon, perhaps, an isolation still unmapped. The going on foot would be either slow or impossible. The cyanide capsules would be triggered before Modesty and Steve Collier could cover a mile. Also, Seff had warned the Moros to stay out of the jungle fringe, for there still remained mines laid by the Japanese to guard their battery from a landing and assault from the rear.

It might be possible to steal one of the two little sailing dinghies under Garcia's charge and then hug the coast, hiding ashore by day from the Moros searching in their launches, and moving on by night. But that would mean getting the boat itself into hiding on the rocky coast...

She left the problem, for it was secondary. Nothing at all could be attempted until the death-capsules had been cut out from their bodies. Already she had considered bribing one of the Moros to help her. She had only her body to bribe with, but it was not this that deterred her. Apart from the risk of the Moro betraying her to Seff, there was the problem of communication. She did not speak the chabacano dialect, the 'bamboo Spanish' of the Moros, and she could not believe that she would be able to explain what had to be done—or that a Moro could do it without piercing the capsule and killing her.

She had not even considered trying to bribe Garcia, for he had no interest in her as a woman. But she had very warily tested the possibility of enlisting his aid, for Garcia was not an enemy. In a different way, he was as innocent as Lucifer. Garcia lived in a very special world of his own. It was a world made possible by Seff, and Garcia's only anxiety was that nothing should disrupt it. Modesty's tentative approach had troubled and bewildered him. Seeing this, she had dropped the attempt before he had begun to understand.

There remained Lucifer. His manner to her was one of kindly amusement, and it was plain that she was his protégé. She had taken the risk of telling him that Seff had placed a killing device in her back. Lucifer had laughed delightedly at her fantasy and shaken his head: 'My servants and I have no need of human ways of destruction, Modesty. You shouldn't try to lie to the Father of Lies himself.'

Along the beach a flash of colour caught her eye. She turned her head. Lucifer was coming towards her, wearing red trunks and taking off a black shirt as he trod the dry sand.

It was not hard to smile a welcome at him. She felt pity and some measure of affection for this physically splendid young man with the tragically deluded mind.

'Shall we swim, Modesty?'

She nodded, and registered that this was the first time he had asked rather than commanded her. That might be significant of a subtle change in his attitude. To test it she sat still, waiting, and after a moment he reached out a hand to help her to her feet.

Beside him she walked into the warm sea, feeling the drag of the broken rollers as they swept round and back. She drew up the skirt of the cheong sam and tucked it between her legs like a loin cloth, knotting the ends of the slashed skirt over one hip. The pull of the breakers faded, and she was waist deep in the quiet stretch of water beyond. Leaning forward, she began to swim lazily towards the raft.

Lucifer surged past her. He was a powerful swimmer. Turning, he submerged, and a moment later she felt his hand on her ankle, drawing her down. She let herself sink, caught his head and forced his chin back, then broke free. They surfaced together, and Lucifer was laughing.

She knew now that he was feeling the tug of her sex, even though he might not be aware of it. This could be dangerous in the long run, for Seff would be driven to act if he saw her influence over Lucifer growing too strong. But in the short run it was good, for Lucifer alone stood between her and dispatch to the 'lower levels'.

She splashed water in his face, then turned and swam for the raft. As she sat on the edge, wringing water from her hair, he drew himself up to sit beside her.

'I like the sun,' he said contentedly. 'And swimming.'

'Yes. It's good.' She looked round the bay. 'I shall miss all this if Seff sends me down to the lower levels.'

Lucifer's chin came up and a slight frown touched his brow. 'That is not for him to decide, Modesty.'

'He wants to send me, though.'

A smile. 'That is because his power is limited, and he cannot see as I see. He mistrusts you. He thinks you are still in rebellion against me.'

'And do you think so?'

'I know you are not,' he answered with complete assurance.

'I'm glad you know it. And I'm glad you've given your new servant, Collier, another chance. Is he working well now?'

'Yes.' Lucifer thought for a moment, then added, 'but he is

slow to learn. I have been busy teaching him all afternoon, but he keeps asking me to show him again.'

In a ground floor room in the front of the house Bowker closed the drawer of a filing cabinet and lit a cigarette. He did not offer one to Collier, who sat with elbows on knees, hands hanging limply, a pale sheen of exhaustion on his face.

Seff and Regina had just entered the room. Regina moved to a couch with her usual slight hobble, sat down, slipped her shoes off, and began to rub her forehead with a menthol stick.

Seff said, 'Are the results satisfactory, Dr. Bowker?'

Bowker nodded towards Collier. 'He's the expert.'

Seff's neck groaned as he turned his head. 'Well, Mr. Collier?'

Collier looked at him with weary loathing. 'Lucifer's extrasensory powers are greater than I've found in anyone I've examined. And the results are bad, from your point of view.'

'Please explain that paradox.'

Collier looked out of the window. 'Most people with e.s.p. have it only in a moderate degree. I mean moderate to the layman. So moderate that it only shows up in statistics. You toss a coin a thousand times and get your subject to predict each result. If he gets twenty per cent better than a chance result on the whole run, that's something to get excited about.'

He paused, looking at Regina and wondering vaguely whether he hated the woman more than he hated Seff. After the vile puppet show last night, he thought it likely.

'You want something different,' he went on. 'You want Lucifer to be at least ninety per cent accurate in predicting death by psychometry. We've taken a run of a thousand envelopes this afternoon, and he picked out thirteen. Then we did the same run again and he picked out fifteen. Seven of them were the same as he'd picked the first time.'

'And what does this indicate, Mr. Collier?'

'I haven't worked out the maths yet, and I can't until we eventually find out what percentage of predictions he's got right. Bowker's tabulation of past results isn't in the best form for mathematical analysis, but as a broad opinion I'd say that Lucifer's accuracy is probably diminishing.'

Collier stopped talking and looked out of the window again, hoping to see a figure in a red cheong sam, not knowing why he hoped, unless it was for reassurance that he was not alone in this nightmare world.

Seff said, 'Forget the maths. We are purely interested in practical results. To what extent can your expertise improve Lucifer's performance?'

'I don't know. For Christ's sake, there aren't any rules in e.s.p. Or if there are we haven't found them yet.'

'Kindly give thought to your language, Mr. Collier. There is a lady present,' Seff said stiffly. He glanced at Regina, who gave him a fond, proud smile. Collier felt sick. 'Surely,' Seff went on, 'you have studied the effect of external influences on the results of e.s.p. experiments?'

Collier shrugged. 'We don't experiment with death-predictions. But for what it's worth, we find that the best results are gained when the subject isn't making any effort. Conscious effort seems to block the faculty. We also find that we can get improved results by training. Lucifer's been having daily sessions with the Rhine cards and other standard techniques since we got here. That's not so long, but I'd have expected an improvement.'

'Perhaps your training is at fault?'

Collier smiled without humour. 'See what results you get if I stop it,' he said grimly. 'Lucifer's going down hill in spite of it.'

'He's right, Seff,' Bowker said quickly. 'Lucifer's tightening up. I've been watching him while Collier's been watching the results. The boy's too tense. Get him relaxed, and I think Collier's training could put him back on the top line for accuracy.'

'Get him relaxed...' Seff echoed slowly. 'That seems to be to your own address, Dr. Bowker. Have you any recommendation?'

'I've tried tranquillisers but they don't help.' Bowker stubbed out his cigarette thoughtfully. 'What impresses me is the way he put a stopper on killing that Blaise girl. There's something there, maybe. I could put it in psychiatric terms, but Jack Wish of all people came up with the idea first, back on Sylt, and he put it simply enough. Lucifer's a big boy. Maybe he needs a girl.'

Regina tittered and a little colour came to her pallid cheeks. 'Apart from the Moro women,' she said coyly, 'there's only Modesty Blaise.'

'That's who I had in mind,' said Bowker.

There was silence. Collier found himself with a seething desire to get up and walk over to Bowker and smash his fist in the man's face. He did not imagine he would be very good at that sort of thing, but neither would Bowker for that matter. And it would be infinitely satisfying to feel something break under his fist. He took a slow, deep breath and tried to relax.

Seff was standing with hands behind his back, rising on his toes and sinking to his heels, lips pursed judicially.

'Might it not be dangerous?' he asked. 'I have in mind that the root cause of Lucifer's paranoia was—ah—intimacy with a woman.'

'It might be dangerous for Blaise,' Bowker said. 'That needn't worry us, since we want her put down anyway. Whatever happens won't remove Lucifer's obsession. That's incurable. At worst, giving him Blaise can do no harm, and at best it can make a hell of a difference to his e.s.p. results. Lucifer needs to haul his ashes, and I'm for giving him the chance.'

'It might reduce his psychic ability,' Collier said hoarsely.

Seff favoured him with a wintry smile. 'You are biased in this matter, Mr. Collier. And you can hardly claim to have statistical experience of the results of intimacy on extrasensory faculties, I think?'

'There's one thing, Seffy...' Regina ventured diffidently.

'Yes, my dear?'

'Well, it isn't just a question of *giving* her to Lucifer, is it?

The poor boy would have said if he wanted her—if he realised it. I mean, she'll have to *co-operate*. Well, really she'll have to *persuade* him, I suppose.'

'I've thought of that,' Bowker said. 'Regina's right. Getting Lucifer to bed is going to take a careful piece of seduction. She can't just throw it at him. But I'd say she's pretty talented, and if she wants to stay alive a little longer she'll damn well have to use her talent.'

Collier wondered how much more hatred his mind could hold without driving him to action that would kill him. Seff was ready, his hand in his jacket pocket, on the transmitter. Regina's hand was in her shapeless handbag.

Eyes on Collier, Seff grinned suddenly. 'I like it, Dr. Bowker. It's really very good indeed. You must warn Mr. Wish about the change of sleeping arrangements to be expected, so that he can reorganise the Moro guards on interior duty. And you, Mr. Collier, will inform Miss Blaise of what she must do.'

'Me?' Collier stared stupidly.

'I feel you are the best person to put the situation to her fully, with all the contingencies involved. I suggest you take a walk on the cliff top with her after dinner tonight. We shall be watching, of course.' Seff's gaunt face flushed with pleasure.

Regina capped the menthol stick and put it away in her handbag beside the slim black oblong of the transmitter. 'Oh dear,' she sighed with tremulous regret. 'What a pity we haven't got the closed circuit television fitted here, Seffy.'

Meals were taken at two well separated tables in the big dining room. Modesty shared one with Bowker, Lucifer and Jack Wish. Collier sat with the Seffs. A Moro woman served what Regina had cooked. This was the time when, if Steve Collier had been Willie Garvin, a sudden move might have been attempted—Willie taking the Seffs and Modesty taking Bowker and Wish, before any transmitter or Wish's gun could be brought into play. Even with Willie this would have been a desperate gamble; without him it was sure death.

Collier dreaded mealtimes. Proximity to the Seffs aroused

194

physical nausea in him. He felt as if in the presence of human decay. At the other table, Modesty Blaise seemed quietly unaware of any strain.

Tonight, after dinner, Lucifer went to his room as usual to play his records for an hour. He had a selection of pieces by Saint-Saëns and Pierné of which he never tired. Seff wiped his mouth on a napkin and looked across at Modesty. 'Mr. Collier will walk with you now, Miss Blaise. He has something to tell you.'

Regina tittered and sipped daintily at her glass of gin and water. Modesty said nothing, but stood up and moved to the door as Collier held it open for her.

A lilac dome of twilight rested on the horizon as they walked the broad expanse between house and cliff top. Four Moro guards were patrolling. Later there would be more.

Collier found himself unable to frame a simple sentence, and it was Modesty who spoke first.

'It's a good chance to talk, anyway. How are you feeling, Steve?'

He shrugged. 'Shattered. In God's name how do you manage to stay so untouched by it all?'

'I'm hardly that. But I've been in trouble before.'

'This bad?'

'That's something we won't know till it's over. Listen Steve, you've got to eat and sleep properly, and stay detached. You're living on your nerves, and if you crack Seff will kill you.'

'Detached?' He gave a short dry laugh. 'How the bloody hell do you do that?'

She stopped, turning to look at him. 'You make an effort, Steve. You starve the imagination and you feed the will.'

'A nice glib formula.'

'Don't feel so damn sorry for yourself. Or for us. And don't quarrel with me, Steve. You're on edge because you've got something to tell me and you don't like it. But just leave it for the moment and try to take in what I'm telling *you*.'

'All right.' He rubbed a hand over his face, glad of the

useless reprieve and contemptuous of his foolish relief. 'How do you starve the imagination and feed the will?'

'Well...' she gestured as if it were self evident, 'every time you find yourself starting to think of what Seff and the others might do to us, you stop sharp. And you switch. You start working out what *we're* going to do.'

'Us?' He stared incredulously. 'Like what, for instance?'

'Like if we can ever get half an hour together, unwatched, undisturbed, I'm going to cut that poison capsule out of your back, and you'll do the same for me—if I haven't killed you doing it. I've got a razor blade.'

Collier's mouth hung open. 'A razor blade,' he said at last in a shaky voice. 'Now there's a fragrant thought. Starve the imagination, you tell me, and then you give me the razor blade bit to reflect on. Oh, I'll sleep like a baby tonight.'

Her teeth showed in the half light as she smiled. 'That's better. I haven't heard a droll word from you since we got here.'

Collier was astonished to find that for the moment he felt better. The tightness had gone from his stomach and the permanent ache in his muscles had faded a little. He said, 'It's hardly a situation for drollery.'

'Never mind the situation. Or rather, the more you can manage to be yourself, the less the situation will hit you.'

'Oh, I'm myself all right. Scared. I want to go home.'

'So do I. Do they watch you all the time?'

'Not exactly. I mean, nobody breathes down my neck, but there's usually someone hovering in sight. Except at night. Then my door's bolted on the outside and a Moro sleeps across it in the passage. The window's barred.'

'It's the same with me. But we might find a way out sometime. At night, I mean. Think about it.'

'It's hardly my line, but all right. What happens after we've got together and done the Dr. Kildare bit with your razor blade—if we ever manage it?'

'Think about that, too. Switch to it any time you find yourself imagining the worst. The more you try, the easier it gets.

You can think about your work with Lucifer, too. That's important if you want to stay alive.'

The mention of Lucifer brought Collier's mind lurching sharply back to what he had to tell her, but she was still speaking. 'We've got two chances, Steve. One is to make a break for ourselves. The other is Willie Garvin.'

'Willie?' Collier was confused, trying to cope with two thoughts at once.

'Yes. Willie saw us taken. He won't be standing still.'

'But Jesus, he hasn't a hope of finding us here, Modesty!'

'That's what Seff and the others believe. A lot of people have made the same kind of mistake about Willie and found it expensive. They count him out unless I'm there to do the thinking. But they're wrong. When Willie Garvin climbs in the ring it's time for people like Seff to duck fast.'

She began to walk slowly on again. Collier moved beside her. Vaguely he was beginning to understand how she was able to remain untouched by the hopelessness of their situation. To her, it was not hopeless. Her mind was totally directed towards the positive concept of winning the game, to the exclusion of fear, anxiety or despair.

It was a good trick, he thought, but she had been learning it all her life. Starve the imagination...

'Look,' he said in a flat voice. 'This thing I've got to tell you. Lucifer's not doing well on the e.s.p. and Bowker thinks you could make a difference. They say you've got to take Lucifer to bed. Or else.'

Her pace did not alter, and when he looked at her he saw only a small frown of concentration on her brow.

'It could be dangerous,' she said after a moment or two.

'Of course it could.' His voice was ragged. 'It was having a girl that triggered off his latent paranoia and first made him think he's the kingpin of Hell. Did you know?'

'Yes. Bowker told me. But I didn't mean that. It's Seff who's dangerous. If I have too much influence over Lucifer, Seff will throw the switch on me.' She was silent for a few paces. 'Still, I can probably handle that side of it.'

197

'What about the other side?' Collier said roughly. 'The horizontal gavotte for two, with Lucifer.'

She stopped again and turned to look at him, holding down her impatience and speaking quietly. 'Don't make a drama of it, Steve. In a spot like this, the big trick is to stay alive for another day. Just that. I'm buying time. I've paid tougher prices in the past, believe me.'

'Well...' He shrugged, suddenly angry at her calm acceptance. 'In that case, have fun.'

She said nothing but stood looking at him with a half exasperated, half resigned smile, until he dropped his eyes, ashamed, and muttered, 'Sorry. I really am a bastard. A jealous bastard, too.'

'Yes, you are a bit. Never mind. What else are you, Steve?'

'Eh?' He was bewildered.

'Well, you're not a metallurgist, we've agreed that. And psychic research isn't a living, is it?'

'Oh! God, no.' He found he was able to smile. 'I'm a mathematician. I used to teach, and then about five years ago I wrote and published a primer. I was lucky. It was taken up by the schools, and I suddenly found myself with a steady income from royalties, about six or seven thousand a year. So I gave up teaching and followed my hobby.'

'Psychic research.'

He nodded. 'I'd been dabbling for years. It started with an interest in the statistical side and developed from there. I turned out to be not bad at it. Apart from being a jealous bastard I'm a sceptical one, too. You have to be if you're going to get anywhere with e.s.p. phenomena.'

'And you're an authority now?'

'I suppose so. I seem to have scratched up a minor reputation in interested circles over the past few years.'

'Why do you tell outsiders you're a metallurgist?'

His grimace was close to a grin. 'Tell them you do psychic research and they'll bend your ear for ever, mainly about ghosts. Everybody's got a friend who's seen one. Statistically, in 63.5 cases it's an aunt. God knows why. But if you tell people you're a metallurgist they stay off your back. Nobody cares'.

'Except Willie Garvin.'

'Yes. Him and his blasted beryllium——' Collier broke off, astonished. 'What the hell are we talking about?'

'This and that. Old times. We've already covered present business, haven't we?'

'I suppose so——'

'*Hey!*' A shout came from the direction of the house. In the deepening twilight they could see the stocky figure of Jack Wish. 'Hey!' he called again. 'Come on in now!'

'That's it, then.' Modesty touched Collier's arm and together they began to move towards the house. There were lights showing from several windows now. The house had its own supply of electricity. There were storage batteries in reserve, but the main supply came from a generator set on the southern flank of the mountain and driven by the deep, narrow stream that coursed down. From the same source, water was pumped to the huge tank on the roof.

Jack Wish had gone back inside, leaving the heavy door open. A Moro leaned against the wall by the door, a Garand rifle slung on his shoulder. On the long, balustraded terrace above, a thin black figure looked down.

Seff. He had been watching them, and his hand would be on the little transmitter in his pocket.

As they went inside——

'About Lucifer,' Modesty said very quietly. 'Does it begin tonight, Steve?'

'Yes.' Carefully he killed the quick flare of his imagination and began to think about the barred window of his room. The bars were only three-quarters of an inch thick. How deeply were they embedded? Perhaps he could lay hands on some kind of tool...

'Yes,' he repeated, almost absently. 'It begins tonight.'

15

'You'll have to play this by ear,' Bowker said. He was showing signs of nervousness now. 'I can't predict how he'll react to any particular approach. But for God's sake don't try a direct one.'

Modesty said curtly, 'Will he be asleep now?'

'Maybe.' Bowker halted outside the door of Lucifer's room and tapped gently. There was no response. 'Looks as if he's asleep.' Bowker bent to draw back one of the two well oiled bolts.

'You lock him in?'

'Yes. He was used to that in the home. He thinks he causes the door to be sealed by his own power.'

'Suppose he wanted to get out?'

'He doesn't. If he tried and the door didn't open, he'd decide he didn't want to, that he was just testing it. He rationalises everything.' Bowker reached up to draw the other bolt. 'Do you want me there for a few minutes, just to put him at ease?'

'No.'

Bowker shrugged and opened the door quietly. She went in, and saw the big double bed and the clutter of ornate furniture in the spacious room. A low wattage bedside light glowed under a red shade. Across the room another door led to a small bathroom and lavatory. Lucifer lay on the bed with the covers pushed back over the foot. He wore black shorts and was on his back, asleep.

The door closed softly. Modesty waited a few seconds then tried cautiously to open it. Bowker had shot the bolts, and the door did not move. She had expected it, but was disappointed to have been proved right. Until a few moments ago she had nourished a slender hope of being able to get out, tonight or another night, and of reaching Steve Collier's room for what he had called the Dr. Kildare bit.

She slipped off her sandals. The yellow silk cheong sam rustled as she moved towards the bed. Shock touched her as she looked down at the fine golden body and the young face beneath the short black hair. The body was tense. She could see the flutter of the taut sinews in the shoulders and arms. The face was set in a curiously noble mask of pain and sorrow. She bent closer, and saw moisture on the cheeks below the closed eyelids.

Deep in the lower levels of Hell, Lucifer flashed across bubbling pits where fire seared the shapeless souls of the damned. Most of the time, through all the long eons, he had found joy in bearing the burden laid upon him as punishment for leading the angelic rebellion. But sometimes it taxed him almost beyond endurance, sometimes he could no longer hold back the pity that welled in him for the writhing creatures he must forever hold in torment. Their agony became his. And Lucifer, Prince of Darkness, wept for them.

Something was drawing him up now, up from the molten gloom and the red glow of fire. He was returning to the upper levels of his kingdom, and a hand was holding his.

Lucifer remoulded his jet-black flesh and fanged face to the shape and texture of his earthly form. He opened his eyes.

Modesty Blaise sat on the edge of the bed, holding his hand tightly and looking down at him. For a moment he felt what in a human might have been surprise, even fear, but then he remembered that he had willed her to come to him, and so she was here. She wore the yellow silk dress, the one he liked best, and she was the most beautiful of all the subjects in his vast dominion.

'You sent for me, Lucifer,' she said, and he could hear the thread of nervousness in her voice.

'Yes. But don't be afraid.'

'It's hard not to be. I'm not like your servants. I'm just a human.'

He pressed her hand. 'I know. But I like to have you with us, and I want you to be happy, Modesty.'

He was glad to feel her hand relax a little, and to see relief touch her face. She said, 'I think you sent for me because you saw into my mind and you knew I wanted to come to you.'

'I knew. But you must tell me the reason yourself.'

'You know everything, you know the reason. I wanted to ... ask you something.'

'Yes. Ask me.'

'But you know, Lucifer.'

His eyes went blank for a moment before he smiled and said, 'Yes. But you must put it into words, Modesty, to show that you're not afraid.'

She had grown tense again, her body twisting a little as if with inner conflict. 'I can't help being afraid. I could only ask you in words if you let me think of you as a man. Not as Lucifer. Just a man, who sometimes goes swimming with me, plays on the beach with me, talks of ... of ordinary things.'

'You may think of me in that way. I won't be angry.'

Modesty was silent, keeping her eyes lowered. So far all was well. He had taken her presence in his bedroom calmly. She had even seen quick pleasure in his eyes when he first opened them. And as they talked he was looking sometimes at her face and sometimes, with the merest hint of unease, at the curves of her body under the thin silk. His hunger was there and could easily be roused, but if she trod carelessly there might be a dangerous reaction.

Acting the part was not difficult. His innocence demanded little subtlety. But choosing the right words was a hazard. She would have to take one delicate step at a time, ready to go forward, ready to draw back.

'If you won't be angry with me, then ...' She lifted her head and let him see a shaky smile. 'If you were a man, I'd want to belong to you, Lucifer.'

A flash of panic came and went swiftly. 'You do belong to me, Modesty,' he said quickly, sternly. 'You know that.'

He had taken the point and deflected it. But he had

not been shaken badly by it; she could press forward
warily.

'I didn't mean belong to you as a subject. I meant...' She
let the sentence hang on air, then continued, 'Have you the
power to be just a man, Lucifer?'

'I must always be Lucifer.' The words were measured, yet
she heard in them a touch of uncertainty. He had more than
half grasped her meaning, and the opposing pressures of
excitement and fear were beginning to stir in him. There was
not yet any strong or dangerous clash between his wanting
and not wanting, but she knew it could only be avoided in the
end by making the initiative his.

'Yes. You must always be Lucifer.' There was a tinge of
sorrow in her voice now. 'The others, your servants, they can
do all things that men do, because you've ordered it so.' She
looked at him with resignation. 'It's so strange. I'm sometimes
frightened that they may want me as a man wants a woman.
Yet I wouldn't be frightened if it were you ... because I know
you would be kind and gentle, and you'd help me.'

His eyes flared, and she drew her hand away before he
could tighten his grip. Standing up, she moved quickly away
from the bed, then turned to look at him. He was propped on
an elbow, staring at her anxiously, his face a conflict of
emotions.

'I'm sorry I've been so foolish,' she said in a low voice. 'I
knew there could be no wrong in Hell. No sin. No guilt.' She
saw his eyes widen a little at her last words. 'No guilt,' she
repeated heavily. 'And because I've been honoured above all
your subjects, because Lucifer has been my friend for a little
while as well as my master, I thought that he might want
me as a woman.'

He was still in the same half lying position, rigid, staring at
her with turmoil in his eyes. She shook her head and twisted
her lips into a forced smile.

'I'll go now,' she said. 'I shouldn't have hoped. I should have
known that Lucifer must always be Lucifer.'

She turned slowly. Now the initiative was his, and she had

tried to strip away from him any sense of guilt. She took two paces towards the door, and still he did not speak. She had given him the initiative but he needed time—more time.

Without turning she said, 'I'd like to take something with me, Lucifer. Just a memory. I'm only a woman, and human. Will you help my pride a little?'

Still he said nothing. She let her instinct take over, and went through with the gamble. Her hands moved to the shoulder buttons of the yellow cheong sam.

'It doesn't matter if you lie,' she said. 'But will you look at me? And tell me—if you had the power to be just a man for tonight, would I please you?'

The silk whispered to the floor about her feet. She stepped away from it and turned to face him, standing erect, without embarrassment or coquetry. The rose-filled light glowed on her long tanned legs, on the narrow waist rising to full firm breasts and wide shoulders.

'Please,' she said. 'Tell me, Lucifer. Just one word ... before I go.'

He looked at her with wonder, and slowly all conflict was erased from his face, leaving only youthful eagerness. The blue eyes danced and his smile was brilliant. He swung his feet to the ground and moved towards her, reaching out his hands.

'Don't go,' he said in a whisper. 'Lucifer must always be Lucifer. But in his own dominion he has the power to be all things, at his pleasure. Tonight it is Lucifer's pleasure to be no more than human—a man.'

Though his whispering voice was confident, she felt his body shaking as he took her in his arms. His kiss was the artless kiss of a boy, and she let it be so for the moment.

'You'll have to help me,' she said softly, her hands gentling him. 'I'm not afraid now, but I want to be good for you.'

'You will be good for me.' He drew her towards the bed.

In the time that followed she guided his awkward love-play, murmuring praise and wonderment, and always making it seem that he was the preceptor and she the novice.

When joy shook his powerful body the first time she knew a strange contentment, growing not from a sense of victory but from the simple gladness of giving.

After that first time Lucifer was gone, and only the man remained; a man who spoke gentle, clumsy endearments and held her close; who had forgotten his eternal burden for a while; who had laid aside fear and guilt, and was supremely unaware of his own gaucheness because she hid it from him; a man whose young strong appetite grew quickly keen again so that he turned to her anew.

It was very late when at last he slept. Modesty lay on her back, holding him in her arms, his head cradled on the softness of her breast and shoulder, and she knew that whatever the end might be she was glad to have given him this night.

Twice each week Garcia would go out in one of the small sailing dinghies and catch a shark.

Now, in the heat of the afternoon sun, he stood outside the little shack where he lived beside the long rocky inlet which probed into the shore a hundred yards north of the bay. He was examining the dead shark, some seven feet long, which he had caught a mile or two out to sea the day before.

'You tow it round the bay?' said Collier.

'Yes, señor. But first wait till he go older a little.'

'Starts to decay?' Collier pinched his nose and flapped a hand in mime.

Garcia nodded. 'Then is best thing of all to make sharks not come. I make tow four times each day. Then is safe to swim. Old shark is there.' He pointed to the mouth of the inlet where the top of a net showed just above the water. 'He is nearly finish. Come apart. Tomorrow this one just right.'

Collier grimaced, sniffing. 'He seems pretty high already. But I still prefer him to some of my table companions. If we could get our black-suited laughing boy in that condition, you'd only need to tow him round once a week.'

'Señor?' Garcia stared, uncomprehending.

'Never mind.' Collier gave a friendly nod and strolled

slowly back along the edge of the inlet. He had been making conversation while waiting for Modesty Blaise, and now he saw her, in red, moving down the slope from the ridge which hid the house from view. They had arranged the meeting with a few quick words soon after breakfast.

There were three Moro guards in sight, one on the ridge and two more on the flat ground beyond the inlet, but Modesty was alone. That was a change, Collier reflected. Lucifer rarely left her side now.

It was three weeks since Modesty had become Lucifer's mistress. At first Collier had felt only relief that she had overcome the immediate danger. Then had followed jealousy and resentment, both acknowledged by him to be juvenile. Now he had reached the stage of wry acceptance.

Lucifer's happiness was manifest. He seemed even taller, and his manner had taken on an added touch of regality. Yet he co-operated in the many sessions of experiments, and this was Modesty's influence at work. Lucifer carried out the experiments for Bowker and Collier with the relaxed, tolerant manner of an adult amusing children.

The improvement in results had been considerable, but Collier had contrived to draw out statistics which were beyond Bowker's understanding and which showed the results to be even better than they were. 'Buy time,' Modesty had said, and Collier was doing that.

His main worry was Seff's evident dislike of Modesty's growing influence over Lucifer. She made no overt use of this, but that it existed was apparent in Lucifer himself. He was less amenable to manipulation by Seff and Bowker now, and from time to time he gave a firm order, as Lucifer, which had to be obeyed. Collier wondered for how long Seff would let this situation develop before deciding that letting Modesty live was a greater disadvantage than it was a benefit.

But for the moment the pressure was off, for Seff was otherwise preoccupied. Another of his victims had agreed to pay, and tonight a pick-up would be made at sea, forty miles to the west. Seff and his colleagues were in conference at this moment. There was not only the pick-up to discuss. Jack Wish had returned after twelve days' absence on the grim business that was his contribution to Seff's scheme, and he had his report to make.

Modesty halted, waiting for Collier as he covered the last few paces between them, then she turned and began to walk slowly with him up the slope towards the cliff top.

'Where's the boyfriend?' Collier asked, and was surprised to find that he spoke without underlying bitterness.

'Asleep.'

'At mid afternoon?' Collier lifted an eyebrow. 'He's usually swimming with you now.'

'He's discovered that there are other things you can do in the afternoon, apart from swimming. And he sleeps like a log afterwards.'

Collier sighed. 'A trip to the moon?'

'Now don't make a big production of it, Steve.'

'I'm not. Much to my amazement, I'm not. Maybe it's because we've been spared any more of those nauseating puppet shows since you took him on.'

'Yes. It's worth it for that. I'm afraid the Seffs don't like it, though.' She looked at him with quick appraisal and gave him a half smile. 'You're doing fine, Steve. That attack of the jitters seems to have passed.'

'Your lecture helped. But don't misjudge me. I still have all the attributes of a fervent coward.'

'You hide them well. In fact I'm getting worried about your new technique with the Seffs. For a moment last night I thought you'd gone just too far.'

'Impossible. They're entirely humourless.'

'That doesn't make them any less dangerous.'

'I know. And I don't forget it. But I have to sit at the same table as the Seffs, and that's an ordeal that unseats the gimbals of the soul. I have to do something to keep my food down.'

It was true that the Seffs were humourless. And, as a counter to his fear and loathing of them, Collier had started to twist their tails for his own satisfaction. His manner to them was donnish and elaborately polite, but the content of his conversation was derisive insult. The Seffs were blind to this.

Despite herself Modesty laughed suddenly, remembering.

After dinner last night, when Lucifer had gone to play his records——

'Have you ever had experience of a true haunting by any chance, Mr. Collier?' Regina quavered as she poured coffee with an unsteady hand.

'A haunting?' Collier rolled the word round his tongue, considered, then continued reluctantly, 'Not a visual experience. No, Mrs. Seff, I would not claim that I had ever *seen* what one might loosely call a ghost or phantom.'

Seff looked up. 'Your emphasis seems to indicate some other kind of experience, Mr. Collier.'

'Perhaps. But I would not care to be dogmatic.' A pause. 'There was an aunt of mine who worked as a conductress on a bus during the war...' Collier shrugged, then sipped his coffee as if unwilling to amplify the story.

'On a bus? What happened?' Regina asked curiously.

'It was a number thirty-six bus.' Collier shook his head and sighed faintly as if troubled by sad memories. 'Plying between Hither Green and Kilburn, if I remember rightly. One night, passing Victoria Station, it was unfortunately destroyed by the blast of a bomb falling close by.' He looked at Regina. 'We have always felt proud of the fact that when my aunt's body was found, she was still holding fast to her ticket punch.'

Modesty saw Bowker catch his breath. He was half delighted, half terrified by Collier's excursions of this nature.

After a few seconds——

'That would probably be a natural reaction rather than a conscious act of—ah—loyal duty,' Seff said, and both Bowker and Modesty relaxed.

'I beg your pardon,' Collier said coldly, 'but my aunt was a very great patriot. Her name was Florence.'

Seff stirred his coffee, frowning. 'What has her name to do with the matter?'

'Nothing. I only mention it as a matter of information

since your good lady displayed interest. But let us say no more.'

Regina looked apologetically at Seff, then turned to Collier again. 'But the haunting...' Her frail voice was baffled. 'What was the haunting, Mr. Collier?'

'Well...' Collier allowed himself to be mollified by her interest. 'I make no firm assertion, Mrs. Seff. But ten years later I was on top of a number thirty-six bus near Victoria, at the very place and on the day and hour that my aunt laid down her life. Ten-thirty, p.m. I was quite alone, yet a dozen times I distinctly heard the ting of a ticket punch, up and down those empty seats.'

Modesty heard Bowker mutter, 'Oh, Christ...'

But the gravity and the reluctance with which Collier had related the absurd story carried remarkable conviction.

'An aural illusion, I would imagine,' said Seff.

'Well, I don't know, Seffy.' Regina took out her menthol stick. 'I remember when I was at school, there was a girl who distinctly saw her aunt...'

Now, as she walked with Collier, Modesty said, 'I know it does you a power of good, but just don't go too far, Steve. The Seffs may have a blind spot, but if Bowker loses control and sniggers you'll be sunk.'

'I'll be careful.'

'Good. Have you had any ideas about escaping?'

'A dozen. All no good. But just now I'm concentrating on the idea of trying to find Seff's main transmitter.'

'Ah.' She was pleased. 'Go on.'

'Well, I thought if that could be put out of action, and if we could somehow steal one of the dinghies and just get a few miles clear we'd be out of range of the portables. Then we could go ashore, cut these bastard poison capsules out of each other, and...' He ran a hand through his hair and shrugged apologetically. 'Sorry, but it's all pretty vague after that. I just thought that if the first part worked we'd have a chance. I'd sooner be slogging through the jungle than just waiting for Seff to put us down.'

They walked on a few paces, and he said, 'All right. I know it's a lousy idea.'

'Is it? I've been looking for the main transmitter myself, and for the same reason.'

He laughed and felt ridiculously pleased. 'I must be learning fast. I think the damn thing's in that big workroom of Seff's. Two days ago I actually got in there—just followed Bowker in when he was going to talk to Seff. They didn't chuck me out. But if it's there, it's hidden.'

Modesty nodded. 'I got in myself, with Lucifer. Just for a few minutes.'

'No luck?'

'Not with the transmitter.'

Collier shot a glance at her. They had reached the cliff top now. She sat down, her legs curled beneath her, and motioned him to do the same.

'I've cut through one bar of my window,' she said absently, looking out over the bay. 'Your turn now, Steve. If you work a couple of hours each night you can do it in ten days.'

He stared at her blankly. 'What do I use—my teeth?'

'On the ground.'

He looked down. Close to his hand was a four-inch half round file.

'I picked it up in Seff's workroom,' she said, 'and he hasn't missed it. Put it under your shirt now and hide it in your room as soon as you get the chance.'

Casually, very conscious of the watching Moros in the background, Collier covered the file with his hand. He reached inside his shirt and scratched his ribs before bringing his empty hand out again.

'Cut through the top of the bar, starting from the outside,' Modesty said, still looking out to sea. 'Plug the cut with spit and dirt when you finish each night.'

'Just the top?'

'Yes. They're long bars. Enough leverage to bend one aside if the top's cut through. Let me know when you're set, and I'll get to you.'

'How?'

'Out of Lucifer's window—the bathroom, where I've cut the bar, then up to the roof, across, and down to your window. I've studied it.'

'Will I need ten days?'

'Pretty well. With a Moro sleeping outside your door it has to be taken quietly. The noise won't be a problem if you get a little grease from the tin Garcia keeps in his shack, and don't use too much pressure when you file. Those bars are only mild steel. All right?'

'All right.' Collier found that his mouth was dry. 'I don't think my salivary glands are working too well, so I might be a bit short of spit. But it's nice to know the bars aren't made of beryllium, isn't it?'

THE twin screws of the cargo boat were still. The first mate came down the bridge ladder to the main deck. In the darkness, John Dall and Willie Garvin stood by the rail. Dall wore a navy blue shirt and wrinkled slacks, with a peaked cap pushed back on his head. Willie Garvin was in black. There was no lightness in the face of either man; but of the two, Dall's face was the harder and grimmer.

The first mate said. 'Just coming up to 2130 hours local time, and we're on the right spot, Mr. Dall.'

'Okay. Go ahead.'

Figures moved in the darkness, and a donkey engine chattered. A derrick swung smoothly round, halted, and the big pear-shaped container suspended from it moved down towards the flat dark surface of the sea.

Samarkand was a ten thousand tonner, a ship of the Cresset Line, which was a part of Dall's empire. She should now have been on her way to San Francisco, but had been held at Yokohama on special instructions. There she had taken on a number of passengers arriving by air. One was the fair-haired Englishman called Garvin, another was the pilot of the Beaver seaplane which now stood in a makeshift hangar on the main deck amidships; there was Dall himself, the big boss, and the rest were a dozen tough, competent-looking men Dall had brought with him.

The *Samarkand*'s captain had fought in the Pacific and later taken part in the Inchon landings of the Korean war. He had seen men of this stamp before, and would have laid long odds that they were ex-marines.

There were weapons in the ship's armoury now, and rumours were rife among the crew. The captain himself was much intrigued and not a little worried, but he hid his anxiety and asked no questions of John Dall. A shrewd man, he had an uneasy suspicion that a situation might arise in which he would receive an order which involved hazarding his ship. If and when that happened he would fight Dall, regardless of the outcome. But until then he was content to hold his peace.

A voice said, 'Let go.' The derrick's cable went slack and the big black container sank beneath the surface.

Dall said, 'Will you give my compliments to the skipper and say I'd like him to head south for two miles then heave to again.'

'South two miles and heave to, Sir.' The first mate vanished into the darkness. Dall leaned on the rail and looked at the small black dinghy which hung from the davits. Only eight feet long, it had a mainsail and a jib and carried a small 3.9 h.p. Mercury outboard engine fitted with a Bray silencer. There was a spare can of petrol in the boat, two bottles of water and some food. A bag six feet long and a small rucksack between them held a Tyne folding canoe, a sports two-seater.

'You can get in with a canoe where you can't take a dinghy,' Willie Garvin had said.

A small black kitbag was propped against the rail beside Willie now. Dall had watched him pack it, and knew that it held a small but potent variety of weapons and combat equipment, including a miniature radio transceiver.

'I still don't see what we'd lose by going in fast and hard with all the boys,' Dall said.

'We can't risk it.' Willie's voice was patient. 'I got to find out about the bugger-factor first. Modesty didn't tip me off for nothing. Besides, you can't go in fast and hard anywhere in these waters unless you want to lose your ship. Ask the skipper.'

Dall lit a thin cigar and broke the match in his fingers. 'It's been a long time since she was taken. A hell of a time. The bugger-factor might have vanished by now.'

'It might not. We've got to play it quiet till we know.'

The ship was moving at half speed. Dall looked out into the

213

blackness and said, 'She could be dead. She could have been dead this last month, Willie.'

'Yes.'

'So then what do you do?'

Willie turned and rested his arms on the rail. In the light from a deck lamp his face was strangely serene. 'If I find she's dead, John, then there'll be no need to keep pussyfooting around. I can 'ave a go.'

'And get yourself killed,' Dall said. 'Call us on the radio and wait for us, Willie. Please.'

'I'll call you.'

'And you'll wait?'

'No. I've 'ad enough waiting.' The voice was soft, but for a moment Dall saw the killing flare of a berserker in Willie's eyes. Then the look was gone and Willie said calmly, 'But I don't think she's dead, John. I'd 'ave a feeling if she was. Anyway, I'll call you as soon as I know the score one way or the other. But don't sweat if I'm not on the air by dawn. It might take a day or two before I can find a way to make contact with Modesty.'

'If you find her at all. If Jack Wish and these others are where you think they are.'

'They can't be far away, not if I've guessed right about the pick-up.'

Dall nodded. Incredulous at first, he was sure now that Willie's guess was right. His eye fell on the small black kitbag. 'You brought in three crates of gear by air to Yokohama,' he said, frowning.

Willie's lips parted a little. It wasn't the grin Dall remembered of old, but it was the nearest Willie ever got to it now. 'That was all the gear and spares we ever used or ever thought we might, John. I'm working blind, so I don't know what we might need.'

'But you're only taking that?' Dall nodded towards the kitbag.

'It's got to be a small boat. I can't take more. But we might want the other stuff later.'

'Later?' Dall stared, shaken. 'Surely to God if you find her alive you'll bring her back?'

Willie looked at him. 'The only sure thing is that we 'aven't got a bloody clue what's wrong. All I can do for a start is make contact with Modesty and find out how she's nailed down. Maybe I can't bring 'er out with me. If it was easy she wouldn't need any 'elp. But she'll know what's to be done, and I've got to 'ave the gear ready for whatever she says.'

Dall started to ask another question, then closed his mouth and shook his head. It was no use trying to understand. Willie Garvin's reasoning was founded in instinct rather than in logic, and it was on a plane where Dall could tread only blindly. He had once heard Tarrant speak about the frustration that came from listening to Modesty and Willie speculate on an opponent's plans. In a void without facts they seemed able to make a series of deductions, wherein they alone could understand the chain of reasoning involved.

So it was with Willie Garvin now. In some curious way he could discern not the details but the shape of the problem that lay ahead.

The ship was hardly moving now. The first mate appeared and said, 'Two miles, Mr. Dall.'

'Okay. We'll have that dinghy lowered.' Dall turned back to Willie. 'How long do we wait for you at the rendezvous?'

'Make it four days. If I'm not with you by then and 'aven't called you on the radio, you can reckon I went wrong somewhere.'

The small boat hung level with the deck. Willie dumped his kitbag in and climbed over the rail. Settling himself in the stern he looked up at Dall. 'Best thing then would be to buy in on another drop. You could play it your own way next time. There won't be a bugger-factor to stop you.'

Dall nodded. He was thinking how long four days could seem, and his head ached with tension. He forced his lips apart in a semblance of a smile and said, 'All right. But do me a favour, Willie. Just don't go wrong this time.'

Willie Garvin lifted his hand in a sketchy salute. The

pulleys creaked, and the little boat slid down to meet the sea.

Pluto and Belial glided smoothly and easily through the liquid night, a thousand feet above the surface of the earth. They were playing The Game, and it gave them pleasure. No human eye could have penetrated the surrounding blackness, but Pluto and Belial were not human and this was their own element in which they moved now. There had been a time when their race lived upon earth, but that was countless eons past.

The Master they adored had taught them The Game, and He would reward them when it was over. He would talk to them, and fondle them, and they would feed on the dead from His own hands.

Together Pluto and Belial climbed, soaring briefly through the air, then swooped down again.

Three miles away a small black triangle of sail swung over before the night breeze as Willie Garvin put the dinghy on a northerly tack. There was a broad sickle of moon in the sky. The lights of the *Samarkand* had dwindled and vanished well over an hour since. He was alone under the great star-pierced dome of blackness which rested on the quiet sea.

Willie Garvin might have felt very small and insignificant in the emptiness, but he did not. It was many years since he had been vulnerable to the atmosphere created by his surroundings; he was aware of it but not disquieted.

Now, sitting with a hand resting lightly on the tiller, he was quietly alert, his thoughts focused on the idea that had taken shape in his mind that evening in Stockholm, an idea based on a blend of knowledge, half-knowledge, instinct, and patient deduction.

He had spent two hours on the phone, first locating and then talking to Dr. Royle, a curator of the British Museum of Natural History and one of the world's foremost experts on the subject that now occupied Willie's mind.

Thank God the line had been good and Dr. Royle had been helpful beyond all expectation, even though he must have been more than curious at the stream of questions from an unknown caller in Stockholm.

'It'd take too long to go over all the details,' Willie had said, 'but believe me, Doc, it's urgent. Life an' death maybe. Can I fire away?'

'I'll answer whatever I can.' The voice, quiet and positive, evoked a comforting confidence.

Dolphins?

Yes. Dr. Royle had carried out many experiments with these cetaceans, and had naturally studied all the work of other experts—Fraser, Kellogg, Schevill, Norris, Lawrence, and a dozen more.

How trainable was the dolphin?

To a very high degree. Some might say an astonishing degree. The dolphin, like other whales, was a mammal which had adapted to an aquatic existence in pre-history. The brain was large, exceptionally convoluted, and in fact bore a remarkable resemblance to the human brain. In the Wirz classification, the highest category of brain development was to be found in man, elephant and Odontocetes. The last included the dolphin. Dogs and even monkeys were graded lower. In short, the dolphin was intelligent, very amenable to training, and seemed to have a great affinity for humans. It was of interest that these creatures loved to play games, and would even show a tendency to sulk if not allowed to display some particular trick of behaviour they had learned.

Could one take a trained dolphin from its home waters to other waters, from the Caribbean to the North Sea for instance, without detriment to its abilities?

That might depend on the species. But the Bottlenose Dolphin had a fairly universal distribution. It would be equally at home in the North Atlantic or the Indian Ocean.

Was it correct that the dolphin's hearing was of a high order?

Ah yes, most certainly. In underwater hearing, the powers of the dolphin were fantastic by human standards. The auditory centres of the brain and the organs of hearing were highly specialised...

Here followed a long and technical explanation. Patiently Willie had sought elucidation of abstruse biological terms. Patiently the abstrusities had been explained to him.

The dolphin could hear sounds not only in the human audio frequencies, from sixteen cycles to fifteen kilocycles per second; it could also detect sounds well into the ultrasonic frequencies, up to a hundred and twenty kilocycles and beyond. This was second only to the bat in range of hearing. And, like the bat, dolphins used sonar or echo-location. They emitted sounds, from low to high frequencies, picked up the reflection of those sounds, and, with the astonishing phase-sensitivity of their two ears, they could pinpoint underwater objects with complete accuracy.

At what range?

Dr. Royle had given this question some thought before answering that nobody had yet made controlled tests as to the precise range of the dolphin's sonar response.

Forgetting sonar response, over what range could a dolphin hear sound underwater?

That would clearly depend on the intensity of the sound. Did Mr. Garvin appreciate that sound travelled through water four times as fast as through air? That the absorption, or attenuation, was far less? That sound waves in water, though having only one sixtieth of the *displacement* amplitude of the same sound waves in air, had sixty times the *pressure* amplitude?

Yes, Mr. Garvin was fairly well up on the physics side. He realised that the range of hearing would depend on the intensity of the sound created. But was there any general information on this, any clues as to the dolphin's range of hearing in terms of distance?

Dr. Royle had pondered for a while, with the natural caution of the scientist dealing in generalities. Certainly there were clues. It was on record that a dolphin in a two hundred metre pool could be attracted by dropping a teaspoonful of water into the pool; it was difficult to translate this accurately in terms of very long distances, but during aerial observation a school of grey whales had been seen to turn suddenly away from a number of killer whales, their enemies, at a distance of several miles. This could be due to echo-location by the creatures, or to their picking up sounds emitted by the killer whales. And the research ship *Calypso* had filmed a sequence in which sperm whales came from many miles away to rescue an injured calf, undoubtedly in response to the calf's distress signals. These signals would be of far less intensity than could be produced electrically, of course; and the hearing of dolphins would certainly not be less acute than that of other whales. Was this kind of clue any help to Mr. Garvin?

A great help. With a suitable underwater transmitter, would Dr. Royle think it possible for a trained dolphin or dolphins to locate the transmitter at a distance of, say, thirty miles? And home in on it?

If the intensity and the frequency were right, the idea was certainly possible. But there was one snag. With an intensity sufficient to be heard by a dolphin at such a distance, it might cause pain and distress as the dolphin drew nearer.

But if the transmitter were so constructed that over a period of two or three hours the intensity diminished?

Ah, then the snag would be overcome. But the question of the transmitter was outside Dr. Royle's field. Mr. Garvin would have to consult a sonar expert as to whether this would be possible.

Willie Garvin, remembering the device in the container he had examined, was able to assure the doctor that there was no technical difficulty about a mechanically reducing intensity. If Dr. Royle could bear with him a little longer he had only three more questions...

First, how deep could a dolphin dive?

Well, normally they skipped along the surface in four or five shallow undulations, and then sounded to about ten fathoms for perhaps five minutes. The Bottlenose Dolphin could sound for thirteen to fifteen minutes. But there was no biological reason why a dolphin could not go deeper than ten fathoms if need be.

Twenty? Thirty fathoms?

Biologically quite possible. More than possible with skilled training.

The second question. Could a dolphin be fitted with some sort of harness, so that it could tow an object behind it?

Certainly, if the object were not too heavy. Dolphins had been fitted with harness in numerous experiments, notably at the U.S. Naval Ordnance Test Station at China Lake, California. They were powerful creatures. The object would have to be floating, or sufficiently near the surface for the dolphin to break surface and breathe, of course.

And finally, could a dolphin be transported to another part of the world by air, in a tank or something of that sort?

No need for a tank. Dolphins had been transported by air on several occasions. They were simply strapped to a foam bed and kept damp with wet blankets. There was a photograph of one in this situation which Mr. Garvin could see if he happened to be in London soon.

Willie had thanked Dr. Royle warmly. The photograph would not be necessary. He had all the information he needed, and was deeply grateful for it.

Now, a little over four weeks later, Willie Garvin sat at the tiller of the small black dinghy moving at two or three knots on the velvet sea. Beyond the horizon to the north lay Mindoro, to the south the Cuyo Islands; ahead, Panay; astern, to the west, the Calamianes. He was a tiny speck in the vast archipelago of the Philippines which rose from the sea in a scattering of thousands of islands, stretching to either side of him for five hundred miles.

He thought about dolphins, and about the container. He needed no technical information on the transmitter, for he had examined the one in the laboratory at Uxbridge. Both container and transmitter were precisely designed to fit the pattern of his ideas. He did not yet know in detail how a dolphin, or dolphins, took the container in tow; but, given their remarkable capacity for training, this would not be difficult to encompass.

When a line was caught in the snap hook on top of the container, tilting the whole thing sideways, the lead shot would begin to trickle out like sand in an hour-glass—except that the lead shot would vanish into the sea, and the container would become progressively lighter over the next ten minutes until at last it floated only a few feet below the surface.

In the heavy time of waiting for word from Dall, Willie had learned more about dolphins. There were even experiments in verbal communication going on now. Successful experiments. Throw three different objects into a pool, call for one of them, and your dolphin would sort out the right object and bring it to you. The limit of a dolphin's ability to learn and to perform had still to be found. But every new fact that Willie discovered fitted neatly into the pattern of the pick-ups.

Dolphins could detect any normal tracer that might secretly be fitted to a container, and they would be trained to react by leaving such a container alone.

A dolphin's sonar faculty was so perfect that it could even differentiate between two species of small fish of the same size. It would easily detect any addition to the exterior of a container; the suspended depth charges, for instance. And it would be conditioned to leave any suspect container alone.

By similar conditioning, dolphins could scour the surrounding waters to ensure that no ship was close by before performing their task. Willie's own small dinghy was a full two miles from the dropping point, and he was not using the outboard motor. The dinghy might not escape detection, but since it was no bigger than a shark, or many another marine creature, it would not be a factor to prohibit a conditioned dolphin from making the pick-up.

In harness, a dolphin could tow one of the normal containers at perhaps three or four knots, once the initial inertia was overcome. With the heavy, gold-bearing container, a simple but effective drive had been added, to operate at a particular depth and when the container was tilted. Possibly more than one dolphin was used anyway, which would give a better speed back to base.

It all fitted, and Willie Garvin knew he was right. He had maddened Tarrant by refusing to give a hint of his ideas, for fear that Tarrant might feel bound to interfere and take official action.

But Dall knew, and if this attempt failed he would remain in the field to take future action.

Willie Garvin looked down at the compass and edged the tiller over to keep the small boat moving in a two mile radius round the dropping point.

It was an hour since the sound had stopped, but Pluto and Belial had already found the big, unalive thing which must be taken to The Master. There were no wrong sounds coming from it, and its shape was right, so they had moved far away before beginning to spiral in again, searching the waters, sending out the creaking groans which would be reflected to their hypersensitive ears from any solid object.

The plaited black nylon rope connecting the harnesses they wore was thirty feet long. They were so used to being linked that even without the harness they tended to swim as a pair. Now they rose briefly to the surface, drew in air, and plunged down in the long dive they had been trained for by their Master.

The sounds they made, varying from creaks to clicks, were reflected back to their ears and gave them the precise position of the big quiet thing that hung in the water. They circled it so that it passed slowly between them, and then felt the sudden weight dragging at their bodies. Now was the time to swim with full strength, forward but rising as the weight grew less.

Ten minutes later and almost a mile away, with their streamlined burden moving smoothly now, the sleek bodies broke the surface. Pluto and Belial could not leap clear of the water, as they would have done without the weight of their load, but that did not matter. They undulated in and out of

222

the water, breathing, then sounded again and drove steadily forward a fathom or two below the surface.

Willie Garvin rose from the thwart, staring ahead. In the moonlight he could see the edge of a broad green streak that coloured the sea. It spread in a wide band across the heading of the dinghy, running to port in the direction of the dropping point, the colour deepening towards the middle of the streak.

The powdered green dye Willie had added to the cavity containing the lead shot was filtering out now. He reached the middle of the spreading green band, brought the boat to starboard and took a careful bearing. The long lane of greenish water extended ahead of him and would guide him for several miles before the canister containing the powder was empty. With the sea calm, dispersal would be slow. He could check his bearing again when the green streak began to fade away.

The wind was steady on the starboard quarter, so he would not need to use the silenced engine. That was good. He trimmed the mainsail and settled back with his arm resting on the tiller.

17

'DON'T wait for me, Lucifer. I just want to fix my hair,' Modesty Blaise said.

'All right.' He smiled at her, then ran along the beach, first over the dry sand and then over the damp sand where the rollers had curved round, their flanks against the cliff, and lapped over part of the beach. A big roller came and Lucifer turned, letting it sweep him up and suck him out past the raft.

Modesty wound her single thick plait of hair into a club and slipped a rubber band over it. She was looking down at a patch of sand between a few low rocks where she and Lucifer usually lay between swims.

Two nights ago a pick-up had been made. Successfully. It was only during the morning of the next day that she had heard by chance that the man who had paid up was John Dall.

Seff, Bowker and Jack Wish had been exultant. So had Modesty Blaise. She knew beyond all doubt that Dall could have done this for one reason only, and she also guessed that when the drop was made Willie Garvin must have been no more than thirty or forty miles from the house where she lay. Garcia's dolphins could not tow a container beyond that limit.

Willie Garvin was still closer now. The patch of sand had been carefully smoothed and its surface bore a few squiggles, as if someone had doodled on it with a finger. The squiggles were Arabic words, and she knew that somehow, from somewhere, Willie Garvin had watched her on the beach the day before, the day following pick-up, and had chosen this as the best place to leave his message.

Since last night she had been alert for a sign from him.

Now it had come. She scrubbed a foot across the scrawl on the sand and made the affirmative sign with a casual movement of her right arm, in case Willie should be watching now—perhaps from one of the peaked, rocky arms of the bay.

Kneeling, she slid from the hem of her dress the rolled cigarette packet on which she had carefully written during the night while Lucifer slept. The Moro guard at the end of the beach was watching Lucifer dive from the raft. She looked for the red stone that the message on the sand had spoken of. It was the size of a football and lay embedded in sand close to the foot of the cliff. Rolling it aside, she slipped the cigarette packet underneath and settled the rock in place.

Rising, she turned and ran down the beach to the water.

Night had drawn its purple-black veil over the bay.

Willie Garvin came slowly to his feet at last. He had spent two hours reaching his goal from the point where he had first hidden the dinghy over forty hours earlier, a mile along the coast to the south and rear of the house.

The journey tonight had been tedious. First there had been the jungle, then the long wait on its fringe while he studied the patrol pattern of the Moro guards, and finally he had spent the last hour on his stomach, inching forward across open ground with only scraps of cover.

Now he stood in the angle formed by the south wing of the house and the stem of the T which ran back to the steep grey mountain behind. He wore his knives in the light leather chest harness under his black shirt, and carried a thin flat box of first aid equipment in the big thigh-pocket of his trousers. Modesty's note, picked up at midnight from under the rock on the beach, had warned him to travel light but to bring every item of medical gear available.

After some thought he had buckled on a holster with a ·44 Magnum for Modesty, but he had left the kitbag with the rest of the combat equipment hidden by the edge of the jungle, where the ground became rocky and the trees sparse.

It was three in the morning.

His hand moved across the angle of the wall and found a black nylon rope, knotted at short intervals. He grinned, not showing his teeth, and began to draw himself up the wall to the barred window above.

As his head rose over the sill he saw the outline of her face through the bars. The shutters and window beyond them had been hinged back within. She reached through, guided his right hand to the top of an end bar, and began to push. The bar gave slightly. Willie hooked his left arm through the other bars and heaved with his right. When the cut bar had moved out three inches at the top he applied sideways pressure until it lay over at an angle.

To squeeze his bulk through the fifteen inch gap took a full minute, with Modesty supporting the weight of his body as he edged his hips through.

He stood in a bathroom, facing her. She wore a man's silk dressing gown, too big for her, and she was holding both his hands tightly. He could not see her face clearly in the darkness.

She let go and closed the shutters. When she put on the light he shot her a look of query, but she smiled.

'It's all right, Willie love.' Her voice was low but not a whisper. 'I have the light on and off half the night. The Moros are used to it. I only closed the shutter so they wouldn't see that bent bar.'

He nodded, jerked a thumb at the inner door and again lifted his eyebrows in query. She opened the door and beckoned him to look. In the soft red light of the bedside lamp Lucifer lay asleep on the bed.

Willie looked slowly from the sleeping figure to Modesty's face at his shoulder. She drew down her lips in a little grimace and shrugged.

Closing the door, she said, 'He won't wake till dawn unless there's an earthquake.' She moved to the bathroom stool and gestured for him to sit on the edge of the bath, then sat looking at him quietly for long seconds before reaching out to lay her cupped hand gently against his cheek.

'Poor Willie.'

'I been a bit worried,' he confessed. 'But it's okay now. What's the score, Princess?'

'Let's have your side first. In short-hand. We haven't too much time, but I must know.'

His story of all that he had thought, assumed, and done since the moment he had last seen her on Sylt was soon told. When he had finished she looked at him soberly for long seconds and said, 'My God, you've done well. I told Steve Collier you wouldn't be standing still, but I put it a lot too low. Does John Dall know about the dolphins?'

'He knows what I figured and he checked up on dolphins 'imself. After that 'e could take the dolphin bit easier than the bit about someone predicting deaths.'

'It's true, though. Lucifer does it.' She nodded towards the door. 'He doesn't know what he's doing. The big brain behind it all is a man called Seff. He spent two years on dry run predictions with Lucifer, and at the same time he was making the containers and dumping them at strategic points around the world in warehouses. It's just about the way we guessed. Lucifer predicts natural deaths. Seff chooses rich victims from people not on the death list, and puts the squeeze on them. Jack Wish takes care of any mistakes Lucifer makes, or any victim who doesn't pay up. You have to know this in case I don't get out, Willie.'

He stared, shaken. 'In case——?'

'Yes. But only in case.' Leaning forward she took his hands. 'Listen carefully, Willie. There's quite a bit to tell.'

She spoke for five minutes, and he did not interrupt. Her account of the way in which Lucifer's precognition had defeated her in combat, in the house on Sylt, brought shock to his eyes; but it was the revelation of the cyanide capsule embedded in her back which hit him hardest. This came early in her story, yet even when she had finished his body was still tense as a giant spring, his grip still hurt her hands, and his tanned face was yellow with pallor.

'God Almighty,' he breathed in a frightful whisper. 'The

bastards! The—the bloody——' He could find no words, and shook his head. 'I'll 'ave them for it, Princess.'

'Yes. But later. You're going to need a steady hand now.' She sat watching him, feeling his grip loosen as he slowly forced his muscles to relax. At last she drew her hands away. He inhaled deeply, then took out the first aid box and opened it.

'We've got no novocaine, Princess. There's morphia, but——'

'No. I'll put myself out, Willie.'

He nodded. 'No scalpel either. Just scissors and tweezers. I'll 'ave to use one of me knives.'

'A razor blade will be easier to handle. I've had one hidden away for a long time now, but we can use Lucifer's.' She opened the bathroom cabinet, took out a safety razor and removed the blade.

Willie washed it carefully in strong antiseptic poured from a flat plastic bottle into a shallow tray, then washed the scissors and tweezers. He laid out swabs, coagulant, a threaded needle and a small bottle of viscous liquid which would form a gel of transparent skin. His movements were brisk and competent now. He scrubbed his hands for several minutes in the basin, then immersed his fingers in the antiseptic.

Modesty said, 'It was a small incision. I don't think there'll be any scar left now, but I can tell you just where to cut.'

She put the bath stool in front of her, knelt down, let the dressing gown fall from her body, and bent forward so that her bare torso rested on the stool. Her left hand reached awkwardly up her back, and she drew the thumbnail against her flesh just to one side of the left shoulderblade.

'There, Willie. With the incision angling to my left.'

He swabbed the area with antiseptic, then his fingers probed her flesh gently. After a few moments he said, 'I can feel it. White, you said?'

'Yes. The capsule's white.' She knelt up and rested her hands in her lap. 'Give me three minutes, Willie.'

228

He sat on the edge of the bath, holding his cleansed hands away from his clothes. Gradually the rise and fall of her breasts grew slower. Her eyes seemed to be fixed on some infinitely distant point. When two minutes had passed her breathing had slowed to such an extent that the movement of her chest was almost imperceptible. By the end of three minutes she might have been a statue carved in ivory, yet there was no rigidity in her erect body. Every muscle slept and was still.

Willie Garvin bent to peer at one eye. The pupil was widely dilated. He cupped a hand to shield it from the light, and there was no reaction. Satisfied, he took her body and eased it gently forward until her torso rested on the low stool once again. Taking the razor blade, he closed the focus of his mind to a pinpoint of concentration.

The first delicate movement of the blade left a thin red line on her back. He cut deeper, swabbed with his free hand and cut again, this time going down through the fatty layer beneath the skin. His incision was an inch long. The flow of blood was minimal and sluggish, for her heartbeat was down to a third of its normal rate in the coma she had induced.

A clearer view would be needed to extract the capsule than had been needed for the insertion. Willie put the razor blade back in the little tray of antiseptic and used two pieces of plaster to draw back the flesh on either side of the incision, holding it open.

Now he could see the muscle fibres. They would split with the grain readily enough, but he had to find the right place. Sweating, he took up the scissors and probed delicately; their points were blunter and less dangerous than the razor blade.

No ... he could feel the capsule a fraction to the left. He withdrew the scissors, swabbed, eased the points into the pink fibre again and opened the scissors slightly. Between the divided fibres he saw the edge of something white, and relief swept him. He lengthened the split, held the scissors open

229

with one hand, and reached for the tweezers. Now it was a matter of teasing the deadly capsule out without rupturing it, and he would have given an eye at this moment in return for a blunt, curved spatula or a pair of good forceps.

Twice the tweezers lost their grip and slipped, but he dared not use any greater pressure with them. Again the tweezers slipped but this time the capsule moved. He was able to take a firmer grip...

At last it was done. The small white capsule of death lay intact on Modesty's tanned back. Willie picked it up, dropped it in the wash-basin, and removed the two strips of plaster.

A dusting of amino acid antiseptic powder. Two stitches of nylon thread. A coating of plastic skin. No dressing.

Willie Garvin sat back on his heels and mopped his sweating face with a towel. He rolled the swabs and plaster in toilet paper and pushed them down the trap of the lavatory. Again he washed his hands, then packed away the first aid kit.

The operation had been so minor as scarcely to merit the word, and her shoulder would stand up to anything short of a severe test; but he had once removed a bullet sunk deep in her thigh, and it had cost him far less in mental stress than the last ten minutes had cost. He looked at the capsule in the basin with sick loathing.

Modesty still knelt with her body bent forward and resting on the low stool, her head turned to one side. The open eyes were blank. Willie lifted her gently until she was kneeling upright. He supported her back with one arm and a knee, taking care to avoid the wound, and began to drive the heel of his other hand rhythmically against her body with a kneading motion, just below the heart. Soon her rate of breathing increased and the heartbeat grew faster.

Three minutes later she was standing, the dressing gown about her, looking at the small white capsule in the basin. She began to shiver, and turned to Willie. Quietly he put his arms about her, holding her until the shivering had passed.

After a little while, her head still on his shoulder, she whispered, 'What's a supernacular wine?'

'Ah ... well, it's a wine worthy of being drunk to the last drop.'

'We'll get a barrel of it once we're home.' She straightened up. He saw that she was smiling and that her face was cleansed of all tension now. 'Thanks, Willie love. It can't have been easy. I hope I can do as well when it's my turn.

'Your turn?'

'There's still Steve Collier. We daren't make a move till we've debugged him, and we can't get to him tonight. I haven't got a way figured out and it's too late, anyway. You'll only just have time to get clear before first light.'

'Oh, Jesus!' Willie stared in horror. 'You mean you're *staying* 'ere?'

'We can't start a rumble. One touch of a switch will kill Steve. And if I disappear it's going to be ten times harder to get to Steve and cut his capsule out.' She watched him absorb the truth of her words. 'Go back to where you hid the boat when you first came here, Willie. Lie low, and check under that red stone on the beach each night for a message from me. When Steve's cut through a bar we can reach him. It should be any day now. I'll tell him to work longer at it. You'd better call John Dall. Don't stay on the air a second longer than you can help. Just tell him okay but wait.'

Willie rubbed his head hard with the heel of his hand, scowling a little. At last he said reluctantly, 'Okay, Princess. D'you want me to leave you the Magnum?'

She thought for a moment. 'It's tempting, but no. The Seffs and Bowker have us covered with their transmitters all the time, even when we're together at meals. Especially then. And Wish is lightning with a gun. I couldn't take all four of them fast enough. There's Lucifer, too. I don't know that his precognition would beat me if he wasn't personally threatened, but I can't risk it. I've nowhere to carry the Magnum, anyway. They only allow me to wear a cheong sam, and that's no good for hiding a gun. I had a bad enough time hiding that nylon rope.' She stood thinking, a finger to her lips. 'Leave the first aid kit, though—just in case I can get to Steve Collier on my own somehow.'

'Okay. How's the back feel now?'

She rotated her shoulder experimentally. 'Good. A little sore locally, but fine generally.' She smiled. 'Better than when Bowker did it.'

Two minutes later Willie Garvin eased himself through the window. Straightening the bar was harder than bending it, but at last it was done well enough to pass casual inspection. When he had climbed to the ground he signalled with three tugs. Modesty drew up the rope she had stolen from Garcia's store and hid it on top of the tall, ornate wardrobe in the bedroom, together with the little first aid box.

Lucifer still slept.

She returned to the bathroom, looked at the smeared white capsule, then picked it up and flushed it down the lavatory. After checking carefully that no sign of Willie's visit remained, she went into the bedroom, slipped the dressing gown off, and put on her green cheong sam to hide the new scar on her back. Keeping this hidden from Lucifer might call for some verbal ingenuity, but she was practised in that now. And discovery by Lucifer would not necessarily be disastrous. The vital thing was to prevent discovery by Seff or his colleagues.

Willie Garvin was two hundred yards into the jungle. Soon he could bear south to the coast and then make his way along the rocky shoreline to the tiny inlet, no more than a crevice, where the dinghy lay.

He eased through some bushes and reached the long natural mound, about five feet high, which ran in a straight line down through the trees to the shore. It was better, he decided, to cross here and follow the ridge of earth down on the far side. He lifted the black kitbag he had picked up on the jungle fringe, rested it on the crest of the low ridge, and let it slide down on to the soft, rotting vegetation on the other side.

Then a section of the mound leapt and roared and struck

him savagely down. After twenty-five years, the Japanese mine set on the far side of the barrier of earth had found prey.

Willie Garvin did not hear the echoes of the explosion rolling through the quiet pre-dawn air.

18

SEFF had shaved and was dressed in his usual black suit. He stood with his back to a large florid picture, a landscape by a painter rightly unknown, which hung at one end of the long room. Regina sat in a chair near him, dressed but with her sparse grey hair hanging loose. Her pallid cheeks held two small pink blotches of excitement.

At the far end of the room Willie Garvin lay crumpled in an armchair. His torn shirt had been stripped off. The two knives had been taken from the sheaths which lay in echelon across his chest, and the belt with the Magnum had been removed from his waist.

Two Moros stood behind him. One was Sangro, the Moro leader, a big man with a flat face and high cheekbones. At his waist hung a bolo, the traditional sword of the Moros, a terrible sabre-like weapon. The red tuft of hair at its hilt marked Sangro as a chief.

Bowker had been bending over the unconscious man. Now he straightened up and said, 'He's coming round. I can't find any damage apart from superficial scratches and bruises.'

Seff glanced at Jack Wish to make sure he still held a gun trained on Garvin. In Seff's mind was a suspicion that Garvin had come to his senses even before he had been carried into the room, and was foxing, hoping for a break.

The blue eyes opened slowly and Willie Garvin looked round the room. Seff allowed a full minute for him to take in the situation, then said, 'Mr. Wish has identified you. I have questions to ask, and you would do well to answer them accurately. First, how did you find us here, Mr. Garvin?'

Willie Garvin rubbed a hand across his eyes and shook his head. 'I was looking for 'er,' he said thickly.

'For Miss Blaise. Yes. I asked *how* you found us.'

Several minutes earlier, as he played unconscious while strength flowed steadily back into his bruised body, Willie Garvin had prepared his answers. They were designed with the twin aims of keeping John Dall's presence nearby a secret, and confirming Seff's natural assumption that Willie Garvin had stumbled on the Japanese mine while making his approach to the house rather than while leaving it.

'I figured things,' Willie said, letting his eyes wander dazedly. 'The loot. Drugs, ice ... then gold. You got someone 'andling all kinds for you. There's not many can do that, not in a big way. I reckoned it 'ad to be Mr. Wu Smith, in Macao.'

Bowker drew in his breath sharply, and Jack Wish looked startled.

'You got information from Mr. Wu Smith?' Seff's high-pitched voice was abrupt.

'Don't be bloody stupid.' Willie looked with bleary eyes. 'I nailed one of 'is blokes in Macao. Off Wu Smith's boat. Soon twisted this location out of 'im. Then I flew to Manila and 'opped from island to island in a small boat.'

'To whom did you confide your suspicions?' Seff asked.

'Eh? Nobody...'

Sangro said, 'Is right about small boat. We find along shore.'

Seff ignored him, still looking at Willie Garvin. 'You came here without telling *anyone* what you had learned?' There was disbelief in Seff's voice.

'Christ, you're dumb.' Willie gave a contemptuous shrug. 'Tell someone, and there'd be about five bleeding navies round 'ere. I reckoned she might still be alive. But you'd knock 'er off if the balloon went up.'

There was silence for a few seconds, then Wish said, 'It figures, Seff. That's the way they work. And if he *had* told anyone you can bet your goddam life we'd know about it by now.'

'That is my conclusion too, Mr. Wish.' Seff spoke absently. After a moment he went on with seeming irrelevance. 'Garvin throws a knife, I believe?'

Wish grinned. 'Like you've never seen a knife thrown before.'

'I see. Dr. Bowker, will you go and fetch Lucifer and Miss Blaise? And send Collier down too, if you please.'

Willie Garvin leaned forward with sudden eagerness. 'She's 'ere? Alive?'

'For the moment, Mr. Garvin. For the moment. Whether that situation continues will lie very much in your own hands.' Seff offered the full pink-and-white range of his dreadful smile.

Modesty Blaise had heard the explosion and known what it must mean. Tormented and shaken, she had mentally savaged herself for failing to warn Willie of the possibility that mines still lay in the jungle. For an hour she had fought to rally her inner resources against the frightful blow of knowing that Willie Garvin was dead.

At first, soon after the explosion, she had heard the house astir. It would not be easy to make the Moros enter the jungle to investigate, but Seff would do it. And then, after an eternity of fighting cold despair, she had heard the Moros returning to the house, heard Jack Wish's voice calling, and known that by some miracle Willie still lived.

Lucifer had slept through it all. Then he had woken and wanted to make love to her. She was smiling, talking, trying to dissuade him, when Bowker came for them and unbolted the door.

As she entered the big room below with Lucifer she made a snap appreciation. Seff stood at the far end with one hand on the transmitter in his pocket. Regina's hand was hidden in her handbag. There was Jack Wish, with a gun, and the two Moros. Any attempt to fight now would be hopeless. Her sweeping glance took in Collier, standing by the wall, his face pale and expressionless. Then she looked at Willie.

He stared with mingled relief and despair, half rose from the chair and said, 'Princess!' Sangro slammed him back into the chair again.

Her own expression as she looked at Willie was one of startled astonishment.

Seff looked at Lucifer and said briskly, 'A very fortunate situation has arisen, Lucifer. We have a rebel here, a friend of Miss Blaise's, who has dared to challenge your authority.'

Lucifer regarded Willie Garvin with little interest. 'Why do you say this is fortunate, Asmodeus?'

A deprecating gesture from Seff. 'As you know, we who consider ourselves your most faithful servants have some doubts that the loyalty displayed by Miss Blaise is genuine. We now have an opportunity to test this. She is expert with a gun, this man Garvin is expert with a throwing-knife. Let us therefore pit them against one another. If she is loyal, your power will give her victory. But if she refuses, or is defeated, it will be proof that the doubts of your trusted servants are justified.'

There was complete silence. Regina was smiling with delight and admiration. Sangro, who had understood enough, was grinning. So was Wish. Collier stood very still, not breathing, praying that Lucifer would reject the twisted logic of the idea, yet knowing with horrible certainty that his pride in Modesty would persuade him to accept the subtle challenge to his omniscience.

It was an evilly brilliant move by Seff. If Willie Garvin died, nothing was lost. If Modesty died, it would be with Lucifer's approval. Willie could be disposed of immediately afterwards. The loss of Modesty as a bedfellow for Lucifer would be a disadvantage; but, now that the ice of sexual inhibition had been broken for Lucifer, it would be easy to bring in a competent girl from Macao to keep him happy. At least, Seff would think so.

Collier forced himself to look at Willie Garvin. He was sitting quite still, staring at Modesty with extraordinary intentness. Collier followed his gaze. She was badly shaken, and trying to hide it from Lucifer, but her fingers twitched and a hand rose to flutter nervously about her mouth.

Lucifer's thoughtful expression became a smile. 'Yes,' he

said. 'Yes, Asmodeus. Modesty will do this, and then you will see.'

'Does she agree?' Seff asked, and the whole room looked at her. The hand fell to her side and she was still, her gaze on Willie Garvin. Collier saw that her lips were compressed in a thin straight line and there was bitter decision in her eyes. In the space of ten seconds she had assessed every factor and accepted the brutal conclusion.

'Too bad,' she said. 'Do your best, Willie.'

'You an' me?' There was utter incredulity on his face. 'What's it *about*? Who's *he*?' A hand jerked in Lucifer's direction.

'Never mind who's what,' Modesty said bleakly. 'It's you, or me, or both. There's no way out and I don't want any favours. So don't be gallant. There's no place for it when you've reached the crunch.'

Through thirty leaden seconds of silence Willie's face slowly hardened, unbelief giving place to bitterness and then to anger.

'I should've stayed 'ome,' he said at last in an ugly voice. He looked slowly round the room, then at Modesty again. 'We could've 'ad a go, you and me. Tried something, and taken a couple of 'em with us. But if you want it this way, okay. It's you or me.'

Light morning mist drifted in patches across the bay.

On the grassy cliff top Willie Garvin squinted up at the new day's sun. 'I'm not 'aving that in me eyes,' he said, and moved round until he stood facing towards the house and a dozen paces from the cliff edge.

Sangro had called the Moros to watch and there was an air of almost festive excitement among them. Bets were being laid and taken. Jack Wish had brought Modesty's Colt ·32 in the belt and holster she had worn on Sylt. There was only a single round in the cylinder now.

She buckled the belt about her waist over the cheong sam and checked the gun while Sangro stood with a Browning automatic rifle pointed at her back. Seff, Regina and Bowker stood with Lucifer some way behind and to one side of her. The Moros were spread out on her flanks.

Willie Garvin stood alone, thirty feet from Modesty, facing her. Jack Wish moved towards him with a throwing-knife, holding it by the haft of dimpled black bone. He slipped it into one of the twin sheaths on Willie's bare chest and said, 'Nice knife, feller.'

'It'll do.'

Wish waved Sangro back and moved away until he stood between the combatants but well clear of the line of fire. He carried his heavy Colt Commander in one hand. With the other he held up a white handkerchief.

'Watch it,' he said. 'When I drop the rag you can make your play.'

Collier, standing a little apart from Seff's group, and with a Moro rifle menacing him, whispered obscene and bitter curses to himself. His overstrung nerves were making his hands and face twitch uncontrollably.

The handkerchief fell. Two hands moved in a blur of speed. Willie Garvin's hand scarcely seemed to touch the knife, yet it was in his grasp, held by the blade, and he was throwing. Modesty ducked as she fired, and steel glinted above her head as the knife flashed past.

Collier saw Willie Garvin stagger. His hand clutched at his bare stomach, then he stood still, crouched a little, head lifted to stare at Modesty. She was frozen in the pose she had fired from, the Colt held at waist height in front of her. A breeze stirred the hem of her green cheong sam.

Collier looked again at Willie and saw that the hand pressed to his stomach was streaked with crimson that crept between his fingers. From the Moros had come a brief outcry of excitement, but now all was quiet, so quiet that even at forty paces Collier could hear the agonised wheeze of Willie's breathing.

Still he did not fall. His voice, cracked with pain, came clearly. *'You didn't 'ave to make it the slow way ...!'*

There was an almost ludicrous note of resentment in the shrill cry.

Willie Garvin turned. Panting, stumbling, doubled over in agony, he went blundering towards the cliff edge. Nobody moved. He lurched over the edge and plunged down head first.

Modesty's hand holding the empty gun fell limply to her side. She walked forward slowly. Seff, Regina, everybody was moving forward now.

Collier retched, spat, wiped a clammy face, and went forward with the rest.

Willie Garvin lay sprawled face down on the wet sand below. Half his body lay across one of the small boulders that jutted above the surface here and there. Blood was on the side of his face and on the rock.

Lucifer said with regal serenity, 'Now you have seen, Asmodeus. Now you have all seen.'

A roller swirled round the curve of the bay and lapped at Willie Garvin's body. Modesty turned and found Collier's eye. 'I had to go for the body,' she said tautly. 'I couldn't risk a head shot. I *couldn't!*'

Collier turned his eyes quickly away, looking down at Willie Garvin again. A big roller was coming. It plucked up the limp figure and swirled on and round, carrying it out past the raft, the limbs trailing and twisting bonelessly like the limbs of a broken doll.

Now the powerful current along the bay's southern arm took charge. Collier saw a flash of brown flesh as a wave lifted the body and rolled it over, sweeping it on past the Moro boats.

Lucifer put an arm about Modesty's shoulders, smiling. 'You must not be disturbed,' he said. 'The time had come for this man to be sent to the lower levels. The power and the decision were mine, Modesty, not yours. I have only used you as my instrument, to satisfy Asmodeus.'

Collier, looking drearily out over the bay, saw the body swallowed up by the rolling white morning mist.

'I thought she did it splendidly,' he said.

To Collier the day seemed endless. He ate no breakfast, and spent the morning in a long and unsatisfactory session of experiments with Lucifer and Bowker. Inwardly he felt shattered. He knew that Modesty had had no choice, that her decision had been no more than realistic. It was no use saying brutally realistic. Here, in this heavy limbo of madness and murder, reality was brutal by definition.

No. There had been no alternative for Modesty. Or at least only the suicidal alternative of trying to take one or two of Seff's crowd with them. It was absurd to be shocked that Modesty had not chosen such an alternative. Yet still Collier was horribly shocked.

He could only pretend to eat lunch, and sat mentally withdrawn from the prosaic conversation between Seff and Regina. After lunch, Modesty and Lucifer disappeared—to their bedroom, no doubt. Seff called Collier to his workroom and showed him the packet of industrial diamonds which had been in the container brought in by Pluto and Belial.

'We are making good progress, Mr. Collier,' Seff said almost genially. 'And it will continue if we all work together. There may be occasional problems, of course. I anticipate that sooner or later somebody may insert an explosive device *inside* a container, which will of course destroy our friends Pluto and Belial. But the explosion will leave no evidence, and Mr. Garcia is very pleased with the way in which the two reserve dolphins are responding to training.' He held up the oilskin-wrapped diamonds. 'Let this remind you of the importance of your work, Mr. Collier. The greater Lucifer's accuracy, the fewer stubborn clients we shall have.'

It was not until half an hour before dusk that Collier saw Modesty again. He was climbing the cliff path from the beach, trying to brace himself for the ordeal of dinner in an hour's time. She came down the path towards him, a Moro trailing some way behind her. Collier halted, not knowing what to say.

She looked at him, unsmiling. 'I know, Steve. Listen. Whatever happens, your job is to stay alive.'

'Like you did?' He had not meant to be brutal but the words were out before he could hold them back.

She surveyed him gravely. 'Not like I did. You won't have that to face. But don't do anything stupid. Don't lose hope. Just stay alive a little longer.' She held his eyes for a long moment, then walked on past him down to the beach.

It was forty minutes later, and he was in the house, when the shot was fired. Seff came from his workroom. Bowker and Wish ran out to find the cause. They returned after five minutes with Sangro and the Moro who had been on duty watching Modesty. The Moro spoke volubly, gesticulating. Sangro translated.

She had been swimming, alone. It was not unusual. Dusk was coming. The Moro had looked up and she was not near the raft. She was over in the current of the southern arm of the bay, and she was swimming with it, swimming hard. The guard had fired once, but the light was bad. He did not think he had hit her. Then she was beyond the moored boats and he could see her no more in the gathering gloom.

'All the boats are there?' Seff asked. 'Including Garvin's dinghy?'

Sangro nodded. Collier stood listening wearily. He was too numb to react.

'Stay alive . . .' she had said. And now, this.

'She flipped,' Jack Wish said, and shook his head. 'Imagine that. She flipped.'

'Killing Garvin shook her,' Bowker muttered thoughtfully. 'She did it, but she couldn't take it.'

'You think this is virtually suicide, Dr. Bowker?' Seff asked.

'Compulsion to escape from a situation. She may have some vague notion that she can get away round the coast, but that's not the real motivation.'

'She flipped,' Jack Wish repeated.

Seff got up and went out of the room. He walked down the corridor into his workroom and slid aside a panel behind one

242

of the benches. Carefully he set the controls of the transmitter that lay behind the panel. Switching on, he allowed thirty seconds for the set to warm up, then pressed the transmitter key. He held it down for a full minute, switched off, closed the panel and walked back to the other room.

'Whatever her motivation,' he said, 'the girl is certainly dead now. We shall have to tell Lucifer that she has transferred briefly to the lower levels. At his own command, of course.' He looked across the room. 'Be warned, Mr. Collier.'

It was only then that Collier's battered, punch-drunk mind realised what Seff had just done.

At fifteen minutes to midnight Modesty Blaise waded into the tiny inlet, little bigger than a large room, where Willie Garvin had first come ashore and hidden the dinghy. Here, the jungle came right down to the rocky shoreline. She had no doubt that this was the place, for Willie had described the position carefully.

Four hours earlier, when the current carried her out of the bay, she had turned south and swum steadily to break free from its grip. She had been carried on westward for over a mile before she was clear and able to turn east again in the darkness. By eleven she had swum in a wide half circle to reach the southern arm of the bay once again, but on the outer side of its embrace now, where no current ran and where the long ridge of twisted rock lay between her and the bay.

The moon had risen, and she had hugged the line where rock met water as she made her way along the length of the ridge and on for another mile, past the flank of the mountain to where the laval rock of the shore jutted out and turned sharply back to form the small inlet.

As she pulled herself up the bank Willie Garvin's hand reached down to help her.

''Allo, Princess. I was wondering about you showing up.' He guided her to a shallow hollow of smooth rock. 'Thought I might 'ave to sit it out for a few days.'

'Now was the best time, Willie love.' The rock was still

warm from the heat of the day. She lay back and breathed deeply. 'Have you called John Dall?'

'No.' He squatted beside her in the moonlight. 'The radio was in me kitbag with the rest of the gear. It went up with the mine.'

'Just so long as you didn't.'

'I was lucky.' He told her briefly what had happened, then put out a hand, coaxing her gently to turn on her face. She rolled over. He unbuttoned the wet silk of the cheong sam and slipped it down to examine her back. The waterproof skin was still intact. 'Did it give you any trouble swimming, Princess?'

'No. The muscle ached a bit for the first half hour, but then even that passed off. How did you make out, Willie?'

'Easy, once I was out of sight an' could take a decent breath. That mist was handy. I was round the end of the point and heading back 'ere before any Moros were on watch again.'

She sat up and buttoned the dress. Willie was a powerful swimmer and would have broken free of the current much faster than she had been able to. She had counted on that.

'You scared me with the blood,' she said. 'For a crazy second I thought I'd hit you.'

His teeth gleamed in the moonlight. 'What us thespians call getting into the skin of the part. Worth an Oscar, that bit on the cliff was. I gave me 'and a good nick on the draw, and a little blood goes a long way.'

'Is the cut all right now?'

'Fine. I could bottom deal a poker hand.'

She drew a long breath. 'I'm glad you read the signals when Seff came up with his idea of a party game. I couldn't put over too much with them all staring at me.'

'It was enough.'

'Yes. But I wasn't sure you knew that there's a big roller every few seconds that would carry you out.'

'I knew. I'd been on the beach before, when I left that message for you.'

'How did the fall go?'

'No sweat. I've landed 'arder with a parachute. It was

244

wet sand, and I picked me spot, then rolled over on that rock.'

'It looked good.' She stood up. 'That's all the breather we've time for, Willie. They didn't find the canoe?'

'No. I hid that soon as I got 'ere the other night.' He vanished into the bushes. It was some few minutes before he returned. The canoe had been hidden well away from the inlet where the dinghy lay. Willie Garvin knew his job. In silence he set down a long canvas bag and a rucksack. Modesty knelt to help him unfasten the straps. They fitted the ash frame of the canoe together and worked the rubberised canvas skin into position.

Five minutes later they were afloat. Modesty sat in the forward seat of the cockpit, Willie behind her. As they fitted the silver spruce paddles together she said, 'Can you get us there?'

'Yes. I know where Dall's lying off a little atoll, an' I know the bearing from 'ere. Checked the chart as soon as I got 'ere.'

'Compass?'

'Strapped on me leg now. It was packed in with the canoe.'

'How far do you think?'

'Thirty-five miles, give or take a mile. We'll 'ave to make a bit of a dogleg to stay clear of the bay, so let's say forty miles. We're lucky at that. It could've been eighty if John and me 'ad picked a rendezvous west of the dropping point.'

'About six hours, then. All good for the waistline. Let's go, Willie love.'

The paddles dipped in unison and the canoe glided out of the inlet, riding smoothly to the calm sea.

'When we get there,' Modesty said, 'we'll have a drink to Garcia. Something supernacular. We might not have made it but for him.'

'Garcia? The one that trains the dolphins?'

'Half man, half fish. I wouldn't wonder if he had gills. Anyway, he has a special method for keeping the area clear of sharks. It's just as well. Blood attracts them, and your hand was bleeding at first.'

There was a silence lasting for six strokes of the paddles. Then—

'Jesus wept,' Willie said in an awed voice. 'Sharks. I 'adn't given them a thought!'

Her shoulders swung rhythmically in front of him, and he heard laughter in her voice. 'I didn't give a thought to warning you of the mines. I guess it's been that kind of a day, Willie.'

19

DALL shook Willie Garvin to wakefulness, waited for him to sit up, put a laden tray on his lap, then sat down on one of the two chairs in the little cabin. It was late afternoon, eleven hours since Modesty and Willie had reached the anchored *Samarkand*, ten hours since they had fallen gratefully asleep.

Willie surveyed the enormous steak topped with fried eggs, and the steaming pot of coffee. He looked up and gave Dall a huge grin. "'Allo, you bloody old billionaire, you. It's a pretty good life, eh?'

Dall lit one of his cigars. 'So far,' he said. 'That's what I want to talk about. Can we stop her going back?'

'No.' Willie cut into the steak and shook his head. 'Might as well save your breath, John. If we go roaring in with your boys, Steve Collier gets croaked. We got to get 'im un-nailed first.'

'A lot of men have died in this business already,' Dall said quietly. 'Collier would be the last—and then only if Seff throws the switch. You want to risk two for one?'

'Collier's a friend.'

'Yours?'

Willie looked up. 'Modesty's. A special friend.'

'I see.' Dall drew on his cigar. He had been feeling anxious and fretful. Now he felt angry, too. 'Sorry if I made you tell me something she wouldn't want me to know.'

'Ah, for Christ's sake, John. When did she ever hide anything?'

Dall grinned wryly. 'Sorry again. A touch of the green eye. Very stupid.' He was thoughtful for a few moments, then went on. 'My hero-rating is around c-minus. But if I were stuck where Collier's stuck, I think I'd rather gamble on my own chances than have Modesty take this kind of crazy risk. Modesty and you,' he amended politely.

Willie waved a fork in amiable dismissal of the acknowledgment. 'What you wanted wouldn't stop 'er,' he said. 'We got the initiative now. A big 'un. Seff reckons we're both dead, so we're as good as playing with marked cards. Besides, she wants to get Lucifer out as well.'

'*What?*' Dall stood up.

Modesty spoke from the doorway. 'That's right. How are you, Johnnie?'

She wore male pyjamas too big for her. Dall knew she had only now put them on for want of a dressing gown, for she always slept raw. Her hair was in two pigtails, her face freshly washed and without make-up. Her eyes were bright and alive. And she was the only woman on earth who sometimes called him Johnnie.

'I'm fine,' Dall said. He threw the cigar out of the port as she came into the cabin, took her in his arms and kissed her hard.

Willie Garvin nodded. 'Millionaires are best,' he said sagely, and returned to his breakfast.

When Dall let her speak she said, 'Mind my back.'

'Oh, God! I forgot——'

'I didn't feel a thing. That nice doctor you've got just took a good look at it and he says it's fine.' She sat down on the bunk. 'Why does Willie get a breakfast and I don't? I'm just as pretty as he is.'

'I thought you were still asleep. I'll shout for some.'

As Dall moved to the door she said, 'I can hold out for five minutes. You were saying something about Lucifer.'

Dall stood still for a moment. Deliberately he took out a fresh cigar, lit it, then sat down. 'This is a policy of confusion,' he said. 'I know. I use it myself. The back, the breakfast, Lucifer——'

She smothered a burst of laughter. 'Honestly John, I wasn't trying to throw you.'

'You haven't.' He did not respond to her smile, and his

manner was taut. 'Let's talk about Lucifer. Getting him out means piling risk on risk. By what kind of logic do you put your neck on the block for a nut-case who's been laying you for the last three weeks?'

For an instant she froze, but then the smile came back and mischief danced in her eyes. 'You big phoney,' she said. 'You're trying to make me mad so we can quarrel. Then you'll storm out and have your ex-marines do this your way. But it won't work, Johnnie. If you want to stop me you'll have to do it in cold blood.'

'And?'

'And I'd rather we stayed friends.' There was no threat in her voice, only affection.

Dall sighed and relaxed. 'Okay,' he said resignedly. 'But that question I asked—I may have put it a little ruggedly, but it's still a good question.'

'Yes. Lucifer's a nut-case,' she said quietly. 'But he hasn't hurt me. He's a sweet nut-case. And he really suffers. If you accept his delusion, he comes out of it pretty well.' She gave a little shrug. 'I'd say if Lucifer did run Hell, it wouldn't be a bad place to end up. But when it comes to the crunch, Seff will kill him because he knows too much, just as he'll kill Steve Collier.'

'All right.' Dall considered, then went on slowly, 'This may sound pretty rough, but the boy's crazy and he can't be cured. Ever. You say he suffers. You really think he's better off alive?'

'I wouldn't know, Johnnie. I don't know what it's like to be dead.'

Her hands were lifted, absently re-plaiting one of the pigtails which had started to come loose. In the big pyjamas she looked like a schoolgirl, and Dall was suddenly overwhelmed by a wave of tenderness and warmth that held nothing of the physical excitement with which his body remembered her so well. It was in no way paternal; he knew that this feeling could not have existed without the physical desire, dormant at this moment, that she stirred in him. It was . . .

Dall's eyes sought Willie Garvin. He saw that Willie had stopped eating and was watching Modesty with an expression Dall could not identify but which in some measure seemed to reflect his own obscure feeling.

For a moment Dall understood dimly the strange yet tremendous bond that lay between these two, but before his thoughts could shape the concept clearly it was gone.

Hiding the weariness that weeks of waiting had wrought in him, Dall stood up. 'Okay, honey,' he said gently. 'I think I've got it now. You have to pull Collier out because he's a friend. And you have to pull Lucifer out because you don't know what it's like to be dead.' He managed a smile. 'Keep it that way.'

Willie Garvin returned to his breakfast. 'Your whiskers keep growing for quite a while after you're dead,' he said reminiscently. 'I found that out when I was knocking around in Rio.'

'You knew a girl there?' said Modesty.

'M'mm. Her old man was an undertaker and she used to 'elp with the business. Stiffs passing through were kept in a cool cellar on army surplus beds. She used to shave 'em after twelve hours, and I used to give a hand. Trouble was, you'd stretch the skin to get a nice smooth stroke with the razor, and it *stayed* stretched. There was a real knack in getting their faces straightened out after you'd finished shaving 'em.'

'Is he kidding?' said Dall, staring.

Modesty lifted her shoulders. 'I always like to think so. But could *you* dream up anything like that?'

Dall shook his head. 'Nobody could.'

'I 'adn't finished,' Willie said with dignity. 'The thing is, I dropped a right clanger the first time I 'elped. I was shaving this stiff, doing a nice job, because the family always like 'em to look right, and I put me knee on the bed to lean across and get busy on the other side of 'is face. The bed sagged in the middle, and 'e sagged a bit with it. That squeezed the air out of 'is lungs, and suddenly 'e was making this 'orrible wailing groan at me.'

Dall said, 'Good God.'

'Rosita told me afterwards that it sometimes 'appened,' said Willie, munching. 'But blimey, I nearly went through the ceiling.'

Modesty eyed him dubiously. 'I'm not sure it's wise, but somebody has to feed you the next line,' she said. 'All right. What was the clanger?'

Willie grimaced. 'Well, I jumped! Rosita didn't 'alf create about 'aving to sew the bloke's ear back on.'

Dall choked on his cigar, then began to laugh helplessly, coughing.

Modesty stood up, struggling against the same compulsion. 'You—you really are disgusting, Willie Garvin,' she said with a feeble attempt at severity. 'How you can sit there eating that steak and telling that story I'll never know.'

Willie gave a deprecating shrug. 'I suppose it's just a gift, Princess,' he said modestly.

Two hours later on the main deck, watched by a dozen or more astonished pairs of very professional eyes, Modesty Blaise tested her shoulder in controlled combat against Willie Garvin.

'All right, Willie love,' she said at last, a little breathlessly, as he got to his feet. 'We'll do it tonight.'

The next few hours saw much activity. At midnight the seaplane had been hoisted on a derrick and lowered to the sea.

Now it was airborne.

The pilot eased forward the grip handles of the control column and levelled out at fifteen thousand feet. The roar of the 450 h.p. Pratt and Whitney engines diminished slightly as the aircraft settled to a steady cruising speed of 130 m.p.h.

It was a Beaver seaplane, a highwing strut-braced monoplane with two doors to the cabin, one on each side. Modesty sat in the co-pilot's seat on the starboard side. She wore her black combat rig and her face was dark with camouflage cream. Her spare Colt ·32 nestled in its holster at her hip.

She looked back through the open door to the passenger cabin where Willie Garvin sat with Dall, and said, 'About ten minutes, Willie.'

'Right.' He got to his feet and without haste began to strap on a black parachute pack.

John Dall watched, feeling his nerves crawl with tension. When the pack was in position on his back, Willie picked up a slim black canvas kitbag about three feet long. A rope was attached to the neck of the bag. He took the free end of the rope and tied it round his thigh with a highwayman's hitch for quick release, then settled awkwardly on the edge of the seat again.

'Fair old night for it,' he said, lifting his voice above the noise of the engine. 'Clear, but not much moon yet. We'll get in nice and easy, I reckon.'

'Unless the Moros are looking up,' Dall said grimly.

'Even then. But they'll be looking out, not up.'

'Not when they hear the plane. They'll watch its lights.'

'Let's 'ope so. We'll be 'alf a mile south of the plane and a good two miles down when we open the 'chutes. The Moros 'll get about ten seconds to spot us, if that.'

Dall shrugged. 'Okay. I'm through arguing.'

Willie glanced forward. Modesty was looking down and ahead now. The sea was an immense dark plain below, reflecting a faint sheen of moonlight and blemished only by the occasional more thickly textured blackness of a tiny island.

The pilot said, 'I'd like to make one dry run, Miss Blaise. God help me if I drop you in the sea or in the wrong place.' He jerked his head slightly to indicate Dall.

'We can't risk a dry run,' Modesty said. 'You're just passing by. Hold your course after the drop, and don't circle back to the ship until you've made twenty miles.' She turned her head to smile at him briefly. 'Don't fret. Just fly her. The drop's our worry.'

The pilot grimaced and gave a nod.

Ahead Modesty picked up the three island specks she had been looking for. A straight bearing from the last two would take the Beaver just north of the bay where the house lay and the Moros kept guard.

'Come to starboard a little,' she said. 'Fine. Now hold that bearing. You'll pick up a few pinpoints of light soon, and that's our target. Don't worry that we're off-shore and north of it. That's the whole idea.'

She got out of the seat and went through to the cabin. Willie helped her strap on the other parachute, then knelt to hitch a second thin black kitbag to her thigh. There was six feet of slack in the rope. He lifted the kitbag and she held it against her chest while he passed a shorter length of rope round to secure it, once again with a quick-release hitch.

He checked that all loose ends were tucked away and that the ripcord housing was clear, then picked up his own padded kitbag, slightly shorter than hers, and held it while she secured it to his chest.

Dall watched as they examined each other closely. It was some relief at least to see the sober care they took to avoid needless risks.

Modesty looked at Dall and said, 'Will you get the doors open, John?'

The doors of the Beaver normally opened outwards, but both had been modified only a few hours earlier. Dall moved to each door in turn, held it against the buffeting wind as he eased it back, and secured it with a hook. With both doors open wind howled through the cabin, and Dall was suddenly glad of the safety line that ran from a strongpoint on the deck to a harness about his chest. The line just allowed him to reach each door.

The pilot called out and waved a hand.

'He's picked up the lights,' Dall said, shouting now against the noise of wind and engine. Modesty nodded and pulled on her helmet. Willie's was already strapped in place. They crouched, one at each door, peering down and ahead.

Looking obliquely through the starboard door where Willie squatted, Dall could just make out the dark mass of land with the jutting point which split in a curving fork to form the bay.

253

Faint light showed from the house. They would pass parallel with the bay's northern arm and over half a mile offshore.

'Hang on tight, Johnnie,' Modesty called, gesturing. 'The plane's going to yaw quite a bit when we go.'

Dall nodded, knelt, and gripped a seat stanchion.

Now her head was turned to watch Willie. He was staring out and down. Slowly his hand came up. Dall looked for a farewell glance from Modesty, but there was none. He felt a pang at the knowledge that for the moment, and perhaps for a long time to come, he had ceased to exist for her. But then he was glad. She had plenty to think about, and what did he expect, for God's sake? Kisses and a valedictory speech?

Willie Garvin's hand chopped down in a signal.

The Beaver yawed and lurched. They were gone, leaving Dall clutching hard on the stanchion with only an after-image on his retina of the headlong dive into emptiness.

It was time to close the doors, if he could, but he knelt staring blankly, unaware of the noise and wind battering his ears, wondering where her endless resources of strength came from.

In the past forty-eight hours a poison capsule had been cut out of her body; she had thought Willie dead, found he was alive, and fought a carefully faked duel; she had made a four hour swim, paddled a canoe for six hours, slept for ten, tested her shoulder in combat, made complex plans and preparations.

And now . . .

Body horizontal, arms and legs spread wide, Modesty felt the familiar sensation of lying unmoving above the earth while a fierce upward gale plucked at her.

She drew her limbs in a little, to the frog position, and made a 180 degree turn. Now she was facing the coast, facing the same way as Willie, and he was in front of her looking back over his shoulder for her.

She knew he had seen her for he faced front and moved into the dereve position, hands pressed against the front of the

254

thighs, legs together and extended parallel to the ground, buttocks lifted so that the upper half of the body was inclined slightly down. Modesty moved into the same position.

Now, in free fall, she was moving forward, flying at forty m.p.h.

Willie held down his forward speed until she came alongside him, then surged forward with her. They were over the sea. The coast lay ahead, with the mountain and jungle to the left and the long ridge of the bay's northern arm extending to the right.

With a slight adjustment of her position she fell back and concentrated on watching Willie. They had been falling for twenty seconds now—falling but driving forward, for the coast was much nearer. It was tempting to look at the coast, to look at the altimeter strapped to her forearm, to judge speed and height and target. But that was Willie's job, for his experience was marginally greater. She saw him extend his left arm so that he side-slipped to the right, adjusting his course, and she followed suit.

He stabilised again, and she resumed the dereve position with him, but a little later, so that she was directly behind him now and perhaps a hundred feet above, the two of them arrowing down obliquely in line ahead.

Still she looked neither down to the coast below nor at the faint light of the house beyond. Her eyes held to Willie's seemingly motionless figure suspended in the sky. The time mechanism in her head had been counting automatically. Fifty seconds since they had jumped.

It would be soon now. She saw Willie stabilise in the frog position, and instantly she made the same move, her hand seeking the ring of her ripcord.

Willie flung out his left arm in a signal, very briefly so that he should not lose stability. She tugged hard on the ripcord, and in the same moment saw the little extractor parachute break free from Willie's pack.

There came the sudden jerk as her own parachute flared above her, a black mushroom. She spared one quick glance up to make sure that it had developed properly. There was little fear of malfunction. Willie had checked and packed both parachutes himself with infinite care.

She saw that his own parachute was fully developed. They were TU parachutes, designed for accurate steering. Two separate gores were blank, cut away to within five feet of the top of the canopy. Near the bottom these blank gores were joined by a long cut-out, eighteen inches deep and running across eleven gores. Air funnelling through the U-shaped cut-out provided motive power for steering.

Willie was pulling on the steering line to bring the blank gores to the rear, for increased forward speed. She copied him, and now both were gliding down at an angle, travelling fast. From her peripheral vision she knew that they were over land now, and that the rising hump of mountain was on their left. The house was directly ahead.

Willie's kitbag fell, to dangle from the rope tied to his thigh. She released her own. Everything would happen very quickly now, for touchdown must be near.

She saw beyond Willie the flat T-shaped roof of the house. He was angling beautifully down towards it with an occasional touch of the steering lines. Modesty followed his course.

Something on the roof moved. A Moro. As if in a moonlit stage scene she saw the man prop his rifle against the far parapet and look idly round. She could not see his face clearly, but suddenly he froze in a grotesque position, staring.

Willie was only fifteen feet above the roof, passing over the nearer parapet. She saw his arm swing, and caught the glitter of steel. The Moro jerked, then crumpled slowly to his knees and fell sideways. Willie tugged at the hitch on his thigh and the kitbag dropped three feet to the roof. A second later he touched down, rolling. The canopy flew out and collapsed as he hit one of the Capewell release buckles.

Her own touchdown now. *And she was too high.*

Self contempt raged through her and was instantly quelled. She had failed to allow for her lighter weight in the final moments of the descent. She would have to spill air and drop.

Willie's face stared up, taut. She was above him now and still moving forward fast.

With a heave on the forward rigging lines she spilled air from the canopy, as if from an inverted bucket submerged under water and suddenly tilted. No time to drop the dangling kitbag. The canopy flapped and crumpled, losing all lift. She dropped just short of the front parapet and hit the Capewell releases in the same moment, for the parachute was still billowing ahead of her, threatening to drag her over the edge.

She was free, rolling hard against the parapet, the kitbag dragging at her leg. Willie was beside her, making a desperate grab for the harness as it slithered over the edge, but he was too late. She knelt up, to see the black nylon clear the first floor terrace and drift down, heaving and bellying like some shapeless monster as it rolled across the open ground below and collapsed at last against a little patch of scrublike bushes.

A minute passed.

From the right, two men appeared, strolling, taking shape as they emerged from the shadows. They were Moros, with sub-machine guns slung on their shoulders. They paused, surveyed the front of the house, then turned to gaze out to sea for a long minute before resuming their patrol. When they moved on, they passed within twenty feet of the patch of scrub where the parachute lay. Then they were lost in the darkness again.

'Strewth...!' Willie Garvin breathed gratefully.

'They might find it next time round. Or the next,' she said in a low voice. 'Sorry, Willie. I didn't allow for being lighter than you.'

He grinned. 'I knew there was something I meant to remind you about. Thought of it when we were at five thousand feet. Fine time.'

They took off their jump helmets. Willie moved to the crumpled Moro, knelt to look closely at him, then nodded to Modesty. The man was dead. With three inches of steel angling down into the base of his neck it was hardly surprising, but Willie Garvin was a cautious man. Satisfied, he jerked his knife free, wiped it on the man's shirt and returned it to the sheath under his open shirt.

Modesty was methodically emptying her kitbag. It held, packed in foam rubber, a Colt AR-15 survival rifle and two hundred rounds of 5.56mm ammunition; rifle and the ten 20-round magazines together weighed less than thirteen pounds. There were six hand grenades, four tear gas bombs, two gas-masks; a nylon cord rope-ladder was coiled round a large leather wallet of medical gear. There was a box of spare ammunition for her Colt, and, in a slim case, a three-foot bow and a thin quiver of steel arrows. The bow was squat and un-orthodox in shape, but made of laminated wood and plastic, and beautifully balanced.

Except for the bow and quiver, Willie's kitbag held a like armoury but included two heavy throwing-knives, four magazines which held cartridges of his own making, and two thirty-inch black metal tubes.

He laid out the equipment against the parapet and slipped the two big knives into sheaths at the back of his belt. Modesty was unrolling the first aid wallet. She took out a flat box, slipped it into her thigh pocket and looked at Willie.

'I'm not sure how long I'll be.'

'Okay, Princess. How long before I come looking?'

'You'll hear soon enough if something goes wrong.'

'No chance of knocking Seff off in 'is room?' he said wistfully.

'None. Bolted door, barred and shuttered window. We'll play it the way we worked out, Willie.' She moved at a crouch across the roof, keeping low. The door of the roof access was set in a bulkhead at the intersection of the T, with steps leading straight down to a corridor below. As she disappeared, Willie picked up one of the black tubes.

He squatted with his back to the parapet, his head just below the edge, and lifted the tube so that it sloped backwards over the coping at a slight angle. Setting his eye to the rubber rimmed eyepiece an inch or two from the lower end of the tube, he pressed a switch. There came a faint humming

258

sound, and he saw the open ground which extended from the house to the cliff edge.

The tube was more than a periscope. It was also a noctoscope, a four-stage cascade image intensifier which magnified weak light rays to give excellent night vision over a range of several hundred yards.

Two figures were patrolling, in the other direction this time. They passed well clear of the patch of scrub, and he watched them until they vanished down the sloping ground which led to the inlet and the bay.

'So long as the bastards don't spot that parachute...' Willie Garvin thought hopefully.

20

MODESTY BLAISE stood in the dimly lit corridor with her back to the wall. The kongo was gripped in her left hand, leaving her right free for the holstered Colt. There was no sound but for the faint creaking of the house itself as the timbers moved fractionally in the humid night air.

She moved on, past the door of the Seffs' bedroom. The creaking made her think of Seff. She intended to kill him, and maybe Willie's method would have been best ... 'Blow the door in with a lump of P.E., then chuck in a grenade for the Seffs to share between 'em.'

But there was Steve Collier, with the capsule embedded in his body, and Bowker had a transmitter to trigger it; there was Lucifer, who lived in his own fantastic prison of the mind, but who had harmed nobody. And there were more than thirty Moros ready and eager to kill. She wanted to have Collier and Lucifer safely under her hand before any killing began.

A hand on the Colt, she peered warily round the corner of the passage which led to Steve Collier's room. A Moro lay asleep on a narrow mattress across the doorway. Moving on, she sank on one knee beside him, the kongo poised ready to strike if he stirred.

Her other hand reached into her shirt pocket and took out a plastic tube holding anaesthetic nose-plugs. She shook one out and held it an inch from the man's nose. In less than a minute his breathing changed and became heavier. She edged the nose-plug closer and slid it into one of his nostrils. Still he did not move. She relaxed and lowered the kongo.

Stepping over the Moro, she eased back the bolts at the top and bottom of the door and opened it slowly. A wedge of light from the passage lay across the room, and in it she saw Steve

Collier asleep on the bed. A sheet covered him to the waist. His chest was naked.

She checked that nothing lay in her path, then closed the door softly. Now the room was dark except for an oblong of starlight at the barred window. She took a pencil torch from her pocket, moved to the bed and knelt down. Her fingers found the lobe of Collier's ear and she pinched lightly.

'It's me, Steve,' she whispered. 'Take it gently, don't make a noise. It's me...'

She pinched harder, still whispering, and felt him start suddenly and then go rigid.

'... no noise, Steve. Don't say anything yet. It's me, darling. Modesty.' She shone the torch briefly on her face, then directed the beam downwards so that it should not be seen through the unshuttered window. Her hand moved to his shoulder and gripped with reassuring pressure. Slowly she felt some of the tension go out of his muscles.

A long exhalation, then his voice, very low: 'I've been calling myself all kinds of a fool for hoping...'

'No. You were right. I'd have told you before I went, but I could only leave you the tiniest hope, in case you gave the game away to Seff. You're not a terribly good actor, darling.'

'I'm no worse than most metallurgists.'

She smiled. 'We won't argue. Turn over, Steve. I'm going to get that damned capsule out.'

He stiffened for a moment, then with an effort relaxed again and turned on his face. She put away the pencil torch and took from under her shirt a broad elastic headband. In the middle of it was fixed a small, squat cylinder; a lamp with a narrow focus. Bending her head, she adjusted the band round her brow and switched on. A six-inch circle of light illuminated part of Collier's back.

She drew the flat box from her thigh pocket, placed it open on the bed, took out a pair of gossamer thin rubber gloves and worked her hands into them very carefully.

'Giving you a small shot of novocaine,' she whispered, and pierced an ampoule with the needle of a hypodermic.

'Your capsule's out?' Collier whispered. 'It must be. Seff sent out a trigger signal on the main transmitter.'

'Yes. Willie had cut mine out before they caught him. He was going away from the house when that mine blew up, not coming in.' She made the injection and sat back on her haunches, waiting for it to take effect.

Collier hesitated, then said, 'Willie?'

'Don't worry. He's alive, too. Up on the roof. A thirty foot fall on to wet sand wouldn't hurt him.'

Collier breathed an astonished oath. 'You fired wide?'

'Just wide enough.'

'How in God's name did he know what to do?'

'I'd signalled him to take a dive while we were still in the room. It was enough for him to guess the rest. He's very intuitive, remember?'

After a moment or two Collier said, 'In this case I'd imagine it was more a matter of each of you knowing exactly how the other's mind works...' His whisper was so serious and reflective that inward laughter rippled through Modesty. He must have sensed it, for he turned his head and looked at her with an apologetic air. 'Sorry. I'll work out the theories later. How the hell did you *get* here?'

'Parachute. We landed on the roof. Now don't talk any more.' She picked up a small scalpel.

Collier rested his face in the crook of his arm and tried to relax. He could feel a numb spot under his shoulder blade, with the fingers of her left hand pressing just outside the anaesthetised area.

Her breathing was quiet and even, and he tried to match his own breathing to it. She was cutting now. He was aware of it though he felt no pain. The scalpel would have to cut through the fatty layer to the muscle fibre beneath, and then she would have to find exactly where the capsule had been embedded. One slip while she was probing, and——

Angrily he swung his thoughts away and began to make mathematical calculations in his head. Take a number. Say 429,748. Find the square root to three decimal places...

Time passed.

'All right,' she whispered, and laid something on a little square of oilskin. From the corner of his eye he saw the capsule and the small forceps she put down beside it. She was swabbing the incision now. He lifted his head a little so that he could see the white plastic capsule clearly.

'Christ,' he said in a shaky voice. 'I didn't know it was possible to hate a *thing* the way I hate that.'

'I know what you mean. Keep still while I put in a couple of stitches. They're not really necessary, but you might have to be rather active over the next few hours.'

'I'm not much better at fisticuffs than I am at acting,' said Collier. 'But perhaps I could shoot somebody? I'd like that.'

'We'll try to arrange it.' Two minutes later she laid a strip of lint over the small wound and secured it with plaster. 'You can get up now, Steve.' She took off the headband, keeping the beam of the lamp low.

Collier sat up and swung his feet to the floor, watching her wrap up the capsule carefully in the oilskin and pack it away in the flat box with the rest of the medical gear.

'Pity I didn't keep mine,' she whispered. 'We'd have a pair.'

Collier held back an hysterical giggle. 'We could ask Seff to sell us a spare one,' he said gravely. 'What now?'

'Get dressed and we'll go. The Moro outside won't wake up. We go along to the end of the passage, then you turn left and head for the stairs to the roof. Willie will be waiting for you up there.'

He stared. 'What about you?'

'I'll be along later. With Lucifer.'

'*Lucifer?*' He mouthed the word. 'For God's sake, you can't get *him* out! It just won't work. He'll start talking, making a noise——'

'I'm going to get him out.'

'He'll blow you, Modesty!'

'You're getting the jargon, aren't you? But you blew me once yourself, remember?' The soft-spoken words were unjust and hurt badly. He knew she had used them deliberately, to stop argument by crushing him. Before he could form an answer she went on, 'Do as I say, Steve. And as Willie says when you get to him. Otherwise you'll wreck the job. Haven't you learned this is our kind of business?'

He nodded grimly. It was true enough, God knew.

She jerked her head towards his clothes and rose to her feet. He pulled on a shirt, trousers and shoes. When he was ready she switched off the headband lamp. A minute later he stepped over the heavily breathing Moro outside the door and followed her along the passage. She pointed left at the junction, waited for him to move, then walked softly on towards Lucifer's room.

As Collier climbed the steps and emerged on to the flat roof a hand caught his arm and dragged him down.

'Blimey,' whispered Willie Garvin's voice, 'you're better at riveting beryllium, matey. This is no time to stand up an' be counted.'

'Sorry.' Collier's eyes adjusted to the gloom. He saw Willie Garvin beckon then crawl away to the front parapet. On hands and knees Collier followed. To one side of the stairs' bulkhead he saw a Moro lying dead with a dark wound in his throat.

At the parapet Willie lifted a black tube, set it to his eye and pressed a switch, scanning slowly as if with a periscope. He switched off, lowered the tube and looked at Collier.

'Modesty gone for Lucifer?'

'Yes. I told her she was crazy. He'll never play.'

'She'll bring him back anyway.'

'By force? She tried that on him once. Didn't she tell you? He's two seconds ahead of time when it comes to defending himself.'

'She told me. It won't make any difference if your ideas about precognition are right, and she seems to 'ave a lot of faith in 'em.'

Collier did not understand. He wiped sweat from his brow and said, 'I still think she's crazy. Why try to get Lucifer out?'

'Why not? She came back for you, didn't she?'

'All right. That was crazy too. But there's a little difference.'

'How?'

Collier was shaken to find that he had no answer to the simple question. No satisfactory answer.

'Because I'll do as I'm told,' he said at last. 'Lucifer won't. So he's that much more dangerous.'

'We didn't drop in to practise a bit of flower arranging,' Willie said mildly, and dismissed the subject. 'You ever fired an AR-15 or thrown a grenade?'

Collier shook his head. 'I don't even know what an AR-15 is. And I'm not bloody well ashamed of it, either.'

A grin split Willie's blackened face and he picked up one of the skeletal rifles. 'That's fair enough. But now's a good time to learn fast. Look, I'll show you, just in case things get 'ot.'

Lucifer glided over a molten and fuming sea, past the face of a soaring red mountain where shrivelled white souls toiled eternally upwards.

But now something was tugging at his mind, a voice was whispering, an unseen hand touching him, drawing him urgently to the upper levels. His face and body dissolved and reformed in the outward appearance of the other Lucifer, the golden Lucifer of the upper levels.

He opened his eyes and a glow spread through him as he saw her face close above him. The face was dark, almost black, as if she had been down to the lower levels herself. But it was still beautiful.

Modesty was back. Yes, he remembered now. She had gone away for a little while, and Asmodeus had said ... what had Asmodeus said? It did not matter.

Modesty was back. He was happy, even though she looked so different. The black clothes she wore evoked something of the lower levels, too. Had she been down there? And why did she rest a hand over his mouth, putting a finger to her own lips? What need was there for silence?

Modesty watched the pleased blue eyes and wondered what

I*

thoughts were moving in his irreparably damaged mind. He took the hand that rested on his mouth and kissed it.

She said in a whisper, 'Please speak very quietly, Lucifer.'

He smiled tolerantly but kept his voice low. 'Why do you ask that?'

'Because there is rebellion in Hell.'

His smile became reassuring. 'No, Modesty. Don't be afraid. The little humans cannot rebel against *me.*'

'Not the little people. Your own servants. Asmodeus plans to dethrone you from the world, to bind you for ever in the lower levels. Please believe me, Lucifer.'

'I know you believe what you say,' he answered, reaching up to touch her cheek. 'But you are wrong, Modesty. Asmodeus and the others cannot destroy me. It would break the eternal law laid down by my celestial colleague when he cast me out from his kingdom.'

She scoured her mind for ways to argue within the terms of his own delusion, though her face showed no sign of stress. 'Of course they can't *destroy* you, Lucifer. But they can destroy your presence here, on the upper levels. They have tried to make me join them. That's why I went away. They plan to rebel as *you* once rebelled. Perhaps your celestial colleague prepared this snare for you in the beginning.'

She did not try to clarify the almost meaningless suggestion; better to let Lucifer build his own framework of plausibility around it. If he would.

Lucifer sat up and put his feet to the floor. She knelt on the bed watching him. He thought for a long time, his face intent. At last he said, 'It could be so. But I do not believe it, Modesty. You are mistaken. I will call a council now, and unravel this matter. It cannot wait.'

He rose and moved to the wardrobe. Modesty got down from the bed and stood between Lucifer and the door. He took out a dark navy shirt, black jeans, sandals, and put them on. As he walked towards her he was smiling again. 'My servants are loyal, Modesty. You will see.'

His arm was moving even before her own hand lashed out

266

in a fierce chop to the side of his neck, just under the ear. He seized her wrist, and only then did surprise come into his eyes as his mind caught up with the precognitive reaction of his muscles.

'Why did you do that?' he asked in wonder.

'Because I must show you that I'm right, Lucifer.' She did not struggle to free her held wrist. 'Remember when you first saw me, and I tried to rebel against you? I was helpless.'

'Of course.' He let her wrist go, his expression curious but untroubled. 'You could never harm me, Modesty.'

'Asmodeus has given me a new power.' She stepped back a pace. Her hand moved to the squeeze-pocket of her slacks and brought out the kongo. 'With this I could harm you, Lucifer. That's what they want. Then they will imprison you on the lower levels so that Asmodeus and his friends can rule here. But I will use it only to show you the power, to show you that on this level I can overcome even Lucifer himself.'

He looked at her with a touch of impatience. 'What do you hope to do with that small thing?'

'Strike you, Lucifer. Take away your senses. If I do that, you'll know I speak truly. You'll know there is rebellion in Hell.'

'But I shall not let you strike me,' he said simply.

She nodded. Her first hope, to convince him by words, had failed. But it had been well worth trying. Too late now to wish that she had drugged him or knocked him out while he slept.

'Try to stop me,' she said. 'Try hard, Lucifer. *Think* hard. How will I strike? Where? What must you do to prevent me?' She was edging sideways now, beginning to circle him. He turned to face her, and she saw a new and increasing concentration in his eyes, the beginnings of tension in the poised body.

'Think, Lucifer,' she whispered again. 'Be ready. Use all your powers. Think *hard* ...'

His arms rose uncertainly in a clumsy posture of defence. Suddenly her hand snaked out. She was out of distance, but he reacted, head jerking back, hand swinging up to block the feint ... late. She stepped in, swaying easily past a groping

267

arm. Her empty hand lunged almost lazily towards his stomach. He barely blocked the lunge, fumbled, caught her wrist with both hands. The kongo swung in a hook to take him on the bicep. One arm fell limply, then the other as the kongo struck again.

His eyes were wide and blank with shock as she swayed sideways, shifted her feet, and hit him under the ear. Even as the blow landed she closed with him, arms wrapped about his chest to take the weight as his knees began to buckle.

He was out, and her one concern now was to keep him upright. Panting, she leaned back a little, thrusting with her leg to push his knees back straight so that he would to some extent support his own weight.

He was balanced precariously now, leaning upon her. She ducked and passed an arm between his legs, letting him fold forward across her shoulders. Thigh and stomach muscles burned as she slowly straightened up with the heavy body across her shoulders in a fireman's hoist.

Once upright, she found the strain more bearable. Part of her mind registered relief that she had chosen this way instead of knocking him out while he slept. To lift that weight from the bed and get it on her shoulders might well have been beyond her. Better, too, that he was dressed now.

She moved to the door, opened it and edged out into the passage, trying to breathe steadily and quietly. The house creaked as she moved along, bowed under her burden.

The door to Seff's bedroom lay on her right now. Turn at the end of the passage and she would be on the last lap.

Abruptly, from somewhere outside the house, there came the sound of three shots fired in quick succession; then, more faintly, voices shouting.

268

21

As if in a nightmare it seemed that the passage grew ever longer with each step that she took.

The stairs to the roof were under her feet at last, but to mount each one called for a giant effort of will. Vaguely she was conscious of doors slamming in the house below.

Another step. Pause. Another...

Lucifer was plucked from her shoulders and she sank down, half out of the open door of the stairs' bulkhead, her muscles relaxing gratefully as she drew in long gulps of air. Lifting her head, she saw Willie crawling backwards across the roof, dragging Lucifer after him towards the parapet. And there was Steve Collier, squatting with his back to it, the noctoscope to his eye.

Strength was flowing back to her now. She got up and moved to the parapet, crouching. The rifle belonging to the dead Moro was now ranged neatly with the other weapons. It was a lever action Marlin ·30-30, with a buckhorn open sight. Lucifer lay unconscious beside Collier now.

She said, still breathing hard, 'Do they know we're up here, Willie?'

'Not yet. Couple of 'em stumbled on the parachute and fired an alarm signal. But they'll look up 'ere when they find Steve and Lucifer gone.'

'There's a dozen of them now,' Collier said, his eye to the tube. 'More coming up from the camp. And the house is buzzing. Lights showing from quite a few windows.'

'Tell me if that bastard Seff comes out on the terrace or anywhere in the open,' Willie said. 'Sooner we get 'im knocked off the better.'

'All right. But I can only cover the front from here. There's a door at the north end of the house and another at the back.'

Modesty said, 'The front's the place to watch until they know we're up here. Then it's going to get tougher. Willie, go and make sure they don't come up the stairs.'

Willie picked up two grenades, a tear gas bomb, and an oblong packet of something soft wrapped in oilskin. As he moved away, Modesty rested one of the AR-15 survival rifles across her knees and set it to semi-automatic. She laid it down beside her and began to string her bow.

Still scanning, Collier said softly, 'Willie tells me the idea was to get down to some little inlet you know of, and leave me there with Lucifer while you two came back to kill Seff and Jack Wish.'

'And Bowker.'

'That has my vote too. But we're blown now.'

'There was always an odds-on chance of that.'

'So what happens?'

'We fight. Maybe we win. But the main thing is not to lose. There's a ship coming in at dawn.'

'Your friend Dall. Willie told me. And then?'

'When whatever Moros are left standing see a ten thousand tonner in the bay I think they'll take to their boats.'

'With Seff and company?'

'We're hoping to make sure they're not among those left standing.'

Collier took his eye from the tube and looked at her. 'I don't usually love girls who are very sure of themselves,' he said politely, 'but I'm happy to make an exception in the present circumstances. I find you very comforting.'

'Good. But it's not going to be a stroll, Steve. We're in for a long, rough fight. And it's the long ones that tell on you, so don't waste any energy—physical or mental. Understand?'

'I grasp the theory.'

'That's a start. We're in a good position and we'll do a lot of damage. But it's a long time till dawn and we can't tell how it's all going to work out. I've set things up, but it'll be for Seff to call the play.'

Below, in front of the house, voices were rising. Collier put his eye to the tube again and pressed the switch. After a moment he said, 'Jack Wish is out there now, talking to Sangro.'

'Anybody looking up this way?'

'No.'

Modesty turned and slowly raised her head above the edge of the parapet. The Moros were spreading out, starting to search the open ground. Some of them would be round at the back of the house soon. It did not matter yet. Jack Wish, a stocky figure in shirt and trousers, was talking to Sangro and gesturing. Two Moros held the parachute canopy.

She balanced the advantage of longer concealment against the advantage of killing Wish now, and decided to hold her hand. Better to let mystery and anxiety work on the nerves for as long as possible. Besides, Jack Wish was not her prime target. Slowly she lowered her head and said to Collier, 'Keep scanning. Tell me if you see Seff. I'll take him on the first offer. Wish is going to be around when trouble breaks, but Seff will stay under cover.'

She laid the bow down on a piece of foam rubber and turned to the medical kit. Collier looked away from the tube for a moment and saw her make an injection in Lucifer's arm.

'What's that?' he asked.

'Scopolamine. He'll come round, but he'll be drowsy. Easy to handle. That's your job, Steve, in between times.'

'My job?'

'Yes. I've told him there's rebellion in Hell. Led by Asmodeus. He'll believe it now. Put it to him again when he comes round. Make him understand that he can be destroyed here, on the upper levels. And that we're fighting for him.'

'God Almighty,' Collier said wearily. 'We *still* have to play up to him?'

'It's the only way to keep him co-operative, and we're going to need that. You've handled him long enough to know the technique.'

'All right.' Collier wiped a hand across his dry lips. 'What a way to spend a war.'

'It might be the hardest part——' She broke off, looking past Collier, her eyes narrowed. He followed her gaze, and was in time to see the figure of a Moro step out through the door on to the roof, a rifle poised in his hands.

A shadow moved, merged briefly with the Moro. There was no sound. Willie Garvin caught the falling rifle and lowered the slack form of the Moro noiselessly to the thick lead sheeting of the roof.

'One,' Modesty said, and Collier realised with a sudden lurch of his stomach that he had just seen a killing. It was as if Modesty sensed his reaction, for she said quietly, 'No. That's two. Willie signed one off as we touched down. Just as well, or you'd be dead by now. Remember that, Steve. Remember that everybody's playing for keeps from now on, and they'll blast us on sight. So make up your mind whether you want to stay alive. And if so, don't think twice when the time comes to pull the trigger.'

He nodded soberly, and raised the tube again.

Below, Jack Wish was shouting towards the house and Bowker's voice was answering from a ground-floor window.

Willie glided across the roof. 'Jap rifle,' he whispered, laying it down beside Modesty with a bandolier of ammunition. 'An Arisaka. They sent one bloke up to look round. Most likely be ten minutes before they miss 'im.'

'Yes. But there'll be two or maybe a bunch next time. If it's only two, try to take them quietly, Willie. The more we get that way the better.'

'Right, Princess.' Willie hefted the big knife he still held in his right hand. The blade was stained now. He turned and moved at a crouch towards the stairs bulkhead again.

Lucifer stirred and made a faint sound. Modesty pushed a piece of foam rubber padding under his head and knelt up, leaning over him, her hand hovering over his mouth. His eyes opened and came slowly into focus.

'It's begun, Lucifer,' she whispered. 'The rebellion.

Asmodeus and the others are trying to find you and cast you down into the lower levels. But Collier's with me, and another friend. We're loyal to you, Lucifer. But we all have to keep very quiet for a little while.'

She went on whispering gently, insistently, watching dull comprehension dawn slowly in his face.

'... soon there'll be a battle, Lucifer. Shooting and explosions. You have to keep low down, you understand?'

His lips moved. 'Armageddon?' he muttered thickly, and despite the drug there was a strange eagerness in his eyes.

She hesitated. Then—— 'No. Not Armageddon yet. It's your own servants who have rebelled, Lucifer. But we'll defeat them.'

'Yes.' He sat up slowly, looking about him, but kept his voice low. 'Yes. The greater power must always conquer the lesser.' The words came laboriously, a little slurred. 'They will be cast down, even as I was cast down from the celestial kingdom before time began.' He paused, then added, 'I shall ... I shall have to create a new and deeper Hell for them.'

'Yes,' she said quickly. 'That's very important, Lucifer. You must give a lot of thought to it.' There was value in giving him something to keep his partly drugged mind occupied.

Lucifer drew up his feet and sat crosslegged, sinking into a sleepy reverie. After a moment she moved away and squatted beside Collier again, her back to the parapet. He stopped scanning for a moment and murmured, 'Very nice. You've done it all for me.'

'Not all. There's a long night ahead. You'll have to keep half an eye on him when the balloon goes up. Knock him cold with a gun-butt if you have to.'

'Me? I'm still wondering how *you* put him out. He was a good second ahead of you last time you tangled with him. Maybe two.'

'Yes. But he was acting by instinct then. All right, I mean by precognition. This time I got him to think, to concentrate on being ahead of me.'

'Ah.' Collier nodded and put his eye to the tube again. So

273

that was what Willie had meant. Forcing Lucifer to act consciously was the surest way to block his precognitive ability.

Collier was pleasantly aware that at this moment he was free from fear. He did not imagine that he owed this to any natural courage. It was partly because he felt the same sense of unreality as on that night in Paris; partly because he had no responsibility except to do as he was told by people who knew what they were about; but above all, his calmness stemmed from the tremendous relief of knowing that he no longer carried in his body the sudden death that had dwelt within him every second for so many long days and nights. Seff, he decided, could take all his transmitters and stuff them up his——

Modesty was asking a question, and Collier's happy imagery was interrupted. When he had scanned carefully and assured her that nobody was watching the roof, Modesty again edged the top of her head over the parapet. This time she stayed there, motionless, the little AR-15 held across her chest. Collier switched off the noctoscope and lowered it. The other survival rifle lay beside him. Willie had shown him how to handle it and how to use a grenade, if and when the time came. He would be told when.

Collier hoped very much that the time would come. With his release from the death capsule, a great flood of pent-up hatred had been loosed within him. Violence was alien to his temperament, but he had a murderous longing now to feel the gun judder in his hands, to spray bullets into Seff and Bowker, into Jack Wish, into Sangro and his Moros. It was, he knew, a most uncivilised longing. But this did not trouble him in the least. Oddly enough, he felt quite certain that Modesty and Willie did not share his primitive urge for vengeance. He was equally certain that they would kill Seff as soon as they could.

There came a faint sound from below the bulkhead, followed at once by a slithering thud, a cry choked off. Then, startlingly loud, a shot. Even as he jumped at the sound it was swallowed by a roar and a flash of flame as something erupted below the bulkhead.

Modesty was kneeling up, the elbow of her supporting arm resting on the parapet as she fired down in quick, economical bursts. Collier turned and knelt beside her, snatching up the other AR-15.

For a moment he could distinguish little. His vision was attuned to the extra light provided by the noctoscope. Now he understood why he had been allotted the task of scanning. Modesty had kept her own vision adjusted to the darkness. As his pupils dilated he saw scattered men running for cover, and three lying still on the ground. Modesty's rifle yapped sharply, three times in quick succession. Two Moros, running together, went down. Another shot followed a man as he hurled himself into the trees to the left. Then the whole area in front of the house was empty, from the stand of low trees on the left to the ridge on the right, and ahead to the cliff edge.

Something cracked like a whip an arm's-length from Collier's head.

Modesty said, 'Down!' He ducked with her behind the shelter of the parapet, realising that the whip-crack sound had been made by a bullet passing near him. This surprised him a little, for he had vaguely imagined that a bullet made a whistling sound. Thinking about it, he saw that the crack would be made by the air coming together after the bullet's passage, as with a whiplash or with lightning.

The deduction pleased him. He saw Willie Garvin dart across from the stairs bulkhead; saw, as Willie swung round, that both the big knives were missing from the sheaths at the back of his belt now.

'Fifteen seconds, Princess. Everybody flat,' Willie said, and extended himself face down, covering the knapsacks of grenades and the packets of plastic explosive with his body. Wondering, Collier went flat beside him.

Modesty was saying, 'Please, Lucifer.'

Collier turned his head and saw that Lucifer still sat cross-legged, hunched, the blue eyes remote. Modesty tugged at him gently, still talking. He looked at her distantly, then lay flat.

275

Willie Garvin said, 'Three of 'em started up the stairs, Princess. I dropped two with the knives but the other got a shot off, so I chucked 'im a grenade.'

'And gas?'

'I went down after an' chucked one bomb along the passage. Set two small charges of P.E. inside the spandrel walls with twenty-second detonators——'

His voice was drowned by a sharp explosion, and a gust of air swept across the roof. The sloping top of the stairs bulkhead jerked up, and the two triangular spandrel walls supporting it collapsed inwards. A few pieces of debris pattered down.

When the smoke cleared Collier saw that the bulkhead had vanished, collapsed inwards to seal off the stairs.

Modesty said, 'That's the end of the easy bit. But at least we've put down nine or ten without too much trouble. Nice job, Willie love. Steve, take a look below. But ease that tube up slowly.'

Collier sat up and lifted the noctoscope. The ground below was still clear of men. Somewhere he could hear Jack Wish's voice bawling hoarsely. Bowker's voice replied from a lower window.

'All clear for the moment,' Collier said. He felt a little light-headed with excitement. 'I imagine they're thinking hard now. From my knowledge of friend Bowker, I have every hope that he's thinking with his bowels.'

It was rewarding to hear Willie chuckle and to see Modesty's eyes rest on him with quick approval.

'Be trying round the back soon,' said Willie, and she nodded. The Moros would work round to the back of the house and try to reach the roof, or perhaps climb the sloping rock face of the mountain, from which they would have an excellent field of fire. But on the rock face they would be sitting targets in the moonlight. Their best move would be to find some way of scaling the walls of the house, so that the defenders on the roof would have to expose themselves to fire down.

Modesty picked up the second noctoscope and passed it to

Willie. The situation was still good. There could be no sudden assault from any direction, and watching the whole perimeter of the T-shaped roof would not be too difficult as long as the tubes were in action. Once they were damaged, which was an increasing possibility, things would get tougher. But that still lay somewhere in the future.

'Steve can 'ave the Colt auto. These'll do me,' Willie said, picking up the Arisaka and the Marlin. He crawled away across the roof and took up a position near the junction of the T, surveyed the ground below on one side of the stem, then moved across to scan the other side.

'Ease that tube to the horizontal and watch the terrace, Steve,' Modesty said 'That's their quickest way up.'

He obeyed, then stiffened. 'One Moro there,' he whispered. 'Sub-machine gun of some kind. He's looking up.'

'Spot him for me.'

'Ten yards to my right. Halfway between the wall and the balustrade. Standing still—no, moving away now. Heading for that drainpipe at the end, I think. For God's sake be careful——!'

The last words were an agonised warning, for he had sensed her movement as she stood upright. There was no sound, but through the tube he saw the Moro jerk suddenly. The sub-machine gun fell, and the man went down. Something long and thin jutted from between his shoulder blades.

A moment later bullets from the stand of trees whined above the parapet, but Modesty was crouched again. Collier snatched the tube to safety and saw her lay down the short bow beside the quiver of arrows.

'Good enough for short range,' she said. 'And quiet. We'll need all our ammunition before we're through.'

277

22

SEFF slid open the panel at the back of his workbench, locked the frequency control, then pressed the transmitter key. He was fully dressed in his black suit and white shirt with a wing collar. The only difference from his normal appearance was the slight bristle on his chin and jowls.

Regina was dressed, too. Her stockings were wrinkled, the seams twisted, but that was usual. On her cheeks were rare high spots of colour, but her manner was as frail as ever. She took the last curler from her thin hair and said regretfully, 'I don't suppose that will kill Mr. Collier now, Seffy.'

Seff nodded, waited another ten seconds, then released the key and switched off. 'You're probably right, my dear. But I thought it wise to activate the capsule, even if the chance of killing Mr. Collier is small.'

'Oh, I certainly agree with you.' Indignation came into her quavering voice. 'I just feel so *annoyed* for you, Seffy, after all the trouble you've taken.'

'We must make the best of it, Regina.' Seff began to take down the puppets hanging from a row of hooks and pack them into a case. 'Unfortunately the situation is not yet clear, so I cannot make any final decision. But I think it likely that we shall have to close down this particular operation.'

'You mean—*all* of it?' Tears trembled in her faded eyes.

'I'm afraid so, my dear. It's quite apparent that the Blaise girl is alive and has returned with a companion or companions. They have not only taken Collier, but Lucifer also. I doubt that Mr. Wish and the Moros can be *selective* in dealing with this matter. And even if Lucifer is left alive, I think it unlikely that he could be of use in the same way as before.'

'Oh, Seffy! I'm so sorry...'

'There, there, my dear. We have a great deal of money

behind us now, and you can rely on me to devise something quite new and equally interesting after a little while.'

'Oh, I know you will, Seffy. But when I think of how you've worked and planned...'

'Don't distress yourself, Regina.' He paused in his work and patted her thin arm. 'We must just take the view that our present work must cease a year or eighteen months sooner than we had hoped.'

'Yes. Yes, I'll think of it that way, Seffy.'

'Good. Now we must be ready to leave tonight if things go badly. Fortunately we can rely on Sangro for transport. He would never dare to incur Mr. Wu Smith's displeasure by deserting us. But—ah—don't mention evacuation to Dr. Bowker or Mr. Wish at this stage, my dear.'

The door opened and Bowker entered. His eyes were red and streaming. He coughed and swore savagely.

'They've sealed off the access to the roof,' he said. 'Can't get at them that way. They dropped a tear gas bomb down before they blew the bulkhead in, but I've got all the upper windows open now, and the gas is clearing.'

He sat on the edge of a bench, took out a cigarette and lit it with shaking hands. 'God, how did she work all this, Seff?'

'Blaise?'

'Well it *is* her, surely?'

'I have no doubt of it. But I do not intend to waste time in useless speculation, Dr. Bowker. She is up there on the roof, well armed. And she did not come alone.'

'No, she didn't. Wish says Garvin's with her.'

'*Garvin?*' For once Seff was startled.

'Yes.'

'What is the reason for his surmise?'

Bowker jerked his head upwards. 'I told him what I'd seen up by the roof access. It was messy. You'd be surprised what a grenade can do. But two of the Moros you sent up to check the roof had bloody great knives in them. Wish says that's Garvin. Blaise can't have killed him in that duel you set up.'

Seff was silent for long seconds. When at last he spoke his

high voice was a little uneven. 'They appear to have been extremely clever.' Turning away, he linked his hands behind his back and began to pace up and down, his joints creaking. 'Mr. Wish is still outside, organising the Moros?'

'Yes.' Bowker rubbed his sore eyes and dragged on his cigarette.

'How are you communicating with him?'

'Bawling from a window, at first. Nobody fancies crossing that open ground. But we're using a runner now. He comes to the end of the dip, then works his way along the foot of the cliff and makes a ten-yard dash for the door at the end of the north wing.'

'That is our only way out?'

Bowker shrugged. 'It's the safest way. Only ten yards of open ground, and the Moros by the ridge give a burst of covering fire when we signal for it.'

Seff pondered. 'Do you think the Moros will be able to finish this matter quickly?'

'How the hell do I know?' Bowker's voice was suddenly shrill. 'And what do you mean, *quickly*? Tomorrow? The next day? For all I know we'll have to *starve* them out!' He swore vilely.

'Kindly be calm, Dr. Bowker. I am very displeased with your manner.' Seff's face had taken on an ugly twist but his voice was even again now. 'I must also insist that you cease using that kind of language in front of my wife.'

Bowker stared open-mouthed, his body going slack with astonishment. 'Jesus!' he said almost hysterically.

'Tomorrow will be far too late.' Seff was pacing again. 'I am quite sure that Blaise and Garvin have acted in this way to prevent Collier and Lucifer being killed. But we must expect more company by dawn. They must have arranged a follow-up.'

Bowker wiped a hand over his lips. He was very frightened. 'We've got to get out, then!'

'Not if we can dispose of our friends on the roof and leave no evidence of their visit. But that we must do. They have too much knowledge of us, Dr. Bowker. We do not want to spend the rest of our lives on the run, do we? It would be distressing for Regina.'

A comment on Regina leapt to Bowker's lips, but he suppressed it. 'I'll get word to Jack Wish, tell him to finish them off fast.'

'By all means convey that instruction to him. And tell him also that I want several drums of petrol brought up here to the house.'

'Petrol?'

'That is what I said, Dr. Bowker. If matters go too slowly we shall have to burn our friends out. You can no doubt get the petrol here by the safe route with suitable covering fire.'

Bowker nodded. Seff's cold assurance had calmed his fear a little. Burn them out. Burn the house under them. Yes. That would do it.

'I'll pass the word to Wish,' he said, and went out of the room.

Willie Garvin put down the noctoscope, waited for his eyes to adjust, then rose quickly, sighting the Arisaka rifle. A Moro was settling against the sloping rock face behind the house, about thirty feet above the ground. Willie fired, saw the man fall, and ducked quickly down behind the parapet again. A burst of automatic fire cracked low over his head, and chips flew from the coping.

He moved along to a new position and slowly raised the tube again.

Lucifer still sat crosslegged near the front parapet, his face blotted out by a gasmask. For ten minutes, while wisps of tear gas seeped from the upper windows, they had all worn gasmasks. Now the air was untainted, but Lucifer would not take his mask off. He had seen the others in them, the black snouted faces with huge round eyes. This was more like his true self, the Lucifer of the lower levels. He had kept the gasmask on.

It was hot on the lead roof. The air lay heavy and humid.

Collier wiped sweat from his brow and put his eye to the tube again. 'Terrace is clear,' he said. 'Ground out front is clear, too.'

'We'll try the north wing again,' Modesty said. He edged the tube down slowly, then crawled after her. Every few minutes they had moved from place to place, keeping check on the three sides of the front span of the house.

Willie Garvin was guarding the back and the stem of the T. A little while ago he had used a grenade, and for a while afterwards somebody had been moaning on the ground below. Collier guessed that there had been a group preparing to climb the wall. Worth a grenade. He had said as much to Modesty and received a disinterested shrug in reply. She had not even looked round when the grenade went off. Presumably what went on at the back was Willie's concern, and he could be trusted to do what was necessary without advice or comment.

Three times she had fired herself, on Collier's spotting. Two more men lay dead or wounded out in front. The third Collier had spotted over the northern edge, and she had been just too late to catch the man as he darted from the house and vanished quickly behind the jutting rock face close by.

Holding the tube almost horizontal, Collier scanned the narrow stretch of ground below. 'Nothing,' he said. 'But somebody seems to be flashing a light from just inside the door. I can see the beam——'

Bullets spattered the parapet and cracked overhead. The tube jerked in his hands. When he lowered it he saw that the casing was shattered.

'It's bust,' he said.

'Yes.' Modesty's blackened face was hard. 'And I'm a fool. They keep giving bursts along this edge. Covering fire for getting in and out of the house. That light you saw was a signal. I should have realised.'

'We had to look anyway,' Collier said reasonably, and was both pleased and surprised to see her teeth show in a sudden smile.

'You sounded very much like Willie then,' she said. 'He always has an out for me when I do things wrong.'

'It wasn't wrong, dammit. But it's a pity. What do we do now?'

'Work by quick glimpses. Stick our heads up and get them down again fast. And keep——'

Something curved over the parapet, leaving a streak of sparks in its wake, and bounced on the lead sheeting of the roof. But even while it still hung in the air Modesty was moving. Her rifle clattered down as she took three long, crouching strides and dived. The missile was a big soup can bound with wire. Her hands caught it on the first bounce, just as the spluttering spark of the fuse vanished into a small hole in the can.

Frozen, Collier saw her roll and throw the dreadful thing in a single movement. It cleared the parapet, and a moment after it had dropped out of sight there came a fierce explosion and a patter of iron shrapnel.

Modesty was by his side again, breathing a little quickly. 'And keep on the move,' she said. 'Don't stick your head up in the same place twice.'

It took Collier a few seconds to register that she was continuing her interrupted sentence. But by then she was away again. He saw her kneeling by the front parapet, pulling the pin from a grenade. She lifted her head, stared for a second, ducked down and scrambled quickly along for a few yards. Again she knelt up, this time leaning over the parapet to look directly down at the first-floor terrace. As she drew back a shot came from below and a Moro voice shouted.

Collier saw her arm swing, heard a clatter as the grenade bounced on the terrace. The grenade sounded its iron blast and there was a brief flash of light. She leaned out over the parapet again. Collier's stomach crawled as she hung there, peering. He heard two shots from Willie at the rear.

She drew back and dropped to cover once more, beckoning Collier to join her. He crawled across, sweat running from his body in the oppressive heat.

'Bomb over the north parapet, attack from the terrace,' she said. 'But it didn't work, and it cost them a few people. Things will probably go quiet for a little while now.'

'Yes. I expect they find you rather discouraging,' Collier said, and drew a forearm across his wet forehead. 'Did they *make* that bomb?'

'Yes. A can filled with black powder from cartridges. A handful of steel bolts for shrapnel. Wire up tight, and fit with a short fuse.'

'It's probably illegal,' said Collier, feeling his throat go dry. 'I hadn't thought about bombs or grenades.'

'They haven't any grenades. I know exactly what they've got. I had four weeks to make an inventory in my head.'

So she had been noting everything, all through those quiet and hopeless days. Grenades tossed up here on to the roof would have murdered them, but she knew the attackers had no grenades. They had made a bomb, though. That was probably Seff's idea. His eyes roved the parapet uneasily.

'I doubt if they'll try another,' Modesty said. 'It's a long, fiddly job making one up. Probably took them an hour.'

'An *hour*?' Collier peered closely at the watch on his wrist. His impression was that they had been on the roof for three hours at least, and that was allowing for the fact that it seemed like a lifetime. But it was only half past two. They had been up here no longer than an hour and a half. He would not have believed that so much could happen in so short a time, and he wondered how old he would be by the time the night was over. Always assuming he was still alive.

Willie was coming towards them, the Arisaka and the other noctoscope in his hands, the Marlin thirty-thirty slung over a shoulder.

'Going very nice,' he said. 'I reckon we can take five.'

'Our tube got smashed,' Modesty said.

'Ah. You'd better 'ave mine. It's a snip at the back.' He passed the tube to Collier, who took it reluctantly and said, 'I'm sick of looking through these bloody things. When do I get to shoot this AR-15 thing?'

284

A grin split Willie's blackened face. 'Listen to 'im. Proper tearaway.'

'Take the tube and start scanning, Steve,' Modesty said. 'You'll get your chance before we're through. There's a long night ahead.'

'Bloody bossy woman,' Collier said moodily but without heat, and heard Willie chuckle.

There was no movement out front or on the terrace. Collier said, 'Who's Michael, by the way?'

'Michael?' Modesty's voice was puzzled.

'Yes. Lucifer said something while I was persuading him to get that gasmask on. You were shooting at the time. He said: "She is my Michael."'

'Blimey . . . !'

Collier looked away from the tube and saw that Willie, lying propped on his elbows, was shaking with laughter.

'Let's share the joke, Willie love,' Modesty said.

'*Saint* Michael.' Willie got his voice under control. 'The bloke with the sword who chucked Lucifer out of 'eaven when 'e rebelled. You're clobbering Lucifer's rebels for 'im now, Princess!'

Collier was delighted by the momentary blank astonishment on Modesty's face. Then he looked across at the still figure in the gasmask, sitting crosslegged a dozen paces away along the parapet. 'Well, at least he's not being difficult.'

'I think he's withdrawn from the situation,' Modesty said. 'Bowker could tell us why.'

'This may seem conceited,' said Collier, 'but I don't require the services of a head-shrinker to tell me that this is a good situation to withdraw from.' He scanned again, then added, 'It's funny, though. I wouldn't want to be out of it. I wonder why?'

'You don't feel scared?' Modesty asked.

He thought, then answered honestly. 'Not at the moment. It's ridiculous, but I don't. I've been scared ever since Sylt—until now.'

Modesty picked up the flat box from the medical kit. She

285

opened it, shone her pencil torch down and said, 'Look, Steve.'

He bent towards her. In one corner of the box was a tiny roll of oilskin. She edged it open with the torch. Collier saw the capsule. It was different now. Seff had thrown the switch. At one corner was a small irregular hole, its edges partly melted as if by an eruption from within. Modesty nudged the capsule, and a trickle of fine white powder emerged, sparkling in the torch beam.

She switched off and closed the box. 'You've had that in you for a long time. It's no wonder you're past feeling scared now.'

Collier nodded. He knew that he wasn't by any means past feeling scared, but he also understood what she meant. Fear was like pain. An abscess was in some way an unclean pain. When it was lanced, the lesser pain of the cut flesh was almost welcome. Perhaps he did feel fear now, but it was a clean, taut, healthy fear, different even in kind to the horror of carrying that vile capsule in his body.

Willie said, 'It'll probably be a while before they try something new, but I'd better get back.' He eased the knapsack of grenades to a more comfortable position on his hip, then crawled away.

'We'll check both wings, Steve,' Modesty said.

Nothing was stirring anywhere round the house, and three minutes later they settled at the front again.

'I should think we must have knocked off about half the opposition,' said Collier. 'When I say *"we"*, I speak loosely, of course.'

'Some may only have taken flesh wounds.'

'True. A third of them out of action, then?'

'About that.'

'Couldn't we scatter a few tear gas bombs and try to get down to that inlet where you were going to leave me with Lucifer? I mean, hide there till Dall arrives with his merry men?'

'No. We're in a good position here. We've done a lot of damage and we can do a lot more as long as they keep coming at us. Getting to the inlet would mean exposing ourselves. You don't choose a running fight against odds when you've got a strongpoint.'

'I suppose not. You talk as if you'd served in an army.'

'I have,' she said, and left it there.

Collier sighed inwardly. This was not the first time she had brought him up short by a simple yet astonishing statement that raised a dozen questions but left them unanswered.

'What do you think their next move will be?' he said.

'I don't know, Steve. We're getting to the tough bit now. So far we've had the initiative. Now it's Seff's turn, and we can only play it by ear.'

They scouted the parapet again. On the northern side, where covering fire had shattered the first tube, Collier kept to one end and slid the remaining tube over very slowly, horizontally. All was quiet on the short stretch of open ground below.

He was uneasily aware that his nerves were growing more tense now that nothing was happening. So much for his recent boast.

Modesty had gone to check that Lucifer was still sunk in his trance-like reverie. When she returned, Collier said, 'You mean to kill Seff?'

'Yes.' Her voice held no emphasis. 'Next to keeping ourselves alive, that's the number one priority.'

'Reprisal?'

'No.' She opened her shirt to let the air cool her sweating body. 'I think maybe that colours Willie's intentions. But for me, Seff is just too bad to be left alive.'

It was true, thought Collier. Seff was like a thing from Lucifer's hell made real. 'What about Wish and Bowker?' he asked.

'They're no better. Maybe a little different, but just as cancerous.'

'And Regina. Will you kill her?'

It was a moment or two before she answered. 'I'll take that as it comes. Let's say I'll be glad if she has a gun in her hand when I see her.'

287

'She's mad, you know,' said Collier. 'So is Seff, for that matter. They're as mad as Lucifer, in a different way.'

'Don't talk bloody nonsense!' Her voice was low and angry. He had not heard her swear before.

'Nonsense?'

'If Lucifer ever killed anyone, which he hasn't, he'd do it without having the slightest idea that it was wrong. You could stick a gun at his head, and he'd still do it. Seff may be mentally sick by medical standards, but he knows exactly what he's doing, and he relishes it. He's just plain evil.'

'You sound fierce on the subject.'

'I am. I've run into a few really bad people. Not sick. Bad. And another thing——' She stopped abruptly.

Collier said, 'Go on.'

She shrugged, her eyes on the gun in her hands. 'It's hard to say without seeming to be a do-gooder, and that's a big laugh. I'm a selfish bitch, on the whole. But I know about criminals and I know about international police work, so I can tell you one fact that you can take for gospel. If Seff lives, he'll kill more people. Why the hell should we let him?'

Collier said, 'I'm not arguing, just asking. Allow me to say that your intentions have my fervent approval.'

'Good. But we've a long way to go yet. Take another look, Steve.'

He slid the tube over the parapet and felt his nerves twitch with shock. Two Moros were staggering across the ten-yard stretch to the north door carrying a thirty-gallon petrol drum in a rope sling.

'Target!' he whispered urgently. 'They're carrying petrol!'

The last word brought her to her feet in a bound, the AR-15 to her shoulder, and to Collier's horror she was standing fully erect. The rifle spoke once, and a man went down, but with the echo of the shot there came an answering volley from the low ridge which edged the beginning of the downward slope some hundred paces beyond the curving face of the mountain.

Collier heard the crack of bullets overhead, the whine of a ricochet, the patter of lead flattening against the parapet. He snatched the tube down, and saw Modesty jerk as she ducked. The survival rifle clattered down, and she fell sideways.

Collier saw blood welling from the side of her head. Then, as if without any interim, he was standing upright, the other AR-15 in his hands, set to automatic. His finger locked on the trigger and the gun juddered as he fired towards the pinpoints of light which sparkled along the edge of the ridge. His whole being was consumed by the rage to destroy, and he was barely conscious of the bullets that whipped about him.

The rifle ceased to vibrate in his hands. He swore incoherently.

The bastard gun had stopped! Why? Jesus, the magazine had run out of course! Where were the spares——?

His legs were scythed from under him. The cut in his back gave a stab of pain as he hit the roof. Willie Garvin held him down with an arm that almost crushed his chest.

'Keep still or I'll knock you cold,' Willie's voice snarled. 'You 'ear me?'

Collier managed to nod. His fury drained from him and he felt only sick and afraid now. Willie let him go and said, 'Hop about with that tube. Give me a shout if they try anything.' With the last word he turned away and knelt over Modesty. His hand went to the carotid artery in her neck, feeling for the pulse. He seemed to relax a little. Carefully he explored her body, then gave his attention to her head.

One side of her camouflage-blackened face was covered in blood now. Willie took a field dressing from his pocket, ripped it open with his teeth, then began to wipe the blood away.

Collier said, 'Is it bad?'

'Don't know yet.' Willie looked up, glaring. 'For Christ's sake get around with that tube, will you?'

23

'It ought to burn like a torch,' said Bowker. 'They've soaked the whole of the upper floor.'

Seff shut the lid of the padded suitcase containing the puppets and the packet of industrial diamonds, and locked it carefully before giving his attention to Bowker. 'I would like a precise report if you please, Dr. Bowker. We must continue to be orderly in our thinking, even under difficulties.'

Bowker was grimy, his shirt clung to his body and he smelt of petrol. Increasing panic had tightened his nerves to breaking point, and his chin trembled as he spoke in jerky sentences.

'The upper floor's flooded with petrol. There's a train of petrol-soaked sheets running down to the ground floor. All the Moros are out with Wish now. He's throwing a ring round the house. We signal for covering fire, light the sheets, and go.'

'That seems to be satisfactory.' Seff opened a drawer and took out two Browning ·380 automatics.

'If I might ask Dr. Bowker something, Seffy...?' Regina said diffidently.

'Of course, my dear, of course.'

Regina looked at Bowker. 'I was just wondering if you had opened all the upper windows to make a nice draught, so that everything will burn well?'

'No! I've shut them,' Bowker said shrilly. 'You don't need a *draught* to help sixty gallons of petrol in a bone dry house, for God's sake! And we don't *want* masses of smoke pouring out to give them cover!' His voice rose even higher. 'The whole idea is to build a furnace under that roof so it sizzles like a hotplate! Drive the bastards off, and shoot them as they climb down.' His voice cracked and he almost screamed, 'Satisfied, you—you bloody old faggot?'

Seff lifted a pacifying hand.

'I think, my dear,' he said, 'that Dr. Bowker has taken the correct action in this matter, though of course you were quite right to ascertain *precisely* what he had done, and why.' Seff smiled toothy approval at his wife, raised one of the Brownings, and shot Bowker twice through the chest.

Stiff-legged, Bowker fell straight back. His shoulders hit the floor. He bounced an inch or two, then lay with arms outspread. For a moment his fingers scrabbled feebly at the floor. A sound came from his throat, and then he was still.

'Oh, what a *horrid* man, Seffy.' Regina's face was flushed. 'Did you hear what he——?'

'Please try to forget it, my dear,' Seff broke in soothingly. 'I suppose we must take people as we find them, and though I deplore Dr. Bowker's outburst, one must admit that he was very useful to us for quite a long time. However, his usefulness is ended, and it would be very foolish to leave any loose ends in closing down this operation.'

'Yes, I see what you mean, Seffy. Are there any other loose ends?'

Seff put on the three safeties carefully, and considered. 'I think Mr. Wish may be useful for a little longer. A few hours. He is a very energetic and experienced man. But once Blaise and her companions have been disposed of...'

Seff's voice trailed off and he stared into space. 'Yes,' he went on at last. 'We have no worries about the Moros. Sangro will obey me, since those are his orders from Mr. Wu Smith, who will want to handle the take from our last pick-up. But I feel Mr. Wish should be caused to withdraw. We shall have to make a completely fresh start, and we don't want to share the capital we have accumulated.'

Seff put the gun in his pocket, checked the other Browning, and moved towards Regina with it.

'I shall have to stay close to Mr. Wish once we are outside,' he said. 'And that, I am afraid, compels me to ask if *you* would be so good as to deal with Mr. Garcia, my dear?'

'Oh, goodness.' Regina put thin fingers to her lips. 'I'd quite forgotten about him.'

'He is certainly a loose end to be—ah—cut off,' said Seff. 'No doubt he will be down at the inlet with the dolphins, as usual, and I feel sure he will not be in any way difficult to deal with. I'm extremely sorry to trouble you with this, Regina——'

'Gracious, it's no trouble, Seffy.' She smiled fondly and took the gun, putting it in the big shabby handbag that lay on the bench. 'Shall I wait down by the dolphin pool for you after I've shot Mr. Garcia?'

'I think that is the best arrangement.' Seff picked up the suitcase and led the way out of the workroom and along the passage to the foot of the stairs. A twisted sheet, dripping with petrol, hung down from the landing above. Other sheets were knotted to it and ran along the passage to the open door leading out of the north wing.

A flashlamp stood on a ledge by the door. Seff picked it up and pointed it out into the moonlit night. He said, 'You have the matches, Regina?'

'Yes, Seffy.' She took a box from her handbag and struck a match. Seff flashed the light three times. A rattle of steady fire began to peck at the parapet directly above. Seff nodded. Regina put the match to one end of the knotted sheets. Flame leapt along the passage.

Together they stepped out of the door and hurried across the short open stretch to the cover afforded by the bulging face of the rock, Seff creaking like an ungreased windlass, Regina hobbling on her corn-ridden feet.

Modesty Blaise twisted her head aside, but the stinging pain would not leave her. She fought her way up through grey layers of unreality. Her face was wet. A hand held her chin, preventing her from turning away from the pain that jabbed at her nose and eyes.

A voice was saying softly. 'Princess ... come on, Princess, snap out of it. Come on now.'

She had to force her arm to move before she could push

away Willie Garvin's hand holding the little bottle of strong smelling salts. Her eyes opened.

'That's better ...' Relief sighed in his voice.

His face came into focus, upside down. She realised that he was kneeling behind her, with her head pillowed on his lap. The bottle was still poised in his hand, ready to thrust under her nose again if she slipped back into unconsciousness.

She lay still, keeping her eyes open and breathing deeply, reaching deep down into the reservoirs of strength. Vision and mind cleared steadily under the driving force of her will.

'How am I, Willie?'

'Lucky.' His teeth showed for a moment. 'You copped a bit that chipped off the parapet.' He held up a ragged piece of stone about three inches long, broken from the edge of the coping. 'You've got a cut along the side of your 'ead, but it's not deep.'

She lifted a hand, exploring. There was a long lump running from just short of the right temple to behind the ear. A narrow strip of plaster lay along the middle of the swelling. Willie would have stopped the bleeding with a coagulant before putting the plaster on.

Her head throbbed. Slowly she took hold of the pain and subdued it, sealing it away in some remote part of her awareness.

'What's happening?' she asked.

'Steve's darting about with the tube, but they all seem to be keeping their 'eads down. Lucifer's still squatting there in 'is gasmask—'aving a think, I suppose. You've only been out for about four minutes.'

She lifted her head and rolled over, coming to her hands and knees.

'Steady, Princess.'

'I'm all right. A bit shaky, but it's passing.' She frowned, and moved a hand about, patting the lead sheeting of the roof. 'Willie, this roof's *hot*.'

He pressed a hand to the lead. They knelt looking at each other, feeling the soft metal grow hotter with the passing

293

seconds. Modesty nodded, and together they crawled to the front parapet where their weapons had first been laid out.

Collier came scuttling towards them from the rear. He looked at Modesty and said, 'Thank God.' Then, quickly— 'They've started a fire. The roof's damn near melting around where the bulkhead was.'

'Yes.' Modesty looked across to the corner where Lucifer sat unmoving. 'What's it like over there, Steve?'

'Not too bad yet.'

'All right. Let him stay there for a moment.' She looked at Willie, a hand to her head. 'Fire. I remember now. They were carrying a drum of petrol in. That's why I had to take a chance.'

'Sure.' Willie was clipping a new magazine to his AR-15. The magazine was marked with a circle of red paint.

Collier slipped the tube over the edge and looked down at the terrace below. 'God, it looks like a furnace glowing through the windows. They've kept them shut to confine the fire. We're sitting on a hotplate.' He withdrew the tube and looked round the roof. There was the smell of burning now, and thin wisps of smoke were rising from crevices where the stairs bulkhead had been blown in. 'If we stay here we'll frizzle, and if we show ourselves they're waiting to pick us off. There's not even enough blasted smoke to give us cover!'

'Willie's going to draw some of them away now,' Modesty said. 'We've been saving this one.'

'Draw them away? How?'

She gestured for him to watch. Willie had backed away from the parapet. He was on one knee, elbow resting on the raised knee as he sighted. His line of fire just cleared the nearby parapet and the distant cliff edge, so he was still screened from any hidden watchers below.

He fired a dozen single shots, aiming carefully, then lowered the rifle.

'Take a look, Steve,' said Modesty. 'The Moro boats.'

Collier eased the tube up and put his eye to the viewer. Two hundred yards beyond the cliff edge, against the southern arm of the bay, the Moro launches were clustered about the wooden landing stage. Pinpoints of flame were showing from the boats and the jetty. The pinpoints grew as he watched.

'Incendiary cartridges,' Modesty said. 'Those boats are the Moros' lifeline. Seff's lifeline, too. Listen.'

They could hear the muffled crackle of flames below them now, but faintly piercing this ominous background came the distant sound of voices shouting urgently from somewhere beyond the ridge to the right.

'Why the hell didn't we do that before?' Collier said, and there was something close to rage in his voice.

'We wanted them to come at us before.' Modesty looked at the spare magazines and grenades. 'Will any of this stuff detonate with the heat, Willie?'

'It'll stand a good bit more than we can, Princess.'

Collier said, 'I can't take great comfort from knowing we'll be dead before the stuff blows up.'

The lead on the roof was too hot to touch with bare skin now, and the air held the furnace-like heat of a steel mill.

'We'll have to stand it till we get more smoke,' Modesty said. 'Jack Wish won't let all the Moros go rushing off to stop the boats burning. He'll send the women, and maybe half the men.' She glanced round the roof. There were still only thin coils of smoke rising beyond the perimeter. 'It would help a lot if a few windows were open. Let's see what a grenade can do.'

'It'll have to explode at window level,' Collier said. 'Can you time it as fine as that?'

'I'll pull the pin and slide one down in an extractor parachute.' She looked at Willie. 'Which way out?'

'The back I reckon, Princess. More confined there, so we can make with the tear gas. Then we drop the ladder down in the angle of the junction.'

Collier ran a dry tongue across cracked lips. He was filthy with grime and he felt suddenly very tired. The early excitement had passed, leaving him empty. He did not feel afraid, only depressed and lethargic.

'Let's get it finished one way or the other,' he said dully, then jerked with shock as Modesty's hand swung hard across his face.

'Get hold of yourself, Steve.' Her voice was sharp.

He sat rigidly, anger sweeping through him. For long seconds he hated her, then slowly it dawned on him that he had just passed through a crisis. He had been on an emotional downswing. Weariness and stress had pushed him into a dark pessimism where he was ready to quit, almost eager to. He wondered how Modesty had known.

As if she had read his thoughts— 'It happens to us all,' she said, and gave him a smile. 'You'll be all right now. Will you go and talk to Lucifer? I don't know if you'll get through to him, but try to prepare him for the idea of climbing down a rope ladder. And take Willie's parachute for him to sit on till we're ready, or he'll start frying soon.'

Collier gathered the black nylon. The air was shimmering with heat now, yet still the flames had not broken free. Modesty was tying a length of cord to the lines of the little extractor parachute. Willie crouched ready with a grenade.

'I reckon the timbers of this place'll be bone dry, Princess,' he said uneasily. 'Might not be much smoke even when the air gets in.'

'No.' She watched Collier crawl away, then looked at Willie and pointed beyond him. 'But there's something we can do about that.'

Regina moved across the rocky ground at the foot of the slope. Her feet hurt and she was wheezing. Looking back, she could just see the upper part of the house. Something exploded at the rear, and next moment a great tongue of flame licked up. A front window burst, and she saw a deep red glow beyond it. The upper floor was a furnace.

Regina nodded. That girl and her friends would soon have to try climbing down. Then they would be killed, and serve them right, too. Clutching her handbag, Regina moved on. She passed an outcrop of rock and came to the long inlet where the dolphins swam, Pluto and Belial and the two under training. Garcia's hut stood on the far side. The light of an oil lamp showed through the wide open door. She could see no shadow moving within. It looked as if Garcia might be out attending to his dolphins. That meant she would have to go right down to the far end of the inlet to find him.

Regina clicked her tongue in annoyance and moved on.

Garcia sat with his trousered legs dangling in the water, an empty basket beside him. He was often in the water, and never bothered to take his clothes off. Garcia did not feel good. Neither did Pluto and Belial; he knew their feelings as surely as he knew his own. They had finished the basket of fish but they were still nervous, still wanted him to come in the water and make a fuss of them. He wished now that he had not sent out the other two dolphins on a ten-mile sonar recall test earlier.

Garcia glanced towards the ridge which hid the house from his sight. Shooting. Noise. Trouble and shouting. Now the glow of fire. Why did they do these things? It made him feel bad, and that always upset Pluto and Belial. He slipped from the rock and stood chest-deep in the water, wading about, letting them nuzzle and buffet him as he fondled them, speaking softly to them in Spanish.

Perhaps it would be good to give them something to do...? Yes. They could make a night run outside the bay for an hour, towing the dead shark. He had harpooned it four days earlier, and it was well decayed now. Pluto and Belial would like to do that. It was not as exciting as The Game, but it would calm them.

Garcia put his arms round Pluto and rolled over in the water, then moved to the bank and pulled himself out. His clothes streamed as he moved to the rough shelter he had built over the dead shark to keep the birds from it. Being wet or dry made no difference to Garcia. He pulled aside one or two planks, took out the twin harness with its connecting rope, forty feet long with a hook in the middle, and trudged back to the water's edge.

Leaving the middle of the rope coiled beside him, he squatted and called Belial. The dolphin leapt joyously out of the water, splashed down, then emerged again with his head thrusting up eagerly. Garcia slipped the harness on. Pluto was already jostling to be harnessed.

'Gently, little one, gently,' Garcia said, and fastened the second webbing strap. 'So. Wait now...' He stood up, and was walking away to fetch the dead shark when a voice spoke.

'Mr. Garcia? Are you there?'

Regina emerged from the shadows, fifty paces away, and came towards him. Garcia's nose wrinkled. He took a chewed match from his pocket and put it between his teeth, waiting. He did not like this woman. He did not like any of them from the house, except perhaps the one they called Collier. The dark girl, she had been all right, too. But she had gone now.

'Oh, Mr. Garcia, there you are.' Regina limped to a halt. He noticed that she had fouled the coil of rope with her foot, but he said nothing. The people from the house did not understand his work at all. He was used to that now. It was no good complaining about anything, for the one called Seff might then send him away, and Pluto and Belial would be alone. They might even die. Garcia's eyes filled with tears at the thought.

The bony woman stood rummaging in her big handbag now. She said, 'Oh dear, what a night, Mr. Garcia. So much trouble. Is everything quite all right down here?'

'Yes, señora.' He was about to tell her that Pluto and Belial were going out for a run, but then her hand came out of the handbag and something hit him with shocking force in the chest. There was a noise, a sharp explosion.

Garcia was reeling, trying to keep his balance, trying to understand. Regina frowned, levelled the gun carefully and fired again. Another hammerblow spun Garcia round in profile to her. As his legs started to buckle he fell forward. There was enough light for her to see that the dead match was still clenched between his teeth as he hit the water.

Pluto and Belial darted away along the pool, sounding to the shallow bottom, and the rope snapped taut behind them.

24

THE heat on the roof was appalling now. Flames licked up out of the windows at front and rear of the house, but there was little smoke and the fire served only to light up the scene.

Collier crouched with Lucifer near one of the corners of the T-shaped junction. Lucifer still had his gasmask on. He squatted on his heels now, for it was too hot to sit. His arms were wrapped round his knees, his head was sunk low. Collier saw that the big powerful hands were shaking. He croaked, 'It's all right, Lucifer. Everything's fine. Not much longer now.'

Just fine, he thought. Except we're being cooked, and if we try to get away we'll be shot. And I wish to God I knew what was happening.

Modesty and Willie came crawling round the corner from where the long stem of the house ran back towards the steep slope of the mountain.

'Keep down,' Modesty said. 'And get your mask on, Steve.' She and Willie pulled their own masks into position. The tear gas bombs were laid out in readiness. Collier saw their hands snatching, their arms swinging. The tear gas bombs vanished into the great well formed by the rear of the house and the mountain.

Collier put his masked face close to Modesty's and shouted: '*Are we going down now?*'

Her head shook. 'No. Making smoke first.'

It was hard to distinguish the muffled words from behind her mask, but she pointed up and back. Collier stared. He knew that she and Willie had taken plastic explosive and detonators, but he did not know why. There was nothing to be seen where she pointed, only the great water tank standing on its tapering framework of steel——

The water tank!

His eyes had been to the ground for hours now, and he had forgotten about the tank. Water ... his parched throat burned with the thought of it.

The explosion surprised him by its quietness. He saw the lattice of steel tilt majestically, as if about to kneel on its two forelegs. It fell true, with a great nerve-jarring crash that shook the roof. The tank itself struck squarely over the place where the stairs bulkhead had been, driving through the debris and the surrounding lead, through the charred timbers and plaster beneath. A tide of water swept across the roof, sizzling, throwing up gouts of steam. It hit the parapet and rolled back, thinning as it spread.

Collier scooped at a pool of water in front of him, splashing his head and neck, letting the already warm water soak into his clothes. The pool dwindled, for now whatever water lay on the roof was draining down the slight pitch and out of small gullies in the parapet at the rear. But much of the water, the better part of five hundred gallons, had poured down through the great hole made by the tank, down into the furnace below.

Willie Garvin shouted something from behind his mask, something about smoke. Collier looked about him. Heavy grey smoke was pouring from the windows now, billowing and spreading. In a matter of seconds he could see no more than a yard or two.

'Right!' A distorted voice was shouting in his ear and a strong hand dragged him forward. He fumbled at the parapet and felt the hooks of the rope ladder. Willie had let it down. Collier straddled the parapet, found a rung with his foot, and began to descend.

Halfway down he realised with a shock of horror that Modesty had told him to take one of the AR-15's. He had kept it in his hands, held it clear of the first wash of water over the roof, but had then stood it against the parapet while he splashed his sweltering head and body. And he had left it there.

No time to go back. He could feel Willie, or somebody, coming down the ladder above him. Collier cursed himself almost hysterically, and went on down. The ladder had been dropped in the north angle of the wall, where there were no windows, so it was clear of danger from the fire, which was still trying to re-establish itself.

Collier's feet touched the ground. He stood waiting, as he had been instructed. A hand fumbled, found his arm. He was hustled along through swirling smoke. It was Willie who had hold of him, he knew by the power of the grip. Where was Modesty, for God's sake? Were they leaving her to cope with Lucifer on her own? Collier tried to pull away, but was rewarded by a wrench that almost lifted him off his feet.

They were close to the lower rock face of the mountain. He could feel it, his hand outstretched sideways. The smoke was thinning a little. Pressure from Willie's grasp brought him to his knees. So they were to crawl now.

An eddy of wind blew the smoke away, and Collier was crushed flat by an inexorable arm. His gasmask facepiece was misted within and coated by grime without, but ahead he could make out the figure of a Moro, half crouched, a heavy revolver in one hand, a neckerchief wrapped over nose and mouth. As Collier reassured himself that the tear gas must still be potent and that the man must be blinded by it, the revolver spoke. A bullet ploughed against stone only a foot to Collier's left, and he felt the sharp pain of a rock splinter hitting his cheek. Then the man fell forward with a curious twist of the body, and lay still.

Collier was pulled to his feet, and on. Willie Garvin paused, bent over the Moro, jerked a black-handled knife from the man's throat, and picked up the Webley revolver.

Two minutes later they were clambering down a dry gully which led through thorn and palms to the sea. Willie Garvin halted, slid a finger under his gasmask and tested the air cautiously. He took the mask off and said, 'Clear of gas 'ere. Wind's carrying it the other way.'

That was why the Moro had not been badly affected. That was why Willie Garvin had had a knife ready in his hand.

With relief Collier took off his own mask. Blood trickled from a shallow gash on his cheek made by the splinter of stone. Willie Garvin wiped his knife on a tuft of coarse grass, jerked his head in a signal and moved on. Collier followed.

They did not emerge from the trees where the forest ended just short of the sea, but moved parallel to the coast, keeping under cover for a quarter of a mile. Here the forest dwindled to scrub, and the scrub to bare rock. They were on the outside of the long, vertically seamed ridge which formed the southern arm of the bay.

Collier looked back. He could not see the house, for it was hidden by the ridge, but he could see flames streaming up like a giant torch, pushing back the darkness. There was little smoke now. Fire had consumed the water.

Willie Garvin moved on, staying low on the slope of the ridge. After two hundred yards he turned and began to mount a sloping crevice which narrowed as it ran to the crest. He moved confidently, as if familiar with the route. Six feet short of the top he went down on all fours, crawling. Collier followed suit. Ten seconds later they were in a little hollow on the crest of the ridge with the bay spread below them.

Collier drew in his breath at sight of the burning house. It was beginning to collapse upon itself now. To his right lay the curve of the bay, with the glowing pyre set back from it. Straight ahead, on the far side, was the northern arm, with the dolphin inlet hidden beyond it. Only fifty yards away, down the slope, lay the wooden landing stage and the narrow path running from it to the Moro camp and on up to the house.

One of the Moro boats was burning fiercely and had been cut adrift. Smoke still poured from another. A dozen men and as many women were clambering desperately from boat to boat, trying to reach the two biggest launches. If there had been any fire on them it was out now.

Willie settled down comfortably on his stomach, watching the scene through a V-shaped depression in the rim of the hollow. 'Right,' he said contentedly. 'Now we just wait for the big boys. Let's 'ave the gun, matey.'

Collier wiped a forearm across his filthy face and muttered, 'Look ... I'm sorry. I could cut my throat. I left the bloody thing on the roof.' He made himself look at Willie, waiting for a blow-torch stare from the bright blue eyes.

Willie Garvin did not turn round. He lay quite still, gazing down the slope. Then the big shoulders shrugged and he said, 'Ah, well.'

'That makes it worse,' said Collier, 'but thanks anyway.' After a moment he went on, a little feverishly, 'It's a peculiar thing, but I don't think it was being roasted and shot at that made me forget the gun. It was my hams.'

'Hams?' Willie turned his head to stare.

'Haunches. I must have been squatting on them for about three hours out of the last four. Or is it four hundred? They seem to have dried out and shrunk, like pemmican. I shall probably have to stump about on twenty-inch legs for the rest of my life, like Toulouse Lautrec.'

Willie grinned and looked down the slope again. 'Not a bad idea. You'll need a disguise if the Princess finds out about forgetting the gun.'

Collier nodded gloomily. 'Was it very important, Willie? I mean, we're tucked away pretty safely here, aren't we?'

'Sure. But this is probably the way Seff 'll come to get to the boats. Jack Wish and the others, too, if they're still alive. I'm supposed to 'ave the AR-15 to knock 'em off.'

'Oh, God. I suppose you couldn't manage with that pistol you took from the Moro a while back?'

Willie picked up the Webley he had laid to hand, and grimaced. 'I'm no good with 'and-guns.' He checked the cylinder, then passed the gun to Collier. 'I've got me sling, and a bit of lead ball ammo. But you can't be sure of a kill with it. Main thing is to get Seff. When 'e comes to the boats I'll slip down till I'm in knife range. You cover me coming back when I've done 'im. That's if they spot me, which they most likely won't. A knife's nice and quiet. I'll get Jack Wish, too, if they're together. With them dead, maybe the Moros won't come at us. Let's 'ope so.'

Collier pinched his eyes. He had made things bad for Willie. 'We haven't a grenade?' he asked.

'Modesty took the two that were left. She was more likely to need 'em.'

Collier shook his head, trying to clear it. His mind was painfully sluggish. 'I can't seem to think straight, Willie. Where is she now? And Lucifer?'

'She took 'im the other way, down to the dolphin pool. She wants to get Garcia.'

'Garcia?' Collier stared, uncomprehending. 'But he's harmless. He doesn't even know what goes on. All he thinks about is the dolphins.'

'I know. I meant she wants to get 'im out. She reckons Seff 'll knock 'im off, so she wants to get Garcia out of the way a bit sharpish. She's mad with 'erself for forgetting about him.'

'I shan't admonish her,' Collier said wearily. 'She's had one or two things on her mind. Oh Christ, Willie, can't she be satisfied with what she's done already? Sometimes I think we're really in hell and tonight's never going to end. If she wanted to look after Garcia, why did she lumber herself with Lucifer while she's doing it?'

'Because she can 'andle Lucifer best.'

'And because she didn't want you to be lumbered with both of us?'

'I wouldn't know.'

'I would,' Collier said bitterly. 'I only wish she wasn't bloody well right.'

Seff was getting a little breathless. His legs ached with the effort of moving over the rough ground in the semi-darkness, and the suitcase seemed to grow heavier with each step. Jack Wish walked beside him, jacketless, the Colt Commander in its holster under his left arm. Wish was soaked in sweat, his face coated with smuts.

'It is very unsatisfactory not to *know* whether Blaise and

Garvin are dead,' Seff said, panting. 'Very unsatisfactory, Mr. Wish.'

'Too bad.' Wish's voice was flat and a little ugly. 'But that's how it is. I've told Sangro to round up his men and get them to the boats. He'll take the walking wounded and use that bolo of his on anyone who can't make it—kind of religious gimmick, or something.'

Seff started to speak, but Wish went on. 'If Blaise and the others are dead, okay. If they got clear, we'd want days to round 'em up. And we ain't got days. So the quicker we pull out, the better.'

Seff halted and put down the case. His voice was higher than usual as he said, 'You arranged this without my instructions, Mr. Wish?'

'Without your instructions. This is my kind of work now, so string along with me until we're clear. Then I'll listen to you again.' The heavy Colt was suddenly in Wish's hand. Seff had not seen the movement; it could only have happened as he blinked his eyes. The round black hole of the barrel menaced him.

'I'll have that gun in your pocket, Seff. You might use it wrong.'

'Really, Mr. Wish——'

'Don't let's argue, huh? You want to leave things tidy and you might overdo it.' Wish reached out and took the Browning from Seff's pocket. He checked the safety catches, then slipped the gun into the waistband of his slacks. 'You got the brains and I got the contacts, Seff. We're still a good team. I wouldn't want you to make a mistake now.'

Slowly Seff picked up the case. He noted that Jack Wish was slipping the Colt Commander into the shoulder holster again. It was fortunate that Regina had a gun. Seff hoped that she would act quickly when he gave the word. He was sure she would. Regina was very reliable . . .

Lucifer lay on a thin blanket of rotting vegetation in a furrow of rock. His earthly body was sore, his earthly face felt as if it were parched and cracking. It was good that Modesty had taken off his mask now and was wiping his face with a scrap of cloth soaked in some cool liquid from a bottle in the little box she carried.

Lucifer opened his eyes and looked up at the sky. The battle against the rebels was almost over now. Modesty had said so. Though shaken to its foundations, Hell had stood firm. The Enemy had failed. There could have been no other outcome, of course, but the battle had drained him of strength. It had taken all his concentrated power. For hours he had been pouring that power into Modesty and into the other faithful servants who fought for him.

She was kneeling over him now, black with grime. He saw a long strip of grubby plaster at her temple, and said, 'I will heal that for you soon.'

'Yes.' She put a hand on his shoulder. 'Listen, Lucifer. Your place is here until I come back. You understand why?' She had found it best to tell Lucifer what must be done and let him devise his own reasons for it.

'I shall rest here and husband my power for the final defeat of the Enemy,' he said quietly.

'Yes.' She unslung the water bottle and knapsack at her hip. The knapsack held only one grenade now, the other had been used as they fought their way from the house. For the last five minutes they had been moving in the fringe of the trees. Now they were in the open, and there was no sign of the Moros. Here, in the furrow of rock, Lucifer was well hidden.

Only a few moments ago she had seen a twisting column of sparks soar up as the roof of the house fell in. The Moros would be gathering their wounded and heading for the boats now. So would Seff and his companions. Perhaps. If, like her, they had forgotten about Garcia. But Willie Garvin would be waiting for them.

She stood up. Her AR-15, with a new magazine, was in her left hand. With her right she eased the Colt ·32 in its holster.

Lucifer was staring intently up at the sky. It was pale with

307

the coming of dawn now. She moved quietly away towards the inlet. Two minutes later she stood at the inner end of the long, natural pool. The dolphins were swimming. She heard them come close, then turn and race towards the net at the far end which barred the way to the sea. An odd wallowing sound seemed to follow them.

Soft-footed she moved round the curved end of the inlet and along the side. She could see the dolphins undulating in and out of the water now. They seemed to be towing something behind them.

No sign of Garcia. She walked soundlessly to the little hut where he lived, and looked through the open door. The hut was empty. She turned towards the pool again. As she did so, two figures emerged from beyond the other side of the hut and she heard Seff's voice say, 'I really cannot understand where Regina has gone——'

She whirled to her left. Seff and Wish stood fifteen paces away, facing her. The rifle in her left hand hung at the trail, useless. Jack Wish's hand blurred towards the big Colt in its Berns-Martin holster. Her own revolver cleared leather and she fired from the hip. Jack Wish seemed to draw his gun and throw it away in the same movement, as the ·32 bullet slammed into his heart. It was over before Seff had fully registered her presence.

She watched the chunky figure of Wish hit the ground and bounce. Her gun moved an inch, to bear on Seff. He gestured, empty-handed, and said in a shrill, anxious voice, 'I am looking for Regina. Have you seen her? She really should be here. It is most extraordinary.'

Something moved in the water. Modesty's gun twitched, but she held her fire. The dolphins were coming to the side. Their dark, sinuous shapes curved round, and they splashed fretfully.

Now she saw that they were harnessed, towing something that came drifting slowly by ... a bony, stockinged leg that vanished into a shapeless bundle of clothes. Regina's leg, with a twist of rope hitched tightly round one ankle. The clothes billowed away for a moment, revealing the wax-white face and the straggle of floating hair.

Seff cried out, a high, wordless whinnying. There came a flurry of water as the dolphins turned away. The rope tightened again, and Regina went gliding after them as they resumed their swimming up and down the long pool.

Seff stood in a grotesque, frozen attitude, his cadaverous face working. 'Regina...?' he croaked incredulously.

The hammer rose as Modesty cocked the Colt to kill him. There was a sound from behind her and she twisted, ducking aside, checking the final pressure on the trigger by a millisecond.

Lucifer.

He gave her a gentle smile, then turned his gaze to Seff and moved steadily past her. He was in her line of fire now. She called out, but he seemed not to hear. She could have overtaken him, but a strange prescience held her back.

Lucifer extended an arm slowly. One strong hand took Seff by the throat. He made no attempt to struggle or escape.

'I have made a new Hell for you, Asmodeus,' Lucifer said in a clear, sad voice. 'I have made a new Hell for you ... and into it I now cast you down utterly, for all time.'

He bent a little and gripped Seff with his free hand by one scrawny thigh, then with a sudden heave lifted the black, sticklike body over his head.

'For all time,' he repeated.

Seff squealed, his limbs jerking, and with sudden dreadful strength Lucifer dashed the creaking figure down upon the seamed rock at his feet.

Willie Garvin looked down on the bay. The boats that remained seaworthy, two big launches and one smaller one, were on the move. They had been ready to sail for more than half an hour now. Presumably they had been waiting for Seff, but Sangro had decided to wait no longer.

There had been no sign of Seff. No sign of any of his colleagues. Willie had given deep thought to the matter of killing

Sangro, but had decided against taking the risk. He might be more urgently needed for other matters. There was that single shot, some ten minutes ago . . .

'You think it was Modesty's gun?' Collier said. It was the third time he had asked the same question.

'Sounded like it,' Willie said patiently. 'She gave me a run-down on everything the Moros carried, and there was nothing as small as a ·32.'

A gleam of light was showing beyond the crest of the mountain, and the steady flames from the burnt-out house seemed paler now with the coming of dawn.

'Dall's ship ought to be 'ere soon,' Willie said.

'And what do we do in the meantime?'

'Wait.'

Collier tried to quell the nervous irritation that Willie's laconic manner evoked in him. 'But Seff and the others might have Modesty in trouble.'

'We'd hear if they did.'

'Shouldn't we go and look for her?'

'No. Wait till it's light. If Seff or any of 'em are still alive they might be laying for us now. So we'll sit tight till we can see what's what. Modesty'll do the same.'

'How the hell do you know she'll do the same?' Collier said thickly. He was almost too tired to speak.

'Because they might be laying for us,' Willie repeated monotonously. Then, with a touch of impatience—'Blimey, we don't go around *asking* for trouble.'

'You don't——?' Collier started to laugh. He was horrified to find that he could not stop, and that his laughter was turning to sobs.

'Steady there, matey,' Willie said kindly, and leaned forward. For the second time that night Collier was slapped hard across the face. It stopped his near-hysteria and at the same time seemed to empty his body of its last vestiges of strength.

He leaned back against the rock behind him. His head fell on his chest, and his eyes closed.

At once Willie was shaking him. Mumbling, Collier forced

310

his eyes open and found that in the last two seconds the sun had risen above the mountain and dawn had filled the bay; the Moro boats had vanished. Willie was standing up, looking towards the curve of the cliff. 'There she is,' he said cheerfully.

Collier put his hands to his head, to prevent any unnecessary movement, and stood up gingerly. 'Is there ... is there an axe buried in my skull?' he asked. 'In the general excitement I didn't notice it before, but I'm sure ...'

His voice trailed away as he saw the figures of Modesty and Lucifer four hundred yards away across the angle of the bay, standing on the white beach at the foot of the cliff path. Enormous relief rose within him. He said, 'If you're going to shout to her, Willie, or make any loud noise, for God's sake shoot me first. I'd rather go quickly.'

Willie grinned, moved forward a little, and waved his arm in a wide arc. After a moment or two Modesty responded. Collier realised she was signalling. It was not semaphore, but some kind of tick-tack system. At this distance her movements were exaggerated, but he had a sudden memory of the moment when Seff had declared that she and Willie must fight; he remembered the little nervous movements, her hand touching an ear, rubbing an eye; the head bowed, lifted, turned away.

Now he understood how she had told Willie to throw the fight and take a dive.

'Seff's dead,' said Willie, shading his eyes. 'So's Regina and Jack Wish.'

'She's been busy,' said Collier.

'No sign of Bowker, but she says not to worry.'

'That's right. If Bowker's still alive he won't do a General Custer. He'll try to make a deal.'

Willie raised his arms and signalled an acknowledgment to Modesty, then started down the slope. Collier followed. As they passed the landing stage and moved on towards the beach he looked back. A white cargo boat was heaving to, half a mile beyond the jaws of the bay, and already two launches were being swung out on the davits.

25

'DR. MARSTON here is your new personal aide,' Collier said. 'He has a boat ready to take you to the ship, Lucifer.'

Lucifer nodded dully. He was quite passive now. Another shot of scopolamine had ensured that.

'You have several ages of creative work ahead of you,' Collier went on, his tired mind trying to construct some kind of logic. 'After this struggle, Hell must be repaired and strengthened. Your faithful servants will also have much to do, all over the world—on the upper levels.'

'Yes.' Lucifer's voice was heavy. 'But Modesty . . . ?'

'Since you have raised her to immortality and made her your chief servant, she will have more to do than anyone. But no doubt you will see her again in a few centuries.'

Lucifer nodded slowly. 'I am accustomed to endure. Tell her that she has Lucifer's heart, and that I shall watch over her.'

Dr. Marston ran a hand through his greying hair, glanced at Collier, received a quick nod, then put a hand on Lucifer's arm and led him away towards the cliff path.

Collier sat down and extended his aching body on the ground, closing his eyes. John Dall gazed after Lucifer and the doctor for several seconds, then said softly, *'Jesus . . .!'*

'I know,' said Collier. 'It gets rather trying. Look, there are a lot of very capable-looking men with guns swarming about this place since your launches roared in. If you're going off on a tour of inspection do you mind telling them that I'm on Modesty's side? I'd hate to get shot now.'

'They won't do that.' Dall surveyed the Englishman. 'You look pretty bushed, Collier. Anything I can get for you?'

'Thank you. I'll have an iron lung, I think.' Collier's manner was cool. He had made up his mind not to like John Dall.

The man was a rival. That he was a millionaire gave him no edge with Modesty, but his personality was immense, and it made Collier feel inadequate.

'We forgot the iron lung,' Dall said. 'I've got a hip flask if that will help. Where are Modesty and Willie?'

'Down at the pool.' Collier sighed. 'She suddenly remembered those poor dolphins, so she and Willie went down to get the harness off them and drop the net so they can get out to sea when they want to.'

'That figures. Those poor dolphins.' Dall began to chuckle, and suddenly Collier found it difficult to maintain his dislike. He opened his eyes and took the flask Dall was holding out to him.

'Sorry if I was terse,' he said, sitting up, 'but I'm feeling a little frayed at the edges. I didn't get much sleep last night.'

'Neither did I,' said Dall. 'I'd sooner have been where you were.'

Collier swallowed a mouthful of brandy, choked a little, and looked up. He was astonished to find that Dall's words made him suddenly very smug and very happy. He had been *there*, hour after hour, through the whole damn lot, doing the most extraordinary things with Modesty Blaise and Willie Garvin, while John Dall had been sitting on his million-dollar arse in a cabin, sweating and wondering.

'It was an interesting night,' he said contentedly, and stood up, handing the flask back to Dall.

'Yes. I'd like to hear chapter and verse sometime.' Dall put the flask away. 'Modesty and Willie tell a poor story.'

'I think shop-talk bores them,' said Collier. 'Shall we see how they're getting on?'

Along the low ridge where the ground began to slope down, four dead Moros lay in a little group.

'All my own work,' said Collier, and pointed back to the house. 'I did it from up there, where the roof used to be, with a gun whose name escapes me at the moment.'

Dall stared. 'Nice shooting.'

'Very nice. I couldn't see them, of course, and I'd gone

313

slightly off my trolley at the time. Modesty says I could never do it again in a million years. That's about how long I'd like it to be before a similar opportunity arises.'

Dall smiled. He had been very curious about Collier, wondering what he had for Modesty. At this moment he looked like a charred scarecrow, but the tired red eyes were intelligent and even now held humour; and the man was highly sensitive. His early coldness had quickly melted in response to Dall's amiable disregard of it. They came to the inlet. Regina, Garcia, Seff and Jack Wish were laid out neatly on a stretch of smooth rock.

'I may not have the details quite right,' said Collier. 'As you say, Modesty tells a poor story. But I gather that *la belle dame* here,' he indicated Regina, 'killed Garcia, and then must have got her foot caught in the dolphins' towing line. She was dragged in and drowned. Lucifer killed Seff rather dramatically by throwing him down from a great height, which was very apt. And our Mr. Wish made the mistake of trying to pull his gun faster than Modesty could pull hers. Willie informs me that's one thing you don't live and learn. Where the hell are they?'

'There's Modesty.' Dall nodded towards the open end of the pool. The net had been cut down now. Modesty stood on the low bank. She wore only a black bra and pants. Her hair hung loose. She was doubled over a little, shaking, staring down into the water.

For a moment fear hit Collier, and then he realised that she was laughing.

Willie Garvin surfaced, spluttering. His arms were wrapped round a dolphin, and his wrathful voice came clearly to Dall and Collier as they moved forward.

'Stop 'eaving about, you stupid gitt! I'm trying to 'elp!'

Another dolphin's head emerged and butted Willie amiably in the back. He lost his grip on the first, and swore. An empty basket floated nearby, and Collier guessed that Willie had been trying to coax the dolphins with the tiny dead fish that Garcia always fed them.

314

Pluto and Belial were both butting at Willie now. Modesty was on her hands and knees, weak with laughter. She lifted a hand, pointing.

'There's ... there's a little fish caught in your hair, Willie love! That's what they're after!'

Willie groped in his hair, plucked out the tiny fish and flung it from him. 'Come on,' he said coaxingly, edging towards one of the dolphins. 'Come to Uncle Willie, there's a good boy.' His voice rose. 'Keep still you bottlenosed burke!'

With an effort Modesty got to her feet. She saw Dall and Collier approaching, waved an arm in greeting, then dived into the pool.

Pluto, or Belial, soared six feet clear of the water, spun in the air, and dived down headfirst within a foot of Willie Garvin as he drew breath to speak. Willie inhaled a mouthful of water, choked, submerged, then surfaced again, glaring with indignation.

As Dall and Collier reached the point where Modesty had dived in it became clear that one of the dolphins had been freed from its harness but the other was proving more difficult, not because it was afraid but because it was in a playful mood.

The next five minutes provided something in the nature of a pantomime, with Willie Garvin as the chosen butt of the dolphins' high spirits. His comments, when they could be heard, were more than florid.

Collier lay on his stomach, watching, almost convulsed. And even Dall, not given to easy laughter, was standing half doubled up with a hand pressed to his side.

At last Collier took a grip on himself and knelt up.

'You—you have to watch it a bit,' he panted. 'Every time you get hysterical they slap your face. It's effective, but it gets a bit depressing after a while.'

Dall nodded, his face growing gradually sober. Willie had a firm grip of the dolphin now, and Modesty was grappling with the strap of the harness. Her face was alive, and full of amusement.

'How do they do it, Collier?' Dall murmured. 'I mean, this ... after that?' His head jerked briefly towards the smoke still rising from the smouldering house, and the ground where so many dead men lay.

'I rather think this follows that,' said Collier. 'Cause and effect. I've never subscribed to the theory of hitting your toe with a hammer because it's so nice when you stop. But they seem to operate a satisfactory parallel.'

'I guess there's a little more to it than that,' Dall said. There was a shadow of envy in his voice. 'But whatever it is, it makes life taste pretty good to them.'

Collier nodded. 'Mine tastes pretty good to me just now,' he said. 'But I wouldn't want to renew the experience. The price comes too high.'

The harness was off at last. The two dolphins sped away, circling exuberantly. Modesty pushed Willie's head under, then turned and swam for the bank. Dall moved to help her out, looking sharply at her temple as she pushed back her hair. The plaster had come off in the water. He saw a long purple lump with the dark line of a cut running along the middle of it.

'Hallo, Johnnie. Sorry I'm wet.' She leaned forward and kissed him quickly. 'You look awfully tired.'

'I'm tired too,' said Collier. 'I need nursing, and sundry other comforts. Like somebody to tell me a story while I'm going to sleep, and somebody to hold my hand all night in case I wake up crying. I wouldn't mind having a teddy bear, too, if the damn thing didn't get in the way.'

Willie Garvin came up with a pile of clothes, his own and Modesty's. 'I knew a nurse in Liverpool once,' he said, pulling on trousers over his wet shorts. 'She'd got a marvellous theory about the best way to sweat out a cold. All you needed was a double bed, four 'ot water bottles. And her. I always seemed to be feeling a cold coming on in those days, but she'd stop 'em dead. Then I got a real cold. A stinker. Felt like death. So Maureen starts a course of crash treatment on me . . .'

He shook his head and held out Modesty's shirt for her to

slip on. 'If she 'adn't caught the cold off me an' flaked out 'erself she'd 've just about killed me.'

Dall grinned and took out a thin cigar. 'Maybe she'd do for Collier if he wants nursing. Look, I don't want to hurry you, but can we go now?'

Modesty nodded. 'Better have your boys clear up Seff and company, John. We're on foreign territory, and we don't want to leave anything around that might cause a lot of fuss.'

'Sure. I've told them that.'

'Good.' She pulled on her slacks. 'Where do we go from here?'

'Lucifer's on the ship with Dr. Marston. I'll see he's well taken care of back home. We four fly in the Beaver to the United States H.Q. at Clark Air Base, Luzon. I'll call Washington from there and tell them there won't be any more death lists. And I guess Tarrant would be pretty glad to have a call from you.' He hesitated. 'Then everyone has a free choice about what they do next. It's finished.'

'Fine.' Modesty laced her boots and stood up. She put a small packet wrapped in oilskin into Dall's hands. 'We got your diamonds back, John. Seff had them with him.'

As they moved up the slope Collier found himself beside Dall. Modesty and Willie were walking a little ahead. To the extent that Collier's ears could catch their words, they seemed to be talking idly about buying a trampoline to install at 'The Treadmill' or in some special room adjoining it. He decided that his exhausted mind must be imagining things.

Once Modesty stumbled and swayed a little, and Willie slipped his arm around her. They walked on, still talking. Collier slowed his pace, and Dall dropped back with him.

'Look,' Collier said slowly. 'I'm too tired to put this delicately, but what exactly happens now—I mean about you, and me, and Modesty?'

'You really want to know?'

'Of course I bloody well do.'

Dall smiled, drew on his cigar, and looked speculatively at the two figures ahead. 'Okay. First thing, we don't have to quarrel. She's not to be fought over. Second thing, she won't come back home with me or go back home with you. She'll go some place with Willie Garvin. She'll take it easy, and she'll sleep alone. Maybe they'll do things, like swim or ride, or sail ... or other things, like go on the town, dance, play roulette. And maybe they won't. They know how to do things, those two. But they know how to be completely idle, and that's a rare art.'

'It's one I could shine at just now ... an art I could encompass with ease.' In his weariness, Collier had a little difficulty in enunciating the words. 'Still, I know what you mean. Go on.'

'Well ... then one day maybe she'll call you,' said Dall. 'Or maybe she'll call me. Or not. Of course, you can figure you're not the kind of guy that waits for a girl to say when. She won't mind. She doesn't reckon to have you on a string, so there'll be no hard feelings. You can always say you're busy.'

'Is that what you'll say?'

Dall laughed. 'I'm always busy. But not that busy, by God.'

'I believe you.' Collier nodded muzzily. So there was nothing to be done, nothing to be said. She would walk her own road. On leaden legs, yet with a strange inner contentment born of hope, he tramped on beside Dall up the slope.